The Dead Time Chronicles

BOOK ONE

Frozen Shadows

A NOVEL

BY

JASON WILCOX

Publisher: Avid C. S.

**The Dead Time Chronicles:
Frozen Shadows**
Third Edition

Publisher: Avid C. S.
2025
First Paperback Edition: 2010
Second Paperback Edition: 2012
Third Paperback Edition: 2025

The Dead Time Chronicles: Frozen Shadows: a novel/ by Jason Wilcox. -3rd. ed.
ISBN (pbk): 978-1-967760-00-8
Printed in the United States of America

Book One
Frozen Shadows

Book Two
Fractured Fate

Book Three
The Final Gate

DEDICATION

For **Michelle**—
my sister, my first reader, my biggest fan, my trusted editor.
Your tireless eyes, patient heart, and invaluable insights
have transformed these pages in ways I never could alone.
Thank you for believing in me, for your unwavering support,
and for guiding me through every sentence.
This book is as much yours as it is mine.

Cast of Characters
Science, Defense, and Solutions (SDS)
- **Caden Gray**—Scientist and field team commander. Oversees the Dead Time project.
- **Bridget**—Therapist and medic; Caden's partner.
- **James**—Skilled member of Caden's field team.
- **Matt**—Skilled member of Caden's field team.
- **Robert**—Director overseeing SDS operations.
- **Allen**—Lead engineer developing experimental technology.
- **Bain**—Field team commander.
- **Palmer**—Skilled member of Bain's field team.
- **Mike**—Skilled member of Bain's field team.
- **Steven**—Scientist and field team commander.
- **Professor Howell**—Scholar of ancient languages and runes.
- **Mags**—Caden's loyal golden retriever.

The Witch's Woods & Beyond
- **Azgiel**—An ancient power long imprisoned.
- **Mauldrin**—A legendary figure from the old war.
- **Maselda (The Witch)**—Mysterious ruler of the forest. Azgiel's wife.
- **Kaz**—A towering, red-skinned demon.
- **Tagen**—A dangerous aniborn.
- **Snyp**—A ruthless warlord.
- **Triaad**—A shadowy figure of immense power.
- **Domblin**—A powerful ally from the old world with knowledge of what once was.

CHAPTER 1

Tagen—The Border

The scream woke him.

Tagen came awake on his side in the dirt, eyes open, mouth closed. Nostrils flaring. He did not move.

His black oily skin pulled the shadow under the rock-shelf and held it. Two breaths wafted steam into the night air before habit caught up and shut them down. He had learned how to breathe silently a long time ago.

The scream had come from inside the trees. That was the wrong direction. Nothing should be coming from those woods.

He rolled up onto his feet. Two short steps carried him deeper into the shadow of the boulder, and he pressed his shoulder to the stone and let the dark take the rest of him.

The woods went quiet behind the scream. The owls, the insects, the small rustlings in the brush, the wind in the high branches—all of it, gone. It was the kind of quiet that felt like a hand had come down on the mouth of the world.

He let his eyes work the shadows one at a time.

Five days, he thought. *Five days Snyp had kept him starving*, and his ribs were sore where they were always sore, and his legs already hurt, and he did not need this. Not tonight.

Something is happening.

He waited. Nothing moved. The Witch's woods rose on his right the way they always rose, a black wall of ancient trees too thick to see ten feet into. On his left was the open country where another aniborn was supposed to be standing his post. Tagen could not hear him either.

A week ago he had watched two demons drift to the edge of the treeline, stare across at him, and drift back. Every aniborn on this border had been on edge ever since.

This felt worse than that.

He sniffed the night. The wind was wrong. There was something under the cold. A sweetness that did not belong in these woods. He went to the nearest trunk and pressed himself against it, and he listened.

A sound came out of the woods. A long low hum, like a struck bell held down at the bottom of its note. It rolled past him and into the meadow at his back and thinned out to nothing.

He stepped off the path. He shifted into shadow form.

The change came slower than it should have. Hungry aniborn did not shadow-form well. His outline thinned and did not finish thinning. He made himself move anyway.

He went along the inside of the treeline toward the sound.

A hundred paces on, he saw the light.

Pale blue, burning in the dirt.

He slowed. He eased closer.

A clearing had opened on the boundary itself. The trees around it had pulled back—leaves curled, bark gone gray, as though something had walked through and pushed them away by being there. In the middle of the cleared ground, a circle of cold blue fire burned in a line cut into the earth. It did not flicker. It held steady, the way a wound holds steady when something is keeping it open.

A body hung above the ground inside the circle. A hand's breadth above it, with nothing under it, arms loose at her sides. White hair falling straight down. Pale skin. Not breathing.

A woman. The Witch.

Tagen's claws dug into the bark before he knew he'd moved.

Only aniborn of his generation had ever seen her. The Witch did not leave the deep of her own woods. She had taken her throne in those trees after the war and she had not come out of them for over a thousand years.

She was here, and she was on his border.

He did not understand what he was looking at, and he had been alive long enough to know when a thing he did not understand was bad.

Around the circle of blue fire, demons stood in a loose ring. Six of them. Heavy, horned, the big ones—soldiers, the kind that used to have a use for being big. They had their faces turned outward into the trees. They had their backs to her body. They were guarding her.

Tagen stared.

Then he saw the seventh.

Inside the ring, between two of the guards, stood a figure taller than the others. Broader. Skin the color of old coals, dark red and catching the blue fire wrong. Black tattoos in the old writing ran down the side of his arms and chest.

Tagen stopped breathing. Being in shadow form, he backed into the boulder behind him, sinking into it until only his face pushed out of the stone.

Kaz.

Kaz had not been seen outside the woods in as long as the Witch had not. Kaz did not come to the border. Kaz stayed in the black of the deep forest with the old powers.

And here he was. Ten paces outside the treeline, his great head tilted toward the Witch's body, his black eyes tracking the trees in the slow easy scan of something at home.

Tagen pressed deeper into the stone.

What is this? What have you brought to my border?

Another scream split the air.

It did not come from a mouth. It came up out of the circle—a sound like metal tearing through water, and at the end of it a white flash swallowed the Witch's body whole and snapped shut. When the light was gone she was no longer hanging in the air. She was on her knees in the dirt, one hand flat against the ground, shoulders shaking.

She was alive, and she had come back from somewhere.

Kaz moved to her. The red demon went down on one knee at her side and set a hand under her elbow.

She said something to him. Her mouth moved. Tagen could see it move. Whatever the words were, the air of the clearing ate them—some part of what had been worked here had taken sound along with the rest of it. Kaz listened. Kaz nodded once. He turned and made a small gesture with two fingers.

Two of the guards broke from the ring and moved out of the clearing, one yellow, one black, heading away from the Witch's woods toward the open land. They were going to cross the border.

Tagen was the only aniborn standing between them and the world beyond.

The order on this border had been the same for a thousand years. Nothing comes out. If you could not stop it, you died trying. There was no third option.

Starving, he would not last three breaths against Kaz himself, let alone two demons with him.

That is the point of you, isn't it? Starve him until he can't hold the line, then send him to die on it. Tidy.

He had been sent to die before. His wits had always kept him alive.

Snyp had put him out here five days without a meal. If Tagen fell tonight, there would not be a mourner in the caves. But a live aniborn carrying what he had just seen was worth more than a dead one had ever been worth to anyone, and between his master's need to punish him and his need to know, Tagen had a chance.

A chance was more than he usually got.

He backed away from the treeline.

He made it fifty paces before he saw the silver.

Low to the ground, between two young saplings, a glint of metal where there should not have been metal. Tagen froze. He strained his red eyes in the thin moonlight.

A preel.

His gut knotted. The beetle-thing was large and it was turning toward him. Preels could see through shadow form. Preels were one of the few things that could. The demons used them as scouts for exactly that reason, and this one was looking right at him.

Its back flushed dark orange, faint at first. The way they colored when they saw.

Tagen moved.

He was on it before it could shriek. He tore open its shell, shoved the broken thing into his mouth, crushed it between his teeth, and swallowed. A thin smoke of venom curled off the cut edge. The taste was foul and full of iron.

The last leg was still going down his throat when something stepped out of the brush behind him.

The preel had been traveling with a handler. Of course it had. Preels never hunted alone.

Tagen was already backing up. He did not know if this one was one of the few demons that could see through shadow form. He was not interested in finding out.

The demon was big. Gray-skinned. Bone-white tattoos ran down his face and his right arm. A double-bladed axe held across his chest with both hands, and along one edge of the blade a thin vein of green crisscrossed in a web.

The demon moved fast, and the axe came down. This one could see him.

Tagen dropped backward into the large tree behind him. He melded into the wood the way he had been trained, and the axe-head came through where his chest had been and struck the trunk. The demon cursed. Tagen came out the far side of the tree already running and already turning.

The second swing caught him in the ribs.

He went sideways off his feet. He slid in the leaves. The demon came down on him for the kill and Tagen got one claw up and raked it across the inside of its thigh, and his venom bloomed black in the wound, and the demon bellowed and staggered to one knee.

"Degnar mekna!" the demon roared. His eyes and his wound lit with flame.

The healing chant. Tagen had heard it many times over many years. He did not wait to watch it work.

He ran.

He ran at a speed he had not known he had left in him. His ribs were wet. His head was ringing. A horn was already blowing somewhere behind him, long and low—the demon on the ground calling others, calling the ring around the Witch, calling whoever else was out here. He did not make it far.

A second demon came in low from the left and slammed him flat. Bones in his left leg and his ribs snapped under the weight of it, and every breath after that came out of him in a ragged wheeze.

The demon's hand clamped his throat and lifted him off the ground as if he weighed nothing. The demon laughed. "Clever, aniborn. But not clever enough." Tagen's feet dangled, and the strength leaked from his limbs as he clawed at the demon's arm. Spots danced in his vision. The hand tightened.

"You're weak," the demon growled.

One word: "Enough."

Everything stopped. Reverence crossed the demon's face. "Maselda…"

The hand loosened. Tagen crashed. Pain sparked through him. He should have been healing already. Malnourished as he was, he healed slowly, the way sick things heal.

Maselda stepped out of the trees with the weight of the forest behind her.

"You bring chaos to my domain," she said, her voice the quiet of a closed door.

Every instinct he had left was telling him to run.

"You're alive," she said. "Do you know why?"

He shook his head.

"Because I allow it."

Pain lanced through him as she flicked her wrist, then dissolved into warmth. His wounds closed, the ache eased. The weakness underneath them stayed where it was.

Her eyes were pale and they did not move. Whatever softness a face could hold, hers was not holding it. "You have seen what happened here tonight."

Tagen didn't dare speak.

"Tell your master what you saw. Tell Snyp that the storm is coming. Tell him it is time."

She faded as though she had never been there. The few demons who had gathered turned back into the forest, leaving only wind in the high branches and the smell of cold earth.

Tagen put his eyes on the mountains. Snyp had to know.

He went low through the trees, away from the border, away from the woods.

He did not stop to look back for a long time. When he finally did, he was miles out and the sky had a thin smear of gray in it and he could not see the woods anymore. Nothing was following. Nothing he could see.

He stood in the shadow of a dead pine and let his hands shake.

Five days without eating. And Kaz. And the Witch out of the forest. And I have to tell Snyp. I have to tell him all of it.

He walked again.

That was when he smelled it.

A scent he had not smelled since before the Witch closed her woods against the world.

He stopped so fast he nearly fell over. He pressed his back to a tree and stood there breathing through his nostrils and trying to decide whether he was losing his mind.

He was not. The scent was there. Faint, almost gone, but there.

It was coming from downslope. Thirty paces, maybe forty. A stand of granite and scrub pine. Something was lying in the grass between the stones.

He crept forward. Breathing shallow. He had had a bad enough night already, and he did not want to add whatever was waiting down there to the rest of it. But the scent—the scent he could not walk past.

He came around the side of the standing stone and saw the body.

A man, lying in the grass.

A human man, on his back in the coarse grass, arms loose at his sides. Unconscious but alive—the chest rose, the chest fell. He was wearing a suit Tagen did not know how to look at. Gold links no bigger than a fingernail, tight as chainmail, with thin wires running under and between them like veins under skin. A wisp of steam lifted off the left shoulder. The metal there had been scorched.

His face was hidden behind a visor of ruined glass. Black score marks burned at the center, cracks running out to the edges. A faint static still crawled along the frame.

Tagen stood over him and stared.

His first thought was to kill it. Human. Alone. Defenseless. A kill was a kill, and a human kill at the end of a night like this one might buy him a mouthful of mercy from Snyp. He raised a claw over the throat.

He stopped.

The smell. So ancient, so familiar. He could not place it.

A blue and white shimmer lit across the suit and vanished.

Magic. The last of it.

On the man. On his throat. On the suit. Two signatures, very faint, fading by the second. One of them he knew. The cold silver one. He had felt it once tonight already. The Witch.

The Witch had touched this man minutes ago.

The heat of her hand was still on his throat, and Tagen did not understand how.

Tagen pulled back so fast he scraped himself on a stone. He stared at the body, and his belly went cold. He did not understand any part of what he was looking at. The Witch had been kneeling in the dirt of a blue-fire circle on the border of her own woods, and she had come back from somewhere, and here was a human lying in the scrub with her touch still cooling on his throat, and none of it fit together. The second signature, the one under hers, Tagen could not name. It was working on the man, he could feel that much—but the hand that had set it there was hidden from him.

But under both magics, there was the scent. Different. Something he still could not place, and yet some old part of him—some part that had been alive a long time—knew the weight of it. Knew not to cross it. Knew to get small and to get away and to never come near it again as long as he lived.

Tagen should have left.

He did not leave.

He could not. Something about the scent of the man himself—under the two magics—kept his feet where they were.

He leaned down, close to the visor. He sniffed.

His black face went still.

No.

He leaned closer. His claw touched the broken face-plate—just touched it, the barest weight of one point of claw against the glass.

The glass gave.

It had been holding itself together out of habit. The lightest pressure finished it. Fragments fell inward in a slow tired collapse, landing on the man's brow and cheeks. The dark frame of the visor stayed where it was. The face under it was open to the night.

Tagen looked at the face and went over backward, scrambling two paces in the dirt before he caught himself.

He looked at it for a long time.

He had seen that face before. Once. Standing on a battlefield two thousand years ago with a hand raised, calling down the wrath of the old powers on an unstoppable army, erasing them from the world with the turn of a wrist. He had never forgotten it. He had never expected to see it again.

"Mauldrin," Tagen whispered, and his own voice came out as a scratch.

The man did not answer. The chest rose. The chest fell. Under the cracked visor he was a mortal thing. Soft. Helpless. A child could have put a knife through him.

How, Tagen thought. *How can this be you? This shouldn't be possible. You vanished two thousand years ago. You had more power in one finger than I have had in my whole body, five times over, and look at you. Mortal. Feeble. Alone, with no one set to watch over you.*

Everything about it was wrong.

He stood up. He took one step back. He took another. He kept his eyes on the face. He kept expecting it to open its eyes and call down the old wrath and end him where he stood. Nothing came. The chest rose. The chest fell. The man breathed on like a man.

Tagen narrowed his eyes.

If you are him, you are too much of a threat to leave.

He dug his claws into the soil and pulled at what power he had. A thick darkness solidified along the ground between them, crawling toward the body. Tagen's red eyes blazed.

The man's eyes opened.

Tagen's concentration broke. The blackness came apart in the air. He shifted to shadow form and was gone before the man could focus enough to know he was there.

He ran.

He ran north. Then west. Then north again. He did not take the straight path to the cave. He could not take the straight path yet. He had to think, and he could not think and run at the same time, and he could not stop running.

Demons out of the forest. The Witch at the border. Kaz walking in the open. Mauldrin alive. Mortal. Lying in the grass.

Snyp was going to hear about the demons. Snyp was going to hear about the Witch and Kaz. The Witch herself had ordered him to carry that news, and even if she had not, Tagen could not have kept it—Snyp could know by morning through other channels, and if Tagen had been at the border and had seen it and had failed to report it, Snyp would take him apart for the pleasure of taking him apart.

Mauldrin, though. Mauldrin was different.

Mauldrin, he could keep.

Snyp did not know the scent of Mauldrin. Snyp had never met him. Only a few aniborn still living had ever seen that face, and most of them were gone. If Tagen did not say the name, no one else would say it either. Not tonight. Maybe not for a while.

If he was the only one who knew—if he was the only aniborn in all the master's service who knew Mauldrin had come back and was lying in the grass somewhere mortal and helpless—then he had something. For the first time in two thousand years, he had something of his own.

With information like that, maybe I finally get out from under Snyp. Maybe I finally get a full meal. Maybe, finally, after all this time.

A new light came into his red eyes.

He ran a little faster.

CHAPTER 2
Caden—SDS Lab, Earlier That Day

"How do you feel?" Allen asked.

Caden flexed his fingers inside the Dead Time suit's glove. The weave moved with him, lighter than he'd expected when Allen had first settled it on his shoulders—and lighter still after ten minutes, as if the material were still making up its mind about what it wanted to be.

"Like I'm about to do something stupid."

"Good," Allen said. "Means you're paying attention."

Caden stood on the blue mark painted at the center of the lab floor, a footprint outlined in tape because Allen believed in tape. The room held the particular quiet of people trying not to breathe too loudly. Six technicians at their monitors. Two cameras. Robert with his hands jammed in his jacket pockets, pretending to be at ease and not quite managing it. Robert had that look he got when he'd already decided something and wasn't ready to say so—a tightness at the corner of the mouth, a slight forward lean in the spine. Caden had learned to read it a long time ago.

The helmet sealed around his head, a single enclosed unit. Through the visor, the lab took on a faint coppery tint. The air inside carried the tang of new electronics and treated cloth—sealed in with him. His breath fogged the glass and faded. The heads-up read battery at one hundred percent, field array at one hundred percent, all circuits nominal. A green line ran steady across the bottom of his vision.

"Remember," Allen said, his voice arriving through the comms as clearly as if he were standing in the helmet with him. "Anything feels off—anything— you abort. One tap on the wrist and you'll be out. Nobody's going to be disappointed."

"Robert's going to be disappointed."

"Robert doesn't count."

Caden heard Robert make a small sound that was supposed to be a laugh.

"All right," Allen said. "On my mark. Three."

Caden let his shoulders drop. Dead Time had always been a theory—a field that stopped a pocket of time. They'd sent plants. Mice. An orange that came back with a bloom of mold along its peel. Six trials, most survived. But this was the first human trial.

"Two."

He thought, for no reason he could name, about Bridget. About her hand on the back of his neck that morning when he'd tried to leave the kitchen without eating. *Eat something,* she'd said. *You can't change the world on tea.*

"One."

Allen hit the switch.

The world stopped.

It stopped the way a record stops when the plug is yanked from the wall. The hum of the fluorescents went dead. The technician at the nearest monitor had been scratching the back of his head; his hand was there in the air now, fingers bent, motionless. Dust at the far end of the room hung in the light, each grain set carefully in its place.

Caden breathed in. His breath moved. Good.

He took a careful step. The green line held steady. His foot came down on the tape mark without disturbing it. He lifted his hand in front of his face and watched his fingers open and close. Good.

We did it, he thought, and let himself have one short breath of pride. *We actually*—

Pain drove behind his eyes like a nail, sharper than any headache he'd ever known. An image flashed in front of him: a warrior in black plate mail, holding a blade with a purple vein running the length of it. Gone before he could fix on it. The afterimage pulsed and faded.

Then the room changed.

It grew grainy at the edges, as if he could see the particles the people and the machines were made of. The grains shifted—all of them, at once—half an inch to the left. The technician's suspended hand pixelated. The monitors pixelated. A breeze he couldn't feel seemed to move through the lab, and the dust began to come apart, wiping outward the way sand wipes when a wave pulls back.

Something pulled at him from inside his chest. Not in the room—in him, behind his breastbone and slightly to the left, a line tied to something very far away. The line went taut. Gravity reconsidered itself.

Caden reached for his wrist.

He didn't make it. A sideways tear took him and dragged him through what felt like cold water. Lights flashed around him in colors he couldn't name. He could almost make out images—he couldn't be sure.

Then it all came to a hard end.

He hit stone.

He hit it hard enough to empty his lungs, which should not have been possible, because stone was not what had been there a half-second before. He was on his hands and knees on a flat surface the size of a bus, gritty with frost and carved with runes worn to ghosts. An altar. He was leaning on an altar. The stone under his glove was colder than anything he'd ever felt, a cold that climbed up through the suit and into his wrist as if the stone were drinking him.

He lifted his head.

He was in a hall. Or what had once been one. The walls were rough black rock and climbed so high his eye lost the ceiling. There was no source of light and yet he could see. Something about the place told him it had been holy once, and that whatever had made it holy had left.

"Mauldrin..."

The whisper came from behind him. He turned hard, heart going, and there was no one. The hall was empty. The word had not been spoken aloud. It had arrived at the back of his skull the way the name of someone you've forgotten arrives when you're trying to remember it. It landed like a forgotten bruise.

The nail behind his eyes drove in again. The black-armored warrior flashed across his vision, the purple-veined blade lifted—and was gone.

The tether yanked. Lights flashed, and he was pulled again through what felt like fluid.

For a heartbeat the world was stretched light and nausea. Then his knees were in dirt, and he was blinking, and the scene in front of him made no sense.

A battlefield.

It was the size of a city, and time lay across it like a sheet of glass. Thousands of men and thousands more demons, caught mid-combat. Horses reared in silence. A banner leaned halfway into its fall. Dust hung in a long golden veil across all of it, each mote set where the light had caught it, waiting for a wind that had stopped coming. Twenty feet from Caden, a demon's black claw hovered a finger's breadth from a soldier's throat. The soldier's eyes were wide. The demon's mouth was open in a scream Caden would never hear.

The sun was rising somewhere. The light had the color of an old bruise.

At the front of the field, one figure stood with his hand out as if conducting the stillness itself.

He wore armor the color of winter iron. A long cloak, dusted and pinned at the shoulder. A sword in his other hand, its edge dark with blood. He carried himself like a man who had been exactly where he was for a long time and meant to be there for as long as he chose. He was tall. He was broader in the shoulder than Caden. The beard and the weathering put him twenty years or more past Caden's age.

But the face—

The face was Caden's.

Caden stopped breathing.

He took half a step toward the man, drawn forward by curiosity—or something older than curiosity. The man in the gray armor did not turn. The man did not see him. His focus was pinned on something deeper in the field.

Something deeper in the field was looking back.

Behind the iron-armored figure, out in the frozen carnage, there was a shape that should not have been there. Caden's eye could not fix it. The edges shifted every time he tried, as if the shape were several possible shapes that hadn't yet chosen one. It was tall. It was the color of heat rising off a summer road. It did not sit inside the stopped time the way everything else did. It moved, slightly, at its outermost edges—the way a flame moves inside a sealed jar.

The shape turned its head.

Not enough to look at him. Just enough to show it knew he was there.

A pressure arrived behind Caden's eyes and stayed. A high, thin note began inside his skull—not a sound, quite, but the shape a sound would make. The green line at the bottom of his visor spiked once and shivered back down.

The shape began to settle. Its outline hardened, a heartbeat at a time, into the silhouette of a great warrior in jagged black armor. It lifted a hand. Its voice came through bone, not air.

"Leave me be."

Power struck.

It struck like a hammer. Caden felt the suit's field shove back against it—it held—and then he was airborne, hurled backward, landing in a heap of dead demons.

For a long moment there was nothing but the pound of his own heart, which in this absence of sound was grotesquely loud, and which he was certain the figure must be able to hear.

The figure gave him no more attention.

Then the air in front of it tore.

There was no other word for it. A line opened in empty space about ten feet from where the figure stood—the length of a person—and it widened, and the widening was a violence. Light of a color Caden had no name for spilled out of the rip. The stillness of the place hated it.

A woman came through.

She came through with effort, as if she were pulling herself forward against a hand that had her by the waist. Her hair was white. Her skin glowed with a soft cold light. Her outline wasn't quite solid—the air at the edge of her trembled, as if she hadn't brought all of herself through, and what was still on the other side was paying a price to keep what was here here.

She set her feet. She lifted her face. She looked at the man in the black armor, and her expression moved through several things quickly, none of them simple, and settled on something like the face a person makes at the graveside of someone they had once loved and now found.

"I am here," she said.

He seemed frozen. He did not look at her.

When he spoke, his voice was hoarse from long disuse, and there was no welcome in it.

"You should not be."

"I know."

"Then be gone. Stop haunting me."

She closed her eyes briefly. Opened them.

"My love. It's me. Look at me."

Hope and dread collided on his face. His shape hardened further—as if her gaze had given him more of himself to hold.

"You tread where time forbids," he rasped.

"Yet here I am."

"How? It's impossible."

He stepped forward, carefully, the way a prisoner moves after too long in a cell. His gaze searched the fraying edges of her.

"Are you severed? They cast you in here?"

Pain flickered across her features.

"I was not condemned."

His jaw tightened. "Then you should not be here. No living soul crosses into stopped time and returns."

Her silver light trembled as the void pressed against her.

"I wove a tether," she said. "I crossed through it. My body still lives."

The air recoiled as if the claim itself offended it.

Caden, low in the pile of bodies, could feel the tension—could almost see the invisible thread pulling her back.

"You gamble with an eternity of imprisonment," He growled.

"I did not come to argue."

Webs of strange electricity snapped around her.

"Humans." Her voice sharpened as her outline dimmed. "They have found a way to cross the threshold."

He frowned. "You mean they are separating from their bodies. Entering as souls, as you have."

She shook her head. "No. They are going to cross whole."

He shifted, moved closer. "That is not possible. Only souls are placed in these Cells."

"That is all we ever knew how to do." Her voice thinned as the void clawed at her edges. "Stopped time was built to imprison souls. It rejects flesh—it does, still—but the humans have found a way."

The space around her twisted violently.

"Even now, it tries to sever the tether binding me to my body. But they have found how to do the impossible."

Another surge from the tear behind her rippled across the battlefield.

"When living flesh forces its way in, the prison resists. It creates a pulse you feel."

His eyes darkened. "The pulses are souls being cast into other Cells. Nothing with physical bodies. I have felt them before."

"Listen to me. No one casts souls into stopped time anymore. Those pulses—" She faded for a moment, flickering out of existence, a few of her words swallowed. "—humans—humans, with physical bodies you can take.

Take and escape this prison."

Her gaze held his.

He reached for her. His fingers passed through fading light.

"The pulses." He spoke quickly now. "I felt one before you entered. I nearly did not notice." His gaze narrowed. "It was different. It was longer. It—"

He stopped.

He stopped because the woman had gone perfectly still—a stillness different from the one around them, the stillness of a hunting thing when the wind changes.

Her head turned.

Slowly.

Caden flattened himself against the bodies. His hands were cold inside the gloves. He did not breathe.

"I did not notice," she murmured, more to herself than to the ghostly warrior. "I was holding the tether. I was holding myself. I did not notice—"

Her head turned another degree.

"There is one here," she said. "Now."

Caden's hand went to his wrist.

He tapped the abort.

He tapped it twice. He tapped it three times.

The suit could not bring him back. Whatever door had opened between him and the lab, the lab was no longer on the other end of it.

The woman lifted her hand—what remained of it, as the vortex behind her dragged more of her away. Her attention settled on him with the weight of water. Something behind his breastbone caught and pulled. His feet left the ground. He skidded across stone on the points of his toes and the backs of his heels, a helpless slide, and then he was off the ground entirely, moving toward her through the air as if she had hooked a line into his chest and was reeling him in.

The tear at her back went violent. It clawed at everything within reach. Electricity slammed into his shoulder and helmet as he was yanked the last distance into her grip, darkening the visor, making it hard to see.

Her hand closed around his throat.

It was cold, and it was strong, and it did not feel like a hand. It felt like the grip of an idea.

Through the burnt glass of the visor he saw the tear behind her pulse. The cold light shuddered. Something on the far side of it was losing its hold. She staggered half a step—the barest falter—and the fingers at his throat tightened by a fraction, and the green line at the bottom of his vision spiked hard.

A spiderwork of fractures bloomed across the visor from center to edge in the space of a breath. A force like a tidal wave pressed them both toward the tear. A figure appeared on the far side, reached through, closed a hand on her arm. She screamed. A flash—and both were gone.

But Caden was going through the tear, pulled in with the woman.

He felt himself pulled into what could only be called a tunnel. Images flashed at him and he couldn't tell whether they were visions or things he was actually seeing:

—A throne room swallowed by fire.

—A city's spine sawn open and left to smoke.

—A creature the size of a car bending over a glowing golden sphere, its surface veined like a living heart.

He wanted to breathe and couldn't. His body stretched, thinned, threaded across places that remembered him. His essence spun like a paper scrap in a drain.

Then he was falling—falling backward through something that was neither air nor stone—and the last thing he saw was a wooded slope coming up fast, grass and roots and the earth beneath them, and he knew he was going to hit, and he was going to hit hard.

CHAPTER 3

Caden—Hillside, Then the Helicopter

Leaves.

That was the first thing. The smell of wet leaves. Not the bottled air of the lab, not the dry cold of the altar—earth, close to his face, warm with rot and green.

He kept his eyes shut.

His head ached in a thin high place behind the eyes. His throat ached in a cold dull place at the front, as though he had swallowed ice and the ice had not finished melting. He let his senses come back to him one at a time. Breath. Weight. The small, sharp pressure of something on his cheek.

Glass.

He moved his head a fraction, and a few fragments rolled down the side of his face. The visor. The whole panel had given up. Whatever had held the cracks together inside stopped time had let go on the way out.

He opened his eyes and blinked the dust from his lashes.

Something moved at the edge of his vision.

Low to the ground. Dark. The size of a man, but darker than a man—black skin the color of wet tar, two red points where eyes should have been. It was crouched near his shoulder. Watching him.

He could not bring it into focus. His vision swam. The thing had edges he could not pin down. For one terrible half-second it stared at him as if it were going to come for his throat.

He blinked.

The shape was gone. A few leaves shivered at the base of a tree five paces off, and then even that was still, and he could not have said for certain it had been there at all.

Hallucination, he thought. He did not believe it.

He sat up.

His neck screamed. He put a hand to it and felt warmth, not blood—a dull, settled soreness that climbed into the back of his head. He coughed, and something loose inside him shifted back into place. He got his elbows under himself, then his knees, and ended with his back against the trunk of a pine. He let his head rest there.

He did not know where he was.

He did not know how long he had been here.

He lifted his left arm and looked at the wrist panel. Half the indicators were dark. The comms light still pulsed—slow, weak, but pulsing—and he thumbed it alive.

"Allen." His voice came out small. "Allen. Come in. Anyone. Come in."

Static.

He tried again. More static. Then, faint and fading in and out, a voice he did not recognize at first—and then did. Allen, very far away.

"—den. Caden.—Holy hell—you—we can't—signal—"

"Allen. I'm down. I don't know where I am. The suit is—the suit went. I'm on the ground."

A long wash of static. Then a different voice. Robert's. Tight and controlled, the way Robert got when he was scared.

"—tracking you. We have a signal. Hold your position. Hold, Caden, do you copy—helicopter is inbound—repeat, inbound, twenty minutes out—"

"Copy," Caden said. "Copy. I'll hold."

The line went to hiss and then to silence.

He let his arm fall.

He sat with his back against the pine for a long time and tried to put the last hour back together. The first of it came easily—the blue tape mark, Allen's voice, the count, the held world, the green line. The sideways tear. After that the sequence began to come apart in his hands. He could find pieces of it. An altar. He was sure of the altar. A battlefield. A face in gray iron. There had been something else there too, something whose shape his memory refused to keep. Every time he reached for it the outline slid sideways, the way a dream fades in the first minutes after waking.

A voice had told him to leave it be.

Had it?

He had the residue of it, not the substance. The feeling of having been held. A coldness in his throat that would not warm. The certainty in his bones that he had been in the company of things that were not hallucinations.

He looked around.

The hill rose at his back. He pushed himself up the slope to see what was on the other side of it. A meadow opened in front of him, long and sloping, dotted with scrub and standing stones. At the far edge, a forest.

He stopped.

The trees there did not sit right against the sky. Too dark. Too tall. Too still—no sway in the high branches, no shift of light through the canopy, though the meadow grass between him and them moved in the wind. Something inside the forest spoke to him without speaking—a whisper at the back of his skull, words he could almost make out and could not. *Come closer.* The hair lifted on his arms. A part of him, somewhere deep, wanted to do exactly that. Wanted to walk straight across the meadow and into the dark of those trees and not stop walking.

He shook his head. He took a long breath through his teeth. Then he turned his back on the woods and went down the hill.

The whispering followed him a few paces and then was gone. His hands were shaking.

The helicopter came over the ridge on the twenty-minute mark, and the sound of the rotors was the most ordinary sound he had ever heard.

James and Matt reached him first.

They came out of the open door before the skids had settled—James low and quick, Matt a step behind him, a hand already going to Caden's shoulder. They had him on his feet between them in a count of three. Neither of them said anything that needed saying. James's mouth was a thin line. Matt was watching the treeline.

They walked him to the chopper. Allen met him at the door with two technicians and a medic behind him, and the medic had Caden out of the top half of the suit in under ninety seconds. Allen crouched over the ruined visor like a man over a wounded child, touching the fractured glass with the flat of one finger, shaking his head slowly.

"What did you do to my suit, Major."

"I don't know."

Allen's head came up. Whatever he saw in Caden's face made him decide not to ask the follow-up. He set the visor into a padded case and closed the case and did not open it again.

They lifted.

The trees fell away below. The clearing where Caden had lain shrank to a pale scar in a green sea. He watched it go.

The dark wood at the meadow's far edge did not shrink. It stayed where it was. As they climbed, it seemed to lean. He turned his face away.

Robert was in the forward jump seat, belted in, turned so he could see Caden. James sat across from him. Matt next to James. The rotors made conversation into short exchanges, mouths close to ears.

Robert leaned forward.

"Tell me."

Caden drew in a breath and let it out.

He told them about the held world. He told them about the sideways tear. He told them about the altar—he had an altar, he was sure of it, he could still feel the cold of it under his palm. He told them about the battlefield and a figure in gray armor.

He did not tell them the figure's face had been his own.

He did not tell them about the warrior in black armor, or about the voice that had said *leave me be.*

He did not tell them about the woman with white hair, or about her hand on his throat, or about the other hand that had closed on her arm and pulled her back through the tear.

He could not have explained why he kept it. It was not a choice, exactly. It was the same kind of pull that makes a wounded animal turn its body to the wall. The part of him that had been in that other place did not want the men in this cabin to know what it had seen. It wanted the knowing kept. He would think later that this was the first lie he had ever told any of them. At the time he did not think of it as a lie at all.

He told them the suit was not safe.

He kept his voice low and level—because he knew Robert—and he told them whatever they had built, they did not understand. The suit had not stopped time. Not only. It had done something else. Something had pulled him. He did not know how far he had gone, or through what, but he had gone somewhere, and he had come back bringing a man who could not account for half of what had happened to him in the intervening hour.

He told them the project needed to be grounded.

No one else went in. Not until they understood.

Robert listened, hands loose on his knees. When Caden stopped, Robert did not answer at once. He looked at Caden a long moment, with that same slight tightness at the corner of the mouth Caden had noticed back in the lab.

Then he said, into the steady thunder of the rotors:

"Or. Alternatively. If the suit is doing something we hadn't accounted for— we need to know what it's doing."

"Robert."

"Hear me out."

"No."

Caden had not meant to say it like that. It came out of him the way a nail comes out of a board—a short, hard sound with a small bright shine on the end of it.

Matt's head came up. James went very still in a way James did not usually go. Allen looked up from his case across the cabin. Robert's expression did not change. Which was how Caden knew Robert had heard it too.

The cabin held the silence between them.

Caden could not stop.

"Absolutely not. We do not put another person into stopped time in that suit until we understand what happened to me. I am telling you. I am not discussing it. You will ground the project, or I will ground it for you."

The cabin went quiet under the rotors.

It was not Caden's voice.

The shape of it—the cadence, the way it landed—none of it was his. Caden did not give orders to Robert. Caden had never given an order to Robert in fifteen years. The two of them had a worn old argument-shape that was almost a game: Caden pushed, Robert pushed back, and they found the answer somewhere between them. This was not that. This had come out of his mouth as if someone else had been doing the speaking and Caden had been along for the ride.

His cheeks went warm.

"Robert." The voice was his again now—tired, sheepish, the voice of a man who had overstepped and felt it. "I'm sorry. That wasn't—I'm not myself. I'm sorry."

Robert studied him another moment. Whatever Robert had seen in that snap—Robert had good eyes, always had—he did not put a name to it out loud. He let his shoulders drop. He gave the small nod that, between them, had always meant *it's fine, we're fine, let's not make a thing of it.*

"You're going to take some leave," Robert said.

"Robert—"

"Leave. A week. At least. Go home. See Bridget. Walk Mags. We'll bring the suit in, we'll do a full diagnostic, we will not put anyone else in it—" he lifted a hand when Caden started to speak—"until we've had time. All right? You and I will talk when you've had time."

Caden opened his mouth to argue and found he did not have the argument in him. He nodded.

"All right."

Matt had not looked away from him the whole time.

Matt was not obvious about it. Matt was never obvious about anything. His face wore the same half-amused expression it wore through most meetings. But his eyes had been on Caden's face from the instant Caden had said *no*, and they stayed on it a few seconds after Robert finished talking. Whatever Matt was working out, he was taking his time.

James was the one who caught Caden's eye.

He did not say anything. He did not lean forward. He just held Caden's gaze across the cabin for one long heartbeat. His face was as calm as it always was. But there was a small specific question in his eyes, and the question was not one Caden could answer, because the question was *who just spoke.*

Caden looked away first.

He turned to the window. The country rolled past beneath the rotors—unfamiliar at first, and then familiar by degrees, sliding eventually into shapes he knew. He thought about the line behind his breastbone that had not been there in the morning. He thought about the cold in his throat. He thought about Bridget waiting at home. He would not be able to tell her much. He never could. Tonight he would tell her even less.

Underneath all of it, very quiet, almost too quiet to notice, something inside his chest said one word. Not in any tongue he knew. Not in any language he had ever heard. But he knew the shape of it, and he knew it was a name, and the name had a hook in him.

He closed his eyes and pretended he had not heard it.
Mauldrin

CHAPTER 4
Tagen—Snyp's Portal Room

The cave smelled the way it always smelled. Wet stone, old smoke, the iron tang under it that came up out of nothing and never went anywhere. Tagen moved through the low corridor with his shoulder near the wall and his claws set careful on the rock so they did not click. Somewhere deeper in, something screamed and stopped screaming. He did not slow.

Five days starving. The Witch had closed the wounds and left the hunger. He could feel where his ribs sat. He could feel the place behind his eyes where the hunger lived and watched.

He stopped at the iron door at the end of the run and put one hand on it.

Behind that door was Snyp.

Behind that door was the part of the night he had been turning over in his head all the way down the mountain. *The Witch out of the woods. Kaz at the border. Demons crossing.* All of it, he had to say. The Witch herself had told him to say it. Snyp would know by morning anyway through the other channels he had, and an aniborn who had stood the border and seen what Tagen had seen and had not come home with it would not be an aniborn long.

What he was not going to say was the rest.

He held the door a moment.

Mauldrin lying in the grass. The smell. The Witch's hand still warm on his throat.

If he said the name in this room, the name stopped being his.

He pushed the door.

The hinges took the weight in a slow groan. The room beyond was lit by torches set low into the cave walls, three of them, the kind of orange light that did not climb. The corners of the room stayed dark. The standing gate at the far wall did not help. It was the same arch it had always been, tall, cut with old marks, and the liquid inside it ran slow and black and gave back nothing of the room. A torch could be lit beside it and the surface would stay the same color it had always been. A man could go up to it and put his hand on the dark of it and not see his own fingers.

Snyp stood in front of the gate with his back to the door.

He was bigger than Tagen. He had always been bigger. The skin on him was the kind of black that caught light wrong and gave it back as a sheen, the way oil on water does, and his shoulders made a wide black shape against the wider black of the gate behind him, only the curve of his shoulder picked out by the orange of the nearest torch. Two flat patches sat high on his skull where horns had been in the life before this one. Snyp was one of the few who had come through the dark matter from the demon side, and the size of him said so.

He was speaking, low, to the messenger.

The messenger filled half the room. A rat-thing the size of a draft horse, scaled in dull brown, hunched on its forelimbs with its long head bent to listen. Triaad's beast. They came through the gate when Triaad had a thing to say, and they went back through it carrying what came in answer. This one tracked Tagen with one wet black eye as he stepped through the door.

Snyp did not turn.

"You came back."

"I came back."

"Why are you not on the border? I didn't summon you."

"There were demons at the border. Kaz was among them. And Maselda." Tagen kept his hands at his sides and his voice low. He did not bow. Bowing too soon was the same as begging, and Snyp ate beggars.

The room changed.

It was a small change and it was a big change. The torches kept their slow steady burn, indifferent. The messenger did not move. But Snyp's shoulders went still in a way the rest of him did not, the way an animal goes still when the wind brings it something it has not smelled in a long time.

He turned his head. Only his head.

The red of his eyes was a deeper red than Tagen's had ever been. Healthy. Fed.

"Say that again."

"The Witch was at the border. On the meadow side of the treeline. There were six guards in a ring. Kaz was inside the ring with her. She was—" He stopped. He thought about how to say it. "She had been working a circle. Cold blue fire, cut into the ground. She was hanging in the air over it, and then she was kneeling in the dirt, and she had come back from somewhere."

Snyp did not speak.

Tagen kept going. He had to keep going. Once he had the rhythm of the part he was going to tell, the part he was not going to tell would stay where he had put it.

"Kaz gestured, and two of them broke from the ring. A yellow and a black. They came out of the trees and into the meadow."

"And you let them."

"There was a preel," Tagen said. "And a handler. They put me down. The Witch herself came out before the demon finished me." He made himself say the next part slow and clear. "She told me to bring the news. She said to tell you. She said to tell you the storm is coming. She said to tell you it is time."

The messenger's head moved a fraction of an inch.

Snyp turned.

He turned the rest of the way around, fluid, and his face when it came into the torchlight was not the face Tagen had been ready for. Anger Tagen had a place for. Anger was the easy one. What Snyp wore now was the other one—the look he got when a thing landed in front of him that was bigger than he was.

"She used those words."

"Those words."

"Tell him it is time."

"Yes."

Snyp held the look another beat. Then he looked at the messenger.

"Go. Now. Word for word, what he just said. Maselda, Kaz at the border, the line crossed, the order. Tell Triaad to send back instructions before this night is out."

The messenger hunched lower. "I have not finished the month's report—"

"This eats the report." Snyp's claws came open at his sides. "Move."

The messenger heaved itself onto its hind legs and went into the gate at a half-run. The black surface took its weight with no sound at all and closed over it. The room got bigger when it was gone, and worse.

Snyp turned back to Tagen.

The look had changed. The bigger-than-him look was gone. It had been replaced with something Tagen knew better.

"You should have killed them."

"I would have died."

"You should have died."

It was said flat. It was meant flat.

"I wasn't going to take Kaz alone, hungry, with two other guards on a clear line to me," Tagen said. "I would have died ten paces in and your news would have gone with me. The Witch let me live so I could carry it. I carried it."

"You were sent to die on that border."

"Then your border is held by the wrong aniborn." The words came out before the part of him that knew better could catch them. He held himself very still after.

Snyp moved.

He covered the floor between them in two strides and Tagen had time to set his feet and not much else. The hand at his throat was the size of a shovel. It lifted him a hand's breadth off the stone and held him there. Tagen did not claw at it. He had clawed at Snyp's hand once when he was younger and Snyp had taken three of his claws off for it, root and all, and the lesson had stuck.

Snyp's face came down close to his.

"You speak to me like that one more time and I will eat your tongue out of your head while you watch."

"Yes, master."

"You think the Witch's word makes you safe in this room."

"No, master."

"You think because she touched you, you came back."

"No, master."

He held him a moment longer. Tagen felt the hunger turn in his stomach like a second creature. His vision began to gray at the edges.

The hand opened.

He went down on one knee on the stone and stayed there a beat longer than he needed to, because going up too fast was how an aniborn took a second blow he could have skipped.

Above him, Snyp had gone back to thinking.

"Kaz on the border," he said, not to Tagen. "Maselda out of the woods. After a thousand years. After a thousand years, both of them, the same night." He pressed the heel of one clawed hand to his temple. "What did she work in that circle?"

Tagen did not answer. The question was not for him.

He kept his head down and his breathing shallow and he thought about a body in the grass and a smell he had not smelled since before the Witch had closed her woods, and he thought about how to keep it where he had put it.

"What else did you see?"

It was not a question. It was a check.

Tagen lifted his head. He kept his eyes on the floor in front of Snyp's foot. He had practiced this part on the run home, and he gave it now the way he had practiced.

"They went west when they crossed. Toward the open country and the human territories. The trees around the circle had gone gray. There was a sound when she came back out of it, a long low note." He paused. "Kaz was moving like he was on a mission. Like he had been told a thing was out there and meant to find it."

"Find what?"

"I don't know." He let himself meet Snyp's eyes for the first time. "He wasn't moving like he was raiding. He wasn't moving for a kill. He was moving like a soldier on an errand."

Snyp turned that over. Tagen could see him turning it over.

"If the Witch sent him out of her trees," Snyp said, slow, "she has sent him out for something." His tongue ran along the edge of his teeth. "Then there is a thing in the open country that is worth a thousand years of stillness to her."

"Yes, master."

"And I want to know what it is before Triaad does."

The room went a shade colder. Tagen did not move. *There it is. There's the part*

35

of you Triaad doesn't know.

"Track Kaz," Snyp said. "Find what he is hunting. Do not engage. Do not be seen. Bring it back to me."

"Yes, master."

"Not to the messenger. Not to the gate. To me. You speak the word to no one else under this stone."

"No one else."

Snyp held the look another beat.

"And you will not go alone."

Tagen's head came up.

"I don't need—"

"You will take a youngling."

The word landed wrong in Tagen's gut.

"A youngling will get me killed."

"A youngling will keep you honest." Snyp smiled with the front of his mouth. "No aniborn of mine goes on a mission like this without backup. Triaad would expect it. I would expect it. Choose one with fight in it. You will want it close when Kaz turns his head."

Tagen kept his face flat. He could feel the shape of what was inside the words and he did not let any of it cross into his face.

"Yes, master."

"Then go choose one." Snyp turned back to the gate. "And Tagen."

"Master."

"If you fail me on this—if you lose Kaz, or if you let what he is hunting walk past you the way you let those two demons walk past you tonight—I will not eat you. I will keep you alive in the back of this cave until you are nothing but mouth and eyes and you will live on my charity for what is left of your life." He did not turn around. "Do we understand each other?"

"We understand each other."

"Get out."

Tagen rose. He kept his back straight until the iron door swung closed behind him. The corridor outside was cooler. He walked twenty paces along the wall before he let himself put his hand on the stone.

He stood there a moment with his eyes closed and let the shake go through his shoulders and down his back and out.

A youngling with fight in it. Close, when Kaz turns his head.

The bigger thought came under it, slow and careful, the way a thing has to come up when there are a hundred ears in a hundred walls listening for it.

He didn't ask. He didn't ask if I saw a man in the grass. He didn't ask if I smelled anything else out there. He didn't think to ask. The Witch and Kaz at the border filled his head and he didn't think to ask.

He pressed his palm flat to the rock.

He does not know.

The youngling pen lay three turns deeper. The air there was warmer and worse, thick with the smell of bodies kept too close together. They slept in heaps. They woke in heaps. They scrabbled when an older aniborn came near, because an older aniborn near a heap of younglings rarely meant anything good for the heap.

Tagen turned the corner into the chamber and a body slammed into his hip.

His hand was around the youngling's throat before either of them had thought about it.

He lifted. The youngling came off its feet, claws raking the air, jaws working at nothing. There was no language in the eyes. There was nothing in them but want. It tried to bite his wrist. It tried to bite the dark. Its lungs ran out before its will did, and the body went slack in his hand.

Tagen held it there.

The room watched.

The hunger turned behind his eyes. *Kill it. Eat it. Five days of nothing, and a fresh kill in your hand.* He could taste it already. He could feel the strength coming back into his shoulders before he had finished the kill.

He could also feel what Snyp had done.

He sent me out to track Kaz. He wants what Kaz is hunting before Triaad does. And he gave me this thing as my partner. A thing that will scream at the wrong time. A thing that will lunge at the wrong moment. A thing that will get me killed inside half a day.

Snyp wants the prize. Snyp also wants me dead.

The two thoughts sat in him side by side and did not fit, and Tagen turned them the way Snyp had turned the Witch over.

Eat the youngling now and he would have his strength back inside an hour. He would also have Snyp on him inside an hour. The mission would end here. He would get the back of the cave—the slow life, mouth and eyes, left to rot. Snyp had promised it twice tonight and Snyp did not promise things twice for nothing.

Take the youngling with him and there was a chance. Small. Real. The chance that he made it close enough to Kaz to see what Kaz was hunting before the youngling blew the recon. The chance that he came back with the prize and the body and the truth of what Snyp had set against him.

Snyp gave me a knife and named it my partner. I'm going to walk it out of the cave and see how it cuts before it cuts for him.

He held it a beat longer.

He set it down.

The youngling crashed onto its hands and knees, ribs heaving. The eyes that came up off the stone were already shifting from animal-empty back to animal-watchful. It hissed at him. It would have lunged again if it had had the air.

Tagen looked at it.

"Snyp says you're coming with me." A pause. "You do as I say. There will be meat."

Stay close, and stay loud, and die first.

He turned for the corridor and started walking. He did not look back. He could hear claws on the stone behind him a half-beat later—too eager, too loud, the scrape of a thing that did not yet know how to move quiet—and he heard them keep up, and that was confirmation enough.

He took the long passage out of the cave. The air at the mouth came down off the slope cold enough to wake the hunger again, and he stood in the opening a moment and let it move through him.

Out there, somewhere, a man lay in the grass with the Witch's hand cooling on his throat. Out there, somewhere, a red-skinned demon walked the open country on a hunt he had not chosen. Out there, Snyp was in his chamber turning over a question with the wrong piece missing from it, and Triaad on the other side of the gate was about to be told a story with a hole in the middle.

The hole was Tagen's.

He had carried it down the mountain and into the chamber and back out, and Snyp had not asked the right question, and the messenger had gone through the gate without the part that mattered.

Behind him, the youngling's claws scraped and went still.

Tagen breathed in through his nose. The night was thin and cold and full of the youngling's stink. Under the stink, for half a breath, he caught a thread of something else. He turned his head a fraction toward the slope behind them.

Nothing. The treeline. A few stars between the branches.

He breathed out. *The youngling on his coat already*, he thought, and looked away.

He stepped out into the night and started walking.

CHAPTER 5

Caden—Home, the Fourth Night of Leave

The cold in his throat had not gone.

It had been four days since the helicopter. Four nights since he had slept all the way through one of them. He stood at the kitchen sink with a mug in his hand and waited for the kettle to settle, and the cold in his throat sat where it had sat since the altar, a dull weight at the base of the front of his neck, and the warmth of the tea did not reach it.

He was getting used to that. He did not want to be getting used to that.

Outside the window the yard was dark. Mags was a pale shape moving through it—circling, sniffing, going about his last patrol of the night the way he had every night since he was a pup. Caden watched him for the comfort of watching him. Mags knew about squirrels and the back gate and the moment Caden picked up his coat. He did not need to know anything else. He never had.

The kettle clicked off behind him.

He poured.

Bridget's voice came from the front room. "You're up again."

"Mags wanted out."

"Mags has been out twice."

He let the silence answer that one. He carried the mug to the doorway and leaned against the frame with his shoulder and looked at her.

She was on the couch with her legs folded under her and a book open on her lap that she had not been reading. The lamp behind her threw her hair into dark amber. She was in a sweater of his she had been borrowing for years. Her eyes were tired and watching him.

"Come sit," she said.

He sat.

The couch took his weight, and Bridget moved her legs to give him room, and he set the mug on the table and put his hand on her knee under the blanket. Her hand came down on top of his and stayed there.

For a little while neither of them said anything.

He let himself have it. The lamp. The blanket. Her warmth against his side. The fire down to coals in the hearth and the small clean tick of the wall clock and the smell of the stew she had cooked at dinner and put away in the fridge an hour ago. He let himself have all of it. He had not been able to sleep, and he had not been able to tell her why he had not been able to sleep, and he could not have either of those things at once tonight.

"Caden."

"Yeah."

"Look at me."

He turned his head.

Her eyes were where they had been. They had not moved. She had been waiting four days for him to put his face in the right place, and he had not done it, and now she had asked, and he had to do it.

"You came home Tuesday morning, after being gone all night being medically checked out, with a goose egg on the side of your head, electrical burns across your shoulder, and a cold you don't have. You said you'd hit a wall on the project and Robert had told you to take a week. That was the whole story I got."

"That's the whole story."

"It's Friday, Caden. You have not slept three hours together since you walked through that door. You stand at the window at three in the morning. You hold a cup of tea without drinking from it. Last night I watched you sit in the kitchen for half an hour with the light off. And in your sleep, you said something I did not understand. It was not a word in any language I know."

"I'm decompressing."

"You're not decompressing. I have watched you decompress for eight years. I know what it looks like."

He looked at the fire.

He had known this was coming. On Tuesday he had thought it might wait until tomorrow, and on Wednesday he had thought it might wait until tomorrow, and on Thursday he had begun to suspect Bridget had decided to give him until Friday and had kept her own count, and now it was Friday, and she had.

"I'm sorry," he said. "I know I've been a ghost. I'll be better."

"That is not what I want from you."

He looked at her.

"What do you want from me?"

"I want you to tell me whether you almost died this week."

He did not answer at once.

He could not tell her about the altar, or about the woman with the white hair, or about the figure with his face on an ancient battlefield. He could not tell her any of it without telling her about all of it, and he could not tell her about all of it. Her clearance did not begin to touch what he had seen. He had agreed to that life when he took the work, and she had agreed to that life when she had stayed with him knowing he would not be able to share most of it. They had eight years of that under them.

"It was a bad week at work," he said. "It is not the first one."

"You are a bad liar."

He took a breath.

"Bridget. You know I cannot. We have done this before."

"We have." Her voice did not rise. It went, if anything, quieter. "We have done it for eight years. I have not pushed. I have not made you sit through an ultimatum every six months the way some women would have. I have let you have your time, because I love you, and because I have known what your father did to your mother. I have known."

"I know you have."

She let that sit.

"Caden. I do not need to know what happened. I am not asking. I have made my peace with not knowing what happens to you when you leave this house, because that is the agreement, and I keep my agreements. But I will not make my peace with a man who walks into our home with a head injury and lies on the couch for four nights pretending he is fine. I cannot. I will not."

He had nothing to say to that.

She watched him.

"Marry me," she said.

He went still.

"Don't," she said. "Don't say anything yet. Listen. I want you to hear me."

He listened.

"I am not asking you to pick a date. I am not asking you to tell me anything you cannot tell me. I am asking you to tell me, tonight, that you intend to be my husband. Whenever the work allows. Whenever the project is over. Whenever the world will let you. The intention. In words. Out loud. Between us."

He opened his mouth.

He could not get a word out of it.

He sat there with his mouth open, and the cold in his throat was a bar of iron, and the word he wanted to say was the simplest word in the language. *Yes.* One syllable. He could not get it across his teeth.

He did not speak.

She watched him try.

"Monday night," she said quietly. "I want you to know what Monday night was for me. Because I think you don't know."

He closed his mouth.

"Matt texted me a little after midnight. He told me not to tell you he had. He said they had lost contact with you. He said he'd keep me updated. An hour later he wrote that they had you. An hour after that he wrote that you were a mess but alive. Then nothing from him. Then a text from your phone that said you'd be at the lab overnight for testing. Then nothing. From either of you. Until you walked through the door Tuesday morning with that bag in your hand."

Caden had not known any of this. Matt had said nothing. The text from his phone, he himself had sent only because Robert had told him to, and he had been so wrung out by the time he sent it that he had not stopped to think who would receive it on the other end, or how she would feel reading it.

"I sat up on this couch," she said. "From ten o'clock Monday night until you came through the door Tuesday morning. I started getting paranoid past midnight. I did not turn on a light because I did not want to give myself away to anyone watching the house. I do not even know whether anyone was watching the house. I sat in the dark and I made tea I did not drink and I waited for the kind of phone call I have rehearsed in my head for eight years. And what I learned, sitting on this couch all night, was that I do not know what I am to you, in writing, if something happens. I do not have a name for it. The hospital would not have called me. The agency would not have called me. Matt texted me because Matt thought I deserved to know. Nobody else did."

He looked at his hands.

"And now," she said, "you are sitting in our front room on a Friday and you cannot say one true thing about your week to me. And you cannot say *yes* to a question I have not asked you to answer in eight years."

The silence held. It held longer than he would have thought a silence could hold and still be a silence. The wall clock ticked. The fire popped once, low. Bridget's eyes filled, and did not spill.

She nodded once.

She stood up.

"I'm going to bed," she said. "Don't follow me."

She walked out of the room. The hall light was off. Her footsteps were quiet on the wood. The bedroom door at the end of the hall closed, and the click of the latch was very small and very final.

He sat where he was.

The fire was nothing now. A few coals. The wall clock kept its tick. Mags was somewhere in the yard.

After a minute he stood up.

He walked the hallway. He stood at the door of the room where they slept. He put his hand on the knob. He could feel the cool brass under his palm, and his hand was shaking, and he could not push the door open. He could not even turn the knob. He stood there for a long time with the door under his hand, and he heard her on the other side of it, a small held sound that was not quite a sob, and his hand stayed where it was. His father had pushed doors open. His father had broken doors. His father had pulled his mother out of rooms by the hair and put her on the floor of the hallway and stood over her, and Caden had been six, and seven, and eight, and ten, and he had crouched under his bed in a room down the hall and listened, and the worst sound in the world was a closed door opening in the middle of a fight.

He took his hand off the knob.

He stepped back from the door.

He went to his office.

The room was dark. He did not turn the light on. He shut the door behind him out of an old habit and stood in the dim of the desk lamp he had left burning that afternoon, and he looked at the wall.

The safe was set into the wall behind a framed map of his old deployment. He had installed the safe the year they bought the house—Bridget knew it was for confidential work and knew to leave it alone, and that had been the end of it between them. He had hung the map over the door a few weeks later, partly to cover the steel and partly so the safe would not sit in the back of either of their minds, a quiet thing in the wall holding its quiet things.

He took the map down. He set it on the desk.

The dial was cold under his fingers.

He had last opened the safe a year or so back, for travel papers. He could not remember the trip. He could remember the dial.

The lock clicked.

He did not open the safe.

He stood with his hand on the cold steel of the handle and did not pull it open. Inside was a stack of government travel papers. A spare sidearm. A box of ammunition. A hard drive. A handful of documents he was not legally permitted to keep at home and had kept anyway, because work was work and home was home and he was the one who decided where the line ran. And, at the back of the safe, in a small velvet box, the ring.

He had bought the ring the month after his adopted mother died and put it in the safe the same week, and he had not picked the box up since. Nine years. He had opened the safe for travel papers and the hard drive and one of those documents he was not supposed to have, and the box had sat through all of it, and he had not touched it. He had not even moved it aside. He had reached around it. Nine years of reaching around it.

He could be ready tonight.

He could turn the handle. He could take the box from the back of the safe. He could carry it down the hall and sit on the floor at the bedroom door and slide the box across the wood, and she would open the door, and he would be on his knees, and he would be the man who asked, and he would not be his father.

He could.

He stood with his hand on the handle.

He had taken two rounds in the side and walked his men out of a place he was not supposed to walk any of them out of. He had carried out missions for SDS that no one could ever know about, and put down men who had earned it without losing sleep over any of them. He had let a room of scientists in white coats put him in a suit nobody understood and throw a switch that peeled him out of time itself, and he had come back from that, too.

And here he was. Nine years without the courage to ask one woman a single question.

He closed the dial without opening the door.

He hung the map back on the wall and squared it with one finger and stepped back.

He did not look at it again.

He went to the front room. He picked up his coat. He whistled for Mags, low, twice—the whistle that meant car. Mags came in from the back yard at a trot, his tail high, ready for whatever was next, because Mags was always ready for whatever was next.

He clipped the leash on, although Mags did not need a leash. Caden needed the leash. He needed to be holding something. They went out into the cold of the porch, and the cold of the yard, and the cold of the driveway, and he opened the back door of the car and Mags jumped in.

He sat in the driver's seat and put his hands on the wheel and did not start the car.

He could go back in.

He could walk back through the front door, and down the hall, and into the office, and turn the dial, and end this tonight.

It would take fifteen minutes.

He started the car.

He pulled out of the driveway. He turned right at the end of the road, with no destination, only the need to be moving away from the closed door inside his own house. Mags lay down across the back seat with a long sigh and put his chin on his paws.

He had been driving five minutes when his phone rang.

He let it ring twice. He did not want to answer. He wanted, more than anything in the world, to turn the car around, walk back into the house, open the safe, and end the silence in his hallway. Whoever was calling, on a Friday night, was not calling about anything that mattered.

The phone rang a third time.

He looked at the screen.

It was Matt.

Matt did not call. Matt texted. If he had picked up the phone and dialed on a Friday night, something had happened.

He answered. "I'm on leave."

"Caden, listen to me."

The voice was Matt's, and was not Matt's. The cadence was wrong. Matt's cadence was lazy and dry. This was clipped.

"Listening."

"Robert sent Steven in. About an hour ago. He is not back."

Caden slowed the car.

"What?"

"Steven. Into stopped time. In one of the Dead Time suits. Robert cleared the floor and put Steven in and hit the switch and Steven has not come back. He should have been back fifty minutes ago. He has not come back."

The cold at the base of Caden's throat tightened to a closed fist.

"That's—Matt. That's not possible. Robert told me on the helicopter we were not going back in until we understood the suit. He told me Monday."

"Yeah."

"He told me Monday."

"Yeah, well." A pause on the line. Matt was choosing words carefully. "There is more in play here than the suit, Caden. I have been pulling on threads I do not like. I cannot say more on this line. But you need to know it before you walk in there. This is not Robert getting impatient about a research timeline. This is something else. There is corruption coming from high up. Higher than I want to say out loud."

Caden looked at the windshield. The road was empty. Mags was asleep in the back. The lab was thirty minutes south.

He pulled to the shoulder.

He sat with his hand on the wheel and the engine running. He thought about Bridget alone in the dark down the hall. He thought about the safe behind the framed map and the velvet box at the back of it. He thought about Steven, who was a kind man with a wife and two children and who had laughed at one of Caden's bad jokes at the holiday party. He thought about Robert, who had looked him in the eye in the helicopter and given him the small nod that, between them, had always meant *we're fine, we're fine, let's not make a thing of it.*

He thought about the voice that had come out of his mouth on the helicopter.

"I'm coming," he said into the phone. "Don't tell anyone I'm coming."

"I won't."

"Matt."

"Yeah."

"Whatever the threads are, whatever you have been getting yourself into, I want a better explanation when you and I have time. But if the corruption is as bad as you say it is, you had better be careful."

"I'm always careful."

"No, you're not."

A short, dry sound that was almost the old Matt. Then he was gone.

Caden hung up. He sat with the phone in his hand and looked at the dark country road in front of him.

He could turn the car around.

He could be back in the office in twenty minutes, with the safe open, with the box in his hand. Bridget would still be awake. The hallway floor outside her door would still be there.

He pulled off the shoulder and pointed the car south.

Mags lifted his head as the car moved, then put it down again. He was used to the work pulling Caden at strange hours. He had been used to it his whole life.

The freeway entrance came up. Caden took it. The car climbed and merged and the speed came up under him, and the house was behind him, and Bridget was behind him, and the safe was where it had always been.

He drove south.

In the back seat Mags slept.

Behind him, in a house he could no longer see, the bedroom door was still closed.

CHAPTER 6
Caden—SDS Lab

The lights of the facility came up over the rise a half-hour after he'd hung up with Matt.

He took the long arc of the access road slower than he needed to. The lot at the front of the building was empty. The lot at the side was empty. Two cars by the loading dock, neither of them Robert's. The floodlights washed the steel-and-glass face of the building flat, the way a stage is lit before the first actor walks on. Caden killed the engine and sat with his hands on the wheel.

Mags lifted his head in the back, looked at him, and put it down again.

His left hand went to the latch of the glovebox before his head had decided anything.

He stopped with his fingers on the chrome.

Matt had said corruption. Matt had said, *higher up than I want to say out loud.* Robert had put a man into stopped time three days after looking him in the eye and saying he would not. The lot in front of the building was empty in a way an SDS lot was not supposed to be.

He opened the glovebox.

Inside, behind the registration packet, was the spare. A compact in a leather paddle holster, two magazines beside it in a small zippered pouch.

He loaded a magazine and chambered a round and set the holster on his belt at the small of his back, under the coat. He closed the glovebox.

If his gut was wrong, the worst thing that happened was he carried a gun he did not draw. He could live with that.

He got out. He left the window cracked for Mags.

He'd taken three steps from the car when a voice came from the dark to his left.

"Caden."

A quiet baritone, low enough that he almost did not hear it. He was already turning before the sound finished, his hand already moving to the small of his back, where the holster now was.

A figure stood under the streetlamp at the edge of the lot. Tall, in a long coat. Long silver hair, pale even in the sodium light. Caden had never seen him before. And yet he had. Always at the corner of his eye, like someone who had been following him across a few missions and precarious situations. Caden had blown it off as mission jitters. The mind trying to make something where there was nothing. Now here the man stood.

"You need to leave this place." The voice did not rise. The man was speaking the way a man speaks who knows he has very little time. "Now. With me. Don't look behind you."

"How do you know my name?"

"I know you better than you know yourself." A pause. The pale blue eyes held Caden's. "Mauldrin."

The cold at the front of Caden's throat—the weight that had lived there since the altar, that had been with him on the helicopter and at the kitchen sink and on the drive—tightened around the name like a hand.

From the cracked window of the car behind him came a sound he had never heard out of Mags before.

Not a bark. Not a warning at the back gate. A low rumble, deep in the chest, the kind of sound a dog makes when something is in the room that the dog does not have a category for. The rumble did not stop. It went on, low and steady, a sound the dog had never made before.

He took half a step back from the man, and his right hand found the grip of the gun under his coat.

"My name is Caden."

"That is what you go by now." The man took one step forward and stopped at the lift of Caden's left hand. "It is not who you are. Listen. The Dead Time project is not what they have told you. It is a cell. Built to hold the worst of the souls that have ever existed. And if you or your team enter, the things inside it can come out—wearing your bodies."

"That's enough."

"Your colleague. Steven. He is already gone. What is wearing his body now is older and worse than anything you have a name for. If you walk in there, you may not walk out as yourself."

Caden drew the gun. He brought it up level. His left hand came in under his right and steadied it, the way it had a hundred times before, and he did it without thinking, the way a man does a thing his body has done long enough to do for him.

"Who are you?"

Something passed over the stranger's face that Caden did not want to see. Not a flinch. Something tired.

"I should have been there," he said. "From the beginning. It was on me to raise you. To keep you. To bring you back to who you are. I was kept from you for all of your growing-up years. But I am here now, and I am almost too late."

"Step back."

The man raised one hand, palm out.

"Stop."

The word landed inside Caden's body like a hand on his chest. His feet were where they had been a half-second ago and they would not move. His arms were where they had been and would not come back. The gun was where it was. He could feel his pulse in his ears.

He stopped breathing for one count, then breathed again because his body went on without him. He could not turn his head. He could not blink. He could feel his own weight on his soles and could not shift.

"I will not force you," the man said. "Though I have thought about it. You were stubborn before. You are stubborn now."

He let out a slow breath. He looked at Caden the way a man looks at a person he has been away from a long time.

"Mauldrin. The day is coming when you will see this for yourself. When you will know there is no other way but to come with me. Until then—I am watching."

He lowered the hand.

The pressure went out of Caden's body at once. He stumbled forward a half-step before he caught himself, the gun still up, his breathing uneven. His eyes had not left the streetlamp.

The streetlamp was empty.

There was no one there. There were no footprints in the gravel where there should have been footprints. The light buzzed faintly above an empty patch of ground. Caden stood with the gun pointed at nothing and listened to the buzz.

In the back of the car, Mags had gone quiet.

His phone went off in his pocket.

He didn't look at it for a long count. When he did, Matt's text was already there, the screen still bright.

Caden, hurry. They're about to abandon Steven. Get in there.

He holstered the gun. He started for the doors.

The corridor inside should have been quiet. The corridor inside was not quiet.

The overhead lights were strobing—a long flash, a long dark, a long flash—and the building's air was wrong. Too thin. Too cold.

Halfway down the hall he stopped.

Steven was standing twenty feet ahead of him.

Caden knew it was Steven because the suit was on him—the gold-link weave, the visor—and because the man inside the suit had Steven's height and the way Steven held his shoulders. The rest did not match. Steven's mouth was open in a scream that was not coming out. His arms were lifted toward Caden, fingers spread. His outline was not steady. He was there, and then he was a half-step to the left of where he had been, and then he was where he had been before, and the lights flashed and he was somewhere new.

He was not seeing Caden. The eyes were on him and were looking through him, at something Caden was glad he could not see.

Caden took one step forward and stopped, because the air between them had a shimmer in it like heat off pavement, and he did not want to put his hand into that shimmer.

The lights flashed once more, a long dark, and when they came back, Steven was gone.

The hall was empty. The air system whispered overhead. Caden could hear his own breath.

He moved.

He shouldered the lab doors open.

The room was a bad version of itself. Eight techs at consoles where there should have been four. Half the screens running red. Robert was in the middle of the floor with his hands on the back of a chair, his knuckles white on the chair-back. His tie was loose. His hair was wet at the temples. He looked up when the doors hit the wall, and the tightness Caden had read at the corner of his mouth on the helicopter was now in his whole face.

"You authorized this." Caden did not raise his voice. He stopped two paces inside the doorway, because he did not trust himself to stand any closer to Robert yet. "Monday. You said Monday. You looked at me on the helicopter and you said we were not putting another person in until we understood the suit."

Robert opened his hands. "Caden—"

"No protocols. No oversight. No me."

"We didn't have time." The hands stayed open. "He should have been back. He should have been back over an hour and a half ago."

"I saw him in the hallway."

Robert's hands went still on the chair-back. His eyes flicked to the door behind Caden, then back.

"You saw him."

"Twenty feet from me. In the Dead Time suit. Half there. He could not see me." Caden took the first step toward the consoles. "He's not in this lab, Robert. He's in your hallway."

Robert turned his head a quarter-inch toward the tech at the nearest screen. The tech was already shaking his head before Robert's eyes reached him. "We don't have anything," the tech said. He glanced at Caden, then back at his monitor. "We aren't picking him up. Anywhere."

Robert looked at the screen. Then at the floor.

"That's not possible." He said it the way a man says a thing he has just decided is not true.

"You've lost him." Caden took another step. "Same as you lost me. What did you think was going to happen?"

A low note went through the room.

Caden felt it in the floor before he heard it—a deep slow tone, a hum the size of a building, the kind of sound that does not come from a speaker. The lights along the ceiling pulsed once, dimmed, came back. Two of the monitors went black.

"Sir," one of the techs said, and stepped away from his console.

The hum dropped. A second sound came through under it—a high broken wail, half a person's voice, half something else, riding the air the way feedback rides a wire.

Steven appeared at the center of the room.

He did not walk in. He was not there, and then he was. His knees were a half-inch off the floor. His head turned, slowly, and his eyes did not catch on anything they passed.

"Where am I?" His voice came through static. The speaker in his helmet was broken. The voice was Steven's, and was not.

"How long has it been?"

The lights flickered. He flickered with them, his outline thinning and coming back.

"Who are all of you?" He turned his head another inch. The voice cracked, weaker. "Where is Maselda? Where is my wife?"

The voice scraped and was gone.

Sparks went up off the console nearest to him. The tech there fell back from her chair. There was a sound like a power line breaking, and Steven was no longer in the center of the room. He was in the far corner, hunched over, his hands on his knees, his back to them. He was breathing hard. He was twitching, small, the way a man twitches when something is moving inside him.

"Steven," Robert said.

The thing in the corner went still.

It straightened. It turned. It moved the wrong way for a man in a body it had been in for three hours—too smooth in the shoulders, too slow in the neck. Its eyes found Caden across the room, and it smiled. The smile did not belong on Steven's face.

"Steven?" it said. It rolled the name in its mouth like something it had never tasted before. "No. My name is Azgiel."

The room held its breath.

The thing that had been Steven looked at Caden, and the smile fell off, and what was underneath it was not human, and was very awake.

"You."

Caden could not make himself answer.

"Mauldrin."

The cold in his throat went solid. His body locked. Nothing in the room was holding him. Whatever was holding him was inside him.

"You put me there." The voice climbed. "You locked me in that prison. Two thousand years. Two thousand years in the cold of stopped time, and you walked back into your life and forgot."

He straightened. Along the gold weave of the suit, a thin halo of blue charge crawled up his shoulder.

Robert's hand cut sideways. "Sedate him."

The nearest scientist moved fast. He was three paces in with the syringe when Azgiel lifted his arm, and the cables along the floor jumped. A length of arc came off the nearest console and took the man in the chest. He went over backward. He hit the tile and did not get up.

The second tech with a syringe froze.

Azgiel was looking at Caden. He took a step. The blue charge along his suit thickened and crawled into his fingers.

"You will pay for what you did."

"Now," Robert said, low, to the tech.

The man moved on the word. Azgiel half-turned, late, and the syringe went into the side of his neck. He looked at it like it had insulted him. He looked back at Caden, and the rage in the face under Steven's skin was not anger at a stranger. It was older than that. It was the rage of a man who had been waiting in the dark for a long time to see one specific face again.

"You can't stop what's coming."

The words came out slurred. His knees went. He went down hard, half on his side, the gold-link weave hissing once against the tile. He did not move.

For a long count, nobody moved.

A monitor at the back of the room ticked. Cold air came down from the vents over their heads. One of the techs put a hand over her mouth and held it there.

Robert wiped his forehead with the flat of his wrist. He did not look at Caden.

"Go home."

Caden stared at him. "Are you joking?"

"Caden." Robert turned, finally, and met his eyes. "Go home."

"Robert—"

"I will explain it in the morning." The look in Robert's eyes was not the look Caden had grown up with for fifteen years. It was the look of a man who had decided something a while ago and had only now run out of room to hide it. "Right now we have to contain this. Right now you have to leave."

Caden looked at the body on the floor.

He looked at the techs. He looked at the consoles. He looked at the corner where the thing wearing Steven's body had hunched over and gone wrong. He looked back at Robert, and he kept his voice level, because he knew Robert, and because losing his voice now would let Robert win.

"In the morning."

"In the morning."

Caden walked out.

He did not look at the corridor where he had seen Steven shimmering in the strobe. He did not look at the parking lot for the man with the silver hair. He did not stop until he was at his car.

He stood at the driver's door with one hand on it, and felt the weight of the holster at the small of his back through the coat, and was glad of it.

Mags lifted his head when the door opened. He thumped his tail, twice, the way he did for every door. There was no rumble in his chest now. Whatever had been outside the car was gone.

Caden put his hand on the soft place between his ears and held it there.

He sat in the driver's seat. He did not start the engine.

The stranger had said the project was a cell. The stranger had said the bodies were being taken. The thing that had come out of Steven had used the name Mauldrin the way the stranger had used it—not as a guess, but as a recognition. Was it Steven? Was it a man who had lost his mind in stopped time? Had he seen and learned things there, the way Caden had?

He sat with his hand on the dog's head, and he thought about Bridget in the dark of the bedroom. He thought about the velvet box at the back of the safe. He thought about a man in gray armor with his face on it standing on a battlefield he had no name for. He thought about Robert, who had looked at him in the lab and given him a look he had never given him before in fifteen years.

He thought about Mags growling at the man under the streetlamp.

He started the car.

He pointed it home.

CHAPTER 7
Bridget—Home

Bridget hadn't been able to sleep after she heard Caden drive away. She got up. The kitchen still needed a little tidying, and tidying was the kind of work her hands knew how to do without help from the rest of her.

She slid the last bowl into the dish rack and wiped a crescent of broth from the stovetop. The kitchen was quiet—only a clock ticking toward another hour and the white noise of the fridge. Caden wasn't home. She reached for the marked-up cookbook she'd used and, out of habit, returned it to the narrow shelf beside the pantry door where she kept them all—spines penciled with notes, tabs bent from years of improvising.

As she eased the book back, something resisted. A slim volume hid behind the row, misplaced long enough to collect a skin of dust. Bridget tugged it free.

Her old field notebook—olive-green oilcloth, corners rubbed pale, the cover crosshatched from hard use. It flexed under her fingers with the stubborn give of canvas, water-resistant once, now frayed. The sight of it pulled an ache through her. A life measured then in triage and plasma, not charts and insurance codes.

She hadn't been looking for it. Yet here it was.

At the kitchen island, she thumbed it open. Pages had stiffened with time and heat; the scrawl inside slanted in long, urgent strokes that pulled the past forward—bleary nights, the mealy taste of adrenaline, the relentless math of seconds and blood loss. She found the dog-eared page almost on instinct, the one she had read and reread until the crease learned the shape of her hand.

She began to read:

Hour nineteen. The tent smells like every other tent. Antiseptic and blood and the inside of a copper kettle. Lanterns swing every time the flap moves, and the cots are full again, and the row by the door is the row no one wants. My hands shake. They have been shaking for two hours. I cannot stop them, so I work around them.

They bring in another. "Major Gray. Two rounds, left side. Lost a lot." I look up before I mean to. **Caden Gray.** *I have never met him, and I already know him. Everyone here knows him. He is the one who carried his men out of the valley after the radio went dead. They tell that story like a prayer.*

On my table he is a body losing pressure. I cut the uniform off him in three strokes. Blood comes through the gauze the way it always comes through the gauze when it is going to come through everything. I press harder. The shaking in my hands evens out. It always evens out when there is something to push against.

Then he opens his eyes. He should not have eyes to open. They are blue and they are clear, and that is worse, somehow, than if they had been glassy. A man should not be that lucid when he is bleeding like that.

"Not on my watch."

I do not know where the smile comes from. It is not a real smile. He needs one anyway.

He tries to smile back. It comes out as something else. "I was supposed to get everyone out."

I have been with his men since dusk. I know what they look like. I know which one will not walk again and which one will not see his daughter and which one keeps asking for the major. "You did get them out," I tell him. I press another layer of gauze. His heart is going under my hand, fast and stubborn, refusing to give up the body it lives in. "They are alive because of you. Do you hear me? They are alive."

He looks at me. The whole tent is moving and shouting around us, and his eyes hold steady on mine like the room has gone quiet for him.

"Do you promise?"

I lean down close enough that he will hear me over everything else. I should not promise. We do not promise. The first thing they teach you is that you do not promise.

"I promise," I tell him.

Something in his face lets go. Not all of it. Enough.

"Call me Caden."

"Okay. Caden."

I set the IV. I stay with him longer than I am supposed to stay with anyone. I tell myself I am watching the line. I am not watching the line. I am watching his chest, and counting it, and waiting for the next one, and the one after that.

I have treated so many men. I have watched them bleed, scream, die. I have learned to let them go.

But this one, I won't forget.

Bridget opened the back door and propped it open for a little cool air, then closed the journal in her palm. The porch light flicked on. Out in the yard, a motion sensor caught a raccoon nosing the fence and clicked off again. The quiet that followed felt larger than the room.

Caden's secrets—and what they demanded—weren't only wearing at their relationship. They were carving lines in him. She knew the signs. She had seen them in other faces over the years. The way a strong back learned how to bow.

She set the journal on the table, thumb still marking the crease, and looked toward the dark hallway as if she might hear a key, a step, some proof that tonight wasn't like the others. Nothing.

She slid the journal onto the top pantry shelf, high enough that she'd have to decide to reach for it next time. Her fingers rested on the spine a moment longer. Enough.

Tomorrow, she would stop letting him keep the worst of it alone. She would name what she saw and ask him to let her in. Not as a therapist with a clipboard, but as the woman who once promised a man on a table that he wasn't done yet.

She left the kitchen and went to the couch. Tonight, she would wait, and she would read his face when he came through the door, and what she did next would follow from that.

CHAPTER 8

Caden—Home Office

Caden walked through the front door, the night's events still clawing at his mind. On the couch, Bridget sat curled beneath a thick blanket. He stopped in the entryway. He had thought she would be in bed. He had been counting on it. The couch was where she had asked him to marry her three hours ago, and he had not been able to answer, and now she was on it again, waiting for him. He hung his jacket and paused, weighed down by what he couldn't yet say.

"Bridget," he started, a mix of apology and resignation.

She looked up, tired yet searching. "It's pretty late," she said—no accusation in her tone.

Caden could have offered excuses, but none of them would have been true. "I know," he said.

Bridget's sigh was soft, almost lost in the crackle of the fire.

Guilt rose. He hated the cycle. He hated his part in it more.

"I'm sorry I left. I shouldn't have. I should've stayed with you," Caden said, moving toward her. He was not about to tell her he had gone to the lab when he was supposed to be on leave, or that a man in a parking lot had told him not to walk in there. That would only make things worse.

Bridget didn't counter. She watched. "You look exhausted."

Caden managed a tired smirk. "I'm okay," he said, and the lie felt thinner than it ever had.

It wasn't just exhaustion.

Something inside him had shifted since Steven came back. Since Azgiel looked at him like he knew him. And Bridget on the couch where she had asked him a question three hours ago. Patient, still waiting, asking nothing of him in this moment.

She stayed steady. "Are you?" Two words, soft enough to land somewhere under his ribs.

She had watched him fray for four days. The shoulders that never came down. The nights he lay beside her with his eyes on the hallway, somewhere else entirely.

"Let me get you some tea or something," she said, rising from the couch. "I'll heat up the water."

"Bridget, there's no need—"

She cut him off. "It's not about need, Caden. It's about wanting to care for you," she said, already on her way to the kitchen.

It was not the lateness. It was the way he was hollowing out from the inside and pretending he was not.

Tonight he was a man at the end of something.

"I'm headed to bed," she said, giving up on the tea. As she passed, her hand brushed through his hair and rested there a beat longer than it needed to. "I'd love for you to join me."

She left him there. He wasn't sure if it hurt more when she had told him not to follow her to bed earlier tonight, or now, when she was inviting him to come. Caden slumped onto the couch, the night sitting on him like a coat he could not get off.

His phone vibrated. He reluctantly looked at it. Matt's name on the screen. He answered. "What now?"

"Caden, listen." Matt's voice was low, steady, and threaded with something Caden didn't hear from Matt often: fear. "I've been digging. Steven's condition isn't an anomaly. It's part of something much larger. Someone at the top of SDS is orchestrating this—it goes beyond Dead Time."

Caden sat up. "How do you know this? Robert said nothing while I was there."

"That's because Robert's part of it," Matt said. "I've got intel from inside SDS. Can't reveal my source, but know this—Steven was the beginning."

Caden pressed the heel of his hand into his eye. "And you're telling me this why…?"

There was a pause on the other end. "Because I trust you, Caden. And if I approached Robert directly, I'd disappear. But you—you've got more at stake here."

"If what you're suggesting stretches beyond Dead Time, or beyond Steven calling himself Azgiel, I need hard evidence. Emails, footage, names—anything you've got. But it better be concrete, and if it isn't, I'm going to ask you to get a psych eval because you sound paranoid."

He ended the call and let the phone fall onto the cushion. He rubbed the back of his neck. The room came back around him in pieces—the tick of the clock, the settle of the house, the small private sounds of a place where someone he loved was trying to sleep.

A soft creak in the hallway floor turned him. Bridget stood at the edge of the room.

"Did you say Azgiel?" she asked.

"Yes, it's work-related," Caden replied.

Bridget came into the room. "Someone is actually calling themselves Azgiel?" Her voice held a quiet, careful curiosity.

"You know I can't discuss the details," Caden said.

She did not push back. She just brushed her hand against the stubble of his jaw. "I know. But it's odd, isn't it? That name."

She paused. "My grandmother used to tell me stories about someone called Azgiel. Strange ones, for a child. And here it is, in your work."

Caden went still. "Bridget…"

"I'm not asking for secrets," she said gently. "Just… why that name?"

He sighed. "I can't."

Bridget studied him a moment longer, then leaned in to press a kiss to his forehead.

"Whatever's going on," she said as she started back toward the bedroom, "please, just be safe."

He watched until the soft click of the bedroom door closed her in.

Caden sank back into the couch. The image of Steven's face going wrong under the visor would not let him go.

Sensing his distress, Mags jumped onto the couch and laid his head across Caden's lap. Caden stroked the dog's fur, slow, useless, comforting all the same.

The man in the parking lot kept coming back to him. The silver hair under the streetlamp. *"You will not walk out as yourself."* Caden had not believed him at the time. He was not sure what he believed now.

"It's all going to be okay," he muttered—but the words felt rehearsed. He'd said them before. After funerals. After nights he couldn't sleep. They used to mean something. Now they felt like something you say when you're trying to convince yourself.

CHAPTER 9

Tagen—Myree Battlefield, Two Thousand Years Past

The battlefield lay under a pale moon. Blood and decay hung in the cold air. Bodies of soldiers and horses lay scattered.

Tagen moved silently through the wreckage, taking in his surroundings. The faint gleam of a distant village wavered on the horizon, an illusion of peace mocking the devastation. He doubted the farmers and villagers conscripted to fight Azgiel's forces had believed they stood a chance. *Humans,* he thought with mild disdain. *Fragile. Ignorant. Yet defiantly resilient.*

From somewhere among the mangled remains came the faintest groan. Tagen's acute hearing picked up the sound immediately—a soldier, clinging to life. Tagen slipped into shadow form, his body disappearing in the mist that flowed smoothly over the blood-soaked ground. He moved like a wraith, unseen by mortals, untouchable by the carnage around him.

Triaad's orders infiltrated his mind: *Find Azgiel. Observe his forces. Witness his fall.*

Tagen allowed himself a moment of satisfaction. Triaad's ambition burned brighter than most. Once Azgiel's most trusted advisor, Triaad had shed his loyalty like a second skin. And Triaad's answer to that broken loyalty was the aniborn—a race forged from dark matter, bound to him by a leash older than any oath.

Tagen was one of his finest. Loyal. Ruthless. Efficient. He let the thought pass through him as his spectral form drifted closer to the groaning soldier.

A rustle in the nearby debris drew his focus. Near the edge of the battlefield, a lone soldier pushed himself upright, his movements slow and labored. Leather armor, scorched and melted by demonic fire, clung to his skin. His hand gripped the hilt of a broken sword as though it could shield him from fate.

Beside the soldier, a dog limped forward, its matted fur slick with blood. The animal's movements were stiff, its body shaking, yet it stood by its master's side.

Then it looked toward Tagen. It could not see him—not fully—but it sensed him, and the growl that came out of it was old.

"What is it, boy?" the soldier asked.

Tagen let his edges sharpen—just enough. The animal yelped in terror, scrambled to its three good legs, and bolted.

The soldier recoiled. "Who's there?"

Tagen materialized for a heartbeat—just enough for the soldier to see him. The man's breath caught. The sword fell out of his hand.

Tagen dissolved again and slipped past him. The campfires were waiting, and Triaad's question was waiting in them. The dying field fell behind him.

The camp sprawled across the desolate terrain, a patchwork of chaos and menace that mirrored the battlefield's devastation. Hulking demons with curled horns and long wings sat around blazing fires; their conversations broke the stillness. The pungent stench of sulfur and burning flesh hung in the air, mingling with the metallic scrape of whetstones on blades.

Tagen drifted along the camp's perimeter, his essence weaving through rocks and debris like smoke. He scanned the hulking figures clustered around the fires. Azgiel's forces were smaller than anticipated.

Two hundred. Perhaps less.

Triaad's estimates had been wildly off. Azgiel's arrogance, once a force to be reckoned with, was now his greatest weakness. The king of demons had overextended, and the cracks in his reign were beginning to show.

A sudden movement snapped Tagen's focus. A cobalt-blue demon, easily triple the size of an average soldier, stomped past him. The creature carried a sword as tall as a man, its edge honed to a razor's sharpness. Its yellow eyes swept the area with deliberate precision.

Tagen shifted his form until he was nothing more than a faint distortion in the air. He stilled everything in himself as the demon lingered close. Some demons had a rare ability to sense aniborn, even in cloaked form. Tagen's survival depended on his ability to remain undetectable.

The cobalt demon finally moved on, and tension left Tagen's form. He resumed his path, phasing through a massive boulder that blocked his way. He closed in on his target.

At the center of the camp stood a large tent, its fabric stitched together from the hides of unknown beasts. It was surrounded by a ring of guards—demons larger and more menacing than the rest.

Azgiel, Tagen thought. The king of demons would be inside that tent, plotting his next move. Tagen's mission was clear: observe, report, and ensure the downfall of the king.

Tagen's sights locked on the king who thought himself untouchable.

Tagen didn't sense the attack until it was too late. A crushing force yanked him from his hiding place, slamming him against the trunk of a tree. Pain exploded through his torso as he solidified, black blood seeping from deep, claw-inflicted wounds.

His vision blurred, but what he saw when it cleared was worse than the pain. A circle of demons stood around him, studying their captive.

And at their center stood the king.

"Azgiel," Tagen muttered before he could stop himself, his voice hoarse and bitter.

The demon king's scarred face moved into something between amusement and contempt.

"At least this one knows my name," Azgiel said. "Let's see if you'll talk before I make an example of you."

Azgiel leaned closer, and the aniborn acted. He shifted into shadow form, slipping free of the demons' grasp. Their claws swiped uselessly at the air as he phased through their weapons.

But escape was fleeting. A massive, green-skinned demon moved with surprising speed. It swung a spiked club at the space Tagen occupied, the force of the strike disrupting his cloaked form. The blow forced him to solidify with a sickening thud. Air rushed from his lungs as pain shot down his body.

The creature towered over him, its rancid breath hot as it leaned closer. "You try that again," it rumbled low, "and I'll rip your legs off."

Tagen glared up at his captor. He'd encountered demons like this before—rare creatures capable of seeing aniborn even when they vanished. A cruel reminder that the dark could fail him.

The circle of demons tightened around him as Azgiel moved forward, his sword gleaming with dark energy. Tagen's mind raced. The odds were stacked against him.

Hours blurred together, marked only by searing pain ripping through his body. He hung limply between two demons. His shadow form was out of reach—his energy too thin to summon it. Normally his body would knit itself back together, the way aniborn always did. Tonight nothing knit. Each gash and fracture stayed raw, black ichor oozing as the energy in him guttered like a dying lamp.

The green-skinned demon bent over him. "You'll break, little creature." Its spiked club dripped with black ichor—Tagen's, splattered across the ground. "They always do."

Tagen lifted his head. "You'll have to do better than that," he said.

The green demon's voice rumbled with amusement. "Oh, I can. But it's more fun when they beg."

Tagen's claws twitched feebly. He spat a mouthful of black blood onto the demon's face, and the fluid sizzled faintly where it landed. The demon recoiled, expression twisting into fury.

"Fine," Tagen croaked. "I'll talk."

Azgiel stepped forward. "Let's hear it, then," his voice a low growl. "What does your cowardly master think he knows?"

Tagen raised his head. "It doesn't matter anymore. Your time is up."

Azgiel's face moved—the smallest hairline of unease. "Speak plainly."

Tagen managed a faint, wry smile. "Triaad sent me to watch you fall. He knows your reinforcements are gone, that your arrogance has left you vulnerable. And soon, it will all be done."

"Triaad? My most trusted advisor? Betray me?" He said it like a joke. The fury underneath it said something else.

Tagen nodded. "He already has," he said, faltering. "I'm here to witness it... your fall... and his rise."

Azgiel's expression hardened. The demons exchanged uneasy glances, their confidence in their king visibly shaken. The only sound was the crackling of the nearby fires.

"You lie," Azgiel growled, stepping closer. "Triaad lacks the cunning or the strength to challenge me. You're no more than a worm spitting lies to save your skin."

Tagen dropped his gaze. He said nothing more, conserving what little energy he had left. The truth was a weapon. He had thrown it. Now he would see whether it landed.

Azgiel raised his blade. The air around it thrummed, dark and wrong. "You'll regret wasting my time."

Before he could strike, a distant horn shattered the moment. The ground shuddered under the force of approaching hoofbeats, and the demons went still. The jeering died. Tagen watched something move through them that he had not seen before in demons—the small, tightening fear of soldiers who had just heard the bell.

Dawn's first rays cut across the battlefield, staining the horizon in orange and violet. From the radiance rose the march of an army, distant at first, but growing louder with each passing minute.

Tagen struggled to focus through his battered vision. The brilliance was blinding, forcing him to squint. At the forefront of the army rode a figure clad in light-gray armor that drank in the dawn and reflected it tenfold. Mauldrin.

Mauldrin's presence struck like a tidal wave. Sleek and rune-etched, his helm gleamed in the rising light. The force of him rippled outward, and the battlefield seemed to bend beneath him.

Raising his hand, Mauldrin made a single gesture. White energy burst outward in an unrelenting wave, engulfing Azgiel's front lines. The demons disintegrated on contact, their screams swallowed by the crackling force. Smoke and ash filled the air. The vanguard was gone.

From the chaos, Azgiel's bellow tore across the field. Blackened, jagged armor reflected the dark energy of the blade in his grip. When Azgiel raised it high, the sword erupted in black flame.

"Forward!" Azgiel's voice thundered, commanding his remaining forces. The demons, though faltering, surged toward the radiant army. Each strike came more desperate than the last—the ferocity of cornered animals, no longer of conquerors.

They had pinned him to a tree with two swords through the meat of his shoulders, one through each side, and left him there to watch. Every attempt at shadow form failed; he was too torn open to pull himself thin. Horror mingled with awe as Mauldrin's soldiers, clad in silver-colored armor, advanced with surgical precision. Their blades cut through Azgiel's demons with a terrible discipline.

Tagen watched every movement of Mauldrin's advance. The power he radiated was beyond anything Tagen had ever seen. Fear coiled inside him, tangled with an unsettling admiration. This was history unfolding before him— the end of Azgiel's era and the dawn of something new.

The radiant commander moved with unstoppable force. With a flick of his wrist, beams of energy erupted from his palm, obliterating clusters of demons at a stroke. Molten trails opened in the ground where his power passed. His focus held to Azgiel and to Azgiel alone.

And then—from behind—something Mauldrin had not accounted for. A horde of demons attacked, smashing him to the ground. He cut through them, but lost sight of Azgiel for that moment.

Azgiel raised his black sword over his head. Mauldrin turned a fraction late. The blade met the gauntlet that came up to stop it, and where the steel touched, two of Mauldrin's fingers came away. Black flame followed the cut, climbing the inside of his arm like ink moving through water.

Mauldrin staggered. For the first time since the dawn, he staggered. He drove his other hand against the wound and a blue flame shut around it. The black kept climbing. He spoke a word Tagen did not know—something old, the syllables of it not native to any tongue Tagen had heard—and the white in him answered. Light cracked through the black. Fingers reformed where there had been none. Azgiel raised the sword again, and the explosion that burst from Mauldrin's hands threw Azgiel across the field.

Tagen felt the wave of it pass through his own body. Even at the edge of the field, even pinned to a tree, even half-dead, the wind that came off Mauldrin smelled of something he had no name for.

So the sword could wound him. The thought arrived clean and useful, the kind of thing Triaad would want to know. The sword could wound him, and he had known the words to take the wound back. Both of those things mattered.

Despite the overwhelming odds, Azgiel stood firm. His blade clashed against Mauldrin's light, the collision sending shockwaves rippling through the battlefield. The two forces locked in a brutal struggle for dominance. Yet, even as Azgiel's fury fueled his attacks, his forces faltered. One by one, his soldiers fell under the relentless advance of Mauldrin's army. The battlefield became a graveyard, the once-roaring demonic horde reduced to scattered remnants.

Mauldrin's power was inexhaustible, his strikes growing stronger with every swing. Azgiel began to falter, his movements slowing with exhaustion. The balance of the battle had shifted, the inevitability of Azgiel's fall hanging heavy in the air.

Pinned and weakened, Tagen could do nothing but watch as the end approached. The clash between the two kings burned itself into his memory. There was something in the way each man fought the other that he could not name—a familiarity, a grief under the violence—but it was not his to name. Not yet.

The battlefield descended into a ghostly silence, broken only by the crackle of dying fires and the occasional groan of the wounded. Dust and ash veiled the desolation in a muted haze. Mauldrin moved through the carnage. Behind him, the lifeless ranks of Azgiel's army stretched in unmoving rows.

At the center of the wreckage knelt Azgiel. His once-mighty frame sagged. The blade in his hand was a ghost of its former power, its black flames sputtering weakly. Blood ran in rivulets down his face, mixing with the dirt that streaked his skin.

"You've lost," Mauldrin said with a quiet thunder that reached across the battlefield. "Your reign of evil ends here."

Azgiel lifted his head, blazing with defiance even as his body betrayed his weakness. He spat blood. "My reign?" he growled. "You bring death and destruction, and yet you claim righteousness? You're no savior, Mauldrin. You're a butcher."

Mauldrin raised his hand. A band of plasma erupted from his palm, winding around Azgiel like a living chain. The chain pulled tight as Azgiel's muscles strained against the bonds. The demon king snarled, his teeth bared in a final act of defiance.

"You'll not kill me," Azgiel said. The mockery in it was real. So was the bait. "You lack the conviction."

Mauldrin's voice was steady. "I don't need to kill you," he said. "Death is too small for what you have done. I am going to lock you between the seconds, brother. You will live. You will not act. You will know every passing year and you will not be able to touch one of them. Your sword I will curse—any who reaches for it will be destroyed—and your name I will leave in the world only as a warning."

With a flick of his fingers, Mauldrin warped the air around them. Azgiel's sword wrenched free from his grip and floated above the field. A second motion, and a slow, glassy tear opened in the air at Azgiel's back—a rent in time itself, the kind of stillness that hummed at the edge of a held breath. Through it, Tagen could see nothing. Only that what was on the other side of it was not the next moment.

"No!" Azgiel roared, his voice thundering across the battlefield. He strained against the bindings that held him, but his strength waned with each passing moment. "This isn't over! Do you hear me, Mauldrin? This isn't over!"

"It is," Mauldrin said, his tone carrying no malice—only certainty.

The rent widened. The bindings of plasma drew Azgiel into it, slow at first and then all at once, the way a drawn breath ends. His shout cut off mid-syllable—not silenced, but suspended, as though the sound itself had been caught between two heartbeats and held there. Then the seam in the air closed, and the place where Azgiel had knelt was empty.

Mauldrin advanced on Azgiel's sword, its steel laced with a purple vein, still tainted by its master's power. His hand passed through the hilt. Blue flames erupted from his palm, and when he reached for it again, his hand closed around it. The violet line at the center flared once, then subsided as he drew the weapon high.

With his free hand, Mauldrin gestured, and the ground heaved and opened before him. The flames surged, encasing the sword in a crystalline cocoon. Mauldrin released it, stepping back as the crystal solidified into a sealed shell. One final motion—a downward flick of his fingers—and the cursed blade plummeted down the chasm and sank to the depths of the world.

The pit sealed itself, leaving no trace of what had been buried beneath. Mauldrin took in the battlefield—now a graveyard of ruin and silence. His brother was not dead. That was the part that would not let him go. His brother would live forever, awake, in a single instant that did not move. Whether that was mercy or a worse cruelty than killing him, Mauldrin would have the rest of his own life to decide.

Mauldrin lowered his hand. The weight that came down on his shoulders in its place was not lighter. It was simply his now.

Above, the sun broke through the haze, casting the battlefield in a harsh, unforgiving glare. Mauldrin stood amongst his remaining army, his presence a beacon of triumph—and sorrow.

Within the burned-over ruin of Azgiel's camp, Tagen shifted, the ache of his body almost worse than the wounds themselves. Desolation lay before him—a battlefield scorched clean of Azgiel's army. The memory of Mauldrin's power had burned itself into him—the wave that took the front lines, Azgiel's sword, the fingers gone and grown back, and the seam in the air that had taken the king and closed without leaving a mark.

The air still popped faintly with residual energy, the remnants of Mauldrin's power lingering like a ghost. Smoke coiled in thin ribbons, carried upward by the morning breeze. Tagen's claws dug into the ground, awe and resentment swirling within him. Mauldrin had triumphed, but he had not killed. That was the part Tagen would not forget. The brother had been spared, and the sparing felt like something more dangerous than a kill.

This place was not safe. Mauldrin's presence pressed down on him like a held weight, and a single look in his direction would end Tagen as easily as Azgiel's vanguard had ended.

Summoning his last reserves, Tagen slipped into invisibility, the effort draining him to the edge of collapse. His silhouette wavered, and he slid into the folds of the surrounding forest. Slower than it should have been. The injuries fought him on every step. The trees took him in anyway.

His mission was complete. Triaad would be pleased—or so Tagen hoped. Truth was a fragile thing in front of the master, easily punished when it did not please him. But what Tagen carried tonight was not a truth Triaad could afford not to hear: the king of demons was alive. Sealed, but alive. The war Triaad had been waiting two ages to win was only beginning.

The first rays of dawn filtered through the canopy, piercing the smoke and illuminating the ruins of Azgiel's army. The carnage stretched behind him like a grim display, but Tagen didn't glance behind. He couldn't afford to. The end of Azgiel's reign heralded a new beginning.

Tagen pressed forward, the forest swallowing him whole as the lingering trace of Mauldrin's energy faded into memory. His master awaited.

CHAPTER 10
Tagen—Forest Border

They had been moving for days.

Tagen had run the youngling north and west of the caves, away from the border, threading the long way back to where Kaz had crossed. The youngling kept up the pace and kept its mouth shut, which was more than Tagen had expected. Kaz knew what he was doing. He had covered his tracks well to keep the rest of his kind from following him, but not well enough to hide the trail from Tagen. He had been tracking for a few thousand years, and few aniborn alive matched him for it.

The forest's canopy was thick, allowing only thin slivers of moonlight to penetrate. The fresh trail cut through it like a wound. Tagen crouched low, peering at the disturbed underbrush ahead. The demons' trail was fresh—Kaz wasn't far.

The youngling shifted impatiently beside him. Tagen glared at the creature. Snyp had paired him with the thing for a reason, and the reason was not protection.

He raised his clawed hand sharply, signaling silence. The youngling stood by, muscles coiled and ready to spring. *Stay*, Tagen mouthed at it. *Stay*. Snyp had been clear: track only. Do not engage. Do not be seen. Tagen advanced, shifting form until he vanished from sight, a phantom gliding between the trees, his senses raw beneath the demonic weight that pressed down over the clearing.

Kaz stood at the clearing's edge, accompanied by the two demons that had crossed the border with him—the yellow and the black, the same pair Kaz had sent across the meadow five nights ago. The clearing showed the wear of a camp used and used again: trampled brush, ash where a fire had been smothered and rebuilt, prints in and out toward the human city downslope. Tagen edged closer.

"We retrieve him swiftly," Kaz said. "The Witch demands absolute discretion. Humans cannot be alerted to our presence."

Tagen's attention sharpened, and he inched closer. *Retrieve whom? The man in the grass? Mauldrin?* He held himself still and waited for a name.

That was when the wind turned.

It came down out of the high branches, a thin shift of air that carried something it should not have carried. Tagen had it for half a breath before he understood what it was.

Aniborn.

Not him. Not the youngling. A third was somewhere out there—behind them, downwind by a long throw, far enough back that he had not picked up the scent on the run in, close enough now that the breeze had finally given him up.

Tagen turned his head a fraction. He kept his body still and let his eyes do the work, scanning the dark between two of the older pines on the rise above the clearing. For a moment there was nothing. Then a piece of the dark moved that should not have moved, and the moonlight caught the outline of a face he had known for the better part of a thousand years.

Gench.

Tagen mouthed the name, and the shape of it in his mouth told him everything Snyp had not.

Gench made runs to the human cities for Snyp, so he was an obvious pick for this kind of work. He was the one Snyp sent when he wanted a thing finished without his own scent on it. Gench did not track for partners. He tracked for corpses, stayed downwind of the kill, and walked in after to take whatever the dying aniborn had been carrying.

Snyp gave me a knife and named it my partner—and sent another knife behind me to take the meat off the bone. Track Kaz. Die on Kaz. Gench takes the news home. Snyp gets it without anyone seeing his hand.

Clean. The cleanest piece of work Snyp had ever set against him. And the realization had stopped him for the breath he could least afford—

The youngling had left his side.

It was already moving. Already cloaked, already low to the ground and flanking Kaz's guards on the wrong side of every order Tagen had given it. Tagen had taken his eyes off it for that single beat, and the beat had been enough. *Fool.* He braced to intercept.

Too late.

The youngling lunged at the black demon. The demon roared in surprise and fury, claws tearing into it. Kaz turned, seizing the youngling. Its neck snapped and the head ripped off in his fist. The body went to ash before it hit the ground.

Tagen was already retreating when the black demon turned toward him. The brute hurled a heavy axe from its belt.

The weapon slammed into Tagen's side, pinning him to a tree trunk. Pain exploded through him. Black blood seeped into the bark. He shifted his form, pulled free of the steel, and collapsed onto the forest floor, the shadow form bleeding out of him as he hit the ground. He did not have the strength left to hold it.

The black demon closed in fast. Its claws grabbed Tagen's shoulder and slammed him down. Tagen gasped, limbs barely answering him. He saw an opening and lashed out, his claws tearing through the throat of the yellow demon coming in on his right. Blood gushed. The demon collapsed, choking on its own venomed wound.

Kaz approached without hurry. Tagen braced himself. He was too depleted to flee.

"You've caused enough trouble." Kaz's voice was quiet. "Maselda will handle you personally."

Past Kaz, the black demon had left them and was crouched over the yellow one, hands pressed to the torn throat. The yellow demon's eyes were glassing already.

Before Tagen could react, Kaz struck. Pain erupted at the back of his skull. The forest went out under him.

Tagen woke to the smell of old leaves and wet bark, every muscle a separate complaint. Massive trees arched overhead, branches braided so close together no moon got through. The Witch's domain.

He tried to move. Roots had grown around his wrists and ankles while he slept. He stopped trying.

Something stirred to his left.

He turned his head as much as the roots allowed, and there—not three paces from him, on his side in the leaves, wrists and ankles bound in the same dark woody coils—was Gench. Still out. Chest moving. A long thread of black blood drying along his jaw where one of Maselda's soldiers had clipped him going down.

They got you too? How?

Tagen turned his eyes back toward the open ground in front of him, and the elegant figure he had been hoping never to see twice in one week was already walking toward him.

Maselda.

She came to a stop just inside the reach of the roots and looked down at him. Her pale eyes did not move. Then the corner of her mouth lifted by a fraction.

"You," she said.

Tagen kept his eyes on the dirt in front of her foot.

"The same one. Twice in one week." Her voice was the quiet of a closed door, the way it had been at the border. There was something else in it now. Not warmth. Closer to the dry amusement a person finds in a thing too foolish to be angry at. "I let you go a few days ago. I gave you a message and a road home. And here you are, on your face in my woods, tied to my roots, with another of your kind beside you bleeding into my soil."

She crouched. She was close enough now that he could feel the cold come off her.

"I find I have a fondness for your spirit, aniborn. I do not say that lightly. Most of your kind would have been ash on the meadow before the sun came up, and most of your kind would not have come back to follow Kaz and put themselves under my hand a second time. That takes a particular kind of stubbornness. I will allow myself to be amused by it. Once."

She did not blink.

"You will take the message back. Again. The same one. Tell your master what you saw in the clearing. Tell him I let you live a second time because I choose to, and not because he has any standing to ask it of me. Tell him to keep his slaves out of my woods. Tell him to stay out of our hair while we do what we have come out to do." The corner of her mouth dropped. "If I find one of you meddling in our affairs a third time, I will not be amused. I will not give a message. I will not give a road. Do you understand me?"

"I understand." His voice came out hoarse.

"Good."

She rose and stepped next to Gench. "But let me make it clear." Her nails dug into his shoulder, releasing a dribble of black blood that brought him awake. He tried to break from her grasp, but couldn't.

Something crawled under Gench's skin, running down his abdomen and into his legs. When the Witch loosened her grip, Gench tried again to break free, but the second he moved his leg, something ripped through the skin of his calves and feet. Large brown roots shot out of his limbs and pulled him flat against the ground. He screamed and thrashed, and the thrashing only fed the roots.

Black blood oozed from Gench's torn flesh. He fought against the roots, and with every move, more roots ripped through him, shooting into the ground from his stomach and hands. His face slammed into the dirt as more came through his cheeks.

He clenched his teeth, grinding them together as another root shot out from his gums. His breath came in shallow, ragged jerks; his eyes rolled back. Therion drew a long dagger with green veins crossing the blade and drove it through Gench's heart. The chest hitched once and stopped. His flesh cracked and dried to ash, leaving only black, rubbery bones behind—the way it always went when an aniborn was killed with one of the Witch's cursed blades.

Maselda had not moved through any of it. She stood over the bones the way a person stands over work she has done before and expects to do again.

"So your master understands," she said, "that the next one comes back as ash, and not on his own legs."

Maselda turned toward the black demon. "Your report, Therion?"

"Domblin moves openly among the humans," Therion said. He did not look up. "We believe he is here to stop us from retrieving As—" He paused. He glanced once at Tagen and let the word fall. "From completing our mission."

Tagen kept his face flat. He filed the half-name away under his tongue with the rest of what he was not going to forget.

Maselda did not smile. "Domblin's resurgence changes nothing. We will reach what we have come for, no matter what he thinks he can stop. Kill Domblin if you must, if he gets in the way." She looked back at Tagen. "And tell Snyp that if he insists on putting his hands into my woods, he can come do it himself. I will receive him at the treeline. He need not send another like you, or another like that one"—she tipped her head toward the small heap of ash— "to learn what I have for him."

She faded into the trees as if she had never stood there. The roots loosened and dropped Tagen to the dirt. Therion hauled him up by the shoulder, claws digging in. "Move," the demon said. He did not look at the small heap of ash where Gench had been.

* * *

Every stride Therion took sent pain through Tagen's battered body. It had been a long walk through the Witch's woods and out across the border into the meadows. Therion was moving cautiously, watching for aniborn on every approach. Tagen let his body go limp. A large leg with three white tattoos on it came up into his face as the demon stepped up a small hill. Tagen took his chance and bit down into the strong flesh.

Therion barely broke stride. He slammed Tagen into the nearest tree hard enough to break the bite, then slammed him again on the recoil. What little strength Tagen had been holding for that moment was spent in it.

"If I weren't ordered to hand you back over, I would kill you right now."

Therion stopped walking. The change in motion came through Tagen's ribs before any of his other senses registered it. He pried one eye open.

They had reached a small clearing inside a stand of pines that Tagen did not know. A flat-topped stone sat in the center of it. Standing beside the stone was another demon.

This one was smaller than Therion. Lean. Gray-skinned, with a thin pattern of white markings down one side of his neck. His eyes were the dim copper of a demon who had spent too long being quiet, and his hands were folded in front of him in the way of a creature waiting for something it had already done a hundred times before.

I know you.

He had seen that face on the meadow side of the Witch's woods more than once. The thin white markings. The copper eyes. One of the two who had drifted to the treeline a week before all of this began, who had stared across at Tagen on his post and drifted back without engaging. Tagen had reported it to Snyp. The whole border had been on edge for days about it. The demon looked comfortable outside of the Witch's woods. In one hand he held a black orb the size of a fist—the kind of thing scouts and messengers had carried in the ancient wars, when there had still been wars worth carrying them in. Tagen had not seen one since.

You were scouting. Learning the ground for a teleport.

Therion crossed to him without a word and dropped Tagen onto the flat stone. The smaller demon's hands came up under Tagen's shoulders before he could fall off the side of it. Therion was already turning back the way they had come.

"Throw him back into the cave with the rest of the wretched creatures," Therion said over his shoulder. "Teleport in, teleport out."

The smaller demon nodded once.

Therion did not look at Tagen again. He moved off into the dark of the trees, and the dark closed around him, and he was gone.

The smaller demon hoisted Tagen onto his shoulder. He moved differently from Therion. Not the heavy stride of a soldier. The steady soft step of a thing that had been crossing this ground for a long time without being seen.

Without warning, a crackling flash tore around them. The next thing Tagen knew, they were at the cave. His stomach turned over once, hard, and would have emptied itself if there had been anything in it to empty.

The demon hurled Tagen forward, and the cave floor caught him. He hit hard. The breath he had been holding went out of him.

He turned his head a fraction and got the smaller demon in the corner of his eye, just long enough to see him lift the orb, and the demon was gone in another crack of light.

Tagen tried to move his arms and legs but nothing answered. He lay there bleeding. If Snyp were there, or one of the older aniborn, Tagen would have a chance, but the younglings that sat at the opening of the cave were ruthless.

The first noise he caught was sniffing. He blacked out for a moment but came back when he felt breath on his face. Only one of his eyes opened. He saw three shadowy figures standing in front of him. They were younglings, each eager to have Tagen for itself. Tagen tried to move and call out. He couldn't. His body would not answer him, and most of his head and face were smashed in.

The creatures made their way to him, and a fight broke out among them the way fights always broke out among younglings when more than one of them found meat at the same time. One of them escaped from the brawl and started crawling toward Tagen. The shadowy creature slipped over the boulder he had landed against. Its claws clicked across the hard surface.

Tagen did not blame them for wanting to eat him. It was what they were. If they had the chance to take down an older aniborn, all the better for them. Tagen was no stranger to that life. He had done the same a few times himself when he was younger.

He prepared to die.

The creature bit into Tagen's foot, teeth slowly ripping in. Not wanting to feel the pain, Tagen tried to relax and let go.

There was no use in fighting.

As the aniborn took its second bite, something pulled the youngling off and the creature was thrown against a wall.

A voice came from above. "You greedy wretches. Do I not feed you enough?" Snyp stood on top of the boulder Tagen was slumped against. His voice was, against everything else in the cave, a comfort. Even if Tagen did not trust the source.

"I might need him alive. You don't eat just any aniborn without my permission." Snyp jumped off the rock and loomed over the creature he had just thrown against the wall. Through the slits of his half-open eyes, Tagen watched. *Get 'em, Snyp. Kill 'em.*

"No. Please, no. Snyp, no." The creature groveled on the floor. Snyp grabbed the creature and killed it, biting into its neck with black teeth. The other two younglings tried to escape but were stopped by five other aniborn.

"As for you two," Snyp said to the creatures, "you shall be Tagen's dinner tonight." Aniborn dragged them deeper into the cave, their screams trailing behind. It had been years since Tagen had been given a whole youngling. He was never permitted to eat this much; normally his portion was a few small scraps and nothing more.

"The Witch spared you again," Snyp said, low. "She must consider you useful—or dangerous."

Tagen kept his head down. He waited until Snyp was close enough that no other ear in the cave could catch what came next.

"Gench is dead," he said.

Snyp went very still.

Tagen kept his voice flat and his eyes on the floor. "He was on the rise above the clearing—downwind, far back. He came in too late. Maselda took him at the same time she took me. She killed him in front of me to make a point." He paused, then said it anyway. "I did not know he was there. I did not know there was a second."

The silence after that was the kind a man could fall into.

Above him, Snyp did not speak for a long moment. Tagen could feel him deciding what face to put on. He had said it once. That was the work done. Snyp would either move on it or pretend he hadn't heard, and either answer would tell Tagen what he needed to know.

When Snyp finally answered, the answer was not about Gench. That was the answer.

"Domblin..." The name slipped from Tagen's split lips. "He walks among the humans. Maselda herself said so."

"Domblin has finally surfaced?" Snyp's voice dropped. "Two powers rising... the balance is breaking under us."

He fixed on Tagen and grew quieter. "This changes everything. You've proven yourself useful twice now, yet failed both times to get what I want. You have one chance to redeem yourself. You will hunt down Domblin. And you will uncover what Kaz was sent to retrieve. Do this," Snyp said, "and you will earn the freedom you have not yet known how to ask for."

Tagen lifted his eyes a fraction. The order he had been given before still stood under this one—bring it to *me*. Not to the messenger. Not to the gate. Snyp had not changed his mind on that. He had only added Domblin to the list. He had not said the name Gench, and he never would.

And he had not given Snyp the rest of Maselda's message—the come-do-it-yourself, the come-to-the-treeline. Not tonight. Snyp had taken the news of Gench in a silence Tagen could not read, and a witch's mockery on top of that was the kind of thing that got an aniborn killed where he lay.

"And if I fail?" Tagen managed.

Snyp leaned close. "You will beg for the mercy of the Witch's woods."

As Snyp released him, Tagen scraped together what voice he had left and asked, "What about the youngling you said would be mine to eat?" He was broken and in no shape to walk the few steps he needed to heal.

With a snarl, Snyp tore an arm off the youngling and tossed it to Tagen.

Tagen pushed himself up and tore into the arm. Snyp had walked away already, dragging the rest of the youngling corpse behind him. His body was restoring. It wasn't enough to bring him back whole, but he was stronger than he had been the last time he walked out of this cave.

Tagen clung to two things: he would not fail, and he would not say the name he was still carrying under his tongue. Not to Snyp. Not yet. The man in the grass, Mauldrin, was still his alone, and now—after Gench—he was more alone with that knowledge than he had been when he set out. That was useful. That, he could work with.

Domblin would lead him to answers, to redemption—and to his brother, Mauldrin. Because if Domblin had been fool enough to come back here, it could only be because he, too, knew Mauldrin had returned.

CHAPTER 11
Caden—SDS Medical Wing

In the bright corridors of the SDS facility, Caden's footsteps echoed. The chasm between his life at home and Steven's cell, somewhere in this building, felt like ground he had no map for.

Robert had called him at six. He had not slept.

"You can come in," Robert had said. No greeting. "Medical clearance first. We'll see how it goes."

"Steven?"

"Sedated. Contained. We have him in one of the containment cells, isolation wing. Heavily sedated. He is not a threat to anyone right now."

Caden had hung up first. He had stood at the kitchen island for a long moment after, looking at the dark window over the sink and the shape of his own face in it, before he had gone to find his coat.

He turned the corner now and the medical wing came up on his right, the lit window of the lab throwing a pale rectangle onto the corridor floor. Allen was already inside, head bent over a tablet, the white of his coat almost too bright under the overheads.

The sterile air heightened his unease. He moved on autopilot, enduring the medical tests Robert was making him sit through before he'd clear him back to work. Caden had pushed Robert all night to be cleared after what had happened with Steven, and his mind worked the night over and over while he waited.

Robert was holding something back. Caden could see it in the half-step the techs took when he passed them in the hall, in the way their eyes went to the floor and stayed there. Whatever they had been told about him this morning, it had not been the truth.

He had something ready for that. A close-range pull, built on his own time and his own equipment—the kind of side project Allen would have lectured him about for an hour. Hover within a few feet of Robert's phone long enough and the app would scrape what it could before the handler caught on. The risk was real. So was the cost of waiting.

Caden sat down in the examination chair, the cold seeping through the thin fabric of his shirt. He had not slept in any way that counted since Tuesday. Every time he closed his eyes, Steven was in the corridor again with his arms out and his mouth open, half there, half somewhere else.

A slap on his back jolted him out of it. Instinct took over; he seized the wrist behind him—too tight, too fast.

"Easy!" Allen gasped, wincing as he tried to wriggle free.

Caden blinked and let go. "Don't sneak up on me like that."

Allen rubbed his wrist with a nervous laugh. "You always were the jumpy type."

Caden didn't smile. "What do you want?"

Allen shifted. The mood went out of him a half-beat slower than it should have. "They've already sent Bain's team in."

Caden's stomach turned. "What?" he said, sitting up straighter, fatigue forgotten.

"Earlier this morning." Allen cleared his throat. "Robert wanted them to be the first back into stopped time. To... test things. I tweaked the array last night—that sensor we used on the orange, the one test where it came back wrong, so we shelved it. I kept working on it. I think I solved what was making it spoil the orange. Robert wanted it tested to see if it would solve the problem we had with you and Steven."

"On a person."

"On a person."

Caden let the silence hold long enough to make Allen want to fill it.

"Robert's been wrong about a lot of things this week."

Allen did not have a response to that. He cleared his throat again and looked at the floor.

Robert had told him on the helicopter that no one else was going in until they understood the suit. He had told him that to his face. He had then put Steven in. Now Bain. The pattern was clear enough. Robert was no longer letting him run the Dead Time project. Caden had been cut out.

"And? How did it go?"

Allen hesitated—long enough for Caden to catch it. "It went fine. No issues."

Caden's expression sharpened. "Then why do you look like you've seen a ghost?"

Allen shrugged. The shrug arrived a moment late. "I guess... sending another person in had me on edge. After Steven."

Caden held the look until Allen broke it.

He needed to be in front of Robert. He stood and went down to the lab. The controlled noise of machines filled the space, but something was wrong with the room. Conversations halted as he passed. Bodies tensed. They knew. He found Robert in the command room, back turned, studying the holographic display of Dead Time's last scan.

Matt's words came back to him. They did not feel as paranoid this morning as they had on the phone last night.

Caden palmed his phone, thumbed the app awake, and let it disappear back into his pocket. He moved toward Robert at a pace that put him close.

"You sent Bain's team in?" Caden asked.

Robert turned, unfazed. "Of course I did."

"Without informing me."

"You're supposed to still be on leave," Robert countered.

"You told me on the helicopter you wouldn't put another person in until we understood the suit. That's twice now. And regardless. This is my project. My team. You don't get to make that call without me."

Robert set his hands on the table, finally meeting his gaze. His expression was unreadable. "I made the call because it needed to be made. We couldn't afford to wait. I run this facility. Not you. I'm not sure what's come over you, Caden, but this new attitude isn't helpful."

"You mean you couldn't afford me questioning your decision."

Neither spoke.

Robert's jaw worked. "It's stable. The Dead Time equipment is stable. You should be thanking Allen."

"You sent Steven in last night, and now he's in a cell. We don't get to call that stable."

"I don't need to justify my decisions to you, Caden."

Caden held the silence for one long count. He watched Robert decide whether to push him, and watched him decide not to. He had seen Robert make that calculation many times over fifteen years. He had never been the one Robert was making it about before.

"All right." He let his shoulders come down. "It's your call. I'm here when you need me on it."

Robert's face moved through something—surprise, maybe relief, maybe the small private satisfaction of a man who had expected a fight and not gotten one. He recovered. "Good. Get some rest. We'll talk about next steps later."

"Let me know when."

Caden walked out.

He kept his pace steady through the door and across the floor and into the corridor, because Robert was watching him through the glass and he was sure of it. He did not check the app until he was around the corner and out of camera reach.

The screen lit. *Access granted.* The phone logs, mail, and messages had been scrubbed to the bone. Too clean. Then a red banner: *Active countermeasure detected.* Robert's phone was already pushing a purge. Caden killed the session before the handler could fingerprint his device.

Almost nothing. The pull had taken a fragment of one calendar entry before the wall came down. A meeting yesterday morning at oh-six-hundred, an hour before Steven came back wrong. Two attendees: Robert and a name Caden did not recognize. No agenda. No location.

He stared at the name for a long moment. He committed it to memory. Then he wiped the app's local cache.

A name was a thread. A thread was something you pulled later, when you had a quiet hour and no one was watching. He did not have either of those things yet.

He still needed the security logs. If Bain's team had really gone in, there should be footage.

He slipped into an empty workstation and opened the encrypted archives. His fingers worked the keys until the screen pulled up the Dead Time excursion footage.

He clicked play. The timestamp marked three hours ago. Bain and the others stood in front of the entry point, suited up.

Then the screen went black for exactly 4.2 seconds.

When it resumed, Bain's team was already back from being in stopped time, and the techs were cheering.

No transition. No visible entry. They were in front of the camera, then they were on the other side of the experience, and the camera had been taken out for the moment they crossed and the moment they came back.

He scrubbed the footage backward. Again. The same missing frames.

His gut tightened. Someone had cut out exactly what he wanted to see.

He tried the backups. A firewall blocked him. The clearance was set above his level.

What, exactly, are they hiding?

Whoever was running the project from the inside was not the man Caden had taken orders from for fifteen years. He could not say yet whether that meant Robert had changed or whether someone above Robert had moved a piece on the board. Either way, the project was no longer his.

He shut the terminal down. He stood up. He did not slam the chair back—he set it under the desk with the same care he'd set it under the desk a hundred times before. If anyone reviewed this workstation's logs, they would find a man who had checked his email and moved on.

Out in the corridor he took the long way back. A junior tech in the break room glanced up; Caden gave him a nod. At the vending machine he bought a bottle of water he did not want.

Inside, something he had been holding off all morning settled into him. Robert had made his choice. Caden had just made his.

He was going to play along. He was going to walk into the morning meeting, take whatever Robert handed him, and act like a man whose project had been stable since Tuesday. He would put off Matt for one more day, and he would lie to Bridget about how he was. People might die between now and the moment he moved. Steven might be one of them.

He had been a field commander long enough to know what those costs felt like. He had been a field commander long enough to know they were the price of being in the room when it mattered.

He was going to be in the room.

CHAPTER 12
Caden—Isolation Wing, Cell 6

He did not go back to his quarters.

There was one thing Caden could still do today that nobody would think to flag him for, because Steven was supposed to be too drugged to say anything worth hearing. Caden was less sure about that than Robert was.

He kept a small camera built into his phone case for exactly this kind of work. He had carried it for years and never once used it on his own people.

Today he would.

At the isolation wing security desk, a guard glanced up, his expression tight with unease.

"No one's allowed down here without clearance," the guard said, his hand brushing his holstered weapon.

"I'm here to see Steven," Caden replied, holding up his ID. He kept his voice level.

The guard read the card, then read Caden, and dropped his hand from the weapon. He sighed and reached into his desk. "He's in Cell 6. Power's out in that section." He handed over a flashlight. "Be careful. Whatever's in there—it isn't Steven anymore."

"Has he had a doctor down here today?"

"Robert came down this morning. Didn't go in. Just looked."

Caden filed that. He took the flashlight and went into the cold hallway, and the only sound was his own boots on the concrete.

He stopped before Cell 6 and put the beam through the narrow window.

A figure was slumped in the back left corner—cross-legged, hands on its knees, not moving.

Steven—or whatever was wearing him.

Caden lowered the flashlight to angle the beam down so it would not glare on the glass, and as he did, something pressed against the window from the inside.

He flinched back hard enough to hit his shoulder against the opposite wall.

A face was on the other side of the glass, white breath fogging it, eyes wide, mouth open in a soundless word that took Caden a half-second to read. Then the face was gone and the breath fog faded, and he swung the flashlight back to the corner.

Steven was still in the corner—cross-legged, hands on his knees, exactly where he had been.

For a long count Caden could not get his breath right.

Two of them. Or one of them, fast enough that he could not see it move. He did not know which option made his hand colder on the flashlight.

He stood there long enough to be sure neither was a hallucination. He knew what no sleep did to him by now, and this was not that. The breath was still on the glass. The fog had been real.

Whatever was in there had wanted him to know it was watching.

The instinct that had walked him out of valleys he was not supposed to walk out of told him to leave.

He went in anyway.

He eased the door open—the hinges took the weight in a long groan—slipped inside, and as he passed under the frame, lifted his hand and pressed the small camera to the underside of the lintel where the guard would not see it. The red dot came on. Recording.

Steven sat cross-legged in the corner, fingers drumming against a drain cover. The flashlight caught the side of his face. He looked sedated and not at all asleep.

"Steven?" Caden's voice was low and even.

At the sound of his name, Steven stopped. He raised his head, slow. The corridor's temperature dropped. A smile spread across his face.

"Steven," he murmured. The voice came through distorted, like a radio under a storm. "That's not my name anymore."

"Then what is your name?"

He clapped once. The sound came back off the walls flat and hollow. "Azgiel." The drugs in him did not touch the way he said it. He fixed on Caden, and the smile turned. "But you already knew that, didn't you, Mauldrin?"

The name struck Caden the way it had struck him in the lab the night before, and that evening on the altar in stopped time. "How do you know that name?" He kept his voice flat. He did not trust what would come out of it if he let it.

Azgiel leaned forward—the motion smoother than the drugs should have allowed and slower than a man would have moved. "How do you not?" he mocked softly. "You've forgotten what you are. How… quaint."

"I don't know what you're talking about."

"Oh, you will," Azgiel said. The edge under the slur. "When destruction is unleashed, the demons will revel, and Mauldrin—" The grin widened. "Will be the toy that shatters first."

"What are you talking about?"

Azgiel settled back. The calm that came over him was worse than the smile had been. "The door you opened, and the door you failed to close. You've already lost, Mauldrin. You're too blind to see it yet."

For a long second, the cell held still.

Then something in the face changed.

The smile slipped off. The shoulders came down. The drumming fingers stopped. Whatever had been driving the face a moment ago was no longer driving it.

His head tilted, slow.

A voice came out of him, smaller than the one that had been in the room. "You again."

Caden's hand tightened on the flashlight.

"You keep coming back," the voice said. "Stop coming back. It is not your body. It was never going to be yours again."

Steven was not looking at him. Whatever was looking out of him was looking at a stretch of empty floor near the door, and tracking something there.

Caden watched and did not interpret. He had been trained, on missions where reading the room wrong could cost someone a leg, not to assemble a story before he had the data for one. Whatever this was—Steven, not Steven, something between—he did not have enough to call it.

His hand had started for the bolt without him. He stopped it.

"Go back," the voice said, soft. "Go back to the cell. Stop reaching."

The mouth shaped a word that did not finish. The eyes drifted off the empty floor, slow, the way a man's eyes drift when he is coming back from somewhere far. They moved across the cell and found Caden, and after a beat they recognized him, and after another beat, something in the body remembered why finding him mattered.

The smile drifted in. Not the sneer. Slower. A little crooked. The smile of a man who was almost surprised to find someone in the room with him.

"You are still here."

A pause. The eyes moved over Caden without urgency, the way a man takes inventory of a room he has already searched.

"They keep finding me. Even in here."

He said it as though Caden had asked him a question. Then he looked at his own hand on the drain cover, the way a man looks at a hand he has gone away from for a while. The fingers started drumming again. The same beat. As if they had been waiting for him to remember they belonged to him.

Caden held very still.

What he knew was that he did not want to be in this cell another minute. What he was not going to let himself decide, standing here, was why.

The lights overhead juddered once and held. A low tremor went through the floor and up into Caden's boots. Azgiel's head snapped upward, listening to something Caden could not hear.

"They're coming," Azgiel whispered.

A blast tore through the facility somewhere above them, and the corridor shook hard enough to throw dust off the ceiling.

Caden's body moved before his head did. He was at the door, hand on the bolt, the corridor at his back. Whatever was wearing Steven's face—whatever any of this was—was on the floor of the cell behind him.

He shut the door. He threw the bolt.

He held the bolt for one heartbeat after it landed, the metal cold under his palm. He could not have said, in that heartbeat, who he had just locked in. Whatever this was, he had been a field commander long enough to know that you closed a door before you understood what was on the other side of it, and you understood it later if you were lucky enough to get a later.

He turned and ran for the corridor.

The guard at the entryway was already in motion, radio in hand.

A voice came over the radio, tight with panic. "Explosion on the third floor! We need backup—now!"

"What's happening?"

"Third-floor labs gone. Looks like a chain reaction." The guard's voice barely registered before the ground shook again.

Before Caden could process the words, a second blast ripped through the corridor.

The steel doors to the isolation wing blew outward with a thunderous roar, hurling Caden into the cold concrete wall. His head struck hard.

The last thing he saw before losing consciousness was the warped steel doors crashing shut again, sealing off the corridor.

When he came to, everything was chaos.

Dust and smoke filled the air, blurring his vision, burning his lungs. A muffled ringing in his ears drowned out the panicked shouts of the guards around him. He could barely make out their hazy forms moving through the smoke.

"Caden? Can you hear me?"

He blinked hard. His head pounded. His limbs were leaden, but he managed a faint nod. A guard knelt beside him, propping him up against the wall. "Stay here. Don't move." The guard disappeared into the smoke.

"Get explosives down here, now!" Robert's voice came down the corridor before he did. His silhouette emerged from the stairwell, sleeves rolled, jaw set. He directed a group of guards prying at the doors with a crowbar.

Caden steadied himself against the wall. Through the smoke he glimpsed scorched and twisted steel blocking the hallway. A light flashed twice, seeping through small holes and gaps in the damaged doors and casting shapes along the walls.

"What is that?" one of the guards muttered, leaning closer to peer through the cracks.

Caden forced himself to his feet, jumping in to help pry the door open.

"Knock it down!" Robert yelled. He motioned sharply, and Caden and a guard delivered a hard kick near the destroyed lock.

Before the others could join in, a low thunder rolled through the corridor. The sound wasn't natural. It vibrated the walls, deep and jarring—a growl from something older than the building. Guards recoiled, clutching their ears.

Steel doors groaned, bending inward as if pulled by an unseen force. A gust of cold wind rushed through the cracks, carrying with it a faint, otherworldly undertone. Then the flashing lights died, plunging the corridor into silence.

"Knock the doors—" Robert began, but a second explosion cut him off.

The blast was devastating. It tore through the corridor with a force that sent everyone flying. Caden was thrown against the concrete wall a second time.

When the dust settled, he squinted at the wreckage. The containment rooms were obliterated. A faint pulsating light deep in the corridor, where Cell 6 had been, flared once and went out.

The damaged doors hung limp from their hinges, bent and mangled beyond recognition. A low resonating sound filled the air, like the remnants of a power that refused to dissipate.

Whatever had been in Cell 6 was no longer in Cell 6. He had locked the door on it himself, and that had not held. Of course it had not held. He had locked Steven in with it.

The corridor went still except for the ticking of metal cooling in the walls. A pounding ache grew in his skull. The room swayed.

His mind went to Bridget on the couch the night before, asking him a question he still had not answered, and the quiet of her face while she waited for him to be ready.

"You're bleeding all over the place," Robert said, looking him up and down. "Someone get him to the infirmary."

He heard the words, but his mind was still on Bridget.

CHAPTER 13
Azgiel—SDS Isolation Wing

The lights above him stuttered.

Cold metal pressed against his spine, and the metal was groaning, and somewhere very far from the metal his army was screaming. He could not tell which sound was happening now. He could not tell, anymore, what now meant.

The white wave was eating the front lines again. He had watched it from the field. He could watch it now. Demons disintegrating mid-charge, the smoke that came after—the smell of his men becoming nothing. Above it all, the figure in light-gray armor that drank the dawn and gave it back tenfold. The hand raised, palm out.

In front of him, on the tile, on the dirt, on the field where it had ended— Mauldrin. Was Mauldrin standing in front of him, talking to him with a light in his hand? His mind could not stay in any moment or place.

Light-gray armor. The runes etched in the helm. The hand raised the way it had been raised at the end, palm out, the mouth already shaping the word that had taken everything from Azgiel and left him alive to know it had been taken.

Azgiel's knuckles whitened on something that might have been grass.

"They're coming," he whispered, and did not know which they he meant. The army he had buried. The army he could call back. The brother who had buried both.

A blast cracked through the building above him, and the dirt was concrete again, and Mauldrin dissolved the way a thing dissolves when the drug holding it together thins for a moment and then thickens. The cage came back around him. Had there been a man standing in front of him?

Sedatives lay on his chest like wet wool. He tried to lift one hand. The hand moved an inch and stopped. His mind worked slow and out of order, parts that did not quite fit each other anymore. Memory and vision braided together, and he could not pull the threads apart.

Two thousand years between the seconds had not taken his awareness. They had taken much. Not that.

Time was moving again. He had not noticed when it had started moving. The noticing was new. The moving was older.

Footsteps in the corridor outside the cell. Heavy. Slow. Not Mauldrin's—Mauldrin's gait he would have known on any floor of any world. These were heavier.

A faint thread of magic drifted through the air.

He knew the thread.

The door clicked open.

A figure came through.

Kaz.

He could not move. His mind told him this was another illusion. The prison had served him a thousand of them across the long centuries—friends, lovers, his wife, all walking through doors that did not open onto anywhere. He had learned, after the first hundred years, not to reach. Reaching at a phantom and closing on nothing was how a god learned to be afraid. Once, near the end of his time in the cell, the reaching had been different. Maselda had come through to him—not as a phantom of the prison, but as something the prison could not make. His hand had still gone through her. But she had been real, and she had told him real things. *Take a human body. Live.* He pushed the thought away.

The phantom came closer. The light caught the red of its skin and the black of the old writing down its arms. The horns scraped the ceiling.

The phantom looked at the corridor first. Then the cell. The soldier's check.

"What have they done to you, sir?"

The voice was not the voice of an illusion. Illusions did not say *sir* the way Kaz said it. Illusions did not have the bend of breath at the end of a word.

A single tremor went through Azgiel's body—the long argument between his will and the sedation finally tipping toward the will. His fingers curled. "The drugs," he croaked. "My army."

"No more."

Kaz dropped to one knee. He pulled a small obsidian vial from his belt. The liquid inside was blood red, and it was not still—it moved against the glass like something alive against the inside of a held breath. He uncorked it.

He poured it over Azgiel's head.

It went into him the way fire goes into dry grass. The sedatives burned. The suppressants burned. The thin wash of stopped-time residue that had been on his skin since they pulled him out of the suit burned. His back arched off the floor. His teeth set so hard he could hear it inside his skull.

When the burning passed, what was left in him was not what the doctors had been holding. The veins ran hotter. The muscle answered. Memory slid back into the grooves it had been pulled from and stayed.

He sat up.

The shadows in the corners of the cell drew back from him and then came in close, the way old dogs come close when the master has been gone too long.

He had forgotten, in the cell of time, what loyalty felt like as a presence in a room.

He turned his hand over and looked at it.

The hand was wrong.

It was the right shape. It was the right number of fingers. It was not his hand. He could feel where the bones did not match the bones he had been born with. He could feel where the muscle was not laid the way his muscle had been laid. The body was strong, and the body was honest, and the body was a mortal one, and there were limits in it where there had been none in him.

A vessel. Not meant to hold what it was holding.

The grin came back. He had not chosen it. The face he was wearing remembered the shape of it.

"Maselda sent you?"

"She felt your return." Kaz had stood. He held himself the way Kaz had always held himself—half a pace back from his king, eyes on the door. "We have been searching since."

"And Mauldrin." Azgiel said it flat. He kept his eyes on his own hand a second longer.

Kaz hesitated. "I saw him leave a moment ago. He did not see me. He was…" The word did not come. "Different."

Azgiel set his hand down on his knee. He let the silence have its weight.

"He did not know me," Azgiel said.

It was not a question. He had been telling himself it was a question—lying on the cold of the floor, arguing with the man in the light-gray armor in his head—but the truth had been there since Mauldrin had turned and walked out of this room. His brother had looked at him the way a man looks at a stranger.

He searched what he had. Memories slid past where he tried to set them. Some of them still missing. Most of them missing. But the shape of what Mauldrin had become was clear enough.

"He is mortal." His voice flattened further. "Fully human now. He has forgotten what he is."

Kaz's shoulders set. "Then he is vulnerable. But still a threat. We need to leave."

"We will leave."

He stood. The body was a half-second slow. He gave it the half-second.

"After I remind Mauldrin who I am and make him pay for what he did."

Kaz bowed his head. He had never argued.

Azgiel turned to face the cell door and the corridor beyond it. He lifted his hands. The chant came up out of him in the language under the language, the one he and his brothers had spoken when they were boys, before any of this had been written. The runes lit on the tile under his bare feet and crawled up the cinderblock walls in lines that wrote themselves out of the dust between molecules.

He clenched the hands closed.

The corridor came apart.

The cell door blew off its hinges and went down the hall the way a leaf goes in a hard wind. The cinderblock wall to either side of the door went with it. Concrete came down the way old paper goes in a flame—edges first, then the body of it. Steel that had been a doorframe twisted into shapes steel did not have names for. The cell that had held him was not a cell anymore. It was the open mouth of the building, blown wide. Twenty feet of corridor lay smoking in front of him, the lights along it flickering, dust still falling out of the ceiling where the ceiling used to be.

Kaz reached for the orb at his belt.

The air changed.

It came down through the corridor like weather. Static along the back of Azgiel's neck. The smell of old rain. He knew the presence before he saw the face.

Domblin.

He came out of the smoke at the far end of the hall. Thirty feet, no more. White hair. A staff that looked like it was made out of light. His face was composed in the way Domblin's face had always composed itself when he was about to do something that would hurt him.

Azgiel laughed.

It came out of him on its own. Half of it was real. Half of it was the body's, the muscle memory of a king who had laughed in front of bigger threats than this and watched them fold.

"Little brother. Look at you."

Domblin lifted the staff. "This ends here."

Kaz lunged.

Domblin did not move, exactly. He shifted—a quarter step that should not have been enough, that was enough—and he was no longer where the lunge had been aimed. Domblin's free hand came up. Kaz took the blow square in the chest and went backward into the cinderblock to Azgiel's right. He hit it hard enough that the wall cracked behind him. He came down on the floor in a heap, three feet from Azgiel's knee, and did not get up.

Azgiel's hand was already lifted. Black filaments poured off his fingers and went down the corridor for his brother's face.

They broke against the air around Domblin and did not reach him. The barrier did not flex. It did not give. It simply was what it was, and his power was what his power was, and the two did not meet.

"You have been gone too long." Domblin's voice was almost gentle. "You are not what you were."

"Come find out what I am."

He raised the hand again. The charge came down through his arm the way it had come down ten thousand times before—the way it had come down on the field at the end, the last time he had stood in front of his brother. It did not fit. The body had no track for it. The current went in and could not find the path out, and when it left him it left him sideways. White arcs cracked off his fingers and went where they wanted. One took the ceiling above the doorframe and brought half of it down. One took the floor between him and Domblin and left a black scar in the tile six feet long. One took the steam pipe in the wall above Kaz's head, and the pipe ruptured, and scalding white came roaring out of it and filled the air to the ceiling.

The hand he had raised it with shook.

Heat came up under the skin of his face. He felt the small vessels in the white of his eye giving way. Something hot tracked down his upper lip. Blood. His own blood. He had not bled in his own body in two thousand years, and he was bleeding in someone else's now.

"Control it!" Kaz shouted from the floor.

He could not. The body was not made to hold him. Not like his old one.

Down the corridor, through the steam, Domblin had still not moved. He raised the staff to vertical. The light along it brightened until the steam around him went transparent.

"You are going back, Azgiel."

The strike came as a single line of white that crossed the thirty feet between them faster than Azgiel could turn. It took him in the sternum. It went through him in a way physical things do not go through a body—it found the inside of him and put a hand on it and bore down. He went to one knee. Inside his chest, on the right, a rib gave with a sound he felt more than heard.

He pushed up. He found, somewhere in the wreckage of the body he was wearing, the old strength—not all of it, not most of it, but enough to set his feet under him and lift his head.

The next strike came harder. It took him in the same place. He stayed standing, but only by dropping his hand to the wall for it.

The world went thin around the edges.

Behind him, the air went hot.

He did not have to turn to know what it was. The heat was the wrong heat. It did not come off the steam, and it did not come off the broken pipe. It came off the place a few feet behind him where the air was no longer air. He had felt that heat from the inside on the day Mauldrin had set him into it. He had felt it from the inside for what passed in his prison for years. The opening had a smell—the smell of a room that had been shut a very long time and was about to be shut again. It had a sound—the sound of a held breath about to be held one more time.

The cell of time, come back for him. Domblin had made it.

"No." It was not defiance now. It was a word a man says when the thing he has spent every waking second dreading is two strides behind him. "No—"

A weight took him from the side.

Kaz, off the floor, into him, full body. The two of them went sideways and down, out of the line the rift had drawn for him. They came down hard against the cinderblock. Kaz already had the orb off his belt as they fell.

"Move," Kaz snarled. "Sir. Move."

Across the wreckage and the steam and the broken floor, Azgiel found Domblin's eyes. Held them.

For one breath there was nothing in either face but the boys they had been at a fire in deep woods, before any of this had been written.

Domblin's jaw worked once.

The orb lit up in Kaz's hand. The light came up around them in a sphere that washed the corridor blue. Azgiel held his brother's gaze a heartbeat longer.

"I will be back for you, little brother."

The sphere closed.

The cell, the corridor, the rift, the man who had been his youngest brother—gone.

He was somewhere else.

CHAPTER 14
Caden—SDS Quarters

He came back into himself in pieces.

First the ceiling—the long fluorescent strip he had walked under a hundred times, looking down at it now from the wrong side. Then his ribs. Then the dull throb behind his right eye, the one that always set in late after a blast. He was on his back on a bed in his own quarters at SDS. Someone had bandaged the gash above his shoulder and left him here. The door was an inch open. Voices in the corridor came through it the way voices come through water.

Bridget. He had been thinking of Bridget when they put him on the gurney, and he was thinking of her now, and his first conscious thought after that was that he had not called her.

A voice broke across the haze—low, urgent, and not from the corridor.

"Mauldrin."

Caden blinked, reality slipping in and out of focus. He tried to clear his head. The room thinned at the edges, going pale at the corners first, the way a photograph goes when something is burning it from the outside in.

"Mauldrin."

The fluorescent strip went out. The ceiling went with it. He was somewhere wide and lightless, and the man was there before Caden could see him—a weight in the dark, a pressure that had not yet decided to be a face. Then it decided. The face was the one from the parking lot last week, and from the corridor an hour ago in the smoke, but bigger now, drawn down into him from above as if the whole of the dark were leaning over him to speak.

"Stay out of stopped time."

Each word landed in him like a hand on a door.

He tried to ask why. He tried to ask who. *Who are you*, he thought into the dark, and the dark answered him with a single word that arrived in his head the way the others had, low and complete and his to keep:

Domblin.

The man was already gone, the dark was already gone, and the ceiling was back. His side lit up with pain from a movement he did not remember making. He was sitting up. He had not decided to sit up.

Stay out. The two words kept turning in him, like a coin a man keeps reaching for in a pocket he forgot was empty.

A single knock—courtesy, not a question—and Robert came through the door with Bain a step behind. Bain shut it. Neither of them looked at the bandage on Caden's shoulder.

"You're awake," Robert said. It was not relief. It was a checked box.

"What happened?"

"That," Robert said, "is what I'd like you to tell me. Why were you in the isolation wing?"

Caden rubbed his temple. The motion sent a low spike through his skull. "I went to check on Steven," he said. "The first blast went off on the floor above me. I was clearing out when the second one came down on the wing. That's all I remember."

Robert held the look a beat too long. "Why were you checking on Steven at all?"

"Because he's my project. I needed to see what stopped time had done to him."

Bain spoke without moving. "And what did you find?"

"Nothing usable. The sedation has him talking past me. But he knows something about what we're doing that we don't know yet, and I'd put money on it."

It was the truth. Most of it. He kept the rest to himself.

Robert's face moved a quarter inch and stopped. It was as much softening as he was capable of, and it changed nothing in his eyes.

"Facility's in lockdown," he said. "Three attacks this morning, all inside the same eight-minute window. Guards and scientists are dead. Dead Time equipment is missing. Steven is gone." He gave the last item the same weight as the others. "He had help on the inside. Until we know who, every man on this team gets monitored."

He drew an injector from his jacket pocket and held it up so Caden could see it. "Starting with you."

Caden looked at it. "A T-13. Robert, that's a prisoner protocol. You don't put one of those in your own people."

"Protocol stopped applying the second someone on the inside started blowing up our building. We're running T-13 on the whole team. The minute we clear you, yours comes back out. Containment, not a verdict."

"After what I've put into this project, you're asking me to prove I'm loyal?"

"I'm not asking."

Bain's weight shifted on his back foot. Caden caught it. "Did Bain get one?"

"He was with me during the explosions." The line came out smooth and rehearsed. "No. He doesn't need one."

Caden could feel the argument building in him, line by line. He let it go. Robert was running the play of a man who knew he was outranked on every metric except the one he was using right now, and Caden knew what it cost to push back on a man like that in a room that had already been decided. He had spent ten years learning that cost. He had to be in the room when this opened up further. He was going to be in the room.

"Fine."

Robert was already moving. The injector clicked once at the base of Caden's skull and he felt the bite of it go in, and then a slow heat under the skin where the chip woke up and started listening.

Robert pressed two more injectors into Caden's hand. "For your team. Anyone who won't take it gets detained."

Caden closed his fingers around them. "And Steven. What aren't you telling me about Steven?"

Robert's voice dropped a half step. "You worry about your team. Steven is mine."

He turned and went. Bain followed without looking at Caden. The door pulled shut behind them with the small, firm sound of a thing being decided.

He stood for a long beat with the injectors warming in his palm and the chip in his neck warming against the bone behind his ear. Mauldrin. The name had come at him four ways now. Domblin in the parking lot last week. The same man, larger, in the dark of his own head ten minutes ago. The thing wearing Steven, in the lab, calling him by it across the room with rage. The voice at the altar. Four different rooms. He could explain one of them. He could explain two if he worked at it. He could not explain four.

He had not let himself sit with that yet. He sat with it now, but only for a moment. He couldn't get sidetracked.

He found Matt pacing the corridor outside his quarters. Matt's shirt was dark across the back. He had been moving for a while.

"What the hell is going on?" Matt said when he saw him. "Half the floor's saying we're compromised. Is that real?"

"It's real." Caden tipped his head toward his door. Matt followed him in. Caden shut the door, set the second injector on the desk, and held up the first so Matt could see it without him having to say what it was. "Robert is putting T-13 into the whole team. Take it or they detain you. Those are the only two options he gave me."

Something went out of Matt's face. A muscle in his jaw caught. "No," he said. "No way in hell."

"Matt—"

"They aren't telling us everything." Matt was already reaching past him. He took the pen off Caden's desk and a sheet from the pad and wrote, fast, while still talking. "I've been pulling at it all morning. I've got pieces. I don't have it all yet, but I've got pieces."

He turned the pad toward Caden.

THEY'RE LISTENING. WATCH YOUR MOUTH IN THIS ROOM.

Caden read it once and did not change his face. "How sure are you?"

Matt pulled the pad back and wrote again, harder this time, the pen indenting through to the next page.

EMAIL CHAIN. BIGGER THAN STEVEN. WE'RE BEING SET UP.

The door came open without a knock.

Three guards. Sidearms drawn but low, not raised. A trained entry. Whoever had sent them had already counted the room and decided how to take it.

"Matt Carson. With us."

Matt did not flinch. He folded the page from the pad once and put it on the desk under Caden's coffee cup with two fingers, not hiding the move from the guards, not making it obvious either. His eyes were on Caden. "We'll talk later," he said.

The cuffs went on. They walked him out. The door pulled shut and the corridor took the sound of their boots and gave the room back to Caden empty.

"You couldn't have just taken it," Caden said to no one. He did not believe himself when he said it.

"Caden."

James was in the doorway. He was looking at the second injector on the desk and not at Caden.

"James." Caden's voice came out more tired than he meant it to. "I don't have the fight in me to make a case for this. I don't have answers to the questions you're going to ask. I just need you to let me put it in."

James studied him a long second. Whatever he saw in Caden's face was apparently enough. He turned his head sideways and tipped it forward. "Sure thing, boss."

Caden put the injector to the soft place behind James's ear and clicked it. James flinched once and rolled his shoulder.

"Thanks," Caden said.

James gave him a look that was not unkind and not entirely his old look, either, and went out.

He set both injectors on the desk side by side. He noticed his hands had gone unsteady. He had not noticed them going. He braced his palms on the counter and waited for them to settle.

His phone was buzzing in his pocket. Not a call—a notification. He pulled it out.

Cell-Camera Offline.

The micro camera he had clipped behind the lintel of Cell 6 less than two hours ago, the one that had been the whole point of going down there alone. The blast had taken it. He had nothing on Steven now. Nothing he could play back.

Behind the alert was the lock screen—a photo of Bridget on the beach below the cliff, the wind in her hair, a year ago and another life ago. He looked at it longer than he needed to. He swiped past it and opened her texts and stared at the blank field.

Caden: *I don't know how much more of this I can take.*

He looked at it. He deleted it letter by letter. He did not want to give her that, not while she was sitting at home alone trying to find the bottom of what he had given her last night. He started again.

Caden: *Thinking of you.*

He sent it before he could second-guess it.

The reply came back inside fifteen seconds.

Bridget: *Always.*

One word. He read it twice. He put the phone in his pocket and kept his hand on it for a moment before he let go.

The lab was running like nothing had happened. That was the strangest part of the morning so far. Equipment hummed at the level it always hummed at. Two techs were running a routine calibration on bench three. A printer was warming up. The building had taken three explosions in eight minutes this morning and the lab had decided, as labs do, that the correct response to a crisis was to keep the machines warm.

"Brogan."

Brogan jumped a quarter inch and caught the stack of tablets before he lost it. He was a man who jumped at his own coffee maker on a normal morning. "Robert and Allen," he said, "in the office." He waved the tablets toward the corridor.

Caden went past him without thanks. He pushed into the office without knocking, because at this point he wasn't sure when he had last knocked at any door in this building.

Robert was at the head of the long table. Allen and Bain were at his shoulders. Between them, on the table, lay a sidearm—a Sig frame, its grip and slide wrapped in the gold Dead Time material the team had spent the last year refining for the suits. Under the office lights the gold had a faint, slow pulse, as if something inside the metal were keeping a heartbeat.

"Caden." Robert did not look up from the weapon. "Good. Sit down. We need you for the next phase."

Caden looked at the gun. He had not authorized it. He had not been told it existed. "What phase?"

Robert tipped a finger at the empty chair across from him. He did not repeat himself.

Caden sat. Allen lifted the weapon off the table the way a museum tech lifts something it has been told not to drop.

"This," Allen said, "is what we've been doing the nights you've been at home. The last test came back good an hour ago. It's a Sig P229 in a Dead Time housing. Integrated, not retrofitted. Still experimental, but it's an evening of the field."

Caden looked at it. "Evening it against what?" It came out colder than he meant.

Robert gave Allen a quarter-nod. Allen took it and did not specify. "Against anything we run into in there. Dead Time equipment has been stolen. We need to be ready for anything."

Bain leaned in. "This is the secrecy, then?"

"Part of it." Allen put the gun back down on the velvet between them. "We're also retiring the suits."

Caden's stomach did a small thing. "Retiring them with what? According to you, you just got them working this morning."

Allen looked at Robert. Robert took the question.

"We're putting the tech into the body," Robert said, even and calm, the way a man says a number he has rehearsed. "Direct integration. The receiver tunes to the nervous system instead of to the suit. No fabric. No oxygen tank. No mask."

The words sat in the room. Caden felt his project—the one he had been the only person at this table able to draw from a blank page eighteen months ago—quietly stop being his project. The suits had been his idea. They had been the part of this work he had argued for in front of the agency, the part that kept the human inside a known boundary. Allen and Robert had spent the time he was at home figuring out how to take the boundary out.

"How long until it's ready," Bain said. He was already on board. Caden noted that. He was going to need to note a lot of things today.

Allen squared the weapon on the velvet. "Two days. Less if Caden gets in."

There it was. They had run him around the perimeter for a week and now they wanted him in the center because two days was not two days without him. He kept his face exactly where it was.

"I'll help."

Robert held the look for a half second longer than the response had earned. "Good."

He had played the play. He had played it because the cost of not playing it was being out of the room.

Bain and Allen stood. Caden caught Robert's elbow before he could move, light enough to be deniable, firm enough to stop him. "About Matt."

Robert looked at Caden's hand on his arm and did not move it. "I'll question him myself. You can sit in. That's the best I'm giving you on this."

It was not enough. Caden took it anyway. He would push the rest later, when he had more weight to push with. "And Steven?"

Robert's face shut. "I told you to leave that one alone."

Caden let go of his arm. Robert went out without looking back. The door shut.

Caden stayed where he was. The chip behind his ear pulsed once with his heartbeat, then again, slow and patient as a thing that intended to stay. He set his palms flat on the table and watched them be steady.

Four threads. Matt had left a folded note under Caden's coffee cup upstairs and Caden had not yet read it. Steven was somewhere outside this building, in the wind, with men who had built four working bombs and known where to set them. Bridget was at home with a question he had not answered. And the name Mauldrin had come at him four ways in a week, and the fourth time it had come from inside his own head, in the dark, in a voice that knew him.

He picked up the gold-wrapped sidearm off the velvet. It was warm. He set it back down.

Then he went to find Allen, and the door of the office did not close behind him, and the lab kept on running as if nothing had happened.

CHAPTER 15
Azgiel—Outside SDS

Azgiel hit the ground.

Pain came up through the heels of his hands first, where they had taken the fall. He had forgotten that pain could live in a place that small. His fingers closed in cold dirt. He drew in a breath, and the breath was full of things he had not smelled in two ages—pine and rot, dust and stone, the iron under-smell of soil that had taken a body once and would take another. His ribs ached around the breath. They were not used to being asked.

He had forgotten the weight of having a body. He had forgotten the way the air pressed back on the skin. For two ages he had been a will with no body to slow it. The body was new. The body was small.

"You alright?"

Kaz's voice. He had not let himself imagine he would hear it again.

He looked up. Kaz was a heavy outline against the trees—broad as he had been, taller than the body Azgiel was now wearing, the old runework on his arms faintly catching what the storm clouds had not taken of the sun. He was not offering a hand. He was watching to see if Azgiel would get up on his own.

Azgiel got up. It cost more than it should have. His thigh shook, took his weight, held. The arm he had used to push off the ground would not stop trembling for a long minute after he was upright. Kaz watched him do all of it and said nothing about any of it, which was worse than if he had.

He was still Azgiel. He was still the will that had leveled kingdoms. The body was new. The will was the same. He told himself that until his spine straightened on its own.

Around him the morning moved. Wind in the canopy. An animal at a long distance, hunting something at a longer distance. Insects holding the silence up like a tent. None of these had existed in the prison, where everything had been one held breath without a chest to hold it.

Here, time was moving him again. He had forgotten how it felt to be carried.

"Five minutes to the Witch's border," Kaz said. He still did not put out a hand. If Azgiel was going to take a throne back, he was going to start by taking five minutes back. Kaz had always been the one who understood that.

Kaz turned and went, quiet for his size. Azgiel followed. By the second hundred paces, his legs had remembered how to be legs.

At the edge of a small clearing, Kaz stopped. He put one heavy hand flat against the trunk of a pine and looked past it without leaning out. Azgiel scanned. Nothing he could see. Plenty he could feel.

"What."

"Aniborn."

The word arrived in him as a half-known thing—a smell from a room he had not been in for a long time. "Tell me."

Kaz did not turn his head from the clearing. "The things you and I caught in the last months of the war. The night before Mauldrin put you in the cell of time. You took one alive. Wretched thing—half a man, all teeth. It told you Triaad had turned on you before Mauldrin ever raised a hand."

Tagen. The name came up in him like a small cold stone working its way out of mud.

"How do you know what happened that night?" His voice came out rougher than he expected. "You were at the kingdom, with my wife."

"It was reported to me," Kaz did not take his eyes off the trees. "Triaad rose after they put you in the cell. He had the aniborn in numbers we had not counted on. He used them to turn the human loyalists first, the way you turn the flank before you take the line. He came for Maselda and the kingdom."

"And you could not stop him?"

Something in Kaz's face went tight. "We stopped him from getting to Maselda. Not the kingdom. We tried. Demons, trolls, the loyal of yours we had left. Triaad had grown into something none of us had measured. By the second year there were not enough of us on the field to be called a line. Maselda took what she could carry and we ran. The survivors came here."

It landed in him slowly. The kingdom—gone. The lines he had drawn on a map all his life—gone. He had walked into the Cell believing the world he was leaving behind was settled—that whatever wars remained had ended with his. While he had hung in the dark, Triaad had come up out of the ground and started a different war and run it for two ages without him. Triaad. His own first advisor. The traitor he had assumed Maselda or Kaz would have squashed inside a season. If any war had still been worth fighting after his fall, it should have been against Mauldrin—his brother, his equal, the one who had earned the right to keep fighting him. Not Triaad. Never Triaad.

Kaz went on at the same low pitch. "It dragged on years. It ended in a standoff because Maselda built wards Triaad could not break. The wards kept his aniborn out. They have also kept us in. Mauldrin and the other kings laid themselves down for eternal rest while it was happening. I do not think they knew about it before they disappeared, so there was no one to stop him."

"How many of us are left."

"Too few. We live in the forest. The aniborn will not go past its outer trees. They run the edges. They do not go in."

Kaz straightened from the tree. He stood a full head over the body Azgiel was now wearing, and he stood that way without comment. "We should move." He looked back at Azgiel a second longer. "Their numbers are up of late. Be ready."

Azgiel nodded. The nod hurt. He followed.

The first scream came from ahead of them and to the right. It went up high and stayed there, wrong all the way. No animal made a sound like that. Nothing born on this world did. Azgiel saw the shape in among the trees—a standing thing, faceless except for two red coals where the eyes ought to be.

It screamed again, and the rest of the woods answered.

"Run."

They ran. Kaz set the pace, and the pace cost more than Azgiel's body wanted to give him. He gave it anyway. The trees came past them in long stripes, the underbrush opening, closing.

It hit him from behind.

He had no time to set his feet. The weight came down across his shoulders, claws into his back through whatever Steven had been wearing, and he went forward into the leaves with a thing on top of him.

He got an arm under it. Its skin was cold and had the wet of something that had crawled out of a wound. It bit. Bit deep. Blood went down across his wrist into the leaves.

He took it by the throat with the other hand. It thrashed against him, drove its claws into his ribs through the cloth, and he kept his grip. He called to the power. It did not come at first. When it came it was slow, and clumsy, and not what it used to be—but it came. The thing in his hand lit from inside. Cracks ran up its throat, opened along its skull, and it burst out of his grip in a splatter. He could feel the body strain around the channel he had just opened in it— bone, blood, nerve, none of it built for what he had just made it carry. He was already spent when the second one took him from the side.

It went for the same arm—the one he had used on the first—and tore into him as if it had been told what to do. He locked his fingers in its hide and could feel that he had nothing left to give.

Kaz had four of his own.

Two were on his back, two in front. He drew his sword off his shoulder in one motion, took both the front two's heads with one cut, and let the bodies fall to ash as he turned. A third he peeled off his arm and threw to the ground and finished where it landed. The last he pulled off his side and held out at the end of his arm by the throat, the way a man holds out a sack he intends to set down somewhere else, and his arm did not shake. He took its head off without ceremony, the way a man takes a head off a thing he has done this to before.

The body folded, hit the ground, and went to black ash in the leaves.

Azgiel reached for the will again. He felt it move down his arms into the throat under his hand, the same shape as before. This time it did not catch. The thing on him was going to take him.

Kaz was already at his shoulder. "Let me." It was not a question. Azgiel eased his grip a quarter inch, and the blade went between his fingers and the thing's neck so close he felt the air of it. The head went one way. The rest went down.

They both stood back. The body folded into itself and was a stain in the leaves.

"Thanks," Azgiel said.

Kaz wiped his blade on the moss. He raised his head. "Up. We need to keep moving."

Azgiel did not answer. He had hesitated. Kaz had not. They had both counted it.

At the edge of the clearing, more of them stood—five, six, more behind those—watching. Not pressing. Watching.

Kaz set his grip on the sword. "They are deciding."

Azgiel flexed his hands. His power was a low thread under his skin. It was not what it had been. It was there.

"Lead," he said. He put a hand on Kaz's arm a moment longer than the gesture needed, because there were not many other ways he had to tell him.

Kaz did not say anything. He stayed where he was a half second past the moment, then turned and went. The aniborn watched them go and did not move.

Azgiel followed him across the line of warded stones at the edge of the clearing—felt the cold pass of Maselda's old work go through him like a hand checking for a pulse—and into the Witch's woods.

Kaz drew the obsidian orb off his belt and woke it. A blue light came up around them. The clearing behind them went away. The next clearing came in around them—older trees, the kind that had been growing in the same spots since before Azgiel had been a king—with morning sun, low and gold, working its way down through the high branches.

A figure came out from under the trees into the light.

Two ages he had carried her face.

"Maselda." His voice did not sound like his own.

She did not run to him. She came to him at a walk, the way a person comes to a thing they have been waiting on so long they no longer want to break it by hurrying. Her feet were bare. The morning had her hair. She came around him in a half-circle—slow, no softness in her face—and took the measure of the body he had come back inside, the body that was not the one she had made a past life with.

He had braced for tears, or for her to put her hands on him at once. She did neither. She stopped a pace in front of him and looked at him the way a craftsman looks at a tool that has come back from war.

"It is you," she said.

"It is me." It came out steadier than he had meant it to. He had been afraid she would not know him in this body. She had known him before he opened his mouth.

"Two thousand years," he said.

"Two thousand years," she said back, very low, and the look in her face moved a fraction.

He closed the last of the distance. He put his arms around her and she came against him and let her weight settle into him for the first time since the morning he had walked out of the kingdom. The smell of her—dry grass, the iron of her wards, the under-smell that was only ever her—went into him and stayed.

He held her. He did not speak. He had thought, in the cell, that if he ever held her again he would say a thousand things to her at once. He could not now find one of them. He put his face into the place where her neck met her shoulder and breathed, and her hand came up against the back of his head and stayed.

"I thought I would never see you again," he said, eventually, into her hair.

She did not answer with words. Her arms tightened around his ribs until he could feel the strength in them—the strength of a woman who had built wards that had held for two ages—and she held him there a long moment, and that said it.

She drew back enough to look at him. Her eyes went over his face the way they had gone over the body the first time—slower, this time, because his face was still his face under what had been done to it—and then her hand came up to his cheek and her thumb went along the bone of it.

She kissed him.

It was a kiss two ages in the wanting. She did not make it small. He did not let her. He had forgotten how she fit against him, and the remembering of it went down through him like water finding a riverbed it had cut and lost. His hand came up into her hair. Her hand stayed at his cheek and then went down to his throat and then to the back of his neck, and she pulled him in until there was no morning between them, no clearing, no body, no two ages—only her, and him, and the fact of having one another in their hands again.

When she pulled back, she did not pull back far. She rested her forehead against his and kept her hand at the back of his neck. He could feel her breath go in and go out against his mouth.

"I have you," she said.

"You have me."

"And I am about to ruin it," she said, "because I have to."

He did not let her go. He kept his hands at her waist. "Then ruin it."

She took a breath. He felt her gather herself the way he had watched her gather herself before a hundred councils—the small straightening in the spine, the small dropping of the shoulders away from the ears, the way she had of putting the wife down for a moment so the war-leader could stand up.

"Triaad has the gate," she said.

He had felt the news coming. He had not braced enough for it. His hands stayed where they were on her, but the ground under him moved.

"The gate to the universe."

"He has held it for an age. Stronghold in the mountains—a cave system, deep, fortified, an army of aniborn between the entrance and the gate itself. He has a captain there who runs his operations on this world. Snyp. Dark-matter demon, came through during the first wave. He is Triaad's hand here. He is the one who has been running the borders against me for an age."

Two thousand years he had been a will without a body, and now he had a body, and the body was holding the woman who had been holding a war alone the entire time. The thought went through him and sat in him and did not move.

"And the rest," he said.

"The rest is us." Her hand had not left the back of his neck. "Less than a thousand. Demons, the trolls who came through the retreat, the old loyalists' children's children. Three of your top generals. Kaz. Strite. Raestal."

"Strite is alive."

"He is alive because I kept him alive." Said even, no warmth in it. He knew that voice. He had heard her use that voice on a council that had crossed her once, eight hundred years before any of this. The council had not crossed her again.

He moved his hands from her waist to her face and held it. He had not let her get more than a hand's width away from him since she had let him kiss her. He did not intend to.

"I am going to take the gate," he said.

"I know you are."

"And then I am going to find Triaad," he said, "and I am going to take him apart with these hands. There is no mercy in me for him. Not for what he has done to you."

Her eyes did not move. The glow he had always known her by came up a shade, the way it had come up a shade in his memory whenever a man across a council table had said a thing she did not agree with. He saw it and his hands tightened on her face without his asking them to.

"No," she said.

"No?"

"No." Quiet. The quiet of a closed door. "We take the gate. With you back I believe we can take the gate. We do not chase Triaad after."

"Maselda—"

"Listen to me." Her hand came up and closed around his wrist where his hand was at her face. Not soft. Not the hand of a woman who had been waiting. The hand of a powerful ruler who had built a fortress that had held for two ages against a god. "I have run this war for twenty centuries without you. I have watched it eat everything I had. I have buried the children of friends who had not been born when you went into the cell. I am telling you, as the one who has been here, that we cannot take both. Not with what we have. The gate is the war. Triaad doesn't matter. Go after him and we lose everything."

He did not move his hand from her face. She did not let go of his wrist.

"I am not going to leave him with anything," he said. "Not a stone. Not a man. Not the air around the man."

"I know," she said. "That is what I am telling you. The man I married would also have wanted that. He also would have been wrong about it."

He looked at her. He looked at her for a long moment. He felt his hand shake against her face and he did not let it.

"Do you wish I had stayed in the cell?" he said.

Her eyes did not move. "No. I have wanted you out of that cell every day of two thousand years. Do not insult me with that question."

"Then trust me through this," he said. "The first part. The gate. We take the gate first, and then you let me bring Triaad to you on a table."

"I trust you," she said. The glow came down a shade. Her thumb moved against the inside of his wrist, slow, the way it had moved against the inside of his wrist at a thousand fires, in a thousand rooms, before any of this had been written. "Trust has not been the question. What I am telling you is that there is already a plan. I have been putting it into place for an age. The gate, and Snyp at the gate, and what holds this planet stops holding it. We take what we can hold. We leave Triaad to himself. He will not come for us through a closed gate."

He pulled her in against him. He did it slowly and on purpose. He put his hand into her hair at the back of her head and held her there and did not say anything for a long count.

He could feel the war-leader in her relax, by degrees, into the wife. He could feel his own war-leader try to do the same and not entirely manage it. They stood like that for a while. The morning kept happening around them.

"Az," she said, quiet, into his chest. "I am not asking you to trust me yet. I am asking you to not decide tonight."

"I will not decide tonight," he said.

"Promise me that."

"I promise you that."

She let her breath out against the cloth at his collar. He kept his hand in her hair. He did not let her go.

Off to their right, somewhere in the trees, Kaz cleared his throat the way someone clears their throat when they have been standing in one spot too long. Maselda's mouth turned at one corner against Azgiel's chest.

"He has been waiting," she said.

"Let him wait a moment longer."

"A moment."

"A moment."

He held her. The morning kept happening. After a while, she drew back enough to look up at him, and the war-leader had come up halfway in her face again, but not all the way—there was a softness around her eyes the war-leader did not own—and she put her hand to his cheek one more time before she stepped out of his arms.

She turned to Kaz.

"Gather them," she said. The look that went with it was the order. "Let them see he has come back."

Kaz inclined his head a quarter inch and went, and the trees closed behind him.

Azgiel watched the place where Kaz had been until the morning had fully taken him. Then he reached for Maselda's hand, and she gave it, and they stood at the edge of the older trees in the morning light without speaking.

He had a war again. He had a wife who had been running it without him and was not handing it back the moment he asked for it. He had a promise, made an hour into being a body, that he was already not certain he could keep.

He closed his fingers around hers and held on.

CHAPTER 16
Bridget—Office

The office clock ticked her toward nine. Caden had gone in. She had told herself sitting at home would be worse than working. The office always appreciated help with the walk-ins, anyway. At nine in the morning she had believed it. By her first patient she did not. Her pen tapped against the open notebook in her lap. Outside, the streetlights were still on. Mist made smears of the neon. The city had started its Saturday morning.

The patient across from her was speaking. She was not entirely hearing him. One word from last night had set itself up under everything else and would not move. Azgiel. It had come out of Caden's mouth on the phone with Matt, late, and Caden had told her it was work. The word should have meant nothing to her. It did not feel like nothing.

She forced herself to focus on him. "The dreams feel real, haunted by hellish creatures," he said, twisting the fabric of his jeans between his fingers. "It's as if the past itself is reaching out, waiting for me to remember. Like all the awful things I've done are catching up to me."

Her grip on the pen tightened. Waiting. She wanted to tell him no, that the past did not wait, that the past in her own life had stopped waiting somewhere around the time Caden put on his jacket this morning and shut the front door behind him. She did not say it. She made a small mark in the margin of her notebook instead and let him keep talking.

It was an old feeling. It was the feeling her grandmother used to talk about. Bridget could be sitting as a grown woman with a license on the wall, and still be eight years old, in a blanket, in front of a fire, listening to a woman who used to know things. She had not thought about the cabin in years. She thought about it now.

The cabin smelled of cedar smoke. The book was on the coffee table where it always was, leather worn pale at the corners, the embossed figure on the cover staring up at the ceiling.

Bridget was eight. She pointed at it. "Grandma. What's that picture?"

Her grandmother paused her knitting. The fire moved on the wall behind her, throwing odd shapes. "That," she said, in the careful voice she used for things she did not want to say wrong, "is a very old story. It's about why shadows do not disappear, even in the face of light."

Bridget pulled the blanket tighter. She did not look away from the figure on the cover. "Why do they stay?"

"Because evil remembers, child." Her grandmother's needles had stopped. "Some things refuse to fade."

A pause. Then: "Would you like to hear it?"

Bridget nodded. The fire was warm. She was cold anyway.

"There was a creature once," her grandmother said, the chair tapping its slow tap, "who could not die. A king, before time itself rejected him. Before the gods cast him out, afraid of what he was becoming." The fire popped. "They trapped him. Not in a prison of walls. In a prison of time. Frozen between the moments. Unable to reach into the world."

"Why?" Bridget barely got the word out over the fire.

"Because if he ever escaped, child, the past would not stay buried." The fire popped again. Bridget flinched and did not look away. "It is said that if Azgiel returns, he will not come alone."

"Will he come back?" Bridget asked.

Her grandmother chose her words. "Unlikely. But if he does, the world will remember him. And he will remember the world. There would be ruin in his path."

Bridget came back to the room. The pen was cold in her fingers. The patient had moved on to something else and she had not noticed. *Azgiel.* A bedtime story. A name on the cover of a book in a basement somewhere under her own house. Last night, Caden had said it on the phone to Matt as if it were a name from a file. The two facts did not fit together. They were going to have to.

Her skin prickled at the back of her neck. She had been a clinician long enough to know the difference between a feeling she could redirect and a feeling that was already true. This one was already true. Some part of her had known the name when she heard Caden say it. Some part of her had been waiting for it since she was eight.

"Do you think memories ever become more real than the present?" he asked.

She held the pen above the page. The professional answer was no. The answer the woman who had sat in her grandmother's blanket would have given was different.

"Sometimes," she said. "Sometimes, yes." She gave him a small smile she did not feel. "But only if we let them."

She turned the page. She straightened. She made herself listen. Underneath, something had begun moving that she was not going to be able to talk back into the dark.

When the patient left, she sat for a moment in the quiet of her own office and let her shoulders go. Then she stood up. The bonsai on the windowsill had gone untended. Branches overgrown. A few leaves curling at the edge. A small thing, on a small sill, looking exactly the way she felt.

I forgot to water it.

She had been shaping it for weeks, one branch at a time, the way she'd been taught—the small ritual that kept the rest of her steady when the rest of her wasn't. She lifted the watering can and poured. The soil drank. "I'm sorry," she said, to the tree, and meant it.

It was not too late for the tree. She set the can down and tried not to read herself into it. She read herself into it anyway.

Her phone buzzed on the desk.

Caden: *Thinking of you.*

Three words. From any other partner on any other morning, three sweet words. From him, this week, after last night—a check-in. A pulse to let her know he was still on the line. She read it twice. She thought about asking him if he was safe. She thought about asking him what Azgiel was. She thought about asking him to come home.

She did what she told her clients to do. She took the words for what they said. She typed back one of her own.

Bridget: *Always.*

She set the phone down. The tension stayed in her shoulders, where it had been since she stepped over the threshold of this office at nine. He was not going to tell her the truth. That did not mean the truth was unavailable to her.

She thought about her grandmother's chest. It was in her own basement, under blankets she had not lifted in years. She could not remember whether the book with the figure on the cover was still in it. Her grandmother had said legends were warnings. Bridget had nodded the way an eight-year-old nods. Then she had grown up, and gone to school, and learned that what an eight-year-old calls a warning a grown woman calls a story.

It might be time to listen the way the eight-year-old had.

She picked up the phone and reopened the day's schedule. She had four more sessions on the books. She moved them. She gave the front desk a flat reason that was not exactly a lie. Then she got her coat.

At the door she paused with her hand on the knob and thought, for a second, about texting Caden where she was going. She did not. He had not told her about Azgiel. She was not going to tell him about the book. Not yet. Not until she had read it for herself.

CHAPTER 17
Caden—Dead Time Test Floor

Caden stood at the edge of the test floor and tried to feel like a man at the edge of a test floor. A week ago he had stood here and felt exactly that. He had thought he understood what he was about to do. He had not.

The act was not holding. The man in the parking lot was still in his head. The silver hair. The hand on his arm. *Stay out of stopped time.* The kind of warning a hallucination did not give you and then walk away into the floodlights.

Under that, the older thing. The cold at the front of his throat that had not warmed up in a week. The line behind his breastbone that the altar had hooked into. The name that sat just under everything else he was trying to think about, the way a bruise sits under a sleeve. He did not say the name to himself. He had stopped saying it to himself. Saying it to himself made it worse.

A week ago, on a helicopter, he had told Robert to ground this project. He had used a voice he had never used on Robert before. Robert had agreed. Then Robert had put Steven in. Then Robert had put Bain's men in this morning. Now Robert was sending two teams in.

He was about to put on the suit he had told them to lock in a case.

On the floor below, the techs moved in clipped lines. Screens up everywhere. Numbers running.

Robert came past him without slowing and went to the cluster around the main console. He did not look up.

The team was assembling at the staging mark. James was already in his suit, sealed at the throat, helmet under his arm. Mike and Palmer in theirs. The gold weave caught the overheads and gave back a slow soft pulse, the way it always did, as if something inside the metal were keeping a heartbeat.

Bain stood apart from the others, still in his clothes, watching the platform. Allen was not in the room. Caden noted both. He had been noting things all morning. He was running a list and he had not yet decided what to do with it.

At the staging rail, a hand came down on his shoulder.

Robert. "Drawer by the switch."

Caden did not turn his head. "Guns."

"Retrofit pair. Allen wants you to fire one in."

"You cleared a live weapon for an in-field test on the first run back."

"Yes."

"Does Bain know?"

"He knows."

Robert was already moving. He did not look at Caden when he said it. He went back to the console and was lost in the cluster of techs. Caden stood at the rail and watched him go.

Across the floor, James caught his eye and lifted his chin at the rack. The suit was hung on it: a single sealed unit, the gold weave running unbroken from the high collar down through the wrists and into the integrated boots, the helmet on its own peg above.

Caden went over. As he came around the rack, James's eyes hooked on Palmer and held a beat too long, a slow private smile that James did not quite let onto his mouth.

"Focus," Caden said, low. "Don't go picking a fight with Palmer. Not today."

James shrugged, the smile not entirely going away.

Caden took the suit down. It was lighter in his hands than it had been a week ago. Allen had probably tweaked the weave. He stepped into it the way he had stepped into it before, one piece, because every seam was a place the field could fail. The weave settled to him. The oxygen pack rode high between the shoulders the way it had a week ago, the same dropped-shoulder weight under the gold—one of the few parts of the rig Allen had not been able to make any lighter.

"Relax," James said. "They're all hotheads. You know how they are."

Caden made a sound that was half a smile and entirely not one. James could see he had the jitters and was trying to crack him up. James had been in the helicopter. James had seen the results of the first test.

Caden lifted the helmet off the peg.

It was heavier than he remembered. He had worn this same helmet across a battlefield a week ago and not noticed its weight until he tried to set it down. He fitted it over his head. The seal closed around his throat with a small soft hiss.

The lab took on a faint coppery tint through the visor. The HUD came up across the bottom of his vision. Battery one hundred. Field array one hundred. The thin green line ran flat along the bottom of the glass.

He looked at the green line for a long count. Last time he had looked at this line, it had spiked twice and a woman had put her hand on his throat. He did not know whether the line had spiked because something had touched the field or because something had touched him.

The team gathered on the platform. The lab quieted by degrees, the way a lab quiets when the people who have been arguing all morning suddenly do not need to. The techs stopped talking. They watched their screens.

"All systems are ready," Allen's voice came over the intercom.

Robert moved to the panel. "In place. Three. Two. One."

He pressed the button.

Sound stopped. Not faded. Stopped. The room and everything in it locked into the position it had been in a half-second before. Robert with his finger on the button. The techs in the small leans of people watching screens. The lights of the consoles in their colors. All of it held.

The silence had a pressure to it. The same pressure as last time. He realized he was holding his breath—waiting, without quite meaning to, for the floor to tear sideways. He let the breath out, carefully. The floor stayed where it was.

Palmer came over the comms first. "Can we move now?"

Bain answered. "Yes. Get a feel for the suits. Adapt fast."

Caden took one step. His suit's field cleared the air ahead of him with a small soft give. The shadows in the room had not moved with the men. They stayed where the men had been a half-second before, a still life of who had stood there. As Bain walked, a thin blackness peeled off behind him and folded back together in his wake, the air bending around the place he had been like ripples in glass that did not quite settle.

"It's the light particles," Bain said. "When you move, you disrupt them. They reform, but not exactly. Like water closing behind you. Slower than water."

"That's interesting," James said.

"Don't give me too much credit," Bain said. "That's Allen's theory. I'm repeating it."

At the other end of the platform, Mike came at Palmer in a slow exaggerated lunge and Palmer met him in a slower one. They were sparring the way men spar when gravity has let go of them by half, all fluid arcs and overcommitted footwork. Palmer launched himself in a long arc at Bain, arms out, hung in the air a beat longer than he had any business hanging, and landed.

Mike laughed. James laughed. Bain made a sound that on him passed for a laugh.

Caden did not laugh.

They did not know. None of them knew. James had pieces of it, the helicopter pieces, but they did not have the altar. They did not have the battlefield. They did not have a hand on the throat. They thought they were inside a tool. A week ago, in this same suit, the tool had reached down a hallway it should not have had and held him by the chest and shown him things. He stood on the platform with men he respected and watched them play, and he could not shake the feeling that the floor was going to open under all of them while he watched.

"Time's up," Bain said over the comms. "On the wrist. One tap. You'll exit."

Caden looked at the soft-plate on the inside of his left wrist. The abort. He had tapped it three times last time. It had not brought him back.

One by one the team tapped and locked, mid-step, as their bodies handed them back to the world. Bain turned to him. "Guns."

Caden nodded and followed him to the drawer. Walking in stopped time felt the way it had felt the first time. Half-weight. The body wanting to glide. He kept his feet on the floor.

At the drawer he made his voice carry on the comms. "How did Steven stay in here as long as he did."

It was not the question Bain expected. Bain looked at him through the visor.

"No one knows," Bain said, lifting one of the retrofit sidearms out of the drawer and sighting at a paper target downrange. "Not even Allen has an answer for that one. Steven's time in there broke every rule we had."

"He was in for hours," Caden said. "He came back as something else."

Bain held the sight on the target. He did not look away from the target. "You going to fire that gun, Caden, or are we having a meeting?"

Caden lifted the sidearm. The HUD line at the bottom of his visor stayed flat.

They fired together. The recoil came up the arm wrong—the kick was barely there, but the round wasn't going anywhere to take it. The two slugs left the barrels and stopped a foot out, hung in nothing, two small bright objects fixed in the air as if pinned to it.

"Well, that's useless," Caden said dryly.

"Completely," Bain agreed, lowering his weapon. "Let's wrap it up."

Bain tapped his wrist. His body locked, mid-half-step, head turned a fraction toward Caden. Caden's own hand went to the soft-plate on the inside of his left wrist. He did not press.

That was when he saw it.

He almost did not. It was a ripple in the half-light by the back machines, the kind of thing that could have been a smear on the visor. His gut went tight before his eye worked out why. He blinked. The ripple was gone. The room had gone charged the way a room goes charged before a thing you cannot see arrives in it.

He had felt the room go charged like this once before. On the battlefield. Right before the figure in the black armor had turned a fraction of a degree and shown him it knew he was there.

The ripple came back. Sharper this time. Something in the corner was gathering. Thickening. He could not have said out of what.

His hand crept on the wrist plate. It did not press. Something—not a thought of his, not exactly—told him to wait. The instruction came from somewhere outside the inside of his head, and that fact alone should have made him press.

He did not press.

The shape held a beat. Then it firmed. Edges. Specifics. A presence in a place.

It opened the way a thing opens that does not have hinges, and filaments came out of it in his direction, and a current the size of a knife edge ran up his spine.

He wanted to run. His legs were locked. They were not locked the way a body locks itself in stopped time. They were locked the way a body locks itself when something has put a hand on the back of its neck. The figure advanced. Not stepped. Each forward motion was the figure dissolving and reforming a yard nearer than it had been a half-second before.

Then it stopped.

It turned its head, if it had a head, toward him.

There was no face on it. Nothing to see.

It was not watching him. It was measuring him.

A filament unspooled from it and stopped four inches from his sternum. His body screamed to move. Nothing in his body answered. The thing hummed at a frequency he could feel in the long bones of his legs. It was not reaching. It was reading him.

The HUD line at the bottom of his visor spiked once and shivered back down.

That was the same.

His fingers found the wrist plate. He tapped it.

The room came back.

Sound moved into the room the way water moves back into a harbor. Lights of consoles. Voices of techs. Robert's hand coming off the panel. Bain's body finishing the half-step it had been frozen in.

Caden looked at the corner.

Empty.

A normal corner.

Inside the suit his hands were shaking. A sweat had broken across his back that the weave was already wicking—and logging, and Allen would read the line of it later. He breathed. He breathed again. He held his hands flat at his sides and made them stop.

It had seen him.

Or it had measured him. The two were not the same. A predator sees what it intends to eat. This thing had paused. It had read him. It had decided something.

Whatever the thing in the corner was, it would be back. Unless he was already losing his mind, the way Steven had. He could not tell which thought he wanted more.

"You forgot to put them back," Robert said.

Caden looked down. The retrofit sidearm was still in his glove. He had not registered taking it out of stopped time. He set it on the rack with care.

Bain set his own beside it. "Doesn't matter. Useless. The round can't carry past the field. Knives might be better. Maybe."

Caden looked up. Palmer was watching him through the visor. The look on

Palmer's face had moved past curiosity. Caden made his face do nothing in particular and kept it doing nothing in particular until Palmer's eyes moved off him. He was not going to tell anyone about the corner. Not Bain. Not James. Not Robert. He was on thin enough ice with the project as it was. He needed his footing back before he opened his mouth.

He cleared his throat. "Or swords," he said, lighter than he felt. "If we're going to wear gold, we should commit to the look."

Bain made a small sound. The corner of the floor was still empty. Caden's eye kept going back to it anyway.

Robert started to say something. Bain spoke over him.

"The bullets hit the target."

Caden cut him a look. "What?" He had watched the rounds hang.

Bain didn't repeat himself. He pointed at the far wall. There were two holes in it, in a tight pair, in a place Caden had not been looking. "When we exited, the rounds finished their path."

Robert was already at the wall. He crouched. He put a finger inside one of the holes and drew it back out. "Through the target. Through the wall. Whatever speed they came back to was a speed we have never put a round at."

"We better hope no one was on the other side of that wall," Caden said. He leaned to look. The hole was small. He could not see what was on the other side of it.

"We can use this," Robert said. The careful in his voice was not careful. "Maybe not the way we wanted. We can use it."

Caden put his back to the rack and let his head drop a fraction. The room tilted. He put a glove flat against the rack and waited for it to stop tilting. The cold at the front of his throat was bigger than it had been in months.

"Everything okay?" Bain's voice came in over the comms.

"Yeah... I just need to get out of this suit." Caden broke the seal at the collar and worked the straps of the oxygen pack with thick fingers as he started for the rack.

Allen had come up next to him without him noticing. "When you're done. Bain and Robert. Lower lab." Allen looked at him a beat longer than the message took. He decided not to say whatever he had thought about saying, and walked off.

Across the floor, Bain had the helmet off and was unstrapping the oxygen pack onto the rack. Robert was still at the wall. Bain's men stood around in their gold weave, easy in it, talking about the experience the way men talk about a thing that has not yet hurt them. Caden envied them. He was surprised at himself for envying them.

Crossing the floor felt longer than the floor. His inner ear was off. He reached Bain and Robert and gave them Allen's message in a voice he had to lower in order to keep the unsteady out of it. Neither asked. Bain looked at him a moment longer than the message had earned. He had heard the unsteady anyway.

He didn't wait for them. He went down to the lower lab and sat in the first metal chair he came to. The chair was cold through the back of the suit and he was grateful for it.

Bain and Robert came in a minute later. They looked at each other. They sat. Allen was at the workbench, doing small things to small equipment, taking his time about it. When he was ready he turned around.

"To get you up to speed," Allen said, "I ran tests on rabbits last night. Before the break-ins." He looked at Caden, then back at the others. "The switch that sends you into stopped time integrates perfectly with a biological system. For the rabbits, we connected it to the base of the spinal cord. One hundred percent success rate."

Bain leaned forward. "And how did you get them out?"

Allen tipped his head at a cage on the bench. Six white rabbits, pink noses going. Each had a thin black band on a hind leg. "Timers on the legs. Set the dwell time. Time runs out, they come back." He paused. "The interesting part was where they came back."

Caden looked up.

Allen had said it without inflection. Allen had not chosen to look at him while he said it. Caden filed that.

Robert leaned in. "Would the human version work the same way?"

"Not exactly," Allen said. "For humans, we've designed a watch-like device. It functions as a remote and master control. Bain and Caden would have the authority to override the team's units if needed."

Robert raised an eyebrow. "And you're telling me you can have this ready within a day?"

"With Caden's help, yes," Allen said. "Once we give our engineers the final specs, they can produce the components quickly. We could start implanting the chips tonight."

Robert had a brief visible fight with himself. "I'm not sure I want a chip going into Matt's spine." He let it sit a beat. "On second thought—do it. In his cell. Restraints on. I want him contained."

Caden tried to keep up. The pounding in his head was louder than the room. The voices on either side of him went under it.

"Caden." Robert's voice came down a long pipe. "You don't look well. Infirmary, then home. I'm strongly recommending you take the rest of your leave."

The room spun for a moment. He used the table to brace himself. "I'm fine."

Robert was not convinced. "You're fine after the infirmary. Allen will walk you over."

Caden nodded. Not that he wanted to.

It was the voice Robert used when the conversation was over.

Bain put a hand on his shoulder on the way past. He did not say anything. He did not need to.

Caden let his shoulders down. Allen put a hand against his back, light, and steered him out of the room.

The thing in the corner had paused for a reason. The reason had been recognition. He had been treating stopped time as a place. He thought, with the slow certainty that came when he had not slept, that stopped time was not a place. It was a cell. And whatever was in it had been waiting a long time to look at one specific face.

Maybe he really had seen Domblin in the parking lot. Maybe Domblin had been right.

CHAPTER 18
Bridget—Home

The basement smelled of dust and damp concrete and years she had not opened lately. Bridget paused at the top of the kitchen stairs with her hand on the rail. The bulb at the bottom of the stairwell was on a chain and it was swinging a little, the way bulbs on chains do in basements, for no reason. The stairs creaked under her on the way down.

She had always hated it down here. Furniture under sheets that looked like people who had stopped moving. Boxes of other lifetimes. Crates she had not touched since she carried them in. Somewhere at the back of all of it, under blankets and old sweaters that smelled of mothballs, was her grandmother's chest.

She bumped a shelf in the dark and the jars on it clinked. Preserves. Brown with age. Her grandmother had canned them the summer before she died, hands stained purple to the second knuckle, humming whatever she had been humming that summer. Bridget had carried them down here. Her grandmother had told her where to put them. She put a hand on the nearest jar and steadied it, and the small ache that lived in her throat for her grandmother woke up the way it always did down here.

The chest was where she remembered, under the blankets, smelling of lavender soap and dust. Carved vines on the lid. Carved symbols among the vines that she had traced with one finger, over and over, when she was eight, half wanting to know what they meant and half certain she did not.

She knelt. She brushed dust off the lid. The latch was stiff. It gave with a small metal sound. She lifted. The smell came up at her: old leather, cedar, dry paper, and underneath all of those, very faint, the perfume her grandmother had worn the last year of her life.

And there it was.

The book was at the bottom. Among folded clothes and curled photographs.

The leather was cracked the way leather cracks under hands that have held it too often. The figure on the cover was looking up at the basement ceiling as if it had been waiting there for her to lift the lid.

Her hand stopped above it. This was the book of her childhood nightmares. Of bedtime stories she had asked for and not been able to sleep after. Of the careful low voice her grandmother had used for things you were not supposed to say aloud. It had been here the whole time.

Her fingers found the leather. The dread of an eight-year-old climbed her spine in the body of a thirty-five-year-old. She named it as it came. Amygdala. Threat response. Old groove. The naming did not stop the feeling, but the feeling did not run her either.

She lifted the book out. It was heavier than she remembered. She set it across her knees and turned the first page. The parchment crackled. Letters in a script she did not know. Claw-shaped. The ink looked wet. It was not wet. She knew it was not wet.

It's awake.

She did not say it. The thought said itself.

Illustrations filled the pages. Meticulous. Cities on fire. Towers folding into themselves under storms. Creatures coming up out of pits in the ground. One battlefield ran across two facing pages, armies of crooked figures locked together under a sky split with lightning. At the center, larger than the rest, the figure from the cover. Azgiel. The man her grandmother had warned about by candlelight. Her grandmother had been right about the size of him.

She stared until the figures blurred. She blinked. They moved a little when she blinked, the way figures in old illustrations sometimes seem to. She told herself they did not move.

It can't be real. Folklore. A bedtime story. A name on a page.

What if it is real?

Her hands were not steady. She pulled out her phone. She needed to warn Caden. He had been carrying something for days he would not put down.

Could he already know what was in this book? Was he tied to it somehow without knowing it?

Her thumb hovered over the screen. She typed.

Caden, I don't know how to explain this, but if Azgiel is real, you need to be careful. You could be in danger...

She read it again. She read it the way Caden would read it. A man on the back of four bad nights, getting a text from his wife about a name from a children's book. He would read it once. He would not read it twice. After that he would file her with the rest of the things he was trying to keep at the edge of the room.

She held the phone for another beat. Then she deleted the message, one tap at a time, until the field was empty. She needed something he would have to look at twice.

She started searching on her phone. Most of what came back was the kind of folklore she had grown up on. Forgotten deities. Tale fragments. Same warnings, same vague edges. After half an hour she found the right kind of dead end. A coastal university. A small collection of ancient languages. One professor with a long bibliography on a script that, in the thumbnails, looked very like the script across her own knees.

If this book was what she was beginning to think it was, it had not been passed down. It had been left.

She drafted an email. She kept it short.

Hello,

I recently came into possession of a book that contains symbols I believe are related to your research. I've attached a clear photograph of one page. I'd be grateful for any insight you can give me, and I'm available at your earliest convenience.

Thank you,

Bridget

She attached the photo. She sent it before she could decide not to.

Then she sat in the basement on the cold floor with the book on her knees and listened to her own breathing.

She carried the book upstairs. It felt fragile in her arms and something else under the fragile that she did not want to name.

The living room had gone dim. Outside, the storm that had been gathering all day had arrived; rain pulled itself across the windows in long sheets. The fire was nearly down to coals. She sank onto the couch and pulled a blanket around her. The light moved on the walls the way it had moved when she was eight in her grandmother's cabin. She opened the book again across her lap. The script caught the low firelight and seemed to shift at the corner of her eye.

She blinked hard. Her vision burned with exhaustion. The warmth settled around her, lulling her toward sleep.

"No," she muttered aloud. "Stay awake."

But the words blurred further, swimming across the page. Her eyelids grew impossibly heavy, drooping against her will. Then—a faint rustle. Cloth brushing carpet.

Bridget turned slowly. She knew—somehow, she knew—exactly who she'd see.

A chill slid through the room, sudden and jarring. Her grandmother stood beside the couch, ghostly pale yet achingly familiar, close enough to touch. She was translucent, moonlight through glass, her eyes hollowed.

"Bridget." The voice was brittle, cracking. "You need to run."

"How…how are you here?" Bridget whispered.

Her grandmother's gaze dropped to the book, face tightening. "It found you through me. It knows our blood. Evil always starts with blood."

Bridget's throat went dry. "I don't understand."

The figure lunged closer, desperation twisting her features. "Run, Bridget! It's waking—"

The book shuddered in her lap. Heat bled through the leather. Ink beaded, the lines swimming as though alive. A pressure clamped around her wrist, crushing, though nothing visible bound her. She tore free with a gasp.

The book toppled to the floor, striking with a heavy slap.

The fire died.

Darkness smothered the room.

A rattling breath filled the room.

Something stirred in the corner—enormous, misshapen. Each step drew the floorboards into groans. She couldn't move. The weight of it pressed her down, closer, closer, until claws gripped her neck.

She opened her mouth to scream—

Bridget jolted awake, lurching upright—the couch, the book, the ordinary room intact. On reflex, she flung the book away. It skidded into the corner with a thud. She gasped, rubbing her neck.

Only fire and quiet remained. But beneath her skin, the phantom ache burned on.

CHAPTER 19
Tagen—Myree War Aftermath (2,000 Years Ago)

Azgiel's demons had not just tortured him. They had taken him apart and not bothered to put the pieces in order. Blood was thick on his tongue. His ribs would not hold his weight, and the dark kept pulling at the edges of his sight, patient, the way a dark thing pulls at a wounded thing.

Even in the wreckage of his own body, what he had seen would not leave him. Mauldrin had come down on Azgiel's camp the way weather comes down on a field. Nothing in front of him had stayed standing. None of that mattered now. He had to move.

From the safety of a hilltop, Tagen glanced back at Azgiel's camp. Light moved through the trees below—tents on fire, some already collapsed into the kind of glowing heaps that had been tents an hour ago. Horses screamed against their tethers, the rope smoking where the heat had reached it.

Mauldrin's men moved through the camp without hurry, lifting shields and weapons off the dead and stacking them. It did not look like victory. It looked like an inventory. Tagen turned away.

Azgiel was defeated. Triaad would reward loyalty. He had to believe that.

Every step pulled at the gash in his side. Blood ran down his leg in a thin warm line. His body would not knit itself the way it should—too drained, the well too low—and he understood, in the cold clear way a wounded thing understands, that he was leaking out his hours.

Halfway to the gate, his legs went out from under him. He hit the dirt face-first and could not push himself up.

He tried again. His arms trembled and folded.

Movement at the treeline. He brought his head up and breathed in. Aniborn.

"It's him," a low, gravelly voice growled.

Two of them came out of the brush.

"Well, well," the second one hissed. "Tagen, bleeding like a mortal. What a pitiful sight."

He kept his voice flat. "Get it over with or take me to Triaad."

The first one showed his teeth. "Still mouthy. Pity. You'd have been fun." He looked at the other. "Master wants him breathing."

Tagen forced himself up onto one knee—not because he could fight, but because going to Triaad on his back was a different kind of death than going on his feet. The nearest aniborn did not give him the chance. He hooked an arm under Tagen's shoulder and heaved him up like a sack.

"Let's move," he barked.

The journey blurred. He tried to keep quiet and could not. He bled the whole way.

Then stone. He hit it shoulder-first and the cold of it came up through the wound in his side and woke him. He pushed up onto an elbow.

A figure stood at the far end of the chamber. Pale. Thin in a way that did not look like hunger.

Triaad.

The master of the aniborn came across the floor in no hurry, each footfall echoing into the high stone of the tower. Tagen's vision tilted, gray closing in at the edges—until Triaad's boot took him in the ribs and slammed him back to the floor and back into himself.

"What happened?" Triaad's voice was sharp the way a cold knife is sharp.

Tagen blinked. The response was wrong. There should have been a different one first. *Welcome back.* Or, *Did Azgiel die screaming?* Not this.

"I...was...captured," Tagen rasped.

"Tortured, by the looks of it," Triaad said, looking him over without interest.

"Yes," Tagen wheezed. He gathered himself for the part he had been carrying back to Triaad like a coin tight in his fist. "But he is gone. Mauldrin won. Azgiel is... dead."

"I already know Azgiel's condition," Triaad said. He waved the news away as if Tagen had brought him a cup of cold water.

Tagen's stomach dropped. *How? How does he already know?*

"Now," Triaad continued, the chill in his voice tightening, "what information did you give Azgiel?"

"I...didn't..." Tagen stammered. "Nothing important..."

Triaad was on him before he saw the movement. A hand closed around his throat and lifted him off the floor, and the strength in those thin fingers was not the strength of a body. "Do not lie to me. I already know what you said."

Triaad's eyes went black to the rim. Something behind Tagen's breastbone began to leak the wrong way, as though Triaad's grip were drinking him through the throat.

"Azgiel isn't dead," Triaad said, close to his ear. "He's locked in a Cell of Time. Mauldrin should have killed him. He did not. So Azgiel will come back, and when he does he will come for me."

He drew Tagen closer, until Tagen could see the small unblinking still of his face. "And because of your mouth, Azgiel's army will rally against me instead of bending the knee. Do you understand what you have undone, or has the pain emptied what little was up there?"

Tagen's mouth opened around something that was not quite a word. Triaad did not wait for it. "You have cost me. Now you will pay it."

Triaad let go. Tagen hit the stone and stayed there.

"You should have let them kill you," Triaad said. "Because by the time I'm done, you'll wish they had."

Triaad lifted a hand. The skin of Tagen's mouth crawled, fused, and sealed. Panic moved up under his ribs and Tagen's claws went to his face—too late, the seal already set, his own breath knocking against the inside of it like a trapped insect.

Triaad smiled. He moved his hand a second time, and the wall behind Tagen began to give. Stone came out of it in slow gray ropes and reached for him, found his ankles, his wrists, his ribs, and went hard. Tagen tried shadow form. The wall ate the attempt and held him tighter for it.

"If you're not dead when I return," Triaad said, from the door, "perhaps I'll make you a slave. Do not expect it. Enjoy the rats."

The door shut. The silence after it was the silence of a place that had been built to hold silences. Somewhere behind the wall, a rat began to scratch.

* * *

Time stopped meaning anything.

The rats came first. They climbed him, tested him, found the soft places at his ankles and his sides where the stone had not quite covered, and they fed. His blood killed them where they bit. Their bodies fell at his feet and rotted there and were replaced by other rats who would not learn. The smell never left.

After the rats, the silences. Long enough that he began to mistake his own held breath for a voice in the dark. Long enough that the memories of the woods, of the camp, of Mauldrin's hand raised above Azgiel—these things stopped feeling like memory and started feeling like the only stories left in the world. He told them to himself. He told them to the rats. The seal kept the words behind his teeth, but the words went on anyway, eating their own tails.

His skin went gray and brittle. Dust settled into the seam of his sealed mouth and into the half-open slits of his eyes and stayed there. He stopped wanting to die. He stopped wanting anything. Wanting was a thing for a creature with a future, and he had been given the wall instead.

A sound came that was not the rats and not the wind. Footsteps. Set down on purpose. Coming closer.

Something in him that had been gone a long time turned its head. He cracked his eyelids—the dust on them gave way like dry crust—and the light hurt. He waited the hurt out. A figure took shape in front of him.

"Are you alive?" a voice said.

The figure resolved into a large aniborn—larger than any Tagen had seen before. Sharp-featured, well-fed, pleased with himself.

"Ah, so you are," the aniborn said. "Good. That makes this much easier."

Tagen's jaw worked behind the seal. The seal did not yield. The sound that came up his throat was not a word.

"I've been assigned a mission," the aniborn continued, pacing leisurely. "A dangerous one. The problem is…" He paused, looking up at Tagen as if remembering he was there. "I need a servant. Someone who knows their way around. Someone expendable."

The aniborn snapped his fingers, and the sound of rattling chains echoed from the corridor. A youngling was dragged in, its shiny black skin glistening with dampness—a clear sign it had recently been freed from a dark matter cell.

"You want it," the aniborn said. He lifted the youngling by the neck. He took the head off in one motion. The body folded. Black blood spread across the stone in a slow, even circle.

"Pledge to me," he said, gesturing at the body, "and I feed you. Enough to heal. Enough to come off that wall. One word and you walk out of this room. Will you serve me without question?"

Tagen pulled. The seal held. His jaw creaked behind it and went nowhere. The aniborn watched him try, and the watching had a faint pleasure in it.

"Let me help you," he said. He raised one claw.

He cut. The seal split along the line where Triaad had set it, and the dry skin under it tore in a way skin tears when it has not been used in a long time. Blood ran down Tagen's chin. Air came in through his open mouth for the first time in he did not know how long, and it tasted like the room.

He shaped the word. It came out cracked.

"Yes," he said.

"Good," the aniborn said. "Would have been a waste to leave you to the rats."

He tore an arm off the corpse and held it to Tagen's mouth. Tagen bit. The meat went down warm and the warmth went somewhere old in him and woke up. With every swallow he could feel the wall begin to give him back.

"What is the mission?" His voice steadied as it came back to him.

The aniborn laughed once and threw the rest of the arm aside. "Hunting rogue demons. One of them has wandered outside the Witch's territory. We cannot get inside her woods—she and her followers have them sealed up tight—but the ones who step out, those we can have. And we will."

Tagen had questions. He kept them. The first thing was off this wall. He could feel his foot beginning to remake itself, the dead bone going dark and damp again, veins threading themselves where there had been only dust. He flexed his fingers, slow, and the joints answered.

"What is your name?" Tagen asked. "If I am going to die beside you I should know whose mistake I died under."

The aniborn grinned. "Snyp. But do not get any ideas—I'm in charge. Triaad is still your master, and I'm his chosen."

Tagen nodded. He flexed his claws and felt the strength still coming back into his hands. The pain was there. The pain mattered less than the fact that nothing was holding him to the wall anymore.

Snyp gestured toward the youngling's remains. "Eat enough to heal. Not more. Triaad's orders—if you grow too strong, I cannot control you."

Tagen kept his face flat and tore into another piece. *Control me. We will see, in time, whose name the room calls when I open my hand.*

He shifted into shadow form and pushed off the wall. The stone fought him on the way through—slow and unwilling, the way old stone fought any form that tried to pass it—but it let him through. His body did not feel like his. Too rigid in some places, too tender in others. But it was his again. A cold draft was finding its way in through the broken stone, and he let it touch him.

"Move," Snyp said, already walking. "We have demons to hunt and I do not plan to fail."

Tagen followed. Snyp walked in front of him as if there could be no other arrangement. Tagen let him think it.

The Witch's woods waited at the end of the corridor, and somewhere inside them, the rest of his life.

CHAPTER 20
Caden—SDS Infirmary

The monitor beeped. The room was lit only by what the equipment threw off—the soft green of the readout, the white of an idle screen, a single LED on the IV stand. Caden surfaced into it the way a swimmer surfaces under thin ice. His eyelids opened halfway. He had dozed off after they hooked him up to all the machines. The lines on the monitor were shaky, uneven, the way his pulse was.

Under the blankets he was cold. Not chilled—cold the way a thing left out is cold. He could not see the clock—it was behind one of the larger machines—and he could not tell, from the dark of the room, whether it was night or whether the door simply had not been opened in a while. He was not sure how long he had been out. Either way, no one was coming.

Static crawled across the monitor. He noticed it with a half-second delay—his thoughts running behind the room. He tried to push up onto an elbow. His body did not respond. From across the room, the slow careful sound of a door being eased open by someone who did not want to be heard.

He tried to call out and could not. Something had closed around the inside of his throat. He pushed against the bed and the bed held him as if it had hands. The dark in the room thickened. Even the green of the monitor went dim. His breath came shallow and would not deepen.

At the edge of his sight, a hunched, indistinct shape. He forced his head sideways an inch, then another, until red eyes came into focus.

"Mauldrin," the voice rasped.

The creature lunged. The air around his ribs bent inward and held. He tried to breathe and nothing in his chest answered. The monitor's jagged line gave up its peaks and went flat, and the small bright tone of it filled the room. Numbness moved up from his feet and met itself at his sternum, and he stopped being in his body so much as next to it. He could feel himself being torn out of it.

His vision narrowed to a pinprick. The pressure on his ribs went away, and the absence of it was so kind that he stopped wanting to fight back. There was no pain. There was no fear. There was only the small bright tone, very far now, and the easy untethered drift of a thing that did not have to stay.

Then a scream cut through him from outside the room. The drift snapped. He was slammed back into his body the way a fish is slammed back into water. Air came into him in a ragged drag.

The hunched thing was already going. It thinned at the edges and slipped through the wall like smoke under a door. Before Caden could understand that part, another figure was standing at the foot of the bed.

Domblin.

"Eyes up," Domblin said. "They are not the harmless things you may believe they are. This is not a hallucination. They will kill you, and they will not need long."

Caden blinked. The room was still wrong. *Another one. Another hallucination. This time trying to convince him it isn't one.* Words came up his throat and got tangled there.

Domblin glanced toward the door warily. "I can't stay long," he said, drawing a white chain from his pocket. A green gem hung from its center. "Take this. It'll keep you safe."

Caden hesitated only a moment before reaching for it. The chain was cold enough to bite. The gem at the center was warm, in the wrong way for a stone. The whole thing was light as a feather and still managed to feel as if it carried weight. Domblin's face went hard. "On. Now."

Caden's fingers fumbled with the clasp. The gem settled against his sternum and bloomed, briefly, with green fire. Something sharp and alive moved through him from collarbone to feet, and the cold that had been in him went out of him as if a window had been opened on it. The chain and the gem dissolved into the air. Only a faint warmth on his chest remained, and a small certain sense, against all reason, that this had been real.

Domblin's stern voice broke through his awe. "And one more thing—don't wait."

"What?" Caden managed.

"Bridget. Marry her. You may never get another chance."

Before Caden could answer, Domblin was gone. The room was quiet again. The monitor beeped, even and disinterested.

Caden pulled the IV from his arm. The sting helped. He swung his legs over the side of the bed and the cold floor under his bare feet did the rest.

Had Domblin been here? The warmth on his sternum said yes. Nothing else in the room said anything. He stood, found his balance, and went out into the hallway. He looked back once. He half-expected something to come through the wall after him.

The overhead lights hummed. The polished floor took the light back at him in a long flat stripe. The corridor was quiet—quiet in a way the corridor was never quiet—and as he came up on the stairwell door, he heard voices through it.

He stopped. He set his ear to the cool of the metal.

"Download the data. We don't have much time," someone said.

"Kill anyone who gets in the way," came another order, sharper and menacing.

Caden eased the door open the width of an eye. Three men inside. A folding table set up against the wall, a laptop on it, a progress bar on the screen. The man in the middle was bald and unhurried. To his right, a wiry blond, twitchy, his hand near the knife strapped to his thigh. The third man stood over a scientist on the floor—bruised face, hands up—pressing the muzzle of a sidearm to the side of the man's head.

"That wasn't the order, Justin," the man with the sidearm said to the bald man.

Caden stepped through and let the door click shut behind him. Soft. Loud enough.

"Who's there?" the blond snapped. The knife was already in his hand. His face changed when he saw who he was looking at.

"Get your hands up slowly," the bald man said, even.

Caden raised his hands. The scientist on the floor was shaking. Caden held the man's eye for a beat and tried to get him to read the small calm in his own.

"What's going on here?" Caden asked evenly. His attention was on the laptop.

Justin smirked. "Maybe you're not as smart as your reputation, Caden—or maybe you simply got cocky."

Caden took a longer look at him. "Do I know you?"

"Doesn't matter," Justin replied, the smile not reaching anything. "But I know you. I know how you operate, and I know how many of mine you have put down. The question tonight is whether you have anything left."

The blond moved before Caden could answer. The knife came at his midsection in a fast underhand.

Caden stepped off the line, took the man's wrist on the way past, and twisted into the shoulder. The blond cried out. The knife rang off the tile. Caden brought an elbow down across his ribs, dropped him onto one knee, and had the blade in his own hand before the man could find his breath.

"Stay down," Caden said. He did not raise his voice. He did not need to.

Justin's grin slipped a hair and held. He flicked two fingers. The third man swung the gun off the scientist and onto Caden. "You're outnumbered," Justin said. "You should have stayed in bed."

Caden ran the room. The angles. The scientist still on the floor. The progress bar on the laptop, almost full.

Justin glanced at the screen. "We've got what we came for." Then, to Caden: "Kill him."

The gunman hesitated. "Our orders…" he began, but Justin cut him off with a flat motion of his hand.

All three of them moved at once. Hoods came up and pulled forward to cover their faces. The air where they had been buckled—a half-second ripple of nothing—and the corridor air closed over the place they had stood.

Caden turned to the man on the floor. The scientist had rolled onto his back and was working at his breathing.

"Are you okay?" Caden asked, crouching beside him.

The man nodded weakly. "They… they took everything. Dead Time research… said it wasn't safe here."

Footsteps in the corridor. Caden came up off his crouch and turned. Robert was halfway down the hallway already, a guard at his shoulder. The guard knelt beside the scientist without being told and started checking him.

"Talk to me, Caden," Robert said. He took the scene in once and let his eyes settle on the smear of blood where the blond had gone down.

"Intruders." Caden gestured at the table where the laptop had been. "They took Dead Time research. They were wearing some version of a Dead Time suit, but not ours. Close, but not ours. They went out of the room without going through the door—just vanished."

Robert's brow furrowed. "Different how?"

"Strange black fabric, with a hood that came over their head and face and connected at the neck. I did not see oxygen tanks either, strangely enough. Maybe the tanks are thinner, or they have built the breathing apparatus into the suit itself."

Robert pressed the radio at his ear. "Surveillance. Pull footage on stairwell five, third floor, last fifteen minutes."

After a pause, a reply came through. "We have an issue. Stairwell five shows a perfect two-minute loop—the live feed was hot-swapped locally. Not a malfunction."

Robert's jaw set. "From inside the building?"

Caden held his eyes. "You know me, Robert."

Robert held the look a moment longer than felt comfortable. Then he nodded once. "With me."

Caden fell in beside him. As they walked, the pieces of the night arranged themselves and refused to settle: the creature in his room, the scientist with a gun to his temple, Domblin's warning about waiting. He was missing the piece in the middle that made the others fit.

In the surveillance room, Robert pointed Caden to a chair. The wall of monitors cycled through angles of the building. A tech at one of the workstations was trying to recover what could be recovered.

Robert watched the screens without speaking. Then: "There."

The frame was distorted, but in the lower corner of it, for a fraction of a second, a foot in black material—there, then gone, the loop resuming over it. Robert's expression went somewhere just short of satisfied.

"That's the trouble," Robert said, leaning back. "Whoever this is knows the building. You don't slip every camera in here without setting off something else."

Caden frowned. "If they were operating in stopped time, they could."

"Agreed. By the sounds of it, they have something," Robert said. "Something at least as good as what we've built. And someone in this building is feeding it to them."

"Who?" Caden pressed, steady. "Do you think it's me?"

One of the guards stepped in. "Sir—about your earlier request. Caden's T-13 dropped at the same instant the loop started. Total cutout."

Robert nodded at the screen. "That's RF shrouding. They jammed your tracker for the duration of the loop. That doesn't clear you—but it narrows the method. Go to Allen. We'll harden your T-13 and pull your raw logs."

Before Caden could answer, the lights cut. The monitors went black. A second of full silence—and then the low rising hum of the backup generator coming online, and the staggered chirp of the systems behind it waking up.

"Generator," Robert said under his breath. He pressed his earpiece. "Security, report." Static answered.

"Security, do you copy?" Robert's voice sharpened. He turned to Caden. "Go to Allen. Stay there until I clear you. Understood?"

Caden felt the wrongness of being sent away from the room with the problem in it. "Robert, I can help with this—"

"Do as I say." Robert turned back to the dark monitors, shoulders tight. Then, almost as an afterthought, he looked back. "Also—Allen finished the new Dead Time chip. Have him put it in while you're there. It's a quick procedure. Spinal block, in and out. We need to be moving faster than we are. We are one misstep from losing all of this."

"Wait—what?" Caden said. The word came out before he could shape it. "How? He was nowhere near it this morning."

Robert dropped his voice. "After he took you to the infirmary, Allen put himself in stopped time and stayed there. He came out for new oxygen tanks, food, and water when he had to, and went back in. You will not recognize him when you see him—he's grown a full beard in there. He would not stop until the new chip was ready. He wanted to give us something the others didn't take."

"That's impossible," Caden murmured. "It's a smart use of the equipment. But that long under, by himself—that's not what the suits are for."

Robert nodded once. "He's dedicated. Right now I need you down there and I need this room. Go."

Caden nodded—not because he agreed with the order. Because the order had already been given. He went to the door and let himself look back from it. Robert had already turned to the dark monitors, fingers tapping a slow pattern on the console.

Something in the room was wrong. Robert's hurry to get him out of it. The silence on the security channel. Allen's sudden, impossible breakthrough on a chip he had not been close to that morning. All of it moving faster than Caden could keep his hands on. Three things, and they did not want to sit in his chest in a row.

He went anyway. He had to follow orders, and he knew where Allen was.

Allen looked unkempt. Beard, longer hair, the slight unsteady look of a man who had spent too many hours on his feet—and only a few hours ago he had walked Caden over to medical without a single hair out of place. The change was jarring.

The procedure took less than a minute. Allen's hands were steady. The chip went in under the skin at the base of his skull with a small even pressure and a sting that was already going by the time Allen taped it. The unease did not go with it.

CHAPTER 21
Tagen—SDS Medical Wing

Tagen moved through the building in shadow, his form a smear the cameras would not see. Footsteps somewhere two corridors over. A vent breathing dry air into a hallway. Snyp's orders ran in his head, where Snyp had set them: find Domblin, bring him back. Domblin was the key to whatever ladder Snyp meant to climb, and Tagen—Tagen had been promised his collar off if he managed it. The promise had felt like a real thing in Snyp's chamber. It felt thinner here.

A new thought had been turning in him since he stepped through the wall. *What if he set Snyp's mission aside and ran his own? Find Mauldrin, take Mauldrin through the gate to Triaad himself.* Triaad would reward an aniborn who handed him Mauldrin and Snyp's treason in one motion. The thought was a treason of its own. He kept turning it anyway. The shape of being his own again was not something he could put down once he had picked it up.

Then there were the demons. He had caught the scent of them already, two scents he should not be smelling in a human building. The Witch's. Kaz's. He did not know yet whether they were here for Domblin or for something else, and not knowing was its own kind of danger. He set them aside. The mission first. The other thoughts could wait. He kept moving—through one wall, through the next—and the walls did not slow him.

The third floor had been hurt. He came up out of the stairwell and the smell hit him before the sight did—chemical, burnt, the sharp under-smell of metal that had been very hot very recently. Glass fragments caught the overhead lights along the corridor floor. The walls had black scorch lines that the cleaning had not yet reached. A piece of doorframe was bent in a direction doorframes did not bend.

He drifted into the room the corridor ended in. A laboratory, or what had been one. The equipment was wreckage. Cables hung from the ceiling like cut tendons. Under the chemical, the iron of blood—old, dried into something.

The room had the look of a place where something had let itself out.

What did this? Domblin? The demons? The humans, doing whatever the humans had been doing here? He set the question aside. The mission did not have room for it.

He left the lab and went back into the corridor. Halfway down it, the trace he was looking for found him—Domblin's, faint but unmistakable, the way Domblin's signature had always read to him. It pulled him forward through the corridors. At a T-junction he stopped. There was an aniborn nearby.

Down the corridor to his left, three men walking together, voices kept low. The tallest had the carriage of a man other men listened to. Behind them, half a step off, the aniborn—in shadow form, unseen by the humans. The placement was familiar. Triaad's people had been working aniborn into the shoulders of powerful humans for as long as Tagen had been alive.

As they passed his junction, the smaller man at the back of the group called forward. "Robert—hold up. I think I've got it." The tall one—Robert—slowed half a step and walked on.

The aniborn flicked Tagen the smallest acknowledging dip of the head as it passed. Tagen let it go by without returning the gesture. It was younger than a thousand years—Tagen could feel it on the air the way an old aniborn can always feel a young one—and one that young would not know Domblin if Domblin had stood in front of it with his name in its hands. They were obedient and they were blind, and Triaad had bred them that way on purpose.

Domblin's trace pulled away from the men, down the cross-corridor. Tagen followed it. It got stronger as he went. Domblin was close.

Then, on the same air as Domblin's, a second trace. He stopped where he was.

There. Confirmation. He breathed in again to be sure of it, the way an aniborn always breathes in twice when the first read is too good to keep. The trace was faint, half-buried under the chemical and the hospital-smell of the corridor, but it was the same trace he had stood over in the grass on the meadow side of the Witch's woods. "Mauldrin," he said, very quietly. After two thousand years of carrying that name under his tongue, it kept tasting strange to say it out loud.

Kaz at the border. Domblin in this building. And the man who had stood on a battlefield two thousand years ago with one hand raised and unmade Azgiel's army between one breath and the next, breathing now somewhere down this hallway, mortal and asleep. The pieces in his head moved and locked.

The opportunity in the air made his claws ache. Snyp had sent him for Domblin—but with Mauldrin here, the other plan was alive again. Take Mauldrin. Carry him through the gate to Triaad himself, and let Triaad weigh that against Snyp's standing instead of the other way around. Mauldrin was mortal in there. If Tagen moved before either of them was ready, he had a chance. If he waited, he had none. Either of these two could end him without breathing hard. The plan needed to be tight, or the corridor he was standing in was the last corridor he would stand in.

Then a worse thought, and a better one.

Why give him to anyone?

If he could take Mauldrin's soul into himself—if he could eat what was in there—there would be no Snyp on the other side of the gate, no Triaad above Snyp, no collar around any part of him. He would be the thing other things came to ask for permission. The thought was insane. It also would not let him go. Whether the eating of Mauldrin's soul would transfer the power of it to him—whether it would give him any of that power at all, or some of it, or all of it, or nothing—he did not know. Eating a soul straight out of a human was a gamble. Most aniborn did not even try. The reliable feed was the youngling, the aniborn flesh; what came out of a human went how it went, and you found out after.

The two traces lay across the corridor—Domblin's going one way, Mauldrin's the other. That was the only kindness the building had done him tonight. If the two of them had been in the same room, he would already be turning around.

Mauldrin's trace ended at a closed door at the hall's end. He went up to it without sound, set himself, and slipped through it.

Inside: a man on a medical bed. Asleep, or close to it. Human. Thin under the blanket. Frail in every way that mattered to the eye. And under that—under the bone and the breath and the slow blink of the monitor—the same weight he had felt in the grass on the meadow, folded into a body that seemed too weak to be holding it. It still did not fit. Mauldrin should not be in this shape, and yet here he was, in this shape. Frail and mortal.

Tagen let himself slip back into the corridor for the length of one breath. He had stood over this same body in the grass and lost his nerve. He was not going to lose it twice. The body was in a bed. It would not be in a bed long. He had to be done with this before it was awake. For the first time since he had set out from the cave, the plan felt like something he could close his hand around.

He pushed through too eager. His shoulder caught the door—a small thing, a thing the wood barely registered—and the door creaked half an inch. He must have come a fraction out of shadow form on the rush of it. He held still, cursed himself in silence, and pulled himself fully back under. After a beat he drew the dark in around the room, and the dark came, and the machines stuttered against it.

He moved on the bed. His claws lengthened against his palms as he came up over the man. As he bent, the man stirred. The head turned. The eyes opened.

"Mauldrin," Tagen said, low. He went. He came down on the man with the full weight of him, and the breath went out of the man under him, and his claws sank in past the breastbone and reached for the thing inside, the flesh untouched, the bonds between body and soul opening one strand at a time under his claws. He could feel what was tethered there—heavier than anything he had ever closed his hand around in another body. Heavier than he had thought a single soul could be.

Yet with that much power under his hands, it felt too easy. Then it was not.

Something inside the man came up to meet him. It was not the small frightened scuttle a soul made when an aniborn put a hand on it. It was steadier than that. It pushed back from underneath in a way Tagen had not felt before, and the answering weight of it sat Tagen back for a half-instant. He snarled and bore down. He drove his claws deeper. Strand by strand, the bonds were giving.

But it still would not give.

White light came up out of the chest under his hands. It came up around his claws and through them and into him, and where it touched him it burned in a way fire did not burn—clear, cold, the kind of light that did not have an opinion about whether it hurt him.

Panic moved up under his ribs. The light brightened. He set his weight against it and the light pushed harder, and his grip on the thing inside the man began to slip. Even slipping, he could feel he had been close—closer than he had any right to be, with the light burning him. The flesh of the youngling Snyp had thrown him in the cave was still in his blood, and without that, his hands would have come off the soul a long minute ago.

Something hit him from the side hard enough to take the room with it. He went across the bed and into a wall. The hit knocked him out of shadow form. He landed on his back, solid, breathing the open air of the room.

Disoriented, Tagen rolled and came up onto his feet.

Domblin.

Domblin stood between him and the bed. Tagen had never met him face to face—only ever felt the signature of him on the air at a distance, the way every aniborn old enough to remember had felt it—but the man in front of him fit that signature the way a body fits a shadow it has cast for a long time. The eyes did not look like a man's eyes in this light. The fight was lost the moment Tagen saw him standing there. Domblin in front of him was not a thing he could meet head-on. Domblin had to be taken from behind, on a moment when his attention was on something else. And worse than that—Mauldrin under his protection now, and Mauldrin himself heavier than anything Tagen had been ready for. Two losses in one room.

Domblin came at him. Tagen did not waste a heartbeat on whether to run. He shifted to shadow as the open hand swept the air where his head had been a half-second before.

He went through the wall. The wall took him and let him through, and he did not look back. Everything in him said the same thing. Run. Domblin and Mauldrin in one room was a fight no aniborn was going to win tonight.

He went out through the building the way water goes out through a sieve, letting nothing slow him. He did not stop until he was through the outer wall and the night air was on him. Only then did he let his form thicken back into something close to a body, and only then did he let himself stop and stand. The mission had been Domblin. He had laid hands on Mauldrin. Domblin had thrown him into a wall—and he had left without his prize. The demons were not far. He could feel that, too—Kaz on the road, the Witch's people somewhere in the spaces around the city, all of them moving toward something he was now, by accident, standing in the middle of. The longer he stayed alone with what he had seen, the shorter the rest of his life was going to be.

So the plan was over. He would give Mauldrin to Snyp. There was no taking that body alone, not with Domblin between him and it, and the only way at it now was an army of aniborn brought down. The thought of handing Mauldrin over after carrying him alone all this time hollowed something inside him. But carrying him alone all the way to a death he could already see the shape of was the worse trade. Better to lose the prize and walk into Snyp's chamber with news no other aniborn could bring. Better to step a rung up out of his slavery on Mauldrin's back than to die for a soul he could not even keep.

Half a win. He had Domblin's location. He had Mauldrin's. He had also been thrown across a room by a man two thousand years older than the body he was standing in. Mauldrin had been stronger than he was ready for. The fear of him was still moving in Tagen's chest. So was something underneath the fear, slower and steadier and worse.

What if I could take that into me? He stood with the thought a moment longer than he should have. Then the practical part of him stepped on it. Going at Mauldrin alone, after tonight, was the same as walking into a furnace and asking it to remember him. He needed the report. Snyp had promised him his collar off for Domblin. Domblin and Mauldrin together would be more than Snyp had asked for. It would be a card Snyp could not refuse to play.

Or it would be a card Snyp would keep for himself, and Tagen would be back at the wall.

Triaad, then. Go around Snyp. Take the news through the gate himself, and take the collar off at the hand of the only one who could lift it.

He did not let himself decide yet. He set the choices down inside him in a row and looked at them, the way Snyp looked at a map.

The uncertainty sat in him like a coal that had not decided yet whether it was going to go out. He moved on. Carefully. Whichever way he chose, the night was longer than he had thought it would be when he came in.

First, the rendezvous with Snyp. He could decide which face to wear into Snyp's chamber on the way. He went into shadow again and let the building fall behind him. As he ran, his body began to mend itself—the cuts on his shoulder closed, the bruise where the wall had taken him went under, the long thin line where Domblin's strike had grazed his ribs sealed and was gone. By the time he reached the treeline, he was whole. Whole, and farther from himself than he had been when he set out.

CHAPTER 22
Tagen—Snyp's Cavern

Tagen came up the long passage into Snyp's caves at a run. Somewhere deeper in, something screamed and stopped screaming, and the rest of the corridor stayed quiet. He did not slow. The screaming was the sound of the caves working as they were meant to work—younglings being kept the way younglings were kept.

The iron door at the end of the run came up out of the dark. He set one hand on it, pushed, and the hinges gave in their slow groan. The room was the way it always was. Three low torches in the walls, the corners dark, the gate at the far end giving back nothing of the orange light that found it. Tagen let his form thicken back into something close to a body as he stepped through.

Snyp was already standing in front of the gate, his back to the door—the wide black shape of his shoulders cut against the wider black of the surface behind him, only the shoulder-line of him picked out by the orange of the nearest torch. He did not turn.

"Report, Tagen." There was a different sharpness under the word that had not been there last time.

Tagen held a beat. He had run what he was going to say over and over in his mind the whole way there, and the question had not gotten any easier. Hold Mauldrin's name and keep something of his own. Give Mauldrin's name and trade it for an army he could not raise alone. There was no third door.

"I found Domblin," he said. He let the silence sit a beat, then added, "And Mauldrin."

The room changed. The torches kept their slow steady burn, indifferent. Snyp did not turn for the length of two heartbeats. When he did, the look on him was not the look of an aniborn whose servant had just brought him a piece of news. It was the look of an animal that had smelled something it had not smelled in a long time.

"Mauldrin." He tasted the word. "After two thousand years. Are you certain?"

"I attacked him." Tagen took a step further into the room. "The body is mortal. Frail in every way that counts—easy to put down, if it were only the body. The soul under it is not." He let that sit, and then he gave Snyp the rest of it the way Snyp would want it. "It is the heaviest soul I have ever closed a hand around. It nearly came out of him under my claws. White light came up out of his chest and burned through me, and even slipping I had been close. He did not heal himself when I came down on him. He did not raise so much as a hand. He did not act like Mauldrin. The body has not woken to what is in it yet. He does not know what he is, or what he can do, or how to reach for any of it."

Snyp moved away from the gate. His claws set down and lifted on the stone in the slow click-click of an aniborn working a problem. "A body that has not woken to the soul inside it," he said, almost to himself. "If Domblin is involved, that window will not stay open. Once the body remembers what it is, we will not get a hand near him."

He stopped pacing. "Domblin."

"Domblin had him under his hand by the time I came up off the floor. The two of them in one room is not a fight one aniborn wins."

Snyp raised a clawed hand, and the ground pulsed as dark matter oozed upward, forming a slow dark map of the place, mirroring the geography of the human city where he'd found Mauldrin.

"Show me," Snyp commanded.

Tagen stepped up to the edge of the map, and it shifted under his hand. Extending a claw, he indicated an area near the city's edge. The substance rippled immediately, reshaping itself into the surrounding terrain.

"Here," Tagen said. The map responded, zooming in as wisps of blackness slithered outward, constructing buildings. Soon, a detailed recreation of the SDS facility stood between them, the windows and the walls of it black-on-black.

Snyp's mouth pulled into something close to a smile as he studied the structure. "This is where you found them?"

"Yes," Tagen said. "Domblin's trace ran one corridor. Mauldrin's ran the other. I took Mauldrin first because he was alone in a bed with a monitor at his elbow. Domblin came through the wall the moment I reached the soul."

"Pathetic." Snyp's claw moved, and the map shifted again, highlighting the streets around the building. "Forget Domblin for now. I will send a team to kill him. Domblin is nothing compared to what Mauldrin is. But together, in one room, you'll have neither." He glanced at Tagen and the look had a small private knife in it. "That part you read correctly."

Snyp gestured, and the map dissolved, seeping back into the floor. "Your mission is now singular: Mauldrin. Capture him at all costs. Do not fail me."

Tagen inclined his head. "Understood."

Snyp smiled. "And if Domblin interferes again…" He paused deliberately, then concluded coldly, "End him."

Tagen nodded again. Inside, the plan he had just been handed him settled into its first hard form. A team after Domblin. Mauldrin to be captured at any cost.

As Tagen turned for the door, Snyp's voice came after him. "There is more." Tagen stopped. "Triaad has given me an order of his own. With the Witch sending Kaz and her demons out in the open, he wants it answered. He has put me at the head of an army of aniborn to put them down."

Tagen kept his face still and let the size of what he had just been told set itself in him. Snyp did not take the field. Snyp had not taken the field since the wars ended and the Witch sealed herself in her woods.

"So, while I am gone," Snyp continued, the clip back in his voice, "you'll handle Mauldrin. And Tagen…" He looked to Tagen. "Return without him, and do not bother returning."

Tagen inclined his head. "I will not fail," he said.

Snyp held the look on him a beat longer, the way an aniborn holds a look when there is more to say and a calculation to make about whether to say it. Then his claw flicked, dismissing him.

Tagen shifted to shadow and went out through the iron door without sound. He did not let himself think yet. The corridor took him, and he ran.

CHAPTER 23
Azgiel—Maselda's Forest Camp

Azgiel sat against a flat-faced stone with his back to the firelight and let the night come the rest of the way down on him.

Maselda's woods made their own running sound. Leaves. The slow creak of older trees settling against each other. Somewhere out beyond the firelight, a small wet rasp of an animal moving in the underbrush. Underneath all of it, the steady current of magic that ran through everything in her domain—older than the trees, slower than the wind, the kind of working a man only registered after he had stood inside it long enough to forget the absence of it.

The Cell had not had any of that. No wind, no distance, no slow click of an ember finding its next dry place to take. He had spent two ages of the world inside one held breath, and the breath had finally let out, and the let-out part of it was what kept catching him by surprise.

He turned his right arm over against the firelight.

The aniborn had bitten him there twice. The first bite had gone deep—he could still feel where it had worked through the cloth and into the meat of him before he had gotten his other hand on its throat. The second bite had gone for the same place.

The wound was healed. Just an ache left, where the muscle had been opened, the way an old man feels a bone that healed wrong twenty winters back. Slow. Honest. The way a mortal heals.

He had not gotten used to that yet.

Across the fire, Kaz sat with a blade across his knees and a stone in his hand and did not look up. The whetstone moved once, paused, moved again. He had always known when to be quiet. It was one of the reasons Azgiel had kept him close, all those ages ago—and watching him sharpen a blade now, in the same patient rhythm Azgiel had heard at a hundred fires before the war, was one of the few things in this new world that felt the way it had used to.

Azgiel stared into the flames. "Tell me, Kaz," he said. "Do you ever regret it? Staying loyal to me?"

Kaz did not look up from the blade. The whetstone moved once more, slow, and stopped. "Never."

A short, bitter sound ran across Azgiel's mouth that he had not asked for. "Even after I lost the war, and the kingdom with it?"

Kaz lifted his eyes. "You made mistakes. We all did. But I saw the man behind those mistakes. The one who fought for something greater. That's why I stayed."

Azgiel watched a knot of resin pop in the fire. "You speak of a man who no longer exists. What am I now, Kaz?" He lifted his hands into the light—hands that were the right shape and the wrong hands all the same. "A lost king of the past? A relic?"

"You're still my king," Kaz said evenly. "And you're the only one who can set things right."

"Make things right," Azgiel repeated. He leaned back against the stone, looking at the stars showing through gaps in the canopy. "A king who has lost his kingdom is no king at all."

"No," Kaz said, rising to his feet. His towering form cast a shadow over Azgiel. "You're the king who built an army strong enough to challenge the kings themselves. The one who fought for a world where demons did not have to live small. And you're the only one who can finish what you started."

Firelight cut hard along the lines of Kaz's face. For a moment Azgiel could see the soldier he had been before the war, before the long unraveling—and the loyalty in him that had outlasted both.

But faith was a fragile thing, and Azgiel wasn't sure he deserved it.

"Sir, if I may. Mauldrin was there when I rescued you."

Azgiel did not answer right away. The word sat in his mouth before he was ready to let it out. Two thousand years, and he had come back into the world a man who had needed rescuing. "Yes." He kept his eyes on the fire. "I vaguely remember him being there."

"Mauldrin?" Maselda walked into the firelight on bare feet. "What do you mean he was there?" Her eyes went between them. "And why am I hearing about it now from the sidelines as I walk up?"

"My apologies." Kaz inclined his head. "There has been a great deal to put before you since we got back."

"I will have my revenge on him," Azgiel said. He let the line sit a moment between them.

"No," Kaz said. "He isn't worth the time. Triaad is the target. Triaad is the one running the universe—the evil behind everything happening right now." He paused, looking at Azgiel hard. "But it is curious why Mauldrin is back, living like a regular human. Weak. There is something wrong there—he was in an eternal sleep."

Maselda lowered herself to the stone beside Azgiel, hip against his hip. She did not speak yet. She let Kaz finish.

"Why he is back," Kaz went on, "why he was not killing you, why he seemed to be oblivious of me standing in the dark—the only conclusion I have come to is Domblin. Since he was there, protecting him. He must have brought him back somehow but failed in the working. Mauldrin did not come back with his power. He did not come back with his memories."

"Domblin and Mauldrin here." Maselda turned the words over in her mouth. "They will have to be dealt with. But I agree they can't be the priority. And by the way you describe him, Mauldrin is no threat at present. If he had his true power, he would have already moved against Triaad."

Azgiel was tapping his knee with his fingers as he listened. "This is perfect." He finally spoke. "We need to get my sword out of the ground. If Mauldrin is really not a threat and doesn't remember who he is, then I can take the sword to him, have him touch it, force the curse he put on it to break. I'll be able to use the sword against Triaad."

Maselda did not answer at once. She watched the fire with the look she wore in council—the one she had worn at the long table at the kingdom, when men had brought her plans and she had taken them apart in her head before saying yes.

"Will he have to draw it?" she said. "Touching it is not enough, is it?"

"He doesn't need to draw it," Azgiel said. He lifted one finger and pressed the air with it, the gesture of a man laying his hand on a hilt. "His touch will break the curse. He set it; he is the only one who can break it; and the moment his hand is on it, the working ends."

"Then this is truly in our favor," Maselda said. "A man who remembers a curse he set will not put his hand on the thing that carries it. A man who does not remember it might."

Kaz had not moved while she spoke. He was holding the whetstone the way he held tools when he was thinking with his hands instead of his mouth. Finally, he stood. "With your permission, my lord. I will go ahead at first light. The pit has not been opened in two ages. There is preparation to be done before we draw what is in it back into the air."

"Go," Azgiel said. "I will follow with Maselda."

Kaz inclined his head a quarter inch and went up the slope toward the village without sound, in the way Kaz had always gone, half a pace beyond what the firelight could hold.

Azgiel sat in the quiet Kaz had left behind. Maselda took his hand in hers. She leaned her temple against the side of his shoulder and put her weight there, the way she had done in throne rooms and on the back of broken hills before any of this.

"First light," he said.

"There is less to do than you think," Maselda said. "The shaft was opened a long time ago. My people went down to it slowly, over the years, and stopped where the curse begins. The blade is at the bottom of a hole that is already dug.

What remains is to lift it."

Azgiel turned his head toward her. "Tonight, then."

"Tonight," Maselda said.

CHAPTER 24

Bridget—Home Office

Bridget ran her thumb along the chipped rim of her mug, staring blankly at her laptop. The search results were the same—scattered myths, vague references, and theories that led nowhere. The professor hadn't responded to her email. She had refreshed the inbox twice in the last ten minutes. She knew she had refreshed it. She did it again.

Maybe she was chasing ghosts. Maybe a woman who had grown up on a grandmother's stories about a frozen king would, of course, hear that king's name in her husband's mouth and start seeing the shape of him in every shadow. That was the reasonable thing. The professional thing. She had told clients a version of it for years. It had not stopped being reasonable just because it was her sitting at the table now.

She closed the laptop. The kitchen ticked around her—the fridge, the clock above the doorway, a faint settle somewhere in the wall. Caden hadn't answered her last text. He had said he would be home by eight and it was almost ten, and the part of her that had been with him for years—long before any of this—was the part that knew when not to text again.

She pushed back from the table and went down the hall toward their room. She saw through a cracked door that his office was a mess. She paused for a moment. If she put his desk back to the way he kept it, maybe she would feel like she was doing something. She normally stayed out of his office, not wanting to see things she wasn't supposed to. But helping had always been her way of steadying herself. She opened the door and stopped in the frame.

The room was worse than what she could see through the crack. Pages spread across the desk and onto the floor. Notes had been taped up the wall above the monitor in three uneven columns, more added at the bottom in marker. Caden did not work like this. Caden made lists. Caden labeled drawers.

She stepped in. The desk lamp was still on. She lifted the nearest page off the top of the pile.

"Azgiel—imprisoned."

The illustration beneath the words was Caden's, in pen—a figure twisted as though something were pulling it from inside. "Steven-Azgiel" was scrawled beneath it in Caden's blocky handwriting.

She set it down and lifted the next. A rougher sketch of a man with a weathered face. Below it, a single word in the same blocky hand: Domblin.

The hair on her forearms came up before she had finished reading the name.

Caden's work had always been dangerous. She had made her peace with that years ago. This was something else. Azgiel's name on a page in her husband's handwriting, beside the figure of a man twisted from the inside. The same name she had grown up hearing in her grandmother's stories. The same name in the book in her grandmother's chest. Three places it had no business being, and all three of them in her life now.

She kept going through the pages. Then she noticed his computer was unlocked.

She knew she shouldn't. She bumped the mouse anyway. The screen woke. Among the cryptic file names, one stood out: **Steven_Test_Record_01**.

She clicked it.

Grainy footage. The lab. Caden was on screen, shoulders set, jaw tight, arguing with someone the camera did not show. There was no sound. She did not need sound. She had watched her husband hold himself like that across a kitchen island enough times to know exactly what kind of conversation it was.

The lights in the lab cut, came back, cut again.

A low vibration came up through the speakers—enough that she felt it in the hand resting on the desk. And then—

Steven appeared. Azgiel.

Steven's body bent at the wrong angles. His limbs jerked the way a marionette jerks when a hand has not yet caught up to what it's doing. His mouth moved, a soundless shape of words she did not want to read.

The footage broke into chaos. Sparks at one of the consoles. Two technicians backing away from the platform. Caden stepping in, not back. And then the thing wearing Steven turned its head and looked at Caden—and said something to him.

The video stopped on the face. Mouth pulled into something that was almost a smile. Eyes on Caden. Bridget pulled her hand back from the desk before she could think about it.

There was another file already open behind it. **Front_Gates_Security**.

She clicked it.

The footage was of a checkpoint. A gate. Concrete. Floodlights. Caden stood near it, body squared, weight forward. And then—a second figure stepped out of the dark on the far side.

Domblin.

She watched the two of them speak. She could not hear it. Domblin held himself the way men hold themselves when they have already decided how a conversation will go. Caden drew his sidearm. Domblin did not flinch. They spoke for a few more seconds—and then Domblin was simply not there. She rewound it. She watched it again, slower. The frame before he disappeared, he turned his head a quarter inch and looked directly at the camera.

And then—he was gone.

She had been watching footage. It felt as if he had been watching her.

A chime pulled her attention back. A notification had opened over the video: "Access anomaly. Confirm credentials."

A second line opened under the first. "Who are you, and what are you searching for?"

She closed the laptop with both hands and held it closed, as though that would help.

The front door opened.

She jumped, and was angry at herself for jumping.

Caden was home. She heard him drop his keys in the dish by the door. The slow heavy step of a man who had not slept in two days. He came down the hall toward the office and stopped in the doorway when he saw her at his desk. "Hey—"

"Who is Domblin?" Bridget cut him off.

Caden stiffened. "Bridget—"

"I watched the videos," she said. Her voice came out steadier than she felt. "Steven convulsing. Azgiel tearing through the lab." The name sat in the room between them like a third person. "Caden, I saw what's happening, and I'm scared."

He pressed a hand against the doorframe. "Bridget, you don't understand—"

"No, I don't," she said. She stepped toward him. "Because you won't—can't talk to me. I know you're trying to protect me, but this isn't just some classified mission, is it? It feels bigger to me."

Caden's eyes went to the floor. "I can't—"

"I know," she interrupted. She rested her palm on his arm. "I understand you can't, but this isn't something you can handle alone."

She held his face for a moment, looking at him the way she did when he was trying to decide how much of the truth she could carry. She squeezed his hand. "I need you to look at something. And... please trust me."

Caden held the look for a beat longer. Whatever he had been holding off all day moved one click in his face. He nodded.

It was only then, with the hall light on him, that she actually saw him. The bruise along the cheekbone. The dried blood at his collar. The gash high on his temple, ragged where someone had not had time to clean it. She did not know how she had missed it.

"Caden..." she whispered when she finally found her voice.

"I'm doing okay," he muttered.

"No, you're not."

She went past him to the bathroom and came back with the first-aid kit.

Caden sighed. "Bridget, really—"

She set the kit on the desk, unopened. "I'm not doing this tonight," she said.

Caden blinked. "Doing what?"

"Playing nurse while you keep me outside the blast radius." She slid the kit toward him. "Your options are the ER, or you tell me enough that I'm not guessing whether something followed you home."

He did not answer right away. The room had gone very quiet.

"I'm not angry," she added, voice steady. "I'm at my limit. Give me at least one truth."

He let his hand drop from the doorframe. His hands flexed once at his sides. "Bridget—"

"I know you can't tell me everything." Her voice softened. "I get that. But I saw the videos. And between what you just told me and what I've uncovered, this isn't some mission gone wrong." She drew a breath. "I have more information about Azgiel. I've been digging into it, trying to piece it together." A pause. Then, softer, "I found a book, Caden. In my grandmother's old chest. It's what I want to show you. I believe it's his story. And it's written in a language I can't understand."

Caden leaned back against the doorframe. "You—what?"

She squeezed his hand. "It's real, Caden. Azgiel, Domblin, everything from those videos—it's not just an experiment gone wrong. This started somewhere a lot older than your project. And I need you to look at the book. Please."

Caden was a long time answering. She watched him weigh it the way she had watched him weigh harder things. Then, slowly, he gave a single, decisive nod. "Okay."

Something gave way in her chest. "I'll go get it," she said. She squeezed his hand and turned for the hall.

Halfway down the hall, the house went quieter than a house should go. The soft mechanical hum she had been hearing all night from the kitchen—the fridge, the clock—thinned. Her own footsteps stopped sounding right against the wood. She kept walking. She did not look back.

CHAPTER 25
Caden—Home

Caden rubbed his temples. His office had gone still in the way rooms went still in the lab when something was about to happen on a monitor. Not fear. Something more like attention—a thing somewhere out beyond the walls of the house turning its head toward him.

He needed a breath of fresh air. He stepped to the porch door, opened it, and went out. The videos. He had not locked the computer. He had not been thinking clearly enough this afternoon to know whether that had been carelessness or something closer to wanting her to find them.

The porch light threw his shadow long across the boards. Robert's words replayed in his mind: "Go home. We'll regroup tomorrow." *Was it a simple dismissal, or was Robert trying to monitor me?*

Bridget deserved more than the half-truths he'd offered so far.

Allen's latest invention sat heavy on his wrist, the Dead Time device a band of black-gold metal that did not quite belong on him. The injection site at the base of his neck pulsed slow against his collar. He had stopped being able to forget about it sometime around the second half of the drive home.

He went back inside. Silence engulfed him again, broken only by the distant hum of the refrigerator. Bridget was somewhere inside, still searching for the book.

But something was off.

He called out, "Bridget?" No response.

He moved down the hall toward the bedroom. The floorboards creaked under his weight.

A soft exhale—not his own—stopped him in his tracks.

A shape shifted in the gloom ahead.

Something brushed the wall. He reached for the switch—and the air ahead of him went thick the way air goes thick before a storm, and something the size of a man hit him and took him off his feet. The hallway tilted. The edges of his vision smeared. Something drove into his chest—not through cloth and skin, through something underneath them. There was no blood. There should have been blood. There was only the heat.

The claws kept going. Past the place where claws stopped. He had felt this once before—the hospital bed, the thing leaning over him, the pull that was not the pull of any animal he knew. This was the same hand. Deeper this time.

The scream caught somewhere short of his mouth. Light came up behind his eyes—white, electrical—and something inside him pulled loose at the seam.

Everything lurched. He was standing in the doorway of the kitchen of his childhood home, seven years old, with his hand on the frame. He had not let himself stand here in thirty years.

The room smelled of whiskey and the linoleum his mother kept too clean. His father's voice was already moving. "You're pathetic! Worthless—like your mother!" A plate came off the wall and hit the floor in pieces. His mother was on the floor in the pieces.

He went at the man. He always went at the man, in this memory, in every version of this memory, fists too small. The man caught him by the shirt and threw him into the cabinets.

He pushed up onto his elbows—and the memory bent. His father's face slid sideways into something else. Skin like wet leather. A grin too wide for a human jaw. The kitchen pulled back from the edges. His mother went with it.

Teeth bared, the creature stalked forward.

The kitchen dropped out from under him. He was somewhere else. Bridget stood before him, her face wet. "You always promise someday…marriage, a place for our vows—but someday never comes, does it, Caden?"

This was the fight they had not had again. Two years ago, the upstairs hallway, late, after a wedding they had been to that he had not been able to enjoy.

"I know, I know…" he stammered, hearing how thin it sounded coming out of his own mouth. He wanted to marry her. He had wanted to marry her almost from the first month. Every time he had walked toward it, the same picture had come up behind his eyes—a man at the bottom of a porch step with a bottle in his hand and a woman bleeding on the kitchen floor—and he had stopped walking. Some part of him had decided, a long time ago, that not putting a ring on her hand was the way to keep that picture from being the next one.

"I'm terrified, Bridget," he snapped, the words coming out before he could shape them. "I can't risk becoming my dad. You mean far too much to me."

Bridget had not had words for him then. She had pulled him into her instead, and held on, and said nothing. He had felt loved. He had also felt the small mean hum underneath the loved, the part of him that had never been able to take a clean kindness without wanting to break it.

That was where the real memory ended. They had stood like that until the ache thinned. Neither of them had brought it up again, not until Bridget had the other night. The ring had stayed in the safe behind the framed map of the coast. He had told himself it was waiting for the right moment. He had known, on some level, that the right moment was a thing he was using.

This time the memory bent. Bridget stirred in his arms, pressing her face close against his ear, and what came out of her was not her voice: "You obviously don't love me enough. You dangle marriage like bait—always out of reach. You're turning into your father, and you refuse to see it."

Each line was something he had said to himself in the dark and never out loud. Her arms cooled around him. The skin against his cheek went slick.

He pulled back. It was no longer Bridget he held, but the grotesque creature once again. "You're mine, Mauldrin." It lunged, claws reaching—

Time stalled. The thing held mid-lunge, claws an inch from his throat. Then the memory fractured again and threw him onto a war-torn battlefield.

Bodies in the dirt. Faces fixed. Smoke that he tasted before he smelled it. Gunfire so close he could not tell which side of his head it was coming off. He knew this one. This was the day that had taken most of his team. It was also the day he had first laid eyes on Bridget, in a triage tent two ridges back, in the moment after he had stopped being sure he was going to live.

He pushed up onto his knees in the dirt of it. Rounds went past him slow, every one of them audible. He reached for men who were not there. The horizon gave at the edges, like film going through heat. It pulled him down again.

"Caden!"

His father's voice. He turned. He was on the front walk of the house he had grown up in, in the uniform he had come home in. His mother ran to greet him, crying, her arms tight around his middle. Behind her, his father came out onto the porch with a half-empty bottle and the look on his face that Caden had spent his teenage years memorizing.

"You think you get to come back here like you're somebody special? Some kind of hero?" his father said, slurring, coming down the steps. "All you've ever done is ruin your mother's life—my life."

He remembered this, exactly. He remembered the part where everything in him had lined up for one moment to put the man in the ground. He remembered, just as clearly, the second after—the one he never told anyone about—when he had looked at the man on the steps and seen, for the first time, what was actually there.

A scared man. A small one. A man who used cruelty because he had nothing else to use. And what had come out of Caden, instead of fists, had been laughter. Bitter and short and surprised. His father had come down the steps at him, missed his footing, and gone down hard onto the walk. Caden had laughed harder.

This time the memory bent again. The mother's embrace constricted around him, the warmth of her going icy and hard. "Laugh while you still can," the creature rasped. "It will be your last." He jerked toward her in disbelief as her face blurred, reshaping itself into the monstrous form—oily skin under the porch light.

He tore loose. There was nowhere to run. The creature advanced. The ground opened beneath him, and he plunged into liquid tar.

Voices came up around him in the dark—some pleading, some accusing, none of them his. A silhouette emerged through the turmoil, reaching out— *Bridget?* He reached for her, fingertips brushing hers. Just as relief bloomed, icy dread touched his neck, and a voice hissed at his ear: "I've found you."

He spun. There was nothing to see. There did not need to be. A cold laugh ran around him, and the memory dropped him. The creature hovered over him—translucent, its ghostly claws plunged into his soul, its wrists encircled by radiant light.

His body had gone far away. He was only barely fastened to it. The creature was methodically tearing him from his flesh. He pulled up his translucent hands; his physical limbs lay unmoving on the floor beneath him. Pain ran the length of him, white and total.

And then, through it, something else. Caden looked past the monstrous figure and saw Bridget—but not the way he had ever seen her. Her physical form was a delicate shell scarcely able to hold the radiant brilliance of her soul, which burned through the cloth and the skin of her like a lamp through paper.

"This is it," the creature growled hungrily. "You're mine."

It pulled. The thing keeping him stitched to his body started to give. Then the warmth on his sternum—the warmth Domblin had put there in the hospital, the gem he had felt go into him as if a window had been opened on a cold room—came up under his ribs. He thrust his translucent hand into the creature's chest. Light came out of him—not from his hand, from somewhere behind his hand—and it went through the creature the way a torch goes through smoke. The gem within him flared once, hard enough that he thought it had broken him, and then went out, and what was left of it dissolved under his skin in slow, cooling shards.

The thing shrieked and went thin at the edges as it hit the far wall. For one beat it was semi-solid—something dark and wet-looking and mostly limb—and then it was not there. Air came back into Caden in a hard drag. A faint green lattice traced under his skin, a slow pulse from sternum to fingertips, fading down to a steady ember somewhere under his ribs.

"Caden?" Bridget's voice came from the other end of the hall.

He turned his head. She stood at the end of the hallway, pale, clutching her phone. Whatever he had seen burning under her skin a moment ago was gone. It was just her. Her face the way it had been every time he had come home from somewhere with blood on him.

"What was that shrieking? What was that green light? Are you okay?" she demanded.

His body did not feel like his. He struggled to speak but could find no words.

She came down the hall fast and dropped to her knees next to him. "Caden, talk to me," she pleaded, fixated on his chest, where the green glow dimmed beneath his skin. "Caden, what's happening to you?"

"I—" he tried, his words breaking apart in his throat.

"I'm calling 911," she announced firmly, though her voice trembled.

"No," Caden managed hoarsely, catching her wrist. "Don't..." *The risk was too great—others might be harmed.*

She put her hand flat over the place on his chest where the warmth had been a moment ago.

"Caden," she said, gripping his sleeve, tears spilling. "What is this? What's happening?"

He brought his hand up to her face. He used his thumb to take the tear off her cheek.

"I want to give you answers," he said, the words coming out wrong-shaped. "But..."

"I know—you can't tell me," she interrupted softly.

"No," he said when he had the breath for it. "I'll tell you everything. But right now, safety first... we need to go."

Her head turned toward the dark end of the hall. "Why? Is it coming back?"

He pushed up on one elbow. She got under his arm and took his weight without being asked. "I don't know. We need to leave. Let's catch a red-eye to the condo. It'll be safe there."

Her brow drew together. "How bad is this? Is it Azgiel? Are we..."

He kissed her instead of answering—hard, the way a man kisses a woman when he has just remembered he could have been about to lose her. "I love you," he whispered against her hair. "We need to go. Grab essentials. I'll explain everything—but first, we leave."

She nodded and went into the bedroom, the book pressed flat against her chest. Caden got up off the floor. Every part of him hurt in a way he could not have named the source of. He moved anyway.

In his office, he opened the wall safe. The hinges complained the way they always did. Boxes. Documents. The spare sidearm. The travel folder. He grabbed his government travel papers—the ones that would put them on any flight at any hour without questions—and knocked a box of ammo off the shelf and onto the floor. Cartridges scattered across the hardwood and rolled.

He went down on one knee to pick them up. The ring was the second thing he saw. It sat there hidden behind items he had not moved in years, a small black box at the back of the safe.

The line from the corrupted memory came back at him whole: *You obviously don't love me enough. You dangle marriage like bait—always out of reach. You're turning into your father, and you refuse to see it.*

Bridget had not said it. Bridget would never say it. The thing in the hallway had pulled it out of somewhere closer than her mouth—his own. He moved to shut the safe. His hand did not finish the motion. There was no time. They had to be in a car. Bridget first; then whatever they had cracked open at SDS.

And still he did not shut the door. He had pictured this a hundred times. He had pictured it on flights home from places he could not tell her about. A small wedding. The two of them, a handful of people who mattered, somewhere with a window and the sea outside it. If this was the night he had been postponing all those years for, he had been postponing it too long.

He took the box. He put it in his pocket. He shut the safe.

CHAPTER 26

Caden—Red-Eye Flight

Caden and Bridget sat side by side, the steady rumble of the engines under them. The cabin was nearly empty—one other passenger at the far end, head tipped against the window. Outside, night went on without breaking. The reading light over Bridget's seat caught the side of her face and showed him every place she had been holding still since she sat down.

He had told her most of it. Steven on the platform, Steven in the cell, the thing in the hallway, Domblin at the gate. He had stopped short of two or three things he could not yet make himself say out loud. Bridget had listened without interrupting, the way she listened to her clients, her hands folded in her lap and her eyes never quite leaving his face. When he finished, she did not say anything for a long moment.

Then she reached into the bag at her feet and brought the book up onto the tray table. The leather was warm. She opened to a page she had marked with a scrap of paper and turned it toward him. An ink illustration filled most of the page—a man drawn with too much in him for the body to hold.

"This," she said, her finger tracing the edges of the image, "is what my grandmother called Azgiel." Her finger stayed on the page. "She used to tell me stories about him when I was a girl. She said it was a warning...a story passed down through our family. That he would come back through time. Your stories seem eerily similar to some of the things she said."

Caden leaned closer to the illustration. The creature's cold, calculating eyes. The wrong look. The look that had come up out of Steven's face on the platform and stayed. "Azgiel," he murmured.

Bridget nodded and gently closed the book. "I've reached out to a professor who specializes in ancient scripts, especially in the language that is in this book. I think there's something deeper in these stories—maybe a warning about what's happening now."

"I want to believe that this is a coincidence, Bridget," Caden finally said. "I need it to be a coincidence. What I have in front of me is hard enough without dragging in something my wife's grandmother already warned about." He looked at the book without touching it. "I keep wanting to put it down and I keep not putting it down."

Bridget straightened a little in her seat. "But what if it's not just a story? What if understanding this could save us—could save you—from whatever's coming? What if your experiments woke something terrifying?"

Caden took the book and opened it to the first marked page, where an illustration of a regal figure. Azgiel—he assumed—stood tall, half a smile on him, a kingdom spread out behind him with people looking up at him the way people look up at a man they trust. "Looks like he was once revered...a king or a guardian, perhaps," Caden said quietly.

He flipped through several pages until he found another image that stood in stark contrast to the first. In this one, Azgiel was bent over the body of a woman lying motionless on the ground. Her face was peaceful, yet unmistakably lifeless. There was something unfinished in the way Azgiel was bent over her, as if he had not yet decided whether to mourn or to do something about it. "Something turned," Caden noted with unease.

The next page revealed a continuation of the tragic scene. Azgiel now stood, his back to the woman. A column of light tore upward out of the woman and into him, the artist drawing the lines so hard they ran past the edges of the page. "It's like he's unleashing some immense power from her...or maybe sealing it within her," Caden guessed.

As he flipped through more pages, Caden came upon a vast, chaotic battle scene. Azgiel was at the center, facing off against a figure radiating a bright, almost blinding light. Both figures hung above a battlefield where smaller warriors clashed in the foreground. "Some kind of last stand," he said quietly.

"Hey," Bridget said with a chuckle, pointing at the glowing figure. "This one almost looks like you. Maybe you're destined to be the hero?" She said it lightly, the way she said things she half-meant. He looked at the figure on the page— the squared shoulders, the set of the jaw—and something cold turned over in him before he could put it away. He gave her the smile she was asking for.

The final image depicted Azgiel cast into darkness, a jagged tear opened in the page itself behind him. His face bore an expression of defiance and rage, yet also a hint of regret. Tendrils enveloped him, pulling him deeper into the abyss.

Caden closed the book slowly. "Rise. Fall. Exile," he said. "That's the shape of it." He looked at Bridget. She was already looking back. Neither of them said anything for a moment. The book sat between them on the tray table, closed, and felt heavier than it had any right to.

Caden paused, seeing her fear, and softened his tone. "Keep researching, Bridget. Keep me in the loop with whatever you find out. If there's anything that can help us make sense of this mess, it would be good to know."

"I will," Bridget replied quietly. She reached out and laced her fingers through his. "We'll figure this out together."

"Of course," he said, trying to mean it. "Whatever happens, we face it together."

He knew what the next morning was going to ask of him. He knew he was going to have to leave her at the condo and walk back into it alone. He let himself not think about it for the length of a runway.

He offered a reassuring smile. "We'll be landing soon. Let's head to the condo," he said. "We can have a quiet night, listening to the waves crashing against the shore. In the morning, maybe we can walk on the beach—like old times." He paused, facing her fully. "But you know, I'm going to have to go back. I have to face this thing, to put whatever evil we unleashed back in the box."

Bridget's grip relaxed along with her body; the familiar way she always steadied herself in the face of difficulty. "A walk on the beach sounds nice," she finally said, the smile small and real.

They leaned back in their seats, her hand still in his. As the plane glided onward through the night, Caden watched the small light on the wing tip blink against the dark and let himself be glad, for one stretch of sky, that she was sitting next to him.

CHAPTER 27
Azgiel—The Pit

Azgiel stood at the edge of a cavernous pit, the last of the daylight going out of the trees behind him. The wind had a bite in it, and the ropes hung over the pit moved with it. Torches sputtered. A crescent moon was just beginning to clear the canopy. From the bottom of the shaft, the slow squeal of strained pulleys came up at him, and underneath it the dry clank of chain on stone.

But none of it was as he remembered.

For two thousand years, he had witnessed only the single instant of his downfall—the battlefield locked in eternal stillness, the ghosts of his past imprisoned in time's cruel grasp. And now, standing here again, where ruin had once stretched as far as the eye could see, there was only forest. Trees had replaced corpses. Thick, intertwined roots choked the ground where rivers of blood once flowed. The rustling leaves had long swallowed the traces of war, and the place where his power had been abolished was now quiet.

He was back. After centuries of staring at this very place, he was finally here—and the world had erased both him and that brutal battle.

"It's down there?" His voice was calm.

"Yes, Lord Azgiel," replied a bark gnome at his side. "The extraction takes time. The wind complicates things."

Azgiel barely heard him. His attention lingered on the pit, its depths swallowing the last golden rays of daylight and absorbing the torchlight. The cool wind pressed against him, carrying the scent of damp earth, of trees and old magic—nothing of war, nothing of fire.

"Azgiel," came Kaz's familiar voice, low. The towering demon pushed through the crowd, his red skin catching the torchlight. He had to duck a low branch on the way in; the last light of evening caught the ragged edges of his wings. "You sent for me?"

"Yes." Azgiel gestured for Kaz to follow as he moved into the forest. He looked over his shoulder, making sure they were alone before speaking. "Mauldrin. We need to talk about how we get him to the blade."

Kaz's nostrils flared, his wings shifting restlessly. "Yes."

Azgiel leaned against a tree. "I've been turning it over." He pushed off the trunk and began to pace. "He doesn't know who he is—that's our advantage. Domblin complicates matters, but Mauldrin's ignorance is exploitable. You'll need to earn his trust—make him believe we're allies. Get him within reach of the blade. He doesn't need to draw it, doesn't need to want it—his hand on the hilt, even for a heartbeat, and the curse he set on it ends. After that, the sword is mine again."

Kaz's wings stilled. "And if Domblin interferes?"

Azgiel hesitated, looked at the ground, then back to Kaz. "Kill him."

Kaz held his eye a moment, then nodded and spread his wings. "I'll return when it's done."

"Be patient," Azgiel said. "Do not give him a reason to wonder about you."

Kaz ascended into the night sky. Azgiel stood motionless, watching until the demon was gone over the canopy. His thoughts returned to the cursed sword, its power gnawing at the edges of his mind.

A jackal-headed creature emerged from the woods, bowing low. "My Lord," he said submissively. "The sword is nearly retrieved."

"Good," Azgiel replied.

He followed the creature to the pit. As they approached, a massive platform began to rise. Encased in crystalline stone, the sword called to him, its purple veins running along its length.

The last light barely reached the clearing now, and the torchlight danced on the crystalline surface, refracting beams of green light onto the gathered group. Maselda stepped down from the platform, her white dress moving against the wind. The demons within reach of her gave her room without being asked. She acknowledged Azgiel with a brief nod before gesturing to the two troll-like creatures assisting her.

Azgiel tapped on the crystalline casing that surrounded it. "Can I break the crystal?"

"Allow me," Maselda said. She drew a thin blade from her belt and traced an intricate line across the crystal surface. A brilliant light flared as the stone cracked with a sound like breaking ice. The sword fell free with a heavy thud. The clearing was now almost fully enveloped in twilight, the fading sunlight replaced by the pale luminescence of the moon.

A troll hurried forward, eager to assist Maselda, and reached out quickly for the hilt before she could stop him. The instant its palm made contact, the air around the blade clapped outward and threw the troll across the clearing. It hit the dirt convulsing and was ash before it stopped moving.

"Fools," Maselda snapped, wrapping the sword in the dark hide one of the trolls held out to her. "Did I not tell you it carried a curse?"

Azgiel's hand hovered near the wrapped blade, the pull of its power almost irresistible. But he held himself back. Not yet.

A blood-curdling scream tore through the clearing, shattering the tense silence. Azgiel spun toward the scream.

Kaz came down hard next to him. "Lord, the aniborn are moving in to attack. I saw them as I was leaving."

A wave of aniborn spilled from the forest as Kaz spoke. In the dark between the trees they were almost shapeless—a moving absence of light with red coals where eyes should have been. Torches sputtered under sudden gusts of wind as faint moonlight reflected off the creatures' undulating, tar slick forms. His demons moved quickly, rallying their weapons as they stormed the battlefield.

"Hide the sword! Summon the rest of our forces—now!" Azgiel barked. Maselda nodded, disappearing into the forest with the wrapped blade in her grasp.

"And you." Azgiel turned to Kaz. "Mauldrin is the priority. Leave this to me. You go."

"No, my lord." Kaz did not raise his voice. There was no argument in his face, only the same flat steadiness he had worn at every fire they had ever shared. "I will fight beside you, and when these are dead I will go."

Azgiel didn't have time to argue with him, so he nodded and moved to face the advancing horde of aniborn. His mortal hands flexed at his sides. The body would not hold what he was about to ask of it. He asked anyway.

CHAPTER 28
Azgiel—Battlefield, Forest Border

Screams carried across the open meadow. The aniborn had broken the treeline.

Azgiel strode forward, the old power moving in him for the first time in two thousand years. His troops parted around him. They remembered him.

Tonight he would give them something fresh to remember.

Raising his hands, Azgiel called inward to the raw power coiled deep within his soul. The wind came up hard around him, and the ground gave a shudder under his boots.

Above, the sky cracked wide, unleashing a firestorm that turned the sky orange. The battlefield below was bathed in this abnormal light, casting ominous silhouettes across Azgiel's warriors.

A collective gasp rose from the ranks. But Azgiel frowned. The fire, his summoned inferno, hung suspended above the battlefield. It hung. It did not fall.

Cracks webbed across Azgiel's hands, blood welling from fresh wounds, seeping into the soil. Smoke rose from his fingertips—his mortal body fraying, rebelling against a power it was never meant to wield.

At his side, Kaz growled low at his shoulder. "My Lord, the sword."

Azgiel turned toward the weapon half-buried in dirt nearby. Acid green light traced the blade's edge, Maselda's magic—a gift of controlled, refined chaos.

He grasped the hilt. Green fire leapt up the length of the blade. "Let nothing live," he commanded.

As they advanced, his army answered as one, their voices thundering together. In response, the aniborn's wails pierced the air.

Carnage erupted across the battlefield.

Azgiel drove forward, ground cracking under the fury of his charge. The world narrowed to what was within reach of his sword. To his right, one of his demons cut a path through the aniborn with a blade that left green fire in the air behind every stroke. To his left, Kaz tore into the line and the line did not hold.

Azgiel barreled straight for the commander—a monstrous aniborn mounted on a beast that resembled a hulking rat. The creature did not engage; he watched, waited, biding his time.

Lifting his free hand, Azgiel called forth his power. Pain seared up his arm, momentarily ignored in the release. Energy gathered, then launched forward in a devastating beam.

The commander was torn from his mount and slammed into the dirt. Something old and pleased moved in Azgiel's chest.

Then the pain truly hit. His arm split open. Staggering, his vision narrowed to a pinprick.

The body was paying more for every strike.

As he fought to keep his focus, the atmosphere changed. Around him, the aniborn melted back into their shadow form, becoming invisible to the naked eye. Azgiel sensed their lurking presence, aware that an attack was imminent yet unable to pinpoint its source.

The assault began. An invisible force drove into his side, throwing him off balance. Another aniborn, unseen and silent, slammed into him, hurling him down hard. Claws he could not see opened his ribs and his shoulder before he could get an arm up.

Then his demons came in, tearing his assailants away with ruthless efficiency. Azgiel got back to his feet.

A demon applied a tarry substance. Smoke curled from his skin where it touched his wounds. The healing was crude and fast and turned his stomach.

No time to dwell. Another aniborn lunged.

Azgiel reacted on instinct, his sword swung, severing the creature's head in one stroke.

Across the field, Snyp had not yet moved. As Azgiel charged, the area around them constricted, with demons drawing in closer, their blades ready, forming a defensive perimeter.

Snyp, towering above the rest, his form hulking with muscle, sneered at Azgiel's advance. Snyp moved like a demon—too powerful, too deliberate to have once been human. "You think you can take me, human?" he taunted, his voice booming across the field.

Azgiel did not reply. His blade clashed with Snyp's claws. He pressed onward, trading strikes with a thing that should not have been outmatching him.

For half a second he thought he had it. Then Snyp smiled, and Azgiel knew he had only been allowed to think it.

A kick sent Azgiel reeling, swiftly followed by a fist to his jaw. His knees bit gravel, his sword skittering out of reach.

Snyp leaped onto Azgiel, massive claws plunging deep into his chest. "You die here," he snarled.

In that moment, on the brink of death, time itself unraveled.

The battlefield around Azgiel shifted, blurring between past and present. He was back in the prison of a war held in stasis, gazing across a battlefield he had lost two thousand years ago—his army, once mighty, now mangled and broken, locked in eternal death throes. Then, the vision shifted forward to a future not yet written.

He saw Caden, trapped and dying, with an aniborn beside him, whispering secrets, watching, waiting.

Power rushed into Azgiel—a maelstrom of energy tearing at the boundaries of his mortal form.

The battlefield exploded in a catastrophic burst. A shockwave tore across the clearing, the ground itself splitting asunder. Aniborn were thrown like rag dolls, the air filled with screams. Above them, the sky cracked open, spreading across the heavens like a shattered glass dome.

From the ground, lightning rose in violent threads, its raw energy flooding the landscape with a blinding, unnerving brilliance.

Amidst this chaos, a blast of pure, uncontrollable destruction erupted from Azgiel. It hit Snyp, carving a gaping hole in his abdomen and shredding the flesh on his back into tatters.

Azgiel could not halt the cataclysm he'd unleashed. His vision blazed with unbearable intensity as his body started to tear apart from within, the energy running past anything the body could hold.

As his senses overwhelmed him and his vision faded to white, the last thing Azgiel registered was Kaz at his side—close, fast, lifting him. Then the white took everything.

CHAPTER 29

Caden—Beachside Condo

Caden woke before dawn. The plans for the morning were already lined up in his head, and he wanted them out of his head before Bridget woke up enough to read his face. He nudged her, told her to go grab breakfast while he handled "some work stuff." She made a face at him over her shoulder, told him he was a terrible liar, and went anyway. The door clicked shut behind her, and he had maybe an hour.

He moved quietly across the condo. The light coming in off the water was the gold-into-pink that only happens here, and only this early. The familiar crash of waves usually settled him. This morning every set sounded like a clock counting down.

He grabbed his phone. Confirmations from James, Bridget's sister, and a priest were stacked on the screen. Everyone was in. Everyone was waiting on him.

One reply hadn't come yet. He paced the length of the kitchen and back, thumbed the screen awake for the third time in a minute, and put the phone face down on the counter. The flight had hollowed him out. He told himself he'd close his eyes for ten minutes.

He made it to the bed. He was out before he hit the pillow.

Something woke him. Not a sound, but a change in the room, the way a room changes when someone has come into it and is choosing not to breathe. He lay still. The fan turned. The waves kept time outside. He listened past those things. A weight shifted at the edge of the bed. The mattress dipped under his foot.

He told his arm to move and it didn't. He told his head to turn and got the same nothing. The order went out and arrived nowhere, like a phone call into dead air. Whatever was on the bed shifted again, closer this time.

He pushed against it the way a man pushes against deep water. His fingers twitched first. Then his neck, by inches. The creature—the same one that had attacked him before—crouched at the foot of the bed.

Neither of them moved. It studied him with the patience of something that had done this before, head tipping the way a dog tips its head at a sound it doesn't recognize. Then it lowered itself further into its haunches, and its claws lengthened against the comforter.

Caden's grip tightened on the sheet. "Bring it on," he growled.

The creature lunged. Something hit it mid-air. He didn't see what. The thing went sideways across the room and into the far wall hard enough to crack plaster. It screamed. The sound went into Caden's teeth. He fought his arm up under him, got himself onto an elbow, turned his head.

A breath came out of the room—deep, animal, displeased—and a man who was not a man stepped forward into the light off the water. He had to bow his head to keep his horns out of the ceiling. His skin was the dark red of old brick. The black of the writing down his arms moved when he moved. The sword in his hand was longer than the headboard of the bed, and the runes along its edge were a green that did not belong indoors.

The thing on the wall held there, claws sunk to the knuckle in plaster. It did not look at the demon. It looked at Caden.

The demon did not raise his voice. He didn't need to. "You're not touching him." The sword came up, level, easy in his hand. "Go back where you came from."

The creature dragged a slow growl up out of itself. Black ran out from where its claws were buried, threading through the plaster like roots looking for water.

Then it came off the wall. The room came apart with it. The demon moved faster than something his size had any right to move. His wings—ragged at the edges, scarred along the bone—snapped open between Caden and the creature, and the sword came down in an arc that pulled green fire along its length and drove the thing back.

Caden willed his body to respond. This time it answered. The two combatants clashed. Claws shrieked against the blade. The dresser went over. The bedframe cried out under his weight as he tried to push up. Green light pulsed across the ceiling like lightning indoors.

The demon shouted a word Caden did not know and threw something. A fistful of fire shaped like a fist. It hit the creature in the chest and folded it into the wall. The wall took most of the impact. The creature took the rest. There was a last sound out of it, sharp and wrong, and then nothing.

The weight pressing on Caden lifted. He dropped back against the mattress and pulled in a breath that hurt going down. His chest heaved. Feeling came back into his hands in a slow tingle, the way a foot wakes up. But before he could get any of that under control, the demon turned toward him.

"My name is Kaz," the demon said. His voice was lower up close—less a sound than something Caden felt in his sternum. "I'll be watching over you." He reached out. The hand was the size of Caden's skull. "You're not ready for

165

this."

Caden tried to speak. His mouth opened around a question and the question stayed in his mouth. Kaz set his palm against Caden's forehead. Power surged through him, pulling him under the way a wave pulls a swimmer who has stopped kicking.

When he woke again, the room was quiet in a way that was wrong. The bed was neatly made. The dresser stood where it had stood when he'd gone to sleep. Sunlight came through the blinds in clean stripes. There were no signs of the fight. No overturned furniture, no scorch marks, no trace of the creature or the demon.

It was as if nothing had happened. Almost. In the corner, low on the wall, a single shallow gouge in the paint marked the place the creature had hit. He stood and went to it. He put his thumb in it. The plaster powder was fresh. He looked at it a long time. Then he wiped his thumb on his shirt and went to find his phone. "Not today," he said, to no one. "Today I'm doing this. The rest of it can wait."

CHAPTER 30
Bridget—Boardwalk Overlook

The note was tucked into the condo door at eye level, folded once. Bridget knew the handwriting before she had it open. Three lines, an arrow drawn at the bottom, no signature. He never signed them. *Meet me at our spot.* She read it twice on the walkway and a third time on the stairs and then she was already moving, the sun already on her shoulders, the note folded small in her palm.

She came down off the boardwalk and stopped where the sand turned from dry to packed. The water was doing the thing it does in the morning where it almost looks combed. She crouched, found a flat stone without looking for one, and skipped it. Four hops. She used to be able to get six.

Standing there with her shoes in her hand brought back the afternoon, years ago now, when he'd said it. Right here. One day. He'd said it the way he said the things he meant, quietly, without looking at her. She had kept it folded somewhere small in herself ever since, the way she had kept the note in her hand. She didn't want to think about why she was thinking about it now. She made herself stop. The morning was the morning. Whatever else was coming could wait its turn.

Something moved on the path up to the overlook, the same path they had walked the day they signed the papers on the condo, the day he had kissed her at the railing and not said anything for a long time after. She started up it.

Caden waited at the cliff's edge. Hands in his pockets. Hair already a wreck from the wind. He had on the shirt she liked and he had not shaved.

"Hey," he said.

She came up the last few steps. "What's all this?"

"A few minutes," he said. "Away from everything."

She tipped her head. "And you couldn't have told me over breakfast?"

He took her hand. He didn't laugh. "Not for this."

And then he was on one knee in front of her, and her hand went to her mouth before she had decided to put it there. He pulled a small box out of his jacket pocket. His hands were not steady. She had never seen his hands not be steady. He opened it. The ring inside was simple—one stone, the band thin— the kind of ring she would have picked herself, which meant he had been paying attention for a long time.

"Bridget," he said. He took a breath. "You're the best part of every day I've had. I don't want to do another one without knowing you're mine for the rest of them. Will you marry me?"

She went down to her knees with him in the sand. She put her hands on either side of his face. "Yes," she said. "Yes. Of course yes. I've been waiting for you a long time, Caden Gray."

Something went out of his shoulders that she hadn't known was in them. He slid the ring onto her finger. She kissed him before he could say anything else, and when she pulled back, she kept her forehead against his, and stayed there a beat longer than she meant to.

"Promise me one thing," she said, eyes still closed. "Promise me we don't wait forever to actually do this."

He didn't answer. He stood, took her hand, and turned her to face the overlook. Down on the beach below them, in a small loose half-circle, were her sister, James, her mother, and the priest, trying not to look like he was watching them.

She stopped. She looked at the beach. She looked at him. "Caden."

"Yeah," he said.

"Right now?"

He shrugged, the small one, the one he did when he was caught at something and not sorry about it. "You said you didn't want a long engagement."

She laughed. The laugh broke a little in the middle. "You are unbelievable."

He pulled her into him. His mouth was at her temple. "I'm done risking this," he said, low enough that no one else would have heard it. "I'm done."

She held onto him. "You won't lose me," she said into his shoulder. "You won't."

They went down to the beach hand in hand. The ceremony was short. The priest had clearly done a lot of these on a lot of beaches and knew how to keep them moving. She heard "Do you take" and she said yes before he'd finished saying it, and her sister laughed, and her mother cried in the embarrassed way her mother always cried. When the priest got to "You may now seal your vows," Caden kissed her like he'd been waiting on permission for a decade.

She barely heard the clapping. She leaned into him while he murmured into her hair, "Forever starts now." A pause. "Well. Technically tomorrow. The priest still has to file the paperwork." Another pause. "So maybe forever starts tomorrow." She felt him smile against her temple. "Close enough."

CHAPTER 31

Caden—On the Beach

The sun was higher now. The beach was still mostly empty, the kind of Sunday morning a stretch of coastline gives you in the off-season, the locals not yet up and the rest of the weekend already driven home. Caden and Bridget sat in the sand, knees drawn up. The world had been narrowed down to the surf and to her, and that was enough. Her head rested on his shoulder, and her thumb was moving in a small absent circle on the back of his hand.

The others had given them space, retreating to the cars beyond the dunes. It was just them now. It had gone quiet around them in the way some mornings do, like the day was holding its breath for them.

Bridget ran her fingers through the damp sand. "There should be agates here," she said. She pushed herself up, brushing sand from her dress, and walked closer to where the waves worked at the shore.

Caden watched as she crouched, her fingers sifting through the wet stones. The way her brow furrowed in focus, the way she bit her lip in concentration. It was a glimpse of the uncomplicated Bridget, the one who could lose herself in the simple joy of looking for something.

She picked up a small, smooth stone and held it up to the sunlight, turning it in her palm. "This one's almost perfect," she said. "But I know there's a better one."

Caden smiled, pushing himself to his feet. "You say that every time."

Bridget laughed. "And I always find one, don't I?"

For a few minutes the rest of it went away. Kaz, the lab, the implant under the skin of his neck, the thing that had crouched at the foot of his bed at dawn, and the demon with red wings who had come for it. None of it. There was only the woman who would spend an hour on a stretch of beach for a stone the size of her thumbnail because finding it would make her happy, and who he had married twenty minutes ago.

He watched as she picked up another stone. "Keep that one," he said.

She raised an eyebrow. "Why?"

"Because this was our first morning as husband and wife," he said. "You should have something to remember it by."

Bridget closed her fingers around the stone and held it there a moment against her sternum. "Okay."

She slipped it into her pocket and took his hand, lacing her fingers through his.

"I wish this could last forever," Bridget said. Her fingers tightened around his by a fraction. He felt the ring he had just put there.

"It will," Caden said. Something in the way he said it made her lift her head off his shoulder. He was looking at the water and he wasn't seeing it. "But I have to leave soon."

Her smile faltered. "You finally have me, and now you're leaving?"

"I'll come back. You stay here at the condo. I'll be back by the end of the week. Friday night," he said. He took both of her hands. "And when I do, we'll plan the real one. The bigger one, with all your friends and family. A honeymoon somewhere far away from all of this." He said it the way a man says something he has been turning over in his head for a long time.

"You're really going." It came out more statement than question.

Caden leaned in, kissed her forehead, kept his lips there a beat. "I have to. This trip was always going to be a short window." He breathed out, pulling back to look at her. "Things are happening that I can't ignore. Coming here was already a risk. The implant in my neck. Robert's using it to track me. If I don't go back soon…" He let it sit.

He'd sent a quick text to Robert the night before, something vague enough to buy him a few hours and not much else. He had no idea how it had landed. He'd killed his phone after meeting James at the gate and not turned it on again. Whatever was waiting for him on the other end of that call, whenever he did turn it on, was going to be loud.

Her brow furrowed. The fear came first. He watched her work through it the way he had watched her work through harder things—quiet, no fuss, the small movement at the corner of her mouth that meant she had decided. "I understand," she said. She leaned in and kissed him. Not soft, not desperate, somewhere in between, the kiss of a person making a promise to herself as much as to him. "This was wonderful. A quiet morning in the middle of what was feeling like a storm. When this is over, I want to sit with you and plan our big wedding. And a honeymoon I won't want to come back from."

She didn't know how true the storm part would prove. He did. He made himself a promise on her behalf, sitting there with her hand in his on a stretch of empty sand: he was going to end this thing before it found its way to her. Whatever ending it cost him.

"I can't wait," he said. He pulled her in against his chest. The world could wait.

After a while neither of them was talking. The waves did the talking. Out past the break, a pelican folded its wings and dropped, came up empty, lifted again. He watched it go and tried not to think about what would be waiting on his phone when he turned it back on.

CHAPTER 32
Bridget—Condo

Bridget sat curled on the couch in the beachside condo. The waves did nothing for the noise inside her head. Her grandmother's book rested on the coffee table between her hands and the window. She had been staring at it for an hour. Now, finally, someone else was going to be the one to open it.

Her phone vibrated.

Professor Howell: *Ms. Bridget, thank you for reaching out. Your book sounds fascinating, and I'd love to see it in person. If you're ever near the university, I'd be happy to meet and discuss it.*

She typed before she could second-guess herself.

Bridget: *I can be there today. I'll get a ride over.*

* * *

The university campus was a stark contrast to the quiet she had left behind. Students hurried across the quad, bundled against the crisp sea breeze, their conversations a low murmur. Bridget drew her coat tighter as she entered the Humanities building.

Professor Howell's office was tucked away at the end of a quiet corridor, the door slightly ajar. She knocked once.

"Professor Howell?" she said, pushing it open.

The professor looked up from a desk buried under ancient scrolls and leather-bound volumes. His face lit up at the sight of the book under her arm. "Ah, Bridget! Come in, come in. I was reviewing some fascinating new documents."

She stepped inside. Books on every wall, an old paper-and-pipe-tobacco smell. Some of the tightness in her shoulders let go. She placed the volume on the desk, symbols pressed into the leather catching the lamplight.

Professor Howell leaned forward and traced a finger across the worn leather binding. "This is remarkable. Where did you say you got this?"

"My grandmother," Bridget said, watching his expression shift from interest to something more careful. "It's been in my family for generations. Can you read it?"

The professor turned the brittle pages. "Some of it," he admitted. "I've seen this kind of script before." His finger paused on a passage. "This is an old dialect, found mostly in a few surviving scrolls. The ones I have speak of Azgiel as a revered leader. A guardian of his people."

"Revered? My grandmother told me he was a tyrant. A monster."

Professor Howell frowned, tapping the page. "That's… unusual. The scrolls I've studied don't mention anything like that. They speak of him with admiration, though they don't go far past it. This portrayal is… different."

Bridget leaned in. "So, was he good or bad?"

The professor took a moment to choose his words. "There's so little written about him that it's impossible to say. History is incomplete at best—and rewritten at worst. He may have been misunderstood, or there may be more to the story than what's survived."

"My grandmother was certain he was dangerous," Bridget said. "She wasn't a woman who got things like that wrong."

Professor Howell paged further, then stopped at an illustration: two figures rendered side by side—one unmistakably Azgiel, the other a woman lying lifeless beside him.

Bridget's brow drew together. "Who is she?"

Professor Howell adjusted his glasses, the awe creeping into his voice before he could check it. "His wife. The text identifies her as Maselda. It says she was murdered—betrayed by a king. But Azgiel brought her back. And not just back—he gave her something. Power."

Bridget stared at the image. Strange symbols had been inked across the woman's body, dense as a second skin. "He… resurrected her?"

"It appears so," Professor Howell murmured, flipping ahead. His brows furrowed. "Here… this—" He pointed. "He lost a war."

Bridget steadied herself against the desk. "My grandmother mentioned something like that."

Professor Howell nodded, reading further. "As a result, he was banished— not killed, but consigned to what this text calls 'the frozen shadows.'"

Bridget felt the cold of the words land before she understood them. "Frozen shadows."

The professor turned to the final pages, his face paling. He turned the book to face her. A single illustration covered the last page—a hand punching through a rip in space, fingers locked around a sword whose edge ran with a thin vein of purple light.

She didn't want to ask. "What does it say?"

Professor Howell read aloud: "'He will return one day when the prison is split again, and he is pulled from the frozen shadows.'"

"Could that be a metaphor?" she said. "For stopped time?"

"It could." He leaned back, rubbing his chin. "If that's true, then time itself—not shadows—is the key."

Her stomach dropped. "Caden's project—the man he spoke of."

Professor Howell looked up, confused. "Who?"

Bridget didn't answer. The pieces were laying themselves down too fast for her to keep up. Caden's veins. His project. The man who had visited him in the parking lot. None of this was coincidence.

Professor Howell flipped to the final passage, reading it in a hushed tone. "'He will come and set the people free, right the wrongs of the universe. His enemies will lie in a waste of death and destruction.'"

Neither of them spoke.

Bridget rolled her thumb against her fingertips, an old grounding tic she used with clients. "So… is Azgiel good or bad?"

Howell hesitated. "We have to remember these are stories. Mythology from cultures that don't exist anymore."

"I'm not asking what they are," she said. "I'm asking what you think."

"I… don't know," he said, looking up at her. "These scrolls seem to say he was, but this book…" He shook his head. "It's conflicting. I really can't say."

Bridget closed the book and lifted it off the desk. Before she could turn for the door, Howell's hand closed on her arm.

"Wait." His grip was firmer than she expected. "There was something on the back. Let me see it again—please."

She handed it back, slower than she meant to. Howell carefully pried at the leather binding, revealing a thin silver rune embedded inside.

Bridget squinted. "What is that?"

Professor Howell turned it over, tilting the carvings to the light. "I don't know." His fingers traced the symbols. "The top word reads 'of heal.' But the bottom section… it's odd. Almost gibberish. If I had to guess, it could say 'danger making.'"

"I don't understand." Bridget reached for it, but Howell held tight.

"One second," he murmured, squinting. "Maybe… *dragner mekina… degnar mekna*—"

The rune flared white under his fingers.

Howell cried out and dropped it. Fire erupted from his eyes—actual fire, the orange of it lighting his cheekbones from the inside. His scream tore through the small office as he collapsed, convulsing.

Bridget lunged forward without thinking. "Professor!"

The flames cut out. Howell gasped, sitting up shakily. Something about him was… different.

"Your eyes," she said, breathless. "There was fire in your eyes."

"Was there?" He pulled the glasses off his face and paused, staring at them as if seeing them for the first time, then set them on the desk. "I… I don't think I need these anymore," he murmured. He flexed his fingers. "The arthritis… it's gone." He looked up at Bridget. "I feel... younger."

Bridget took a step back. The therapist part of her, the part that had spent years learning to read a face, was already telling her something was wrong. "Professor, what's happening to you?"

Professor Howell turned back toward the book, his fingers brushing the pages like he was afraid to wake them. "Bridget," he said, voice unsteady, "this isn't just mythology. These runes—they're real."

She studied his face. The shape of it was the same, but everything inside the shape had moved a quarter inch. "Professor... are you still yourself?"

Howell blinked, almost amused. "Of course, I am. Who else would I be?"

That was what unsettled her. Twenty minutes ago he had taken a careful breath before standing up. Now he sat across from her with color in his cheeks and the loose skin at his throat tightened by something she didn't have a word for.

The rune lay between them on the desk.

Howell rubbed his face and looked at his hands again. He let out a short laugh. "My hands. My back. My eyes. I don't feel anything. Anywhere." At last, he met her eyes, pleading. "Bridget, don't you see? This isn't history. It's power. Real, tangible power."

She reached for the book. Somewhere in the chaos it had fallen open. On the last page, the ink stood stark against the yellowed parchment. The illustration she'd seen earlier—a hand thrusting through a tear in space, fingers clenched around a sword—looked different now.

The lines had sharpened. The shading had deepened. The hand no longer read as a drawing. It read as a photograph of a hand. And in the blackness behind the tear, for one heartbeat, something seemed to move.

She told herself it was a drawing.

What if it's not?

Her legs found her. She grabbed the book, slammed it shut, and pressed it to her chest as if pressure could hold a lid on what was inside. Her skin had gone cold.

Professor Howell barely noticed. He was still staring at his hands, turning them in the lamplight. "I need to study this," he muttered. "I need more time with it. Bridget, do you understand what this is?" His voice dropped to something pleading. "You have to let me keep it."

She shook her head and inched toward the door. "No. I—I can't." She didn't know what any of this was. She only knew the book scared her. She didn't want to be in this office anymore.

"Bridget, wait." Howell came around the desk faster than a man his age should have been able to move.

She flinched. "No!" The force of her own voice startled her. Howell went rigid, hand hovering between them. His face fell—not in anger, but in something closer to disappointment.

"Bridget," he tried again softly. "You saw it, didn't you? You felt it. We can't

175

ignore what happened."

She was already at the door. "I'm ignoring it," she said. The book bit into her ribs through her coat. "I shouldn't have come."

She stepped into the hall, walked too fast for the first ten paces and then made herself slow down, and pushed out into the cold salt air.

CHAPTER 33
Caden—Flight 239

The hum of the plane engines vibrated through the cabin. Caden leaned back in his seat and let out a deep breath. They had been stuck in the airport most of the day, flight delayed for mechanical issues. Robert still hadn't called. That was unlike him. His thumb worked along the edges of the new Dead Time watch on his wrist. He wasn't sure what to make of it. An engineering marvel and a leash. A small dial. A few buttons. The simplest piece of technology he had ever been afraid of.

James nudged him with his elbow. "You're glaring at that thing like it insulted your mom."

"Just thinking," Caden said, eyes on the window.

The sky outside was a deep, clean blue, streaked with thin cloud. The horizon went on as far as he could see. But the unease in his chest would not settle. He had learned, over the last year, to trust that feeling.

A child's voice carried from a few rows back. "Mom, I saw a bird explode!" He said it the way kids said things—a fact someone needed to hear.

The mother shushed him absently. "Don't be silly, sweetheart."

"I'm not," the boy insisted, a small finger jabbing out the window. "Right there! It was flying, and then—poof!"

Caden's gaze snapped to the boy's window. Nothing—empty sky. But the boy's words had landed.

"Caden?" James said. "You good?"

"I don't know." He scanned the sky. There—above the wing—a faint warp in the air, like heat off pavement, riding too close to be weather.

"There," he said. "Tell me you see that."

James squinted, leaning closer to the window. "What am I looking for?"

"That shimmer. It's a cloaking device."

"A jet?"

"Has to be."

Before James could answer, a heavy metallic clank rang through the cabin. The plane shuddered. Passengers screamed as a grappling hook tore the emergency exit door clean off its frame. Air knifed through the cabin. Oxygen masks dropped. The torn door tumbled into the engine and the engine lit up—a fireball blooming against the blue sky.

"Brace!" Caden shouted, locking his hand on the armrest as the plane tilted into the decompression.

Time seized. Wind, cries, even the flex of mask straps—stopped.

The shift left his ears ringing. Passengers hung mid-scream, hair and clothes pulled toward the open exit and held there. Luggage floated in the aisle along the line of the breach. The fire on the wing stood frozen in its own shape—orange and yellow tongues caught mid-curl.

He tried to say James's name, but stopped when his voice didn't come. The air didn't vibrate. Nothing carried.

James gestured urgently, mouthing the words, *Dead Time*. Without their Dead Time suits—and the integrated microphones designed for communication—they couldn't speak.

Caden nodded. The first moments in stopped time still felt like stepping out of a plane mid-flight—the body refusing the input, the lungs forgetting their job. The shock was already passing.

He reached for his wrist device. They hadn't activated the Dead Time equipment themselves—someone else had. And whoever it was, they weren't alone.

From a jet hovering nearby, two figures stepped out. Its outline wavered as if half-cloaked, and the figures wore sleek black Dead Time suits.

Caden tapped James's arm and pointed. They didn't need to speak; they had run enough drills together to know the shape of an attack when one was unfolding.

The men moved with precision, boots gripping the motionless wing as they advanced toward the open exit. Behind them, two more figures followed. Their path warped the air the way a brush drags color through wet paint. They carried knives that gleamed faintly.

Caden eased to his feet and motioned James up. They moved slow— anything fast in stopped time read as a flag. They crept down the aisle, weaving around suspended passengers and debris.

The first suited figure swung in through the breach. Caden lunged. His shoulder hit the man square in the chest, driving him back into the doorframe. The man's knife slipped from his grip and hung in the air where he had let go of it.

The man recovered and charged, fists ready. He swung hard, but Caden ducked under the blow and countered with a jab, knuckles slamming into the man's helmet. The impact knocked him into the seats.

Through the visor's reflective surface, Caden caught a glimpse of the man's face—or what little he could make out. Justin. Had to be—the same bald man who had broken into the facility and attacked the scientist.

Behind him, James engaged a second figure, grappling with him near the row of seats. In the narrow aisle every move was a fight for leverage. James slammed the man into the overhead compartment, cracks spidering through the plastic from the impact.

Caden turned just as the third and fourth men cleared the breach. He drove his shoulder into the nearest one, dumping him back out onto the wing. The fourth was faster—already moving sideways before Caden was square.

Stopped time did something to a fight. Every blow landed softer than it should have. Mass moved differently in here. They had to throw their whole bodies behind every strike to make it count. The attackers were trained. Caden and James were desperate. Desperate won.

The attackers shifted. They stopped trying to land hits and started trying to land hands. The one James had pinned twisted free with a hand that went straight for the watch on James's wrist. James caught the wrist before it reached him and threw an elbow that put the man back against the wall, but not before a second attacker came in low and clamped onto his other arm.

Caden saw it then. They were reaching for wrists.

"The watches," he mouthed at James, but James couldn't see him. James was busy.

The man on James's left got his hand under the cuff and worked something Caden couldn't see. The watch came off. James lurched after it. The man stepped back fast and slapped a flat black device against James's neck where the implant sat under the skin. A faint wavering ran across James's shoulders, and James went still—hands locked mid-grab, chest mid-breath, eyes open, his face caught in the shape of recognition without action.

Caden understood as it happened. The device on the neck had killed the implant. Whatever it had been built for, it had done it. James was out—not just dropped from this bubble, but out of Dead Time entirely.

The third attacker was already coming for him.

Caden brought his arm in tight against his ribs and met the man square. The hand that went for his wrist found his elbow instead. He drove a knee up into the man's gut and twisted free. The man staggered. Caden caught him by the front of the suit and slammed him into the seatback hard enough that the man's helmet cracked against the metal frame and his hands forgot what they were doing for a second. Long enough.

The other two were already pulling back. They had what they came for. Justin—the bald one in the visor—paused at the breach and looked back at Caden the way a man looks at a problem he has decided to leave for later. Then he was through the opening and on the wing.

Caden went after them. He cleared the breach onto the wing and caught the last man before he could close the distance to the jet. His tackle sent the attacker off the wing into open air. The man clawed at nothing. Stopped time held him there like he was kicking through tar—going nowhere, as long as his watch held the field. He could stay in there days if he wanted—until thirst or hunger pushed him to hit the switch and accept the fall waiting for him in normal time. Caden did not envy the math.

The man's helmet lit up—yelling into his comms, mouth working, no sound. One of his comrades broke from the jet and came at Caden across the wing. Caden dropped low and drove a kick up under the man's ribs. The kick sent him over Caden's shoulder and off the wing. He went into open air the same way the first one had. Both of them hung there, mouths open in silent shouts, hands reaching for a hold the air would not give them. Two men with the same choice, and the same answer waiting at the end of it.

The last two reached the jet. One of them glanced back—it was Justin. He sealed the hatch behind them. Caden sprinted to the nearly invisible aircraft and pounded his fists against the hatch. The cloaking made the jet hard to read. He couldn't tell what was hull and what was sky. One bad step and he would be off the side of it with nothing but five thousand feet under him.

He stepped back. Through the breach he could see James inside the cabin, locked in place mid-motion, hand still half-extended toward the wrist they had taken from him. Justin had a working watch in his pocket now. A prototype. Caden didn't need to think about what that meant for the office. He already knew.

His attention went back to the two men suspended beneath the wing. They clawed at nothing, helmets bobbing, mouths open in soundless prayer.

He thought about going for them—pulling them in, holding them for questioning. He couldn't. Any wrong step on the wing and he was joining them.

He climbed back into the cabin. Methodically, he moved through the plane, settling passengers back into their seats, snapping their belts. His hands worked. His head wouldn't stop running the fight.

In the cockpit doorway, a flight attendant was caught mid-step, half through the door. Caden moved her aside and hauled James into the cockpit beside the pilots.

In stopped time, James weighed almost nothing. Featherlight, awkward—a man-shaped bag of static.

He pressed the button on his wrist.

Sound came back like a wall. Screams. Masks snapping against faces. Metal stressing and popping. The wave of it buckled his knees; he caught himself on the console.

Outside, the attackers' jet peeled away, then swung back. Caden barely had time to shout, "Duck!" as the first spray of bullets punched through the cockpit windows and tore the control panels open. Glass and sparks flew. The pilots slumped forward, dead before they had time to know it.

James grabbed Caden's arm. "They're coming back!"

The plane lurched. Alarms screamed from the wrecked panel. Smoke pushed up out of it and stung Caden's eyes. The floor pitched forward as the nose started to drop. Outside the cracked window, the attackers' jet circled back.

"We have to stop it!" James shouted.

Caden pointed at the wrecked panel. "We've got bigger problems."

The plane shuddered again. A groan ran the length of the fuselage as the damaged engine coughed once and died. Smoke poured off the wing. The nose dipped.

The pilots were gone. The instrument panel sparked at random and answered nothing.

"Nothing's working," Caden said.

James caught his shoulder. "Plan?"

Caden stared at the ground rushing up. "We activate Dead Time—right before we crash. Time it wrong and we're paste."

James reached for his wrist on reflex and found bare skin. He looked at the cabin behind them—the passengers, the kids—and let the reach finish on the empty wrist. "Okay. You'll have to do it."

They turned back to the window. Fields rolled up at them—green, brown, green again—closer every second. Caden's thumb hovered over the wrist switch.

James covered his eyes.

The plane's shadow rushed up to meet the plane. Caden slammed the switch.

The screaming cut out. Torn papers hung mid-flutter. A cup tipped halfway off a tray and held there. Beside him in the cockpit, James had gone motionless—eyes half-shut, hand suspended where it had been when Caden hit the switch. Until that moment, Caden had not been certain the neck-zap had killed James's implant. Now he knew.

He took them one by one. Unbuckle, lift, carry, lay down in the field, turn around, do it again. In stopped time the bodies were nearly weightless—easy to lift, awkward to balance. Outside the cabin the field sat fixed in its own moment, stalks of grass mid-bend in a wind that had stopped blowing. He moved through it the way you move through a museum after closing—alone, the whole world watching.

After setting a young woman down in the grass and turning back for the next, Caden glanced at the wing. The fire stood there in the shape it had been wearing when time stopped. He looked closer. It wasn't holding its color the way it should have. As he moved his head, the flame shifted—yellow to orange to a deep red and, at one angle, a thin shock of green.

He held his hand near it. There should have been heat. There wasn't. Something pulled at his fingertips instead—faint, steady, the way a magnet pulls iron through cloth. He reached out and touched the flame.

It wasn't hot. It wasn't cold. It was alive, and it answered him. Energy ran from his fingertips up into his chest. The flame darkened where he was touching it, the way a coal goes dim under a draft. It pulsed once.

He pulled his hand back. His fingers were unmarked. The hum stayed under his skin.

He shoved the question of the flame down where he kept the rest of them.

181

The attackers were gone, and he needed to keep moving.

He worked through the cabin one row at a time. The flight had been only partly full. Small mercies.

After all the passengers were down, he carried James out last and set him in the grass near the plane. He wanted to do one more sweep. The thought of missing someone—of finding out later that someone had died because he had walked past their row—was not something he was willing to leave the plane with. He climbed back into the cabin.

Trays upended. Debris hanging in the aisle. A half-drunk soda hovering an inch above its cup.

And then, he sensed it.

At first it was nothing. A distortion at the edge of his vision, near the rear of the cabin.

His body locked. The distortion grew. The metal of the overheads and the rims of the windows curved toward it as if drawn.

It was not a trick of the eye. The distortion thickened, pooled, and pulled itself into a shape—a body without face or features, but a body. Its edges had the slick of oil on water; reflections broke and reformed across them. Nothing in stopped time was supposed to move. This did.

He understood, finally. He had glimpsed this thing the last time he was in stopped time, and now it was here in front of him. It was something locked inside stopped time, and it was trying to get out. Like Steven. Like Azgiel.

He tried to move. His muscles wouldn't answer.

The figure came toward him. The air bent around it. There was no sound.

"Mauldrin," it said, not in the air but in the place behind his sternum where the cold had been living for a week. The word answered something inside him before his mind had caught up to it. A piece of himself recognized the name as if it had always been his.

One of the creature's limbs stretched out and stopped an inch from his chest. He felt the pull of it deep behind his ribs.

Every nerve in him said run. He couldn't. It wasn't fear holding him in place. It was the thing in front of him.

The silence made it bigger. Each second stretched.

It was not watching him. It was measuring him.

He wanted to scream and couldn't. The pull behind his sternum was the same pull he had felt at the wing flame, magnified—only now it wasn't coming from outside him. It was coming from somewhere under his ribs. Somewhere he had not asked about, that had been quietly there for a week, the way an ember sits in a banked fire.

He went toward it instead of away from it.

He didn't know what he was reaching for. He reached anyway. There was a warmth high on his sternum—quiet, certain, present the way a hand on the small of his back was present—and he leaned his attention into it the way a drowning man leans into the surface of the water.

Something gave.

Not all the way. A finger of his right hand twitched. Then his whole hand. A breath went into him that wasn't the breath he had been holding.

The creature hadn't moved. Whatever was happening inside Caden was not visible to it yet. He could feel its attention on him, narrow and patient. He had a window of one or two seconds before the thing decided what it was going to do with him.

He used them.

He moved. The lock on his body broke in pieces—knee first, then hip, then the rest of him in a graceless lurch toward the breach. He didn't look back. He hit the wing at a half-run, dropped to the grass, and kept moving. Twenty yards. Forty. He stopped only when he was past James, and turned.

It was standing in the doorway. A limb reaching toward him through the breach. The thing was bigger now, or seemed bigger from outside, the way a fire seen through a window seems larger than the room it's burning in.

He hit his switch.

Sound came back. The plane was already going down.

The plane hit. The impact tore the earth open and sent fire boiling up into the sky.

The shockwave knocked them flat. Heat rolled over them. Debris came down for what felt like a long time.

Caden rolled onto his back. His ears rang. Smoke and fire and the new shape of the field.

A few feet away in the grass, James pushed up onto his hands and looked at the wreckage burning where the plane had been. Caden saw the moment he caught up to it—the small landing of a man realizing he had been carried out of something he hadn't been awake for.

Caden pushed himself up onto an elbow. "James."

James found him. "What—" He looked at the wreckage. He looked at the people lying in the grass between them. He looked at his own bare wrist where the watch had been. He flexed his fingers, twice, the way a man checks that his hand still belongs to him. "All of this. For the watch."

"Both watches. Mine, they didn't get." Caden held his wrist up. The Dead Time band sat where it had been the whole flight, scratched along one edge from where someone's hand had grabbed at it.

"And there's something else." Caden touched his own neck where the device had been on James's. "They put something on you. After they took the watch. I think it killed your implant."

James lifted a hand to the side of his throat. He didn't say anything for a beat. He didn't need to. The look on his face did it.

James's face changed. The disorientation went out of it and something tighter took its place. "The office."

Caden didn't say anything. He was watching the wreckage. Nothing moved in it. He told himself nothing had followed him out.

He pulled his phone out and dialed Robert. Voicemail. Tried again. Same.

The passengers in the grass were starting to come around. Cries rose as the shock faded—a woman calling a name that Caden couldn't make out, a man trying to sit up and not managing it. James looked at them and then back at Caden.

"We can't leave them."

"We can't stay either." Caden hit a different number. The line clicked on the second ring.

"Caden." The guard's voice came through tight, breathless. Background noise that did not sound like the lobby of a corporate building. "Where are you?"

"Crashed. A few blocks east of the office. Listen—they took James's watch. They're going for the rest of the prototypes."

A pause. Then: "They're already in. We're under attack. Three minutes ago. I've got eyes on six of them, more inside."

Caden closed his eyes for a second. "Tell Robert. If you can reach him."

"I can't. He's not answering." The line behind the guard's voice broke up briefly with what sounded like a door being forced. "Caden, get here."

"Coming." He ended the call.

He stared at the phone for one breath. Two. He opened the text thread to Bridget.

He thought about what he could tell her. He thought about what he could not. He thought about her sitting in the condo, worried about him. He thought about whether she was safe at all. He knew he didn't have time to waste on a text. He took the time anyway.

Caden: *James and I are okay. Don't worry. Can't talk. A lot is happening. It's not safe to text you what's going on. Stay inside. Lock the doors. Don't open it for anyone. I'll get back to you when I can. Love you.—Caden*

He sent it before he could weigh it any longer. He killed the screen and pushed up onto his feet.

James was already up on one knee. "What's the plan?"

Caden looked east. He couldn't see the office from here—the field rolled up into a stand of trees, and city blocks past that—but he knew the line. Three blocks, maybe four. By car they'd hit traffic from the crash within a minute. On foot they'd be running into the same crowd in the other direction.

He looked at his watch.

"They're inside the office right now. We don't have time." He held up the watch between them. "I stop time. I carry you. We're there in under a minute on foot, no traffic, no crowd."

James stared at him. "Do it."

Caden hit the switch.

The world stilled. The smoke from the wreck stopped climbing and held its shape against the sky like something carved. The cries in the grass cut out. Beside Caden, James froze mid-breath, eyes half-closed, the line of his shoulders dropping into the soft posture of a body without anyone home in it.

Caden caught him under the arm and lifted.

He took the first step. The grass under his boots gave no sound back. Somewhere past the trees, blocks east, the office was either burning or about to. He did not know which. He was about to find out.

CHAPTER 34

Bridget—Condo

Bridget pulled the condo door shut behind her. The click was a small sound. It did nothing for the noise inside her head.

Howell's eyes lighting up. The way he had stood from his chair like a man twenty years younger. The last page of the book—a hand coming through, a sword with a vein of purple along its edge. She kept stacking the pieces. They didn't fit any of the shapes she knew.

She set the book on the coffee table. Her hands shook as she set it down. Some part of her was waiting for it to do something.

She needed air. She needed to be in a room that did not have the book in it.

Her phone buzzed against the counter.

Mom: *Turn on the news. Check Flight 239.*

Flight 239?

She grabbed the remote. The screen came up on a news anchor mid-sentence, his face the careful, grave register they used when there was a body count attached.

"Breaking news this morning: Flight 239, a commercial airliner, has crashed in a rural area just outside the city. Miraculously, almost all passengers and crew survived, but the circumstances surrounding the crash are mystifying authorities."

Her knuckles went white on the remote.

"Eyewitnesses reported catastrophic engine failure mid-flight. Some even described seeing the exit door being torn away as the plane began its descent. Yet, inexplicably, the expected disaster did not occur."

The shot cut to a passenger on the side of a road, a silver thermal blanket pulled around her shoulders, voice unsteady. "One moment, we were all bracing for the worst, and the next... we were standing unharmed on the ground. It's like the crash never happened."

Caden.

Dead Time. The project. The veins under his skin. The thing he had told her, in pieces, on the plane out here. People standing unharmed on the ground after a crash that should have killed them.

It had to be him.

She dialed him. Voicemail.

She typed.

Bridget: *Caden, I saw the news. Please tell me you're okay.*

She watched the screen for a reply. None came.

The condo felt smaller. Her gaze went to the book on the coffee table. The text in it had described a man pulled out of frozen shadow when the prison was split. Caden's project split time. Caden had said the man—the stranger in a parking lot, Domblin—had told him to stay out of stopped time.

She did not want to follow the line her thinking was drawing. She followed it anyway.

The book had said Azgiel would return through a fracture in time. The rune in the back of it had taken Howell's arthritis away in a breath. If the rune could do that, the book itself was a question she did not want to ask alone.

For a moment she thought about taking the book with her. Instinct said no. If the book was anything close to what she was beginning to think it was, the safest place for it right now was a closed cover, on a coffee table, in a room she was leaving.

She grabbed her coat and bag. If he was not going to answer, she would go to him. She would walk if she had to.

Her hand was on the door handle when the phone buzzed. His name on the screen.

Caden: *James and I are okay. Don't worry. Can't talk. A lot is happening. It's not safe to text you what's going on. Stay inside. Lock the doors. Don't open it for anyone. I'll get back to you when I can. Love you.—Caden*

She read it twice. Typed back.

Bridget: *Caden? Where are you? Are you safe? Am I not safe?*

Nothing.

Something was very wrong.

She was not staying in this condo to wait it out. She opened the door. The salt air pushed in around her ankles.

She picked up her keys. If he would not answer, she would find him.

CHAPTER 35

Tagen—Snyp's Chamber

Tagen approached Snyp's chamber, the crunch of bones echoing along the dim corridor. The cavern opened into a grotesque throne room where Snyp lounged on a seat of fused remains, his sharp teeth ripping at a youngling bred for nothing but meat. Black blood striped the stone at his feet. Snyp's blood. His body was restoring itself, but it was still badly torn.

Tagen paused at the threshold. Cells lined the walls, crammed with humans no one would miss—drifters, criminals, outcasts. Their trapped souls were unstable as dying embers, the dark matter working into them. Some aniborn writhed in agony, their transformations nearly complete. Others sagged lifeless, husks already gnawed by waiting creatures. Their cries did not lift Snyp's head from his meal.

Snyp looked up, swallowing the chunk of flesh he'd torn free. "What news do you bring, Tagen?" The voice was easy. The claw on the armrest was not.

Tagen kept his eyes on the floor a beat. Hunger and envy moved in him together, the way they always did in this room. "I have a way to take Mauldrin," he said.

Snyp's brow lifted. "Go on."

"I followed him into a time cell."

The half-eaten limb stilled in his claw. "You entered a time cell." He said it flat, the way a man repeats a thing he wants to hear once more before he believes it. "You could have been torn out of yourself in there. Left as a watcher, with nothing to watch with."

Tagen kept his head inclined. "Mauldrin went in. I went after him."

Snyp worked something out from between his teeth with a claw. He did not speak for a long beat. He did not need to remind Tagen what lived in those cells. They both knew.

"One of them was in there with him," Tagen said. "It did not look at me."

Snyp's claws stilled. "It did not look at you?"

"Mauldrin was the target," Tagen said. "I was nothing to it in comparison. It held still until it had a way at him, and then it bent the cell around him until I thought it had him. He was weaker in there than I have ever seen him. His power did not come up until he was out."

Snyp's claws started a slow tap against the bone of his throne. "And you stood and watched."

"I watched. The cell sharpened what the creature had on him. It almost broke him with a word—his own name, said back to him. If I take younglings in, ones we have shaped, we can have him there. We can carry him out."

Snyp let his teeth show. "Brave. Or stupid. Maybe both." He took another tear off the meat in his hand and chewed slow. "It could have unmade you in there."

"But it didn't."

Snyp let his eyes slide off and back. "If he weakens in there, we use it. But the creature—if it decides to look at you next, it does not have to look back."

"I know," Tagen said.

Snyp nodded. "Ten younglings. No more. Take only the ones that have learned to keep their teeth shut. If you bring him back to me, you bring him back whole."

Tagen let the next thing settle in his throat before he spoke it. "One more thing. Kaz has been around. Watching over him. He attacked me once, when I went for Mauldrin and Domblin was nowhere I could see."

Snyp stiffened. "Kaz? He must have left quickly after we attacked the Witch."

Tagen weighed it, then asked anyway. "Did the attack not go well?" Snyp's wounds answered before he did.

Snyp bared his teeth and changed the topic. "Demons cannot enter time cells."

"No." Tagen let it go. "That's what makes it even better to go after Mauldrin in the cell of time. Kaz can't follow him in there and can't protect him. I do not yet know why Kaz is involved or why he would protect Mauldrin and not kill him. But we'll watch our step if he's around. The moment Mauldrin goes into a cell of time, Kaz can't follow."

Snyp came up off the throne and paced. "Kaz is a knot we do not need. If he stands between us and Mauldrin, the knot comes out. Domblin hasn't been a problem?"

"No, whatever you did to get Domblin away worked," Tagen said. "When I had found Mauldrin again, Domblin was absent. Kaz didn't show up until later."

Snyp grunted. "Domblin is a thorn. But he stops being our thorn—Triaad is coming for him. Mauldrin first. Take him fast. Be gone before Triaad arrives."

Snyp waved a claw. The bones of the throne re-set themselves under him with a slow grind, and he sat into them like a man settling into a chair he had built. "Take the younglings. Shape them. Avoid Kaz and Domblin. Kill them if you have to. Stay clear of the creatures in the cells. Sacrifice the younglings if it comes to that. But get Mauldrin. And don't let Triaad know we have him."

"Yes, my lord," Tagen said, bowing—though what he wanted was to put a claw through Snyp's throat while the body around it was still healing. The plan Snyp had just laid out was Tagen's plan. He had not needed to be told to do any of it. But Triaad coming changed everything. He would have to move faster. If he wanted Mauldrin to be his and not Snyp's, he had no time at all.

He left the room. The screaming farther in the tunnels worked its way through him as he walked, the way it always did, low and steady, a sound the cave made the way a furnace made heat. He went faster. The creature from the cell of time stayed with him—the way its head had not turned. The way nothing in it had thought he was worth turning for. He did not know what it would do the second time. He did not need to know yet.

He came around the last bend into the cavern of younglings. The smell of them met him first—too many bodies, too long since they had been fed. They came up off the floor as one when they saw him, eyes wide and yellow.

"Who wants to feast?" He said.

The room came at him in a wave of teeth and claws and noise. He held his ground and let it break around him, and when it had broken, he picked the ten with the most fight left in their eyes and enough mind left to take an order.

CHAPTER 36
Caden—City Streets

Caden moved through the back streets and alleys at a hard run, James slung over his shoulder in a fireman's carry. In stopped time the body weighed almost nothing, but the awkwardness slowed him at every corner. He kept his line east. The streetlights along the cross streets stood frozen in their orange, the late afternoon caught in them. Three blocks. Maybe four.

He came around the last corner with a view down the block toward the office, and stopped.

The building was caught in the middle of coming apart. A bloom of fire was held against the front face of it where one wall used to be, the orange of it locked into the shape of expanding without expanding. Concrete dust hung in the air like fog that had forgotten how to fall. Window glass was an inch out of its frames everywhere along the second and third floors, going nowhere yet.

He was too late. There was nothing he could do for any of it from out here. Inside the bubble he could walk the street and look at it for an hour and the building would still come apart the second he flipped the switch.

He set James down against the alley wall, propped him so he wouldn't fall when time started again, and hit the switch.

The world resumed in one moment. Sound came at him like a wall—the concussion of the blast hitting his chest, glass coming apart somewhere down the block, the shouts and horns of a city catching up to what had just happened to it. The pressure wave reached the alley a half-second behind the sound. It threw both of them against the brick at his back, hard enough that he felt his teeth lock. Debris came past the mouth of the alley sideways. A car out on the street that had been mid-turn caught the leading edge of the blast on its rear quarter and went into a slow spin into the curb on the far side, metal and glass coming with it.

Glass kept raining out of a storefront somewhere up the street. In Caden's ears, everything past five feet was muffled and underwater.

191

"James." He coughed it more than he said it.

James was already pushing himself off the wall, one hand at the side of his face. He pulled a piece of glass out of his cheek, made a sound that was not quite a word, and dropped the shard onto the asphalt. "I'll live."

"Me too." Caden looked toward the orange light coming up the block. "The office is gone."

They got to their feet. The whole block was rubble. There was no other word for it. Where the SDS building had been, a quarter of one corner was still standing—four floors of broken concrete and bent rebar holding up nothing. The rest had come down into the street. Fires worked through the wreckage in slow patches, the way they did with plenty of fuel and no one putting them out.

Caden moved toward it, picking around toppled streetlights and a half-buried car door. Somewhere under him, the ground was not behaving like ground.

Shapes moved in the smoke ahead—people, two of them, then three—and the noise they were making did not carry very far through the fire.

His phone went off in his pocket. Unknown number. He answered it because the alternative was thinking. "Yeah."

"Caden, it's Matt," came the voice on the other end, breathless. "Are you near the office?"

"I'm standing in what's left of it," Caden said. "Where are you?"

"Listen—there's something I need to tell you. It's about Robert. You can't trust him."

Caden held the phone tighter. "Say that again."

"Not over the phone. The corner of Fourth and Denk—there's a building with a hole in the side. Come in through the wall. I'll be there."

"Matt, the office just—"

"There's nothing in that rubble for you. I promise. Come."

The line went dead.

Caden lowered the phone. He looked at the wreckage of his life's work, then at James. "Stay. Pull anyone out who's still in there. I'll be back."

"To where?"

"To find Matt." Caden was already moving.

The rubble had a logic to it the way collapsed buildings did—paths through it that wanted to be paths, paths through it that did not. Caden took the ones that wanted to be. The heat off the fires came at his face in waves. He had to go past the SDS building to get to Matt's rendezvous. He kept moving. The smoke went into his lungs in a way he could feel for an hour after.

Something moved in the smoke ahead.

He stopped. "Hey."

A figure came forward through the haze. The way it moved was wrong before he could place why—too smooth in the shoulders, too slow in the neck, the same wrong he had seen in the lab three days ago. Then it straightened and turned, and the smoke thinned around it, and his stomach went cold.

"Steven." He said it before he had decided to say anything.

Steven's face was a wreck of cuts and burns, and as Caden watched, the wounds were closing. A cut along the jaw closed in front of him. A burn at the temple lost its color and went to skin. He had never seen a body do that. He could not look away from it, and he could not look at it for long.

"You shouldn't be here," Steven said, his voice hollow and unfamiliar.

"Steven. What happened to you. How are you—" He could not finish the sentence. He had locked the man in a cell three days ago.

Something passed across Steven's face—pain or something else, gone before Caden could read it. "Leave," he said, sharper. "It is not safe for you here."

"Not until you tell me what you are."

Steven took a step back. "You would not understand it if I told you."

Above them, a beam let go. A long, low groan worked its way down through the steel and the concrete and out into the air. The ground under Caden's feet shifted. He stumbled—and Steven's hand was already on his arm, holding him out of the drop, the grip wrong in a way Caden could not have placed if he'd had a year to think about it.

"Go," Steven said.

And then he was gone—back into the smoke before Caden had finished setting his feet.

"Caden!" a voice called out from behind.

He turned. James was working his way through the rubble at a hard clip, his face the color of stone. "We need to move."

"Steven was just—" He looked back at the haze. There was nothing in it. Whoever or whatever Steven was now, he was gone.

He stood with it a moment. Then a glint above caught the corner of his eye—something on the upper floors of what was left of the building. He stepped carefully across a beam to get a better angle on it.

The fourth floor. He had been on the fourth floor twice in his career and only because Robert had asked. What was up there now, exposed by the side wall coming off, were canisters—ten feet tall, lined against the back wall, full of a clear liquid he had no name for. Something dark, like a living tar, moved inside each one. Not floating. Moving the way a thing inside a body moves. One of the canisters was cracked along its midline, and the dark inside it was working at the crack from the wrong side.

"Caden." James was at his shoulder. "We have to move."

Caden pointed up. "You ever seen those?"

James followed the line of his arm. He looked at the canisters a long second. "No. What the hell were they doing on our fourth floor."

They did not get to answer the question. The cracked canister gave with a sound like a tree splitting, and a column of clear liquid came out of it in a single rush, the dark inside the liquid riding the column down like a thing that had been waiting for a door. It hit what was left of the third floor and kept moving—over the edge of the broken floor in a slow black flood, dropping onto the Dead Time lab below.

The black hit the gold suits hanging on the rack by the main console. The suits drank it. There was no other word for it. Sparks came up the leads, and then the whole console arc-flashed in a cone of blue-white that lit the underside of the rubble like daylight, and Caden felt the static come up his arms, lifting the hair on the back of his neck.

"Caden, we've got to go!" James shouted, pulling at his arm.

They did not get to. The arc-flash widened and went silent—which was the wrong way for an arc to go—and a soft pressure rolled out of the lab, across the rubble, and put Caden a step back without touching him.

Then the air in front of the rack opened.

It started as a point of light. Inside a breath it was the size of a fist. Inside two it was the size of a man. The rubble around the lab began to lift—paper first, the way it always was paper first, then the lighter office gear, then sections of broken drywall, all of it pulled toward the opening and gone into it.

"It's a rift," Caden said, and the rush of air around them ate the back half of the words. "Between stopped and real."

James grabbed his arm, yanking him back. "Whatever it is, we need to move—now!"

The pull set into them. Caden's boots went out from under him on loose grit. James caught him by the collar and they ran. Behind them the opening kept widening. He heard a car go past them in the air. He heard a streetlamp tear out of its base. He heard, somewhere to his left, the side of a building two doors down lose part of itself.

The light reached its peak—white, hot, and wrong—and then the sound stopped. All of it. The fires, the alarms three blocks over, the wind. They were running in a silence that pressed at his eardrums. When he risked a look back, the opening was gone. Where it had been was a crater, smooth-walled, perfect, in the floor of the lab.

Whatever had just opened in that lab, it was not finished.

CHAPTER 37
Azgiel—Maselda's Treetop Village

A breeze came across the canopy and found Azgiel on the balcony of Maselda's home. It carried pine, and rain somewhere off to the west, and the long warmth of a day winding down. The treetop village sprawled beneath the canopy—a marvel of careful work. Bridges of woven branches and fortified wood stretched between the massive trunks, the curves of them set into the trees themselves so the eye took a beat to find the seam. Each dwelling bore carved symbols, etched with protective magic.

It was not his castle. Triaad held that one now. He had not stood in this kind of quiet in centuries. It was not the penetrating absence of stopped time. It held sounds, but it felt soft. And it sat oddly in him.

"Do you approve?" Maselda's voice came from behind him. There was hope in it, and underneath the hope something she did not show often.

He turned. "You built it out of the trees themselves. It's remarkable."

"We had to," she said. "After Triaad. After the wars. This was the only way any of us were going to be left."

The name still moved something in him he had thought he had finished moving. Below them, an Anubite walked the path with its long jackal head bent low, going somewhere on its own business.

"And they're safe here. All of them."

"For now." She came up to the railing beside him, her arm against his. "The Anubites have the tunnels under us. The bark gnomes burrow at the base of the trees. The trolls have the lake. The rest live up here, in the branches." She looked out over the bridges. "It holds. For now."

He read her face for a long beat. He had not seen her tired this way before. "Worried about Kaz?"

Maselda did not answer right away. "Not yet. Kaz has always come back, even when the coming back was the worst choice in front of him."

195

Without Kaz, Mauldrin was on his own. Without Mauldrin, the sword was on its own. He let himself sit with that a beat. Then he stopped letting himself.

"I can't stay," he said. "I have to find him. If something has gone wrong with Kaz, sitting up here doesn't help him."

Her hand found his on the railing. "You don't know what's out there now. Two thousand years is not a thing you walk back into."

"I'll learn it as I go. Every hour we wait, Triaad builds his empire. The sword—"

"I know," she interrupted. "The sword is the key. And Mauldrin is the only one who can free it. But if you fall—" Her voice tightened. "I got you back, Azgiel. I'm not going to lose you again."

That stopped him. He could be a warrior in a great many rooms. He could not be one in this room.

"I'll come back," he promised. "I swear it."

Maselda pressed something small and cool into his palm. A charm, the kind she made by hand. "For luck. So you remember where you have to come back to." She kissed him.

He closed his fingers around the charm. He raised his hands. The air around him took on the old, familiar tension—the kind that came up before the world bent for him.

"Stay alive," she said.

Her face was the last thing he saw before the village folded itself away from him. He used an obsidian sphere to open a portal to the edge of her woods, stepped past the barrier, and used the sphere one more time before any aniborn could find him.

He came back to himself in a cold room. Broken walls and bent metal. The same room, near enough—where he had been kept, where he had nearly killed Domblin the last time the two of them stood in it. His boots came down on broken glass. The sound was the only sound in the place.

He took the room in. Dust hung in the low light coming through a hole in the outer wall the size of a man.

"Don't move, or I'll shoot!" a voice barked, shattering the stillness.

He turned. A short man in a security uniform stood ten paces away with a handgun pointed at his chest. The hands holding it were not steady. The face above them was wet with sweat, even in the cold.

"Steven?" the man said.

He let one corner of his mouth lift. "You don't know what you're looking at."

He started toward the guard. The guard's grip went looser, not tighter. "Stay back. I'll—"

He raised his hand. A short, hard pulse left his palm and took the guard off his feet. The guard hit the back wall with a sound that ended him before he reached the floor.

He let the hand fall. He had no time for any of this. Kaz first. If Kaz was not already with Mauldrin, the plan had a hole in it that he could not yet see the size of.

Footsteps in the corridor, with a voice over them.

"—not responding. If he's not down here I'll circle back through the other wing by Matt's cell." Closer. He pressed himself flat against the wall.

The man came around the corner—tall, lean, the uniform crisp on him in a way that did not match how he was holding himself. He saw Azgiel and the radio in his hand was at his mouth before the rest of him caught up. "Steven's here, sir."

Another delay.

The guard's free hand moved to the sidearm at his belt. "Don't—"

"I don't have time for you," Azgiel said, and he raised his hand to finish the sentence the way the first one had finished—and the building took the moment from him. An explosion tore through the corridor.

The blast took the corridor at the far end. He had a blue field up around himself before he had decided to put one up—older instinct than thinking. The wave came through. Fire came with it. The guard never finished the cry.

The force was bigger than he had room for. The field thinned. The field went. He was thrown.

He came back to a body that hurt. Concrete sat on his chest. More of it pinned his left arm. He could feel the weight of it before he could see anything. He opened his eyes. The room came in slow.

A piece of rebar slid free of the ceiling above him and came down on his left hand. His fingers went under it. The pain ran up his arm in a single bright line.

He pulled what was left of himself together. The rubble groaned and shifted off him, slow, slab by slab, until there was room enough for him to climb out.

He came up to his knees breathing hard. Blood ran off his ruined hand into the dust. He closed his eyes and pulled. Old work. The kind a body forgets and remembers in the same breath. Bone moved. Skin moved. The hand came back to him in three breaths, and the ache that stayed under it after was a thing he had not had to feel in centuries.

A reminder of how thin this body still was.

A voice called out behind him. "Hello."

He turned. A figure was working its way through the smoke toward him—tall, lean, dark hair gone everywhere from the blast. He recognized the figure, but the man was thinner than the memory he had been carrying.

Mauldrin.

"You shouldn't be here," he said. He let none of the rest of it through into his voice.

Mauldrin came forward another step. "Steven. What happened to you? How are you—" He could not finish.

The dust on the ground around him moved before he had thought to move it. He let his hand still it. He drew himself up. "Leave," he said. "It is not safe for you here."

"Not until you tell me what you are."

He could not have this conversation in this rubble with this man right now. There would be a time for it later. There had to be. "You would not understand it if I told you," he said.

Above them, the rest of the corridor decided what it was going to do. Another section gave—somewhere over the western wing, by the sound of it—and the floor under them rocked. He went sideways into a pillar and held it as debris came down past him.

Mauldrin's foot went out from under him on the plaster. He dropped to a knee on a section that did not have much floor left under it. Azgiel's hand was on his arm before he had thought about putting it there—the same hand he had once raised against this man, set now under his elbow to keep him from going through.

"Go," he said. He let him go.

The man in front of him was a thinner copy of the man who had locked him in stopped time. Mortal now. Thinner. Slower. And yet there was something in the eyes—the same eyes—and Azgiel could not look at it for long.

He turned and walked into the smoke without another word. He did not look back. He could feel Mauldrin watching him until the smoke took him, and then he could not feel it, which was worse.

He picked his way through the wreckage and tried to think. He needed a quiet place to put himself back together. Without one, Domblin or any other old name could find him here and end this. Kaz first. The sword after that. Everything else could wait. Ahead, the upper floors of a building had come down across the street, and underneath them the lower frame of a parking garage was still standing.

He moved toward it. He could not stay long. Kaz was not with Mauldrin. Something in the plan had broken.

He moved through the empty floors. A large van sat near the back of the second level, its body grey under a coat of ash. He checked the lot for movement, found none, pulled the side door open. Oil and old leather. He climbed in and let the bed of the van take his weight.

Something in the air shifted. He sat up. A low pull came on, somewhere behind him, and his ears caught a noise underneath the noise of the building settling.

"What now?" he said to no one. He swung out of the van and turned toward it. At the far end of the lot, the cars closest to the open side of the structure had started to shake on their suspensions, slow at first, then less slow.

Across the gap, on what was left of the fourth floor of the building he had just come out of, the air was open. Round. Bright at the edge. He knew the feel before his head named it.

A door into stopped time. Open. With nothing holding it open.

The noise climbed. The opening widened. Light came off it in pulses he could feel through his teeth. Debris off the wreckage came up off the floor and went sideways through the air toward it—paper, lighter rubble, then a section of broken wall that had been holding up nothing.

A crack came from the lot. The car directly in front of him squealed once, dragged sideways across the concrete, then lifted three feet off the ground and started for the opening.

Behind him the van started to slide. He turned and put a hand on the frame. The frame slid out from under his hand. The van came up off the floor like something insulted to be on it, twisted in the air, and went into the opening.

A chunk of ceiling came down at him. He stepped past it. Stay in control. Stay in control. Older parts of him already wanted to be elsewhere. Mauldrin had not opened it. Domblin had not opened it. No one had. It had nothing telling it where to stop.

He moved deeper into the structure. Cars came up around him as he went, twisting in the air on their way past. A streetlamp from outside tore out of its base in a shower of orange sparks and crossed the lot at the height of his head. He kept his eyes on the exit. A sedan tore loose nearby and came at him, and he put a hand out and shoved at the air, and the sedan went past him close enough to take the cuff of his coat with it.

A pressure wave came off the opening that he could not see. He felt it in his bones. He went back a step. The lot tilted on him for too long.

When the lot leveled, the opening was twice the size. The light coming off it was no longer one color. The concrete under his boots was cracking in long thin lines. Smaller debris—signage, pipework, a steel desk that had no business being airborne—went past him toward the opening.

He had not come here to be eaten by an unmade door. He moved for the nearest exit, picking around debris, leaning into the pull of the opening with his shoulder set against it.

A boom came from behind him, deeper than the others. He looked back— an SUV had missed the opening by less than a foot and come down on the concrete below in a flat shape that did not look like a vehicle anymore. The opening took one last hard pulse of light.

Then it folded in on itself, and was not there. He slowed. Where the parking lot had been around him was a ring of broken wall and smoking debris.

"Are you okay over there?" a voice called, somewhere outside the lot. The voice did something in him before the rest of him caught up to it. He had heard it before. Recently. He moved across the structure to the opposite side, away from where the opening had been, and looked through the broken outer wall.

Robert.

The man was down on one knee at a split in the rubble, working at it with his hands—pulling someone out, by the look of it. Survivors moved slow on either side of him, half-stunned, picking themselves up by inches.

"I'm going to get you some help," Robert said to whoever was under his hands, and stood, and looked around himself. He moved fast and clean. Azgiel watched from behind the broken wall as the man crossed the street toward a row of fire trucks at the edge of the rubble.

Robert flagged two firefighters and pointed back at the rubble. The smaller of them broke off at a run. Robert started back toward the building. Halfway across, he stopped. He had seen something. He had seen Azgiel.

Spotted. Time to go.

He did not go. He held where he was. Intrigue caught him. He watched Robert's face change—surprise to something steadier. There was something in this man he had marked the first time, in the lab, in the hour after he had come up out of the cell. He had not had time then to learn what it was. He had time now.

He moved behind a pillar as Robert came in through the broken outer wall. Footsteps echoed wrong off the bent metal of the lot. Robert was moving too fast for the floor he was on—he hit a patch of soot and went sideways into the side of a small white car, hard enough to leave a dent in the hood. He pushed himself upright with a grunt.

After that he slowed. He swept the lot in sections, the way a man with training swept the area. He came up to the ledge and looked out over it. "Where did you go, Steven?"

"I'm not going to make this easy for you," Azgiel said, and let the voice carry the way it could when he wanted it to. "I don't think I'll be showing myself yet."

Robert spun toward the sound. "Steven. I'm not here to hurt you. I want to help."

A short laugh got out of Azgiel before he had decided to let it. "Your lies wear the truth on the outside of them. Like a child come in from the yard with mud to his ears, swearing he never went near the puddle."

"Steven. You've known me longer than most of the men in that building. You sat at my right hand for ten years. Let me help you."

"Stop begging." He felt it underneath the begging—something in Robert that should not have been in a human at all. Faint. There. He turned the thought over and set it aside. *A waste.* "You don't know who I am. You don't even remember my real name."

"What are you talking about? We've worked together for fifteen years. We've put men in the ground together—"

"You still think I'm Steven. After you're the one who pulled me out of a Cell of Time."

Robert shook his head. "Cell of Time? Steven, you're not making sense—"

He let his head go back. "You're blind, Robert. You will never see what is in front of you."

"Then tell me," Robert demanded. "Who are you, really?"

He jumped, light, onto the roof of the car Robert had just dented. The hood of the car gave under him by less than a finger. Robert went back two steps and came up in a fighter's stance.

"That is the question," Azgiel said. "Since you're asking. My name is Azgiel. I was put in a Cell of Time, and I was kept there."

Robert's hands came down. "I still don't know what that is. Humor me. How?"

"For doing the things your precious Caden would call evil."

Robert took a step closer. "Caden put you there. That's—that's not a thing."

The smile went out of him. "You have no idea what Caden is. Or what he did to me. Better, maybe, that you don't."

Robert moved. He came in fast and low for a man his size, aiming to put Azgiel into the side of the car. He let him close. He caught the wrist on the way past, turned it, and put Robert face-down on the windshield. The windshield gave with a sound like ice. Robert made a noise into the broken glass that was not a word.

He stepped back. "I'll give you one more chance, Robert. Stand with me. I have things to give a man like you that you do not yet know to want. A world that will amaze you."

Robert came up off the glass with blood on his face. "You are out of your mind."

The corner of his mouth lifted. "Maybe. The offer stands. Don't waste it."

Robert's answer was another lunge. He turned every strike, picked his moment, took an arm and put him down. He set a knee on his chest.

"You're out of your depth," Azgiel said. "Maybe it's time you saw the truth."

He set his palm on Robert's forehead. The current that went through it was small. What it carried was not. Old battles. Old courts. Old names. Robert's back came up off the concrete in a slow arch. His eyes opened too wide and would not close.

He lifted the hand. "That should clarify a few things."

Robert tried to sit up. He did not get there. "I don't—"

"You probably never will. My business is somewhere else tonight. If you put yourself in front of it again, I will move you out of the way the same way I move anything else."

Robert came at him again. He did not have to. He chose to. Azgiel respected that more than he wanted to. He set his weight, drew his fist back, and let what was in his arm come up into his fist. A blue-white field gathered along the knuckles. *Too much. Let it be too much.* He pulled the blow as it left him, the field along his knuckles bleeding off into the air at the last fraction of an inch.

The punch landed under what was left of the field. The sound of it carried across the lot. Robert went off his feet and into the concrete pillar behind him hard enough that the pillar took the shape of his shoulder for a moment before the dust of it came down. He slid down the pillar to the floor and did not get up.

Azgiel crossed to him and crouched. He laid a hand on Robert's chest. It moved. Once. Again. Slow, but moving. He stood. He let the field around his hand fade until it was hand again. Far off, sirens. Closer in, a fire still working.

The lot was quiet otherwise.

"You'll have a long evening when you wake up, Robert," he said, more to himself than to the man on the concrete. "I hope you put it to use."

Kaz. Kaz first. He told himself that on the way out of the lot, and again at the stairwell, and a third time in the dark of the street. The third time it almost held.

CHAPTER 38
Caden—On the Street

Caden hit redial as he came around the corner away from the SDS rubble. James had stayed with the rescue at the building. Caden had told him he would not be long. He was already not believing it.

The line connected on the second ring.

"Caden. Glad you called back." Matt's voice, choppy through the static.

"Fourth and Denk. I'm two blocks out."

"No good. I had to move. It's too dangerous to stay there—for both of us."

In the distance, sirens stacked on top of each other as more emergency vehicles came down on the SDS block.

"Where?" Caden said.

"If I were you, I'd leave now," Matt said, sharper. "We can meet later."

Two police cars came around the far corner and braked hard at the curb in front of him. Doors opened on both sides. Officers were out before the cars had finished rocking on their suspensions. One of them pointed at Caden and said something to the others Caden could not catch.

He turned a quarter step, kept the phone where it was. "How about you tell me what's really going on? No more games. We've known each other too long for this."

"Hands where I can see them!"

He froze. More cruisers arrived behind the first two, sirens cutting off in mid-wail. Officers came out with weapons drawn. Through the phone he could hear Matt saying his name once, twice. The words were too far down the line to reach him.

"What's your name?" The closest officer came forward with a printed sheet held up at chest height. Three more behind him with their pistols leveled.

"There's been a mistake." Caden raised his hands halfway, slow. "I'm with you. I'm here to help." He was already counting the gun under his jacket. If they searched him, the situation was going to find a worse shape than it already had.

"It's him. Take him into custody."

He caught the page in the man's hand as the officer walked past. A photo of himself. Name. Age. Height. Weight.

"Wait—" He shifted toward the officer.

"He's got a gun!"

That was all it took. He went for the Dead Time switch on his wrist, and an officer hit him from behind before his hand got there. He went down on the pavement on a knee and a hip and a hand, the phone leaving his other hand and skidding under a cruiser. He pushed off and snagged it, throwing it back in his pocket. A cuff closed on his left wrist. The world contracted to the cold metal and the cold concrete and the next move.

He twisted on the ground, took the officer down by the arm of the cuff, drove the man's face into the pavement. He came up under another officer's swinging baton. He swept that one's leg from under him, and the man went over backwards and hit the curb.

A third came in with a club. Caden caught it on the upswing, used the man's own weight to walk him forward into a kick that took him off his feet.

A pistol hammer went back somewhere on his right. He kicked a chunk of broken curb at the officer's face—not to hit, to break the line of sight. The officer flinched, and Caden was on him before the gun came back level. He took the gun. Let it fall.

The first officer was still attached to the cuff on his wrist. The man would not let go of it. Another came in with a nightstick. Caden grabbed the stop sign at the corner with his free hand for leverage and slung the cuffed officer in a half-arc into the second one. They went down in a tangle.

They're doing their job. Don't kill them. He held the thought and let it slow him.

Three more came at him at once. He went into them low. One overcommitted. Caden put him into the metal pole he had just used. A shot cracked from somewhere behind him and the pole rang. He felt it in his teeth.

Enough.

He kicked the shooter's wrist sideways and felt the bone go. Took him by the collar before he dropped, drove two fingers into the side of his neck—hard enough to put him out, not hard enough to kill—and dragged him toward the alley as the rest of the line tried to find an angle that did not include their own man's body in the way.

He shoved the unconscious officer back at them at the mouth of the alley and ran.

A brick wall at the end. He pushed off his lead foot, snagged the bottom rung of a fire ladder, pulled himself over the top. As he came down on the far side a sting went into his shoulder. He reached back. A tranquilizer dart, the feathers wet from his own sweat. He pulled it out and dropped it.

The drug was already in him. His legs went heavy three steps in. The sound of the alley dropped a register. He was running on a body that was not entirely his anymore.

A car braked at the curb. A door opened. A man got out fast.

"Caden."

Matt. Of course it was Matt.

His knees gave. Matt took his weight before he hit the ground. Caden went into the back seat of the car and the back seat went away from him in pieces.

* * *

He came back in pieces too.

A leather couch. The smooth of it cool against the side of his face. The smell of new paint and old coffee and something else under both. He pushed himself up on an elbow. The room held still.

"Good. You're awake."

Matt. Across the room, in a folding chair, hands loose on his knees. A whiteboard behind him crowded with maps and pinned notes. A man Caden did not know was in the doorway, going out, not in. The door clicked behind him.

Caden sat up the rest of the way. He looked down at his wrist. The cuff was gone, but it had left a band of dark bruising under it. He turned his hand over and watched it not stop hurting.

"Where did you bring me?"

"My team's base. I heard the commotion through the phone. I came and got you."

He drew a long breath and let the headache fall back behind it. He could not afford to look as taken apart as he was. Not in this room.

"Your base? What base? How did you get out of your cell?"

A beat. "Some of my men got me out."

"Your men?"

"My men."

"You've been building a team? Behind my back?"

The corner of Matt's mouth lifted. "Don't act so surprised. You were starting to see it by the end."

"No," Caden said. "I wasn't. I knew you had channels for intel. I didn't know you had this." He looked at the whiteboard. The maps were of the city. Some of the markings were on places he knew. Some he did not. "What are you doing with them?"

Matt opened his arms to the room. "All of this—for one purpose. To take down SDS. To take down what's running it."

The words landed where they were meant to land.

"You're the bomb."

Matt did not answer right away. When he did his voice was quieter than Caden had ever heard it. "Yes. I planted the bomb. It was necessary."

"Necessary." Caden was on his feet without remembering standing. "There were people in that building, Matt. Our people. People you knew by name. You don't get to use that word."

"You don't have it all yet. Listen to me." Matt held up a hand. "Robert is not who you think. He's been taking orders from above him. T.R.I.A.A.D.—that's the name on the orders. The plan is to clear out anyone they've decided is unfit for the world they want to build. They've engineered a substance to rewrite DNA. Once they have their template, they intend to use Dead Time and the rest of it to wipe whole populations off the map."

Caden's hands closed at his sides. "That's insane. Robert would never put his name to anything like that."

"You're too trusting. You've always been too trusting. You don't question the people closest to you."

Memory ran without his permission. Matt in his office at an off-hour. Robert at the briefing, hands not quite steady. Doubt slid in under the rest of it. Stay rational. Stay where you are.

"So you blew up the building," Caden said. "Because of a conspiracy."

"That building was a hub. Taking it down was step one. We planted records in the rubble. When the dig comes through it, the records come up with it, and the rest of it has to come with them."

"And when it does, you put a new government in place? That's what this is? Power?"

"It's not about power. It's about replacing what's broken with what isn't. We hold elections. We make sure the people who win are people who can lead."

"By rigging the process."

Matt's face went tight. "The system is already rigged. This is the only way."

"Even if you're right." Caden's voice came up a half-step. "Even if every word of it is true. People are dead. You lied to me. To James. To everyone in that office. You don't walk that back."

Matt stood. His tone softened a quarter, no more. "I know. I had to. But— I brought you here because I want you with me. You're my friend. I need you on this team."

Caden looked at him a long second. Hurt and rage worked through him in alternating pulses, neither one winning. "You betrayed me, Matt. You betrayed everything we stood for."

The room went taut. Matt reached into his jacket and brought out a pistol. He did not point it at Caden. He did not have to. "Don't get any ideas. I didn't bring you here for a fight."

A letter opener lay on the side table at Caden's hip. He clocked the distance to it, the distance from it to Matt, the angle of Matt's gun hand. The numbers were not in his favor. They were not far out of it either.

"I can't believe you're the spy," Caden said. "After everything we've been through. Was it your men on the plane? Was that you?"

"That wasn't supposed to happen." Matt almost said it like an apology. "Justin got carried away. The order was to retrieve your watches. Not to bring the plane down."

"Justin. The bald one in your team's gear who broke into SDS." It was not a question.

"He's overzealous. He's also the reason we're as far along as we are."

"He's a lunatic." Caden made himself laugh once. "How do you know he isn't running you? Planting evidence to point you the way he wants you pointed."

"You're wrong about him. Justin would never betray me."

"Same way you'd never betray me?"

Matt flinched. He covered it.

"I'm not arguing with you, Caden. I'm offering you a choice. Come in with me, or stay where you are and watch it burn. It's about to get bad. For you. For James. For Bridget. For everyone you've got. Once it starts there's no closing it."

His fingers were on the letter opener before the rest of him had decided. He threw it. The blade left his hand fast and level.

It froze midair.

Matt's wrist was at the Dead Time switch on his arm. They were both inside stopped time now, and Matt had the gun hand free. Caden had a half-second on him and a worse weapon. He used the half-second.

He came under the line of the gun and took Matt off his feet. They went down together. Matt was strong and trained, and Caden was both of those and angrier. He pinned him face-down. Knee against the back of his neck. Took the gun. Reached for his own switch and brought time back.

The world resumed in the small sounds of the room—the hum of the building, the air moving in a vent, the man under his knee breathing through his teeth.

"Why didn't you come to me when you first thought you had this," Caden said. "Before the bomb. Before the bodies. Before any of it."

"You wouldn't have listened." Matt's mouth was against the floor. "You're not listening now."

The betrayal came down on him then in a slow weight, settling along his shoulders, fitting itself to him for the wear. "I can't trust you, Matt. Not after this." Even if Matt was right about Robert, this wasn't the way.

"Then disappear. When this comes out, you'll be a target."

He let Matt up. He kept the gun. His hands were shaking and he did not care.

"If you're lying about any of this," he said, "I'll come for you. Next time I won't stop."

Matt rubbed his neck. "I'm not lying. You'll see. When it comes, my offer still stands."

Caden did not answer him. He walked out of the room.

In the hallway he hit the switch on his wrist and the corridor went into the quiet of stopped time around him. The overhead lights held their flicker. The shadows under them stayed where they were. He moved past two doors before he saw them.

He stopped.

The air at the far end of the hall was wrong. He squinted into it until his eyes resolved them: eight figures, holding to the walls and the floor and the ceiling, black as oil, their joints bent in places joints did not bend.

One of them screamed.

The sound went through his head sideways. Not through his ears. He had his hand on the switch before he knew he had moved it. The sound cut. Time came back in.

The hallway was empty.

He stood with his hand on the wall to stop his breath from going where it wanted to go. Focus. Move.

He went toward the stairwell door.

A motion at the corner of his eye. He looked up. One of the black creatures was on the ceiling above him, half-there, half-not, the rest of it filling in as he watched.

Hallucination. He told himself the word.

It moved.

He grabbed a lamp off a console table and threw it. The thing came off the ceiling sideways out of the path of it. The lamp hit the wall and broke. The thing did not break.

"Stay back."

A door three down the corridor opened. A guard came out with a sidearm up. "Halt!"

"Wait—"

The thing dropped off the ceiling onto the guard's shoulders. The guard's body locked up under it. The scream was short. The skin of his face went the color of paper. Dark lines spread up out of his collar and across his cheek. He went down. The pistol hit the floor and slid.

Caden ran.

He hit the exit door at speed and went through it.

A red shape stood on the stairs.

Kaz. The same demon from the beach condo. Wings folded high on his back, the shape of them taking up half the landing. He looked at Caden once. Then he was past him, through the door, pulling it off its hinges as he went. Caden heard a sound from the hall behind him that he did not want to put a name to.

Do I follow him. Do I run.

He ran.

He took the stairs two at a time and came out into an alley behind the building. A man in black tactical gear had a pistol on him before his foot hit the asphalt.

"Freeze!"

Amateur.

Caden was inside the man's reach in two steps. He took the wrist, took the gun, took the man's leg out from under him with a sweep. The man went down whimpering, hands up. Caden put the gun on him.

"Stay down. Or you don't get up."

He moved. The drug was out of his system, mostly; what was in him now was the shake of something else, every sense turned up too far, the seams of the world showing where they should not show. He had to get a cab. He had to get to the airport. Bridget. He had to get to Bridget.

The thought of losing her closed around his throat and would not let go.

I'm coming for you.

CHAPTER 39
Caden—City Streets

A block from Matt's building he slowed his pace. If Matt's people were going to come for him, they were already coming. Running drew eyes and the eyes drew sirens and the sirens drew the rest of the world.

The street he was on had not been kept up in a long time. Trash piled along the curbs. A line of cars at the edge of the asphalt that had not moved in months, two of them on rims. From a side street up ahead, a man's voice and a woman's voice working their way up an argument neither of them was going to win.

A low car went past him with its windows down. Three men inside in dark jackets, not looking at him on purpose. He kept his head down and kept walking. The last thing he could afford right now was a cop responding to a call.

His phone buzzed. He had it at his ear on the second pulse.

"Caden." Her voice came at him in a rush, words running together. "Tell me where you are."

"I'm not sure." He stepped around a collapsed garbage bag. Something in it moved. He moved faster. "I'm coming back to you. I'll be there tonight."

"Tell me where to meet you. I'll come get you. We'll go home together."

"That's too far. You'd have to fly to me." He glanced behind him for the third time in a block. Empty street. "I'm getting to the airport. I'll catch the next flight. I'll explain when we're together."

"I'm at the airport," Bridget said.

He stopped walking.

"I flew out. I'm here. Tell me where you are. I'll rent a car and pick you up." Background voices came through her end of the line. He'd been so out of his head he hadn't placed it until now. She was already in a terminal.

"I told you not to come."

"After you survived a plane crash? Did you really think I'd sit in the condo and wait for you? Come on, Caden. When have I ever sat for that?"

She had not. The first time he had met her, it had been at the military hospital, and she had been the first person through every door, every time, regardless of what was on the other side of it.

"Fine," he said. "Get us tickets back to the condo. It's safer there. I'll be at the airport in an hour. We'll talk when we're somewhere we can."

"Does this have to do with the building? It's all over the news. Or with Azgiel—is he in this?" There was fear in her voice now. He had not heard it from her before.

"I'll explain when I see you. I promise. Right now I just need you to trust me."

A long pause on her end of the line. Then a breath. "An hour."

"An hour."

"I'll get the tickets." Her voice clipped on the words.

"I love you."

"Love you too."

She hung up.

Two cabs idled at the curb in front of a bar across the main street. He crossed to them. The first driver took one look at him and reached over to lock his door. The second only nodded.

The driver said nothing the whole ride. That suited Caden. He needed the silence to put the inside of his head back in some kind of order. The city went past the window in lights and the lights went past faster than he could read them. Am I being followed. Did Matt put a tracker on me. No way to know. He couldn't afford to assume he wasn't.

When the cab pulled up to the airport she was already on her feet, coming off a concrete bench by the doors. She came at him at a run and got her arms around him before he had the door of the cab fully closed.

"I got the tickets. You're lucky. Plane leaves soon." She started pulling on him as she spoke.

"Glad I made it." He let his face rest against her hair for a second longer than he should have, ignoring her pull. The last few days fell off him. He picked them back up. "Let's go."

They went through the airport quiet, side by side. Caden had his eyes everywhere. Security barely looked up when they came past. No alerts on the boards. No one at the gate doing more than processing tickets. It made no sense to him, and he made himself accept that it did not have to make sense for them to use it. His SDS badge got him and the gun through screening without a second look. Nothing on the system flagged him. His face should have been on every screen in this terminal after what had happened on that street. None of it was. That was wrong, and he knew it was wrong, and he kept walking.

The flight was tight. He had asked her to keep talk to a minimum and she had agreed, and the agreement put a weight between them that neither one of them put down. She watched the window. He watched the seat-back in front of him and tried to think.

When they landed he rented a car at the counter and let her drive. She did better behind a wheel when she had something to hold onto, and right now, after a day like she had had, she needed something to hold onto. He sat in the passenger seat with the gun he had taken from the guard tucked under his jacket and a hand on her knee.

She started telling him about the professor before they were out of the lot.

"He changed, Caden. After he touched the rune in the book. His eyes— there was fire in them. Real fire."

He listened. He did not interrupt. The car got onto the highway and the lights of the lot fell away behind them.

"The book," she said. "It calls Azgiel a guardian and a tyrant in the same paragraph. It says he comes back through a fracture in time. Caden, what if what came out of stopped time at SDS—what if it's him."

The thought went into him and did not come back out. He worked through it and tried to fit it against what he had seen in the smoke, in the corridor, on the fourth floor.

"You're saying what we let out of stopped time is Azgiel."

"I'm pretty sure it is."

He rubbed his temples with his free hand. "Then SDS opened a door we didn't know was there. And what came through is something we don't know how to put back."

The road hissed under them. He rolled his shoulders to put the tightness somewhere else. "There is too much happening at once. I don't know what the next move is. I know the next move has to be keeping you safe. Azgiel is bigger than I can carry tonight. He'll have to wait."

She was quiet. Then: "What about your end. The plane crash. The building."

"I don't know where to start." He sighed it. "The building on the news was SDS. Matt brought it down. He thinks Robert is part of something bigger— that the people running the agency are working a plan to engineer a 'better' world. They're rewriting DNA. He kidnapped me. I got out."

He waited for the disbelief in her face. It did not come. Her hands tightened on the wheel until her knuckles went pale.

"You've been through a lot," she said. "What do you think?"

"I don't know what I think. I've seen enough to make me question all of it. I can't make Matt's methods sit right." His voice gave out for a second. "I'm a wanted man, Bridget. That's why getting you somewhere safe is the only thing that matters right now."

"It feels like everything has come apart in three days." Her voice held even. "I love you. We'll get through it the way we've gotten through everything else."

He looked over at her. The light off the dash put her in profile. The line of her jaw and the loose strand of hair at her temple and the steady, set way she was driving.

The condo came up at the end of the road. She turned in. The driveway lights were on, low and warm, the way she always set them before she left. She put the car in park and turned to him.

"I want to be here for you," she said. "It's a lot. I'm here."

"Thank you."

"Always."

He leaned across the console. She met him halfway. He kissed her, soft at first. The promise in it was the kind of promise he had no business making and made anyway.

A crack split the air.

She jerked. Her body slammed back against the seat. The windshield in front of her took on a starburst of fracture and the glass behind her shoulder went red.

"No—" The word came out before he had decided to make it one.

He pulled her down across the console and into him. He had his hand on the wound before the rest of him had caught up. The blood was warm. It was coming through his fingers faster than he could close on it.

"Bridget. Stay with me. Stay with me."

Her eyes were on his. They were full of water. "I—I don't want to die." Her voice was already going thin. "Caden—"

"You're not going to. You're going to be fine. Hold on."

She tried to say something else. The words did not arrive. The breath she was working on did not finish. Her body went heavy in his arms in the way bodies go heavy.

He could not move. The weight of her against his chest broke something he did not have a word for. The silence was loud. His hands were red and shaking when he brought them up to her face.

"Bridget." His voice came out hollow. "I'm sorry. I'm sorry. I failed you."

A second shot punched through the windshield. The seat-back beside his head erupted in stuffing and torn cloth. He's still out there.

He laid her back across the seat as gently as a man with shaking hands could lay anything. His clothes were soaked through with her. The warmth of her was already going. He felt the moment it started to leave.

The grief that had been in his chest a second ago was something else now. It was a thing with a job to do.

He pulled the pistol from under his jacket and shouldered the door open. A round took the doorframe an inch from his ear. He went low, came around the back of the car, and stayed in the cover of the trunk while he scanned the dim of the driveway.

A twig snapped to his left.

He pivoted and fired twice. A figure crumpled into the grass at the edge of the property and tried to crawl, one arm working, the rest of him not.

Rage came up into Caden as a kind of clarity. He walked the figure down across the lawn, and he emptied the rest of the magazine into him in a steady cadence, one after the other, each shot a punctuation he did not have words for.

The slide locked back. He stood over the body a moment longer, then holstered the pistol.

The man on the ground was a kid. Twenty at the outside. His face was fixed in a grimace that was already going slack. Caden looked at him and tried to make his head do the thing where it figured out who had sent him. SDS, looking for the man who had brought down their building. Matt's people, cleaning up the friend who would not come in. T.R.I.A.A.D., taking out the loose end before the records came up. Some piece of the agency he did not yet have a name for. He couldn't sort it. Not now. He couldn't even hold the question.

A rifle lay across the kid's chest. Caden picked it up. Walked back to the car.

He opened the door. Slid in. Looked at the love of his life.

She had been the color of life a few minutes ago. She was not anymore.

He brushed the strand of hair off her face. "I'm sorry."

His phone vibrated against his hip. He almost threw it. The name on the screen stopped him.

James.

He opened the message.

James: The president has been assassinated.

A video had loaded under the line of text. He pressed it.

Grainy footage. A figure in dark gear moving through a hallway, stepping over fallen guards without breaking stride, not slowing, not hurrying. He drew a pistol at the door of an office. The door opened. He raised the pistol. He fired once. Inside, a man dropped.

Justin.

The man from the plane. The man at SDS. Now this.

The video kept playing and he stopped seeing it. His eyes were back on Bridget. The rest of the world was something happening to other people, far down a corridor.

The phone slid out of his hand.

Headlights came up the road at the bottom of the driveway. He did not move. Whoever it was, whatever they were, they could come.

He pulled the Dead Time switch off his wrist and threw it into the dirt at his feet. The little metal sound it made was the only sound on the property.

Then it wasn't.

The treeline at the edge of the property started moving. Not in wind. In bodies. A low rumble worked up out of the ground under his feet, the kind of sound a thing makes when it is too big to make any other sound.

A cry split the night, a sound that was not from a throat shaped like a throat.

He turned toward it. He did not turn fast enough. Claws came at him from the side and took him off his feet. The ground hit him hard. The air went out of him. He did not get to push himself up. They were on him before he could try.

Cold hands. Black. The grip on his wrists colder than skin had any business being.

"Mauldrin."

The whisper came from one of them. He did not see which.

"No—" He thrashed under the weight of them. His body strained and did not move them an inch. The claws went deeper. Is this it?

A flare ripped across the dark.

It came so bright his eyelids stayed orange when he closed them. The creatures shrieked at the same instant, a sound that ran up and out of every direction at once. The cold hands were gone off him. The weight was gone. He could feel his arms again.

He pushed up to his knees, coughing, trying to find air. His vision came back in pieces. A figure stood in the center of the light, a staff in his hand, the head of the staff still spitting small blue arcs.

"Get up," the figure said. Calm. Not loud.

Domblin.

He got his hand on the side of the car and pulled himself up. He leaned on it. His body had taken too much. His head was going in and out.

"You—are you real. Am I dreaming?"

"I am very real," Domblin said, coming closer, the same easy authority. "And I am here to help you. We do not have time for you to work this out."

Caden's hands shook at his sides. He set his jaw against it. "What were those things?"

"Aniborn. They were sent for you. They serve a master older and worse than I have time to explain to you here."

He looked at the trees. Things were still in them. He could see the shapes of them in the spaces between. The light from Domblin's staff held them off and they did not like it and they were not leaving.

"You expect me to trust you," Caden said. His own voice came out harder than he had meant it to. "You show up out of nothing and tell me to come?"

"I expect you to stay alive. Right now, that is what trusting me looks like."

A terrifying scream tore through the dark. The aniborn started forward. From every line of cover at once, a low murmur started up in a language he did not know. They came in fast.

Domblin pivoted on the ball of his foot and brought the staff up. The air around them rang with something Caden could feel in his molars. A shield of light went up around the two of them in a sphere. The aniborn that hit it bounced.

"We are out of time," Domblin said. "If you stay, they will kill you."

Caden did not move. "I'm not leaving Bridget."

"Mauldrin—"

A sound from the brush. Something heavier than the rest of them.

A shape came forward out of the dark, slow and careful, every movement of it for the hunt. It crouched at the edge of the driveway, just outside the headlights. Its body was wet-black, slick, the surface of it moving on its own. The other aniborn had spread in a half-ring at the edge of the headlights. Waiting on him.

He knew it. He had seen it before, in the lab, on the beach.

"Mauldrin." The word from its mouth came out like a piece of metal dragging across stone. The headlights of the car flickered at the sound.

Domblin set himself between the creature and Caden.

"You're not going to touch him, Tagen."

The creature held still a beat. Surprised, maybe, that Domblin had its name.

"One way or another." Tagen's voice came out distorted and wrong. "He'll be mine." The air went colder around him as he came another step in. "Triaad is on his way."

"Triaad is not getting near him either," Domblin said. He tightened his grip on the staff. The light around them brightened.

Caden stayed by Bridget's body. The exhaustion and the grief had locked the rest of his body up. He watched all of it from a distance that should not have been possible, given that he was three steps from the creature.

"Triaad is coming for you," Tagen said. There was an arrogance in the rasp of it. "I'll take Mauldrin before he gets here." Black roots came up out of the ground at the creature's feet. They moved out across the dirt in lines, slow and patient, every one of them coming on for Domblin and Caden.

Domblin's face hardened. Light flared off his hand and burned the roots back from where they were reaching. He shifted his stance. "You are not taking him. Not tonight. Not ever."

Caden tried to move and could not. The night had landed on him in full. "What is happening?" He got the words out against the side of the car.

Domblin turned to him. The voice that came out of him was not asking.

"Sleep now."

"What—no—"

Domblin's hand moved in a small precise arc.

Caden's eyelids weighed more than he could lift. He fought it. The fight did not last. The unconscious took him in one downward pull.

The last thing he saw was Domblin raising the staff as the creatures lunged.

CHAPTER 40

Azgiel—City Park

The park had emptied out before the dark had finished coming on. The paths were lined with old trees, the kind that had been growing here long enough to stop noticing the city around them. Azgiel moved through them at a hard walk. He had been on his feet for hours, working a scent trail that kept thinning and coming back. The scents of Kaz and of Mauldrin had braided together, faint at first, then less faint. He was close.

Beyond the far edge of the park, a few blocks of low-rise commercial held against the sky in silhouette. The buildings had not been kept up. Half the windows were dark.

"Turn around slowly. Or I will shoot you."

He stopped. He turned his head in the direction of the voice.

Twelve men stepped out from cover in a half-circle, body armor over dark fatigues, helmets that hid their faces, semi-automatic rifles up and steady. The closest of them keyed a mic at his shoulder.

"Confirmed. It's him."

Azgiel let one corner of his mouth lift. Mortals. He read them the way a man read a chessboard. Their weight was on their lead feet. Their hands were too tight on their grips. Their armor and their hardware would have been a problem for a man. They were not the problem they thought they were.

"Who do you think I am?" he said.

"Steven Torn."

Azgiel laughed once. "And who might you be?"

"You don't need that information."

He tilted his head. "What's the plan, then. Are you going to stand here all night holding those, or are you going to use them?"

"Shut up."

"Come now. You can't answer a simple question?"

The man at the front of the line said nothing. After two thousand years in a

217

cell, even the back-and-forth of soldiers passing time was novel. He did not have time for it. He took a few seconds of it anyway.

The lead man's earpiece crackled. His face shifted under the helmet. "What? The president is dead? Confirmed?"

A pause.

"Understood. Lock the city down." His hand came up. "This is over. Come with us, or we shoot."

The smile went off Azgiel's face. He turned his back to them.

"Gentlemen, this has been entertaining." He started walking. "I have other business."

"Stop. Last warning."

He kept walking.

"Your choice."

The first shot was a warning round, set wide on purpose. The second was not. He felt it coming a half-second before it arrived. He turned, raised a hand, and caught the bullet between two fingers. He held it there long enough to be sure they had seen him do it. Then he turned the hand over.

The bullet became a small white flower in his palm.

He let it fall. The petals turned in the air on the way down and settled in the grass.

The half-circle of men did not move for a long beat.

"Fire."

The line let go at once. The air around him cracked open in a hail. He raised both hands. A small ripple of pressure went out from him in a sphere. Every round that came into it stopped, hung, then went the way it had come.

Three of the men went down where they stood. The rest of the rounds met armor and threw the men backwards into the dirt.

One of the soldiers came up off the grass with a knife in his hand and ran at him. Azgiel let him close. The knife came at his ribs in a hard overhand. He was not where the knife came down. He stepped past, caught the wrist, let the man's own momentum carry him onto his front. The blade hit the side of Azgiel's other hand and broke into pieces.

Three of the others were already running for the treeline. He let them.

One of the wounded on the ground had pulled the pin on a grenade and underhanded it at his feet. He saw the curve of the throw before the pin came clear. He had the field up before the grenade landed.

The blast lifted him off the grass and set him back down. Fire wrapped around the field and rolled off it. The smoke cleared.

Bodies in the grass. A small fire in the underbrush at the path's edge. The trees nearest to him had taken the heat and were starting to come back to themselves, the leaves on the lower branches gone black at the tips.

He looked down. Warm wet at his thigh. He pulled the fabric of his pants open. A piece of metal the length of a pencil had gone in a half-inch under the skin. He worked it out with his fingers and dropped it. The wound began to close.

The closing was slower than it should have been. He watched the skin work and felt the ache go on after the skin had finished.

My power is still thin, he thought. Healing takes longer than it should. I can't afford to take any more damage in this body.

A heavy shape came down behind him. He did not have to turn.

"Sir," Kaz said. The wings folded with a low rasp. "I did not expect you here."

"I have been trying to find you. I came to help with Mauldrin. You have been hard to track."

Kaz's expression was grim. "Good news and bad."

"Go."

"The bad. The aniborn know about Mauldrin. They have been hunting him."

"And the good."

"I have been able to keep them off him twice. I think he is starting to understand we are not the threat."

Azgiel inclined his head. "Where is he now?"

A beat. "I lost him again. Each time the aniborn came at me, by the time I was clear of them, he was already gone. I was trying to pick him back up when I caught your scent."

He started to answer.

The crack of a rifle went off behind them. A round took him through the shoulder and turned him a quarter step. The pain came a beat after the blow. Kaz was airborne before the round had finished traveling, hunting the angle the shot had come from.

Azgiel turned. One of the wounded had crawled back into a firing position. The man got off another round. It hit Kaz in the wing, then the chest. Kaz did not slow. He came down on the man like a piece of weather and took the rifle out of his hands with the sword. It went in two pieces, and the man's fingers went with them.

The man tried to scream and Kaz did not let him. The sword came up and went down once. Kaz lifted what was left of him and threw it into the brush.

He turned back to Azgiel, sheathing the blade. Rolled the shoulder of the wing that had taken the round. The wing flexed and held. "Let's move."

"How long has it been since you lost him?"

"An hour."

Azgiel set his hand against his shoulder and felt the wound finish. The blood already on the front of his shirt was going to stay there. He stepped over a body. "Which way?"

Kaz spread his hands. "Faster by air. It is dark enough now."

"Go."

Kaz took him under both arms and beat his wings down once, hard, and the city dropped away. The lurch took Azgiel's stomach for a second and he set it aside. His mind was already on Mauldrin. The boy who had been a man who had been a king, who did not yet know any of those things. The plan was still the plan. He had to get to him before Triaad's people did.

* * *

They came down hours later on a stretch of coast. A modest building stood at the edge of the dunes—three or four units of beach condominiums, the kind built for retirees and weekend renters. A car sat in the driveway of the unit nearest the building, the windshield holed in two places, the driver's door hanging open. The headlights were still on.

"Is he in there?" Azgiel slowed at the edge of the property and let his gaze settle on the car. "Wait. Do you feel that?"

Kaz growled low in his chest. "Domblin has been here. The trail runs strange. I can't tell whether they are still inside."

He went toward the open door of the condo first. Kaz came in behind him. The boards under Kaz creaked.

The room was a wreck. Black streaks ran along the floor in lines, like something had been dragged through and burned as it went. A whole section of one wall was gone—pulled out and not pushed in, by the look of the damage. A shattered television was set into the opposite wall at chest height like a piece of art. Two skeletons lay on the floor at the far side of the room, the bones gone soft, the surfaces gleaming wet.

He had seen Domblin's work before. This was Domblin's work.

"Sir." Kaz had his head down, looking at something on the floor near the couch. He bent and lifted a leather-bound book out of the wreckage.

"What is it?"

Kaz turned it in his hands. "It's Cerilia's. She wrote it to make you sound like a terrifying monster to your enemies."

Azgiel was at his side in three steps. "Maselda's sister?"

"Yes." Kaz opened the cover. "She made it after the war with Mauldrin. A book to hold your story. Something her line could pass on. She was killed before the second war ended. Her children were never accounted for."

"How does it come to be here?" Azgiel took the book from him and turned the pages. They were old. The hand that had written the early pages was Cerilia's. He would have known it anywhere. Kaz moved away to look through the rest of the room.

"Look at the back," Azgiel said. "Her children's names. Her grandchildren's. They keep going. They stop—"

Kaz cut him off. "That's Mauldrin's wife. Bridget." He had stopped at the broken doorframe. He pointed with his sword toward the car in the driveway. His voice came out lower than usual. "She's gone."

Azgiel set the book down on the table by the couch. He went past Kaz faster than he meant to. Out the door. Across the gravel. He came around the open car door and dropped into a crouch.

She was on her side across the seats. The window above her had a hole in it. Her hair was dark with blood at the temple. The front of her shirt was the kind of red that did not stop being red. He laid a hand under her chin and tilted her head up gently. He thumbed one eyelid open.

"You are sure it is her?"

"I am." Kaz came up at his shoulder. "I saw them together while trailing Mauldrin."

Azgiel held still for a count of three. He did not move the hand under her jaw. He set the other hand on her chest and let the line of his palm settle against the bone of her sternum. He began to chant, low, the way he had not chanted in two thousand years. The words came back to him as old words do.

A blue light spread out of his palm. It moved along her, slow, the way light moved across water. Her skin took the blue, then her muscle, then deeper. The structure of her was visible in the light for a moment. A heart not moving in its place, and at the center of the heart, a small white spark, the size of a grain.

Still there. Just.

He lifted his hand. The light went with it. The spark stayed in the dark of her where he could not see it now, but where he had felt it.

He stood up. His expression had set hard.

"There is still time," he said. "Get us to Maselda. Now."

Kaz had the obsidian orb out of his pouch before Azgiel had finished the sentence. He cradled it in both clawed hands. The air around him drew tight and began to bend. The light off it rippled in a way Azgiel could feel through his teeth.

He bent and took Bridget into his arms. She weighed less than she should have. He stepped into the bend in the air with her, Kaz at his side.

The driveway behind them held its small ruin—broken glass on the gravel, the dark of her blood on the seat of the car, the headlights still on in the night, the open front door of the condo, the book on the table inside. The portal closed behind them with the sound of a small door shutting in another room.

Then the property was quiet. The wind off the water came up the slope and worked through the broken window of the condo. The fire in the underbrush had not started. The world held still and waited.

CHAPTER 41
Caden—Cabin in the Pines

The lights were out when Caden woke. His head felt split. He blinked at a ceiling he did not know and listened, and the silence held. He sat up slowly.

Then it hit him. Bridget.

The driveway. The weight of her in his arms going wrong. Her eyes on him while the words she was working on did not arrive. The warmth of her leaving. He closed his hands into fists and the bedframe groaned under them.

The room came in around him a piece at a time. Rough log walls. A dresser that was not his. A single window with the dark pressed up against it. The air had the close, woodsmoke smell of a place that had been shut up a long time.

A dream. Tell yourself it was a dream. Dead Time. Matt. Robert. The things in the corridor. Bridget on the seat of the car.

He shifted, and a sharp little point of pain flared at the side of his neck. He reached up. A small, raised lump under the skin. The same lump that had been there since he woke up in the lab. Not a dream. None of it.

"No." The word came out of him and kept coming. He drove his fist into the headboard. The wood split. He hit it again. He went on hitting it until his throat had nothing left in it.

When there was nothing left in him, he fell back against the mattress. The tears came without sound. "Bridget." He said it to the dark. "What did I do?"

Light through the window. Not the moon. A pale, moving light somewhere out among the trees, low and small, the way a lantern moves when someone is walking with it.

He pushed himself off the bed. The pistol was on the dresser. He picked it up. The cold of the grip put him back in his body. He pulled a spare magazine from the cargo pocket on his thigh. Whatever was out there knew something he did not.

He let himself out the door without a sound. The light moved between the trunks, brightening, fading, brightening again. Pine needles gave under his boots. He worked his way toward it, putting each foot down carefully.

Voices. Low, two of them, pitched to keep from carrying. He went still and listened. The first voice was one he knew. Domblin.

He moved closer, tree to tree, until he could pick the words out of the dark.

"The whole thing has turned into a mess," Domblin said. "If only I'd been able to spend the years I needed mentoring Mauldrin instead of being locked away. The aniborn know about him now. They've unknowingly released Azgiel, and Mauldrin shows no sign yet of waking to who he is. He's weak."

Caden flinched. Mauldrin. The same name the silver-haired man had spoken in the parking lot. The same name the thing wearing Steven had used in the lab. Twice now strangers had spoken it like a recognition. He did not know what to do with that.

The other voice answered, deep enough that Caden felt it in his sternum before he heard it. "We must keep hope. Is Triaad aware of Mauldrin?"

"No," Domblin replied. "The creatures tell me they're keeping it from him. But they told Triaad about me, and he's on his way here. That's why I called for you."

Caden eased forward another step. The light came from a small flame Domblin held in his palm, no bigger than a candle, but enough to outline what Domblin was talking to. The thing across from him was the size of a barn. White-gray scales, a long reptilian head laid low to the ground so the two of them could meet at eye level, and eyes the wrong shade of blue, lit from inside. Its tail moved once, slow, snapping a hand-thick branch underneath it.

"What's the plan?" the creature growled.

Domblin sighed. "When Triaad comes, he'll find me. But if he learns of Mauldrin, it's over. Everything falls apart."

"Then build a protective ring around this area," the creature suggested. "Keep Mauldrin hidden and allow your capture. That'll distract Triaad long enough for me to summon help."

Domblin nodded. "But what happens if Mauldrin crosses the ring? The ring is what holds the aniborn off him. Outside it, he is a candle in the wind."

"Then teach him to stay inside it," the creature replied.

Domblin let out a sound that might have been a laugh in another life. "If he is anything like he used to be, he will not listen."

The words went into Caden. Why him? Who was Triaad?

He shifted his weight to see better. A twig went under his heel with a sound like a small bone. He froze. It was already too late.

The cold of the thing reached him before he turned. When he did, it was already there, three paces off, watching him without blinking. The same kind of creature that had come through the lab corridor and come through the building. This one was thinner. Worse.

He brought the pistol up and fired. The round hit. Black, oily blood splashed his cheek and stank of something burning. The creature did not slow. It came across the gap before he could line up another shot and put him into a tree. The bark broke against his back.

Stars went across his vision. Claws closed on his throat. The edges of the world started going to gray. Then a flash, hot enough that he felt it through his eyelids, and the weight came off him.

The creature shrieked and threw itself sideways. Caden went down to one knee, pulling air in through a throat that felt half its size. He brought his arm up against the brightness and squinted past it. Domblin stood at the edge of the clearing, lit from inside, the air around him moving like heat off pavement.

The thing came again. Domblin opened his hand and a staff came into it the way a memory comes back. He swung once. The blow caught the creature across the skull and threw arcs of light across the clearing. The thing staggered, screamed, and was not there anymore.

"They are getting desperate." Domblin said it more to the air than to Caden. The staff in his hand came apart into points of light and went out one by one as they drifted up. He turned, offered a hand, and pulled Caden onto his feet. "And now they know exactly where you are."

Caden looked past him. The huge thing he had seen across the clearing was gone. The only sign of it was a span of crushed undergrowth and the faint, dry-warm smell of something that had been there a moment ago.

His chest worked. His hands shook. The light around Domblin was already going, the way a coal goes.

"Thank you for saving me," Caden said, his voice hoarse. "Tell me what this is. All of it. Who is Mauldrin? Why do you keep saying it like it is my name?"

Domblin's eyes did not leave him. "There is not time. The first thing is to get you behind a wall."

He knelt and started drawing in the dirt with one finger. A blue flame followed the line. He spoke under his breath, the same handful of syllables on a loop, and then opened both hands and pushed them apart. The flame ran outward from the line as if the ground itself had been waiting for the signal.

The ring rolled out through the trees, taking in a few acres of forest, then went pale and was almost gone. What was left was a thin blue thread of light at ankle height that did not burn the leaves it ran across.

"This barrier will protect you from the aniborn," Domblin said, getting back to his feet. "So long as you are inside this line, the aniborn cannot touch you."

Caden looked at the line. "And if I cross it?"

"Then they have you," Domblin said. "Your life is the line."

Caden nodded once. He did not have anything else in him. He followed Domblin back to the cabin.

Domblin stopped on the threshold and turned around. "Hear me. I will not be here long. Triaad is coming. When he comes, I face him by myself. You stay in this cabin. Whatever you see through that window, whatever you hear, you do not come out. He cannot see you. Tell me you understand."

Caden had ten questions for every breath. He had also been pulled out from under a creature's claws by this man inside the same hour. He nodded.

Then the dam in his chest gave. "Who are you? One minute I am with Bridget. The next I am in a cabin I have never seen with things in the woods that should not exist and a name I have never heard called at me like it is mine. Just—give me one straight answer."

Domblin's shoulders went down half an inch. "My name is Domblin. I am the one who brought you back." He let it sit. "Mauldrin. I have watched you most of your life from a distance and kept you out of sight of the things that wanted to find you."

"Brought me back," Caden repeated. "What does that even mean?"

Domblin began to pace the floorboards. "You were once a king, a ruler of worlds—"

"Stop." Caden pushed off the bed and took a step away from him. "I don't care about kings. I don't care about planets. Bridget is dead." His voice cracked on her name. The room felt too small. "You're telling me I ruled worlds, but I couldn't save the one person who mattered?"

Domblin held his gaze. "I know you're in pain. But this matters. You were a protector of this world—the planet Myree—and countless others." His tone remained steady, though sorrow lingered beneath it. "You were betrayed by one of our brothers. A war followed—a war you won—but it came at a terrible cost. Fighting your own brother devastated you, and after the battle, you and the others chose to leave this mortal life, placing yourselves into eternal rest."

He stopped pacing. "Getting you back into a body cost more than I have words for. I crossed worlds for the means to do it. And now that you are walking around in one, the balance has tipped. The aniborn know you are alive. They will spend every one of themselves to put you back in the ground before you remember what you are."

Caden sat down on the edge of the bed. He gripped the frame to keep his hands from doing anything else. "So I am supposed to take all that on faith? That I ran worlds. That there is a war I am supposed to walk into."

Domblin did not flinch. "Every world there is. And you are at the center of it whether you would prefer to be or not."

Caden's hands opened and closed at his sides. "And Bridget? Did this take her from me?"

Something gave in Domblin's face. "Yes." He did not make it sound like anything but the truth. "I am sorry for her, Caden. I am. But what was done to her does not have to be the end of it. You still have work in front of you. There is still a way to make some of this right."

The grief tried to come back up. He pushed it down with the next breath. "So what are you proposing I do?"

"Stay here," Domblin said. "The barrier will protect you from the aniborn, but only if you don't leave. You have food here, and the Guardian you saw earlier will return in a few days to take you somewhere safer."

"What if they get to me first?"

"They will not. Not while you are inside the line."

Before Caden could ask anything else, the floor moved. The walls of the cabin took a hit of wind hard enough to flex the windows in their frames. Domblin's face closed.

"He is here," he said.

Caden was at the window in two strides. A shape stood at the tree line and was the tree line. It moved forward into the clearing and what came with it broke a category his mind had been carrying around since he was a child. A dragon. Larger than the cabin, larger than any building he had been raised to think of as large. Black scales that caught the moonlight like wet stone. A man in dark armor sat in the joint of its shoulders as if he had been born there.

Domblin went out the door. The staff came back into his hand, white this time, a hard cold light that put every needle on every tree into relief. He walked toward the line. Halfway there he stopped and stood for one breath the way a man stands before he walks into water he knows is over his head. Caden, watching from the window, understood it the way you understand a thing you do not have a word for: Domblin already knew how this ended for him.

The dragon hit the line and the ground bucked. Blue current pulsed across the air where it had struck. The dragon held off a beat, lifted one foreclaw, and laid it slow against the barrier as if testing the shape of the thing in front of it. Blue light forked around the claws. The shield held. Domblin held. He drove the staff into the dirt with both hands and a wall of light surged up out of it. The dragon recoiled, jaws snapping closed an inch from the shield. The ground rang under their feet.

The tail came around and laid itself across the shield with a sound like a hammer on a bell. The shield held. Claws raked it. The shield held. Domblin did not move.

The rider spoke. His voice carried out across the clearing the way thunder carries—slow, and as if from somewhere larger than where he was sitting. "Domblin, your time is over. Surrender now, and I'll grant you a swift death. This barrier will not hold you if I will it to come down."

Domblin answered without raising his voice. "Turn around, Triaad. Or answer for everything."

Then he walked through his own barrier as if it were not there.

The dragon gave ground a single step—whether on its own or at its rider's command, Caden could not tell. For one long beat the rider did not speak. He sat the dragon's shoulders and watched what Domblin would do next.

The dragon came on. Each strike of its claws Domblin met and turned. Caden's hand was on the door handle without him deciding it should be. He took it off again. Stay inside. Stay inside. The dragon lunged once more and Domblin drove the staff down a second time and another wave of light rolled out of it across the dirt.

The dragon did not stop coming. The blow that finally landed took Domblin off his feet and threw him across the dirt. Before he had drawn the next breath, the dragon's talons closed around him and lifted.

Caden was through the door before he registered moving. He stopped on the porch, pistol up. "Domblin!" he shouted, aiming at the dragon's rider.

Domblin's head turned in the dragon's grip. "Stay inside!" The words never crossed the air. They went straight into Caden's head, urgent and clear. Before Caden could move, Domblin flicked his wrist, and an invisible force hurled him backward through the doorway. Caden crashed onto the cabin floor as the door banged shut behind him.

He came up off the floor and threw himself at the door. The handle did not move. He hit the door with the side of his fist and shouted Domblin's name into the wood. The door did not move. He went to the window. The dragon was already in the air, wings working the night, climbing fast, and the figure in its claws went smaller and smaller until the trees took him.

Behind him, the door let go. The latch clicked. The door drifted open as if a hand had stopped holding it closed. Caden staggered out into the clearing and stared at a sky that had nothing in it. He turned a slow circle, looking at the dark line of the trees on every side. Domblin was gone.

He went back inside and closed the door behind him without making a sound. He sat down on the edge of the bed and the last of him went out of him. Everything was gone.

CHAPTER 42
Caden—Cabin Perimeter

Two birds traded notes outside the window. The morning was gentle. Inside, the room stayed cold. None of what was outside had reached the inside of him. He sat up. Last night was still on him the way a wet coat stays on after you have come in out of the rain.

Her blood was still on his hands. He had not noticed in the dark. He noticed now. The grief came up under his ribs and pushed at the back of his eyes and he swallowed it down. He got to his feet and went out into the morning, putting one foot ahead of the other. He made his way around the cabin to the iron pump.

He worked the handle until the water came. It came cold enough to hurt. He held his hands under it and watched the rust-brown of her blood thin out and run pale and run clear. Her face came up in him while he stood there. Not the still one. The one that had been looking at him in the front seat of the car. He let the water keep running.

The cold did nothing for what was hollow in him.

When he came back to the cabin, the door stood half open. He had closed it. Just inside, on the floor, sat a wooden tray. Cured meat. A cluster of dark berries. Two pieces of fruit he could not name. He stopped where he was.

He looked out at the trees. Nothing moved in them. The clearing wore last night the way a body wears bruises—a pine snapped halfway up its trunk and laid out across the ground, the dirt torn open in long furrows where the dragon had set its weight. His stomach turned over on itself, empty.

He picked the tray up and set it on the table. He had no use for it. He needed answers more than he needed food. He took the pistol off the dresser and went back outside. His hands were not steady. He noticed it the way you notice something about someone else.

The thin blue thread of Domblin's line still ran around the cabin. Caden walked its perimeter slow, the line at the edge of his boots, and stopped where Domblin had been standing when the dragon took him. Something in the grass caught the morning. The staff.

He paced the line, looking at it. Do not cross. Domblin's voice. Your life is the line. He paced again. He stopped. He stepped over.

A crack went through the morning, sharp as ice giving way under a man. The blue line went black around the whole cabin. A thin ring of smoke lifted off it and was nothing. The line was gone.

A cold draft moved through the trees and lifted the hair on his arms. He spoke to himself, low. "Caden. You've been in the woods a thousand times. Nothing here you haven't walked past before." He did not believe it as he said it.

The cabin behind him looked smaller than it should have, as if the distance between him and it were stretching while he stood still. He gripped the pistol and went down on one knee beside the staff. Even unmoving in the grass, the thing put pressure on the air around it. He reached out and closed his hand around the shaft.

The staff was nothing like anything he had been raised on. Not wood, not metal. The surface of it moved the way fog moves trapped behind glass—slow, alive. The moment his hand closed on it, it brightened. It knew him.

It put him back in the moment with the wing flame in stopped time, when something he could not name had answered something in him. This was the same pull, only larger. Whatever was packed into the staff was straining against the shape of it. And then, with no warning, the shape gave. It went off in his hand the way fireflies lift off a field at dusk—a cloud of small lights climbing into the air, and one by one going out. The staff was gone.

He stared at his empty palms. Something at the edge of his vision moved. He raised his head. A pale shape was drifting between the trunks, soundless, no brighter than a lantern through fog. He squinted. Inside the pale, the suggestion of a figure. A woman.

She came clear in front of him before he could move, the way a face comes clear in a dim room when you stop trying to see it. She reached out. Her hand laid flat against his chest.

A voice came from no single place—from the trees, from inside his head, from behind his ribs. "Come to me."

The world smeared. Every shape he could see dragged sideways into every other shape, and something with the temperature of river water pulled him through it.

He came out of it into the side of a tree. The bark took skin off his shoulder. He caught himself, brought the pistol up, breathed.

The forest he was in was not the forest he had been in. The ground was cracked open, dry as old skin. The trees stood gnarled and bare, with no green left in any of them. The sun was gone. Whatever light there was came from somewhere he could not find.

Movement above him—quick, soundless. A shape was climbing the tree at his back. He took two steps clear of the trunk and looked up. Something sat on a low branch, watching. It wasn't like the creatures that had attacked him before. This one had the head of a dog, its long snout lined with sharp, wolf-like teeth. The creature cocked its head, as though studying him with a chilling intelligence.

Caden gave ground. More shapes were sliding between the trunks now, nearer with each second. He brought the pistol up at the one above him and squeezed.

The bullet did not get a foot from the barrel. A pale light blossomed around it and held it where it was. The round quivered in midair, sheathed in a soft glow that took the shape of a hand—slender fingers closing around it the way a person closes a hand around a moth. From those fingers the light grew, climbed an unseen line back to a wrist, an arm, a shoulder, until the whole figure of a woman stood drawn out of thin air in the dead grass.

She had come through into the world the way someone comes through a curtain. She tilted her head and looked at the bullet cradled between her fingers like something a child had brought her. The round flickered there—half present, half not—trying to decide if it still existed.

Black ran into her fingertips and started up the back of her hand. Whatever she was made of was draining into the bullet. The metal of it softened, went bright as molten glass, then came apart into beads that lifted upward instead of falling and thinned out against the sky and were gone.

The bullet gone, the pale light came back into her. Only then did she look at him. Her eyes stayed on his too long for strangers.

"Mauldrin," she said, her voice pitched low and weighted with something that sounded like grief sat down a long time ago. "You've finally come."

Caden's throat closed on what he was trying to say. "Why does everyone call me that? My name is Caden."

"It is the name I knew you by," she said. "Before you were born as Caden."

"Before I was born," he said. The words came out without much in them.

"Yes." Her face softened. "Before you were brought back into the body you stand in. You were a king once. You watched over this world. And now you are back among us."

"And who are you?" Caden asked.

"You may call me the Witch," she said. "That is how you knew me in your past life."

"I don't remember any other life."

She gave him a small smile that did not match the rest of her face. "That is the way of it. I was told you would not. Perhaps something I have for you will help. Call it a gift, for your return."

She raised a hand and beckoned. Out of the dead trees on every side, shapes began to step forward into the open. Caden brought the pistol up between him and them in a single motion.

The nearest was a small, green-skinned thing, hunched, with claws longer than its arms. Every part of it looked dangerous, but when the muzzle swung onto it the creature gave a startled, birdlike chirp and held very still. Before Caden's finger reached the trigger, the Witch raised her hand and the pistol came apart in his grip and was nothing but air.

"Please." Her voice did not rise. "Do not harm my family. They look terrible to your eye. They will not lay a hand on you. They are glad you have come."

Caden's eyes moved across the crowd and stopped on a shape he knew. The big red demon from the corridor. Kaz. He was carrying something wrapped in a length of worn cloth, holding it the way a man holds something heavy and important at once. He came up beside the Witch and laid the bundle across her hands. She turned with it to Caden.

"This was yours," she said, drawing the cloth back. A long, ornate sword. The blade slept inside a sheath that had the look of dragonhide, segmented and dark. The hilt was carved over with patterns Caden could not quite hold in his eye.

He took the sword from her after a beat. It was heavier than it should have been. As if part of the weight was not metal.

The Witch stepped aside so the demon could come forward. Caden found his voice steadier than he expected. "Thank you. For pulling me out of the corridor. And the building."

Kaz lowered his head a fraction in answer. "The things in the building. We call them aniborn," he said. His voice came up out of his chest the way thunder comes up out of a mountain.

Caden gave the demon a short nod. There was an odd small comfort in standing inside the same air as him. He turned his attention back to the sword, peeled the rest of the cloth off it, and reached for the hilt. His fingers went through the hilt as if it were not there.

He looked up at the Witch. "I can't grip it. How am I supposed to draw it?"

Something in her face went a long way off. The warmth that had been in her was not in her now. "It must respect you before it lets you wield it. It does not allow itself to be drawn by hands it has not chosen."

Caden looked down at the hilt his hand had just passed through.

"It is time you went," she said. "You are no longer safe here."

"How do I get back?" he said. He kept his eyes on her.

"Turn around." She lifted a finger past his shoulder.

He turned. The pale light went off around him a second time, and the river-cold pull came back through him. The cabin stood ten feet in front of him. The same plain log walls. Living trees in their right colors on every side of it. He spun back to ask her how she had done it. She was gone. The dead forest was gone. The crowd of her family was gone. He stood alone in his own clearing, in his own morning, with the wrapped sword in his hand.

CHAPTER 43
Caden—Treeline

A twig snapped at the edge of the trees. Caden went still. He gripped the sheath of the sword tighter, for whatever good a sheath was. A figure stood half-hidden under one of the firs. The shape of him was a shape Caden knew.

"Steven?" The word came out of him before he had time to weigh it. He blinked, expecting the figure to thin out and be nothing. The figure walked forward instead. Behind him, Kaz stepped out from the trees without making a sound, his bulk filling the gap between the trunks.

"What do you want?" Caden brought the sheathed sword up across his chest.

The thing wearing Steven's face smiled at him. The smile was too even. "Your sword has come back to you. Good. It is good to see it in your hand again, my king."

Caden's eyes narrowed. "What did you just call me?"

He did not answer. He moved. Between one breath and the next he was no longer where he had been. He was a foot in front of Caden. Caden took a half step back without meaning to.

"How did you do that?"

"This place is not safe for you." Azgiel let the question pass him by. "Aniborn are coming, and there will be more of them than two of us can hold. Kaz and I will keep what we can of you. But we move now. Whatever the Witch put around you was never going to hold long."

Caden did not move. He kept his eyes on the man's eyes. "Who are you? Or what?"

The smile thinned out and went away. "I am Azgiel. I was an archangel once, a warrior of the celestial order. Domblin set a trick for me a long time ago. He sealed me into a Cell of Time and stripped most of what I had. He did it to keep me out of his way. The only door open to me was this body. Walking out of that cell wearing a man cost me what I had left."

"If you are not Steven," Caden said, "where is Steven?"

"He is in the cell I came out of." Azgiel said it the way a man says a thing he is sorry about.

"So you and Domblin are not on the same side."

"No," Azgiel said, and the word came out colder than the rest of him. "Given the chance, he would put me in the ground."

"Then tell me why I should believe a word out of your mouth."

"Consider it this way." Azgiel waved Kaz a step closer. "Domblin put me in that cell so I could not interfere. He could have stopped what happened to Bridget. He chose not to. If he had not put me in there, I could have. And the aniborn at your house? His."

Caden's mouth went dry. "How does that work? He stood between me and one of them last night. I watched him do it. And then there was a man on a dragon who took him—"

"It is a performance," Azgiel said. "Tell me—did you watch them kill him? Or did they fly off with him into the dark and you took on faith that he was finished? If they were truly his enemies, his body would be in the dirt at your feet right now."

Caden's jaw tightened. "No. Not that I saw."

"And have you ever watched Domblin kill one of those dark things?" Kaz said. He let it sit in the air.

Caden tried to put one in his memory. He could not. "No. I have not."

"When I came through that wall in the corridor, I came to kill them," Kaz said. The way he said it did not leave room to argue.

"A week ago I would have laughed at every word out of either of you." Caden looked from Azgiel to Kaz and back. "The last seven days have ruined every category I had for what is true. Convince me this is not the next lie."

"You will see soon," Azgiel said. "When they come for you, you will watch us put them down without a pause. Domblin. The aniborn. The humans who carry their water. Every one of them had a hand in your wife's death. They are working together. They want what you carry inside you."

"They are close," Kaz said. "We have to move."

Caden did not know what to take on. If any of what Azgiel said held, he had spent his last hour with Domblin owing his life to the wrong man. But the body in front of him had walked out of Steven's body. Whatever else was true, that was not nothing.

"If any of that is true," he said, "then Domblin—"

"We argue it on the way," Azgiel said. "The aniborn will not stop on the trail to wait for you to make up your mind."

Kaz drew his blade. The sound of it leaving the sheath cut through the trees.

"How are we doing this?" Caden said. "I don't have a gun. I cannot draw this thing." He swallowed. "Can we outrun them?"

Azgiel shook his head. "No. But that rise of stone up ahead." He lifted his chin toward it. "We can hold there."

They moved. As they went, Azgiel plucked a single leaf from a low branch. "Watch this." He held it up by the stem. The leaf turned in the air on a wind that was not there. As Caden watched, the green ran out of it. What was left went translucent, hardening into something that caught light like glass. The leaf swelled in his fingers, growing under its own power, until Azgiel was holding a thin globe by a stem.

"Take it." He pressed it into Caden's palm.

Caden looked at the thing in his hand. Smooth, cool, the curve of a small fishbowl, and along its surface the ridges of the original leaf. "How did you—"

"It is not magic, before you ask." Azgiel kept walking. The boulders came up around them. "Everything you see—leaves, stone, the air between us—is the same stuff arranged in different ways. With enough power, and the discipline to do it, you tell those pieces to be something else, and they are."

"You are telling me you rearranged its molecules," Caden said. The scientist in him sat up before the rest of him got there.

"Exactly," Azgiel replied. "You were once the king of this world. If you can unlock the mind you used to have, you'll have more power than you can imagine. Enough to draw that sword and lead us out of this."

"How do I unlock anything?" Caden said.

"Start by dropping the bulb," Azgiel said.

Kaz fell in beside them, a head taller than Caden, his blade ready. Caden looked at the small clear globe in his palm. He opened his fingers.

The bulb touched the dirt. Green lightning leapt up out of the ground in a single hard line and locked onto it. Something tore through Caden as it did— he staggered. The colors of the world washed sideways, blurred, came back. He blinked the world into focus again. A green dome stood over the three of them, half clear, half lit, curving away in every direction.

"What is this?" Caden put his hand against the curve of it. The surface was smooth and cool, the way the inside of a shell is smooth.

"It will hold. For a while." Azgiel did not look at his own hands. "And you did it. Not me."

"No. You did. You have to have."

Azgiel shook his head. "You will see. It is the same thing you will reach for to draw the sword and get the three of us out of here."

A scream came from beyond the curve of the dome. Caden looked past the boulders into the trees. The trunks themselves looked wrong, leaning the wrong way, and out from between them stepped one he had seen before. Tagen.

Kaz let out a growl deep in his chest. Tagen leaned a hand against a pine. The trunk groaned under the touch. A shower of needles came loose. Tagen smiled. His fangs had gone black at the gum.

"Draw the sword," Azgiel said sharply. Kaz moved a step forward, blade up.

Another scream from the other side. Caden turned in time to see a thin, wiry one throw itself headfirst into the dome. The hit rolled across the surface in a slow ripple. The dome did not give.

Azgiel's hand closed on Caden's shoulder and turned him back. "Draw the sword."

Caden reached for the hilt and his hand passed through it the way it had in the dead forest. He swept his hand through the empty hilt twice more. "It is not there. I cannot get a grip on it."

Outside the curve, the count of them was rising. They moved in a slow circle around the dome, the way a pack of wild things moves around a fire. Another body hit the wall and the dome made a loud brittle pop. A crack opened on its inner face. Black tendrils, thin as roots, started to grow through the crack and feel their way across the surface like veins.

"You can do this," Azgiel said. "Get your hand on the sword."

Caden wiped his palms on his thighs. He held the sheath up between them. He tried to put the rest of the world somewhere else. He tried for the same pull he had felt in the fire on the plane and standing over Domblin's staff in the grass—that quiet answering thing in him that knew before he knew. The hilt sat there in the air, alive.

He reached. Cold needles ran along his skin. The sword answered—watching, waiting, the way a thing waits that has gone hungry a long time. Whatever was packed into it pushed him back and pulled him in at the same time. There was a promise in it. There was a price. He felt the price in the same instant he felt the promise. Stain. Ruin. Something he would not be able to wash off afterward. He yanked his hand back as if the blade had reached into him through the air.

Green light flared at his left. Kaz had driven his blade into the band of black roots crawling across the dome. Green fire ran the length of the roots and back along the strand to the aniborn that had set them. The thing outside the dome screamed. The sound went through the trees and kept going.

Another body hit the dome and broke a piece of it off. The chunk fell, hit the dirt, and was nothing. One creature folded itself wrong and slipped through the gap. Kaz turned in place. His blade went through the thing's neck and shoulder in one stroke. Its black flesh sprayed across the leaves and went to paste, and what was left in the leaves was a small lattice of bones the color of coal.

"Draw it," Azgiel barked.

"I can't." Caden's voice cracked on it.

Azgiel's fist closed in the front of his shirt and shoved him a step back. "You can. You will." He brought his face close. "What have they done to you? This is your world, Mauldrin. You used to know it the way a man knows his own hands. Find that and take it back. Draw the sword. Or you die here."

Before Caden could move, Azgiel shoved him backward against the dome's curve. The sword's hilt brushed the inside of the wall. Where the hilt touched the dome, the dome began to come apart, pulling back from it like skin off a flame.

"Kaz!" Azgiel shouted. "We've got a problem." He shoved Caden behind him, turning to face the advancing aniborn. "Stay between us. If you haven't grown fearful enough to draw that sword yet, you soon will."

The dome failed. The aniborn came over what was left of it. Azgiel caught the first one across the throat. Its claws tore his arm open. The wounds closed before the blood had time to run. Smoke lifted off his hand as the creature came apart in his grip and went to ash. The ones behind it pulled up short. They stared at him the way wild animals stare at a thing they cannot fit into any category they have.

Kaz waded in. His blade moved through them like a man cutting brush. One leapt up onto his back and put its teeth into his shoulder. Kaz pivoted, drove the thing into the nearest boulder hard enough to crack the stone, and ran his blade through its chest.

Tagen came through the press of bodies in a single low rush and took Caden off his feet. The ground came up under his shoulders. Tagen had him already moving before Caden had registered being hit, dragging him back through the bodies of the rest of the pack. "Azgiel—" Caden tried for the rest of it. Whatever Tagen's grip was doing to him crawled up through his chest and took the breath out of him. His mouth kept moving. Nothing came out.

Azgiel jabbed a finger at the sword in Caden's slack hand. "Kaz! The sword. If they get it into the cave with him, we are not getting it back."

Kaz did not pause. He drove forward into the pack, blade taking them down in heavy, cutting arcs. They closed on him from every side, snapping, climbing each other to reach him. Behind that wall of bodies, Caden was already dragged clear of Kaz, Tagen's grip locked around his right leg, the ground going by under his back.

Azgiel's hand was on Caden's wrist before he saw it move. The grip was hot enough to feel through his sleeve. Heat ran up his arm in a hard line.

Then the world came apart.

It went the way it had gone the first time he had stepped into stopped time. Reality cracked—actually cracked, glass under a hammer, in every direction at once. Through the cracks ran images he could not place. Places. Faces. Moments lifted out of order. Threads of time pulling free of one another. There was no measure for how long it lasted.

The cracks closed. The world set itself back into its frame. Azgiel was not there.

He had no time to make sense of any of it. Hands were on him again, hard hands, dragging him backward over the dirt. Tagen. His arms would not work. His head would not work.

There was no time for any of the questions in him.

Azgiel was gone. Tagen had him. And whatever was at the end of the trail Tagen was hauling him down had been waiting a long time.

CHAPTER 44

Azgiel—Cave Mouth

Azgiel had Caden by the wrist when the aniborn took him. "Caden!" he roared, pulling—and the wrist went out of his hand. The creatures came in shoulder to shoulder, all teeth and reach, and the current of them carried him backward off his feet.

He fought. The mass of them took him under. They clawed at him, climbed each other to reach him, and the dirt and the bodies closed over his head. He tried for one last look at Caden. He did not get one.

Claws went into his chest. They went past flesh and past bone and reached for the part of him the body was wrapped around. The edges of his sight thinned. The cold he had not felt in two ages came up close to him and put its hand on him, and the door he had been on the wrong side of for so long stood open at his back.

Then, deep in him, something shifted. His soul moved a fraction inside the body he was wearing. Power came up through him—not what he had been once, but more than the body had let him hold until now.

He flexed. Energy blew outward from him in one hard burst. The aniborn nearest him went to ash where they stood. The ones behind those came apart at the edges and fell back, screaming, blind.

Blood ran hot down his arms. The dust on him went to paste. The body had paid for what he had just done—the muscle scorched, the bones aching where the power had run through them. He told the body to mend itself. It mended what it could. The rest stayed open.

He pushed himself to his feet bleeding. The pain flared, and underneath the pain his senses opened the way they had used to open. The air, the dirt under his boots, the weight of water above him—he felt them the way a man feels his own hand. A storm was working itself together over the trees. He could feel the charge in it, gathered and waiting.

The ones still standing gathered for another rush. He raised his hand. He opened his palm to the sky. He closed his fingers on the charge above him. Blood ran down his arm. The body shook under what he was asking it to carry.

He pulled.

Lightning came down. It came in white threads, then in one column, and the air burst around it. The pack came apart. What had been a wave of bodies a heartbeat before went to black sludge across the dirt. The ground smoked under him where the strike had landed.

He went down on one knee. The body had been further burned by what he had just put through it. Something inside him frayed. He held himself there a moment, then forced himself up and let the body do what it could to mend.

When the smoke thinned, he looked for Kaz. Kaz was already pushing himself up out of the dirt, bloodied to the shoulder but on his feet. He gave Azgiel a tired nod. Azgiel let his shoulders down a fraction.

Kaz came over. He rolled his shoulders. "They took him," he said. "Do we go after—"

"No." Azgiel cut him off. He did not argue it. He did not soften it.

Kaz held that a moment. "You're certain?"

Azgiel looked at him until Kaz stopped asking. He owed Kaz nothing in the way of an explanation, and Kaz did not need one. "The war is only beginning," he said. He turned toward the line of trees and the dark beyond them. "We are not ready for Triaad. And that is where they are taking him."

CHAPTER 45

Caden—The Dark Matter Prison

Tagen moved fast. He hauled Caden through the trees by one leg, and sticks and rock tore the back of him as the ground went past. Caden clawed at the dirt for anything to hold. There was nothing in the dirt to hold. The grip on his ankle did not loosen by so much as a finger. The world above him blurred and went dark.

They were in a cave before he understood they had stopped being in the woods. He did not know how long the run had taken. The light from outside cut off. The air went wet and close. The stone under him went from hard to slick, and then to something soft that gave under his weight and stank. Tagen stopped and threw him.

He hit the floor and slid. The sword went out of his hand and clattered into the dark somewhere he could not place. Behind him, a sound came that was not water and not stone—a wet rushing, a closing, the kind of sound a throat makes. Then silence.

He pushed himself up. He held his hands out in front of him, blind. Somewhere far back in the cave, water dripped at a steady count. The count did not slow and did not stop, and he found after a minute that he was breathing in time with it.

A scream came through the stone. Not the high scrape of an aniborn—a human throat.

Someone else is here.

It came again, thinner, from somewhere on the other side of the wall.

He moved toward the sound and his feet went out from under him in the slime. He went down on a hand. The wall came up under his fingers when he reached for it. It was soft. It clung. When he pulled his hand back, it pulled back with him for a fraction of a second before it let go.

He kept the wall under his shoulder and walked. He went around the room slow, keeping his weight on the foot that was on solid floor. The room was small. It was four-cornered. There was no door. There was no break of any kind in the wall, anywhere along its run.

It was not a cave. It was a cell. The wet sound he had heard at his back was the door sealing.

He came back toward the center. His foot caught on a low place in the floor. He went down on a knee and ran a hand over it. A shallow dip. Two inches deep. His fingertips struck cold metal, half-buried in the slime. Smooth. Oval. Held in place by what was packed around it.

He worked his fingers down around it and pulled. The shape came up enough for him to know it. The sheath. The sword.

The hilt was buried deep, but the slime around it was pulling back from the metal—the way it had pulled back from the dome in the woods. The sword was eating its way clear of the cell on its own. If he could get a hand on the hilt, he could go through whatever was left of the wall.

He clawed at the rock around the sheath. His fingers tore. The hilt sat there in the slime, throbbing slow under his hand the way a thing throbs that knows it is being reached for.

His hand went through it. He tried again. His hand went through it again. The sheath sat solid under his palm. The hilt did not. It was the way it had been in the dome, and the way it had been in the dead grass before that.

Why can't I hold it?

His fingers throbbed. The skin had gone off them in patches. Everything from the last few days came up in him at once and went looking for a place to land.

He hit the floor with both fists. A sound came out of him that he did not recognize. The walls gave it back to him.

When he had nothing left, he let himself slump against the wall. The slime took the shape of his back. He did not move away from it. Whatever was in it was already in him, the way it had been working in him since Tagen took hold of his leg.

He stared into the dark. There was no way out. He let his head go back against the wall and stayed there.

CHAPTER 46
Tagen—Triaad's Fortress

Tagen rose from the bed. The frame gave a small creak under him. He went to the window and pushed it open. Cool sea air came in. For the first time since he had been put in this room nearly a month ago, sun cut through the clouds. Hundreds of feet below, waves came in against the cliffs and the sound of them came up the wall.

The room was a wealthy man's room. Carved dresser. Polished floor. Furniture set carefully along the walls. None of it sat right with him. Servitude was what Tagen knew. Beating was what Tagen knew. He could not look at any of this and not see the calculation in it.

The door opened. A young woman came in between two large guards. She carried a tray of black, soft food and set it on the dresser. She left without speaking.

"Thank you," Tagen said to her back, pleasant. He hoped the kindness would reach the right ears. The woman did not react. The door closed.

He looked at the tray. The same meal every morning—black biscuits, a thick paste. He was not used to eating on a schedule. Aniborn did not need to. But the meals were doing something. He felt heavier in the body than he had in a long time. Younger. He could not put a date on the last time he had felt younger.

He flicked a piece off the tray and out the window. Birds went after it before it had finished falling, screeching at one another. At least someone wanted it.

He ate the rest. He did not know yet whether he was being kept for reward or for punishment, and a body that had been fed could weather either better than one that had not.

The door opened behind him. A young man in clean silver chainmail came in. He was too polished for the rest of the room.

"Triaad will see you now." The voice was deeper than the body it came out of. "If you'll come with me."

Tagen stood. He brushed his hands. "Did my message reach him? Does he know why I came?"

"Yes," the man said. "He has known since the day you arrived."

"And it took him this long to—"

"No more questions." He motioned for Tagen to follow. "This way."

Tagen hesitated, then went. Six guards stood in the hallway. One of them held a set of chains. The body in him went tight before the rest of him caught up.

"The chains aren't for you," the servant said. "They're for Domblin in the next room."

"Domblin is still alive?" Tagen could not keep the surprise out of it. Triaad had taken Domblin nearly a month ago. Tagen had been carrying the assumption all that time that he was dead. "I don't have to see him, do I?"

The guard nearest to him smirked. "You'll get over it."

When the door to Domblin's room opened, Tagen went to shadow form before he stepped through. Shadow was harder to feel out. He slipped in behind the guards and held the wall.

Domblin sat in a heavy carved chair, wearing a torn white robe. The room around him was the same kind of room Tagen had been kept in. The same furniture. The same window.

Were they both prisoners?

If this was how Triaad kept prisoners, what had the last month been for him?

"You won't be a problem for us, will you, Domblin?" one of the guards asked, holding the chains.

Domblin smiled, easy. "I suppose I'll behave."

"Glad to hear it." The guard raised the shackles. The metal in them shifted as it moved—gray, then black, then brown, then gray again. "These won't hurt you, old man." He fastened them to Domblin's wrists.

Domblin looked down at his wrists. He gave the chain a small testing pull. "What are these made of?"

"Dark matter and steel," the guard replied.

Domblin's face went still. He did not fight the chains. He did not move when the guard tugged at them either. "Where are we going?"

"Triaad wants to see you."

Tagen kept to shadow and followed. Domblin walked ahead between the guards, the white of his robe loud against the black of their armor. They went down a long stairwell and came out in a courtyard.

Two onyx-scaled dragons lay along the far wall. The larger of the two he knew on sight. It was the beast Triaad rode.

Past the courtyard, through the wide gate of the castle, a city was visible. He had not been told it would be there. Vehicles moved between the towers without touching the ground. The lines of them were clean, unfamiliar, the curves of a thing built right. He had been told this world had been left a wasteland after Azgiel's reign. The city outside the gate was not a wasteland.

Triaad rebuilt all of this.

The procession continued into the oldest part of the castle. The wooden doors at the end of the hall opened slow under the weight of them, and beyond was a long chamber lined with black marble pillars. The light in the chamber came from scattered candles, and the candles did not reach the ceiling.

The guards fastened Domblin's chains to a bolt set into the floor and went out. Tagen held to the wall in shadow.

Domblin's robe gave off a faint glow against the dim. The chains clinked when he shifted, and the marble carried the sound up.

A low chuckle came down from the top of the long flight of stairs. The throne up there was hard to see in the candlelight, but the sound made the shape of who was in it. Triaad. Tagen, in shadow against the wall, went still.

"I've been waiting to see you," Domblin said calmly despite the chains that bound him.

"You have?" Triaad said. The mockery in it was easy. "And what makes you think I have been waiting for you?"

Domblin tilted his head a fraction. "You went to a great deal of trouble to capture me. I had assumed you wanted more than to let me rot in that room."

A cold laugh came down through the chamber. "I wanted nothing to do with you," Triaad said. The words carried an old contempt, distant and patient. "I had every intention of leaving you in that room. Your last prison did not hold you well enough. That one would. At least there, you would be out of my sight."

Triaad shifted in the throne. The pale green of his eyes caught the candlelight.

Tagen could not put together why Triaad had taken Domblin alive. Every previous time, Domblin had broken out. Why not finish him this time?

Domblin's voice sharpened. "Then why pull me out now? Did my last attempt to escape make too much noise? Or are you planning to put me in one of your dark-matter chambers and turn me into one of your slaves?"

Triaad chuckled again. The sound went up Tagen's spine. "No. I have plenty of aniborn to manage their own creations. I do not need another strong one." He said it as if it were nothing.

Something landed in Tagen at that.

Aniborn managing their own creations.

It explained more about Snyp than Tagen wanted to think about all at once. He looked toward the throne, and his unease worked at him from the inside out.

Does Triaad know I am here?

"What do you want with me, then?" Domblin pressed.

Triaad leaned forward. The candlelight caught more of him. "I have an informant," he said. Casual. Almost confiding. "Someone who has been feeding me information about what you have been doing on Myree."

Domblin's face did not move. The line of his shoulders did. "And who might that be?"

"Are you worried about what he'll tell me?" Triaad asked, sarcasm laced in his words.

Domblin shifted. The chains rattled. Tagen had to move now. He slid along the wall toward the foot of the throne. The candles he passed dimmed, and two of them went out, and there was no wind in the room.

Tagen took form at the base of the throne. He spoke low. Each word he laid down with care. "There is more to what Domblin was doing on Myree than you have been told." He kept it beneath Domblin's hearing from the floor of the chamber. "We found Mauldrin there. And Domblin was protecting him."

"Why am I only hearing this now?" Triaad's voice came down through the chamber. Tagen went back to shadow before he could think to do it.

After a beat of quiet, he took form again on the other side of the throne. "Snyp kept this from you." He kept his voice as low as before. "He has Mauldrin in one of the chambers. He is trying to turn him into an aniborn. He means to consume him for the power. Enough power to come up against you."

Triaad's knuckles whitened on the arms of the throne. "Snyp has been hiding this from me." The venom in it was real.

Tagen waited a beat, then went on. "There is a problem with it, in your favor. Mauldrin will not turn. He has been in the chamber nearly two months. The transformation has not taken."

Saying it out loud sat in him sideways. He had crossed a line he could not walk back over. If Snyp learned of this, death would be the kindest thing in the room.

Triaad's attention came back to Domblin. "Would you like to know the trouble your friend Mauldrin is in?"

Domblin did not blink. "I don't know what you are talking about. Mauldrin is gone. Has been for a very long time."

"Let's not play games." Triaad leaned back. "Would you like to know where he is, or not?"

"I left him in a place where your aniborn couldn't touch him," Domblin said.

Tagen could not help the small noise that came out of him.

If only you knew. Mauldrin ruined his own protection.

"He has been captured," Triaad said. The cold in it was even. "As we speak, he is in a chamber filled with dark matter. The transformation is underway."

Domblin's chains rattled. He pulled against them. The light off his robe rose the way a lamp rises when the wick is lifted. The chamber brightened. The marble of the walls and floor groaned around him. The chains began to scream, and the gray of them ran toward black.

"Fool." Triaad lifted a hand. The chains went quiet. His voice carried something heavier than sound, and the chamber settled under it. "You should know by now you have no power here."

Something turned over in Tagen.

Why does he not kill him?

The hesitation. The slow handling of it. None of it was the Triaad Tagen had served. Something about him sat different in his own skin than it had before.

Triaad came down the stairs. He moved without hurry, the way a man moves who has never had to.

"Now," Triaad said. The calm in it was a kind of warning. "Tell me. Was it you who brought Mauldrin back from his eternal grave?"

Domblin remained silent.

Triaad smiled, small. "Almost a century since I last saw you. I always regretted that you would not fight for me. You would have made an excellent general."

"I would never join you," Domblin said. He did not raise his voice. "I chose good a long time ago. I will not follow what you are."

Triaad snorted. "Good and evil," he said. "Where did you find such a small idea? There is no good. There is no evil. There is only power. There is only what a man is willing to do. Your laws hold men back from what they could be. That is what your laws are for."

He circled Domblin slow. "If anyone deserves the word evil, it is your kind."

Domblin held his eye. "They follow you because you sold them a savior. I see what you are. A coward. Hiding behind lies and a power that was never yours."

Triaad shifted his weight. He tilted his head a fraction. He flicked his hand. Domblin hit the floor hard. The sound he made filled the chamber.

"I will let you live," Triaad said. "So you can watch me turn Mauldrin into my follower."

Tagen watched. The anger in him sat under the fear and would not stay still.

Why does Domblin get to live after all he has done?

He pushed it down. Triaad was already moving on.

"Ready the dragon," Triaad said. "And open the gate."

Tagen followed. Each step weighed more than the one before. He had stepped past the line where he could turn around.

The front doors opened and sunlight came through them in a hard slant. Two guards came in with the dragon between them, leading it on heavy ropes set around the upper neck. The obsidian of its scales gave back the light as a dull metal gleam. The floor took the weight of every footfall and gave it back through Tagen's feet.

The dragon bellowed. The marble took the sound and gave it back. As the guards brought it closer to Domblin, it lurched and snapped. Its teeth closed on one of Domblin's chains and the link broke with a sharp pop. Domblin moved fast enough to keep clear of the second strike.

It struck at him twice more. Each bite missed by inches. The guards heaved on the ropes. The beast jerked back against them, head whipping aside, and let itself be drawn off.

Tagen caught himself hoping the next strike would land.

Triaad came forward. The armor on him was midnight black with a wash of deep red through the obsidian, and Tagen knew it for the same dark matter that ran through Domblin's chains.

He swung up into the saddle without looking at it.

"Tagen," Triaad called. "You're coming with me."

The fear came up over the anger. The betrayal of Snyp sat in him heavy. But there was no door behind him anymore. He moved toward the dragon. He stood close to the foot of it. He forced his breathing to steady.

"Take Domblin back to his room," Triaad said. "Keep him there until I return."

The guards moved. They hauled Domblin to his feet. Triaad pulled the reins. The dragon's tail lashed across the chamber. It crouched, and in one push it cleared the floor and went through the gate behind the throne.

Tagen hesitated at the edge of the gate. The surface ran like a slow liquid, blue under purple, and it pulled at him without touching him. The cold off it was the cold of deep winter.

He stood at the lip of it. Through it was Snyp, and Snyp finding out what he had just done. Behind it was Triaad finding out he had refused. There was no third door.

The pull of the gate grew stronger. He looked back once at the chamber. Then at the moving surface in front of him.

Snyp was a fool. He would never carry the power to overthrow Triaad. He had been carrying that knowledge for longer than he had let himself say it.

It is time to follow my true master.

Cold liquid enveloped Tagen as the gate consumed him whole.

CHAPTER 47

Caden—Snyp's Cave

How long had he been in here? Days. Weeks. He had stopped being able to tell. The light had been gone long enough that time had stopped meaning anything. He could not have said whether it was today or tomorrow. He could not have said the year.

His eyes burned. His skin hurt where it touched anything.

Every so often a scream tore loose somewhere through the wall. Or a moan. Raw, hollow. He had begun to wait for them. They were the only thing that came in that meant something living was on the other side of the stone.

When he tried to put together how he had come here, his head felt like it might split. Pieces of his time at SDS came back to him in flashes that would not hold long enough to look at. The end of the agency came back to him in pieces too, scattered, in no order. And under those, other pieces. A life he had not lived. A life where he had been called Mauldrin. None of it sat together.

The one piece that came back whole, every time, was Bridget dying. Her body in his arms. The blood soaking through her clothes into his hands. It would not let him go.

Am I dead? Is this what death is? Is this hell?

Sometimes there was a thing in the room with him. The sense of being watched moved across the back of his neck. He thought he could hear movement. More than once, he thought he could hear breathing. Whenever he turned toward it there was nothing there. Only the slick walls and the dark and the count of the water dripping somewhere.

The thing in the walls fed on what he was losing.

He shivered. The walls had a slow movement under their sheen, the way water moves under its own surface. The dark matter was in every crack of the stone. It clung the way tar clings. There were voices in it that he could not make into words, and they scratched at the back of his mind in a language he was almost learning.

"You are holding on to a lie." The voice came from beyond the wall.

Caden went still. His hands closed. He knew the voice before he turned to it.

Domblin.

The old man stood on the other side of the moving wall. His face was even. His silver hair did not move with anything around it.

"You are not real," Caden said. He shook his head. "This place is doing something to my mind."

Domblin came closer. "Then why am I the only thing in here that makes sense?"

He wanted to fight it. He wanted to put the whole thing aside. The voices in the walls came up louder. They wove into one another, and the language they made was not one he had been taught, and yet under it all he could feel the shape of the word they were making.

Mauldrin.

The name landed on him and stayed.

"You still think you are just Caden," Domblin said. Softer now. "That the life you built is enough to bury the rest? Tell me. Why do you remember battles you never fought? Why do you dream of faces you have never met?"

Caden pressed his fingers to his temples. "They are not my memories. They cannot be."

Domblin crouched in front of him. His face was grave. "You were always stubborn. You are running out of time."

The whispers shifted. They formed something new, something more whole.

A brotherly bond meant to withstand time. Shattered.

A battlefield, bathed in fire.

A throne room, old and crumbling.

A woman's scream.

A blade, dripping with blood—his blood.

Azgiel's face filled with rage, his voice roaring Mauldrin's name.

The moment the curse was placed upon the sword.

The moment he placed it.

Caden gasped. His body shook as the memories came forward—no longer pieces but one whole, unbearable thing.

I did this.

I am Mauldrin.

It went into him and stayed there.

He had sealed Azgiel between the seconds. He had laid a curse on the very sword Azgiel now wanted him to take up. He had done it to end what his brother had wrought across the worlds. He was not Caden alone. He was not Mauldrin alone. He was both.

His whole life had been built on the belief that he was in charge of where it went. He was not sure now that he ever had been. He had been walking through the part the past had set out for him long before he knew the past was there.

"Accept it," Domblin urged. "Or watch everything fall apart."

He knew.

He could not run from it. He could not put it down. This was who he was. Mauldrin was not a ghost of the old world.

He was him.

Clarity came up in him. Power moved with it—old power, his power, ready to come back to a hand that had once known how to hold it. He had only begun to put the broken pieces of who he had been into one shape when the dark matter around him shifted.

It came over him without warning. It closed around him. Mauldrin fought it. His mind became a battlefield again. The dark matter did not stop. It clawed at the memories that had just surfaced. It pulled them off him one by one—the battles, the throne room, the scream, the dripping blade—and tore them out of him before he could set them deep enough to keep.

The pain split his thoughts. He lost ground to the dark coming up over him, the dark that wanted to erase the thing he had only just begun to understand. The self he had held for a moment dissolved out of his hands.

He reached for anything to anchor him. In the middle of all of it, one thing was burning bright that the dark matter could not reach. Bridget. Her smile. As clear as if she were standing in front of him in the cell. The image held him to the floor of the world. Love and loss the substance had no claim on.

He held to the last piece of his human life and would not let it go. Bridget's memory became the room he could stand in. The dark matter pulled back, full for now. A thin silence settled in its place. He was battered. He was tired. The things he had just learned about himself were scattered out of him again. The one thing the dark could not take was her.

When Caden came to, the cell was quiet. Domblin was gone. He had never been there. The dark matter still moved across his skin, working at him as it had been since he was thrown into the room. He held to Bridget the way a drowning man holds to a rope.

It was all he had left.

The rest of his mind was empty. Stripped clean.

CHAPTER 48
Caden—Vision in the Cell

A scream came through the wall. High. A woman.

He came up off the floor before he knew he had moved. The sound stayed in his head longer than it should have, and his head was empty enough to hold it. The dark matter had taken the rest. He could not have said how long he had been in this room. He could not have said his own age. He could have said the name Bridget. That was the only name the cell had not gotten out of him.

He stood. The image of her came up behind his eyes the way light comes up under a door. It was less memory than presence. He could almost smell the flowery perfume she had worn on a Sunday morning he could not place. The wanting in him grew larger than the room. A heat lit in his chest and spread out through his arms. It had an edge on it that warmth did not have.

The walls shifted. Other images came up under the one he was holding, and they did not belong to him—himself in armor he had not owned, Azgiel beside him, a wide country bending to the lift of a hand. Fire pulled out of stone. Wind shaped to a will. A throne he had sat on. None of it sat in him as a memory. It sat in him as a room he had walked into by accident.

"Bridget." He pushed the other images back. He said her name out loud, and the saying of it held him to the floor.

The fire under his ribs leaned harder. The room thinned. He was not in the cell. He was in a wooded place he did not know, and she was there in front of him, alive. Her smile was the one he knew. The rest of her was not. She moved in a way the Bridget he had loved had not moved. Her skin had a low glow under it.

The creatures around her—the green-skinned thing with too-long claws, the jackal-headed one, the others—stood close to her in the careful, lowered way a body stands close to something it serves.

The vision did not feel like a dream. It felt like a door someone had opened on the other side, and Bridget was through it, and she had heard him.

"Bridget," he said. His voice came up out of him deeper than it had a right to. Her face turned toward him. Her eyes found him.

The walls of the cell screamed.

The sound went into the back of his skull and stayed. The image of her began to thin. He reached for it with the part of him that knew how to reach, and the dark matter slid over the place he was reaching from. It worked at the edges of her until the edges were gone. Then it took the rest.

He leaned against the wall. The cold came back up through his shoulders. He could not have said how long he had stood there. He could have said her name.

A thin seam of light cut through the stone in front of him.

It widened. It made the shape of a door, and then it was a door, and then the door came open with a sound like a struck bell. The light past it filled the cell. He had to put his arm over his eyes.

The dark matter on the walls drew back in soft pulled-out sheets, the way mud comes off a boot, and what was under it was rough stone, ordinary stone, the first ordinary thing he had seen in he did not know how long.

A figure stood in the doorway. White cloak. Light came off her in a way light did not come off people. He could not look directly at her.

"Follow me." The voice was a woman's, low and carrying. *Bridget?*

When he looked up, she was already down the corridor—a thin pale shape moving away from him. Something in him that had been lying down for weeks stood up.

His foot struck something on the floor. The sword. He had forgotten it was in the room with him. He bent and caught the wrapped hilt—the cloth, not the metal; he had never been able to touch the metal—and he carried the bundle out of the cell at a run. Some of what the dark matter had taken from him was starting to come back.

The figure stayed ahead of him. She turned at each branching of the tunnels and was already gone before he reached the turn. His legs burned. He did not slow.

Behind him, a low gurgling rose. He looked back once. The slick of dark matter was coming up the tunnel after him, fast, climbing the walls in long flat sheets where the figure's light had stripped it back. Where the light reached, it could not follow. Where the light did not reach, it owned the stone.

The smell of the air changed. He could smell trees. Wet leaves. The cave opened on a stand of old growth, and he came out of it under a sky.

The light pulled away from him across the clearing and up a hill. He went after it. He pushed the last of what was in his legs into the hill. He cleared the top, and just as he came around the trunk of a wide old tree, the light went out.

His hands went into mud. The cold of it slapped him fully awake. He stayed there a beat, looking at the place where the light had been.

Was that her? Or did I make her?

He pushed up onto his knees and looked down at his arms. The veins under the skin ran black. Like ink had been poured through him and stopped there.

"What did they do to me?" His fingers shook against the skin.

A scream cut the trees behind him. He went low against the trunk and looked back toward the cave. Nothing at the mouth of it. Yet.

Run. The word came in a voice that sounded like Bridget's, in the back of his head. It came hard. He looked for her on the ground around him and did not find her.

A roar tore open the cave mouth and an aniborn came out of it on a wash of fire, landing twisted in the dirt. Behind the aniborn came the head of the dragon—black scales, an old hardness in the line of the jaw. He knew the dragon. It was the dragon that had taken Domblin from the cabin. The memory came up sharp and his head ached at the seam of it.

Rage came up in him fast enough that he almost stepped out from behind the tree. The feeling was not his—it ran heavier than his, older than his, and it wanted out. The part of him that had stayed alive in the cell pulled him back. Not yet.

He held against the trunk. Watched.

The dragon dragged itself the rest of the way out, claws cutting long grooves into the dirt. Its rider sat the shoulders the way a man sits a chair he owns.

"Snyp." Triaad's voice came across the clearing. The trees took it and gave it back. "There is no use to this. Accept what you have done."

Snyp came up out of nothing near the dragon's feet—a thin black shape pulling itself into form. His voice was a hiss against stone. "Tagen is lying to you. He is trying to turn you against me—"

Triaad cut him off with a small motion of the hand. "I am done with your lying. Tagen has the cave."

The dragon made a sound that was not a roar and not a growl. Its ears flattened. It pulled back and let out a torrent of fire straight onto Snyp.

The flames pinned him to the ground. They should have ended him. They did not. The dirt under him went black, not from the fire—from threads of something oily that spread out from his body and ate at the soil.

A blast of dark roots erupted under the flames and threw the fire back into the dragon's face. The beast screamed and reared, smoke coming up off its scales.

"If you want a fight," Snyp said, coming up onto his feet, "I will give you one."

Snyp threw his arms forward. Roots ran out of him across the clearing, opening the ground, lifting rocks and earth in heavy arcs. The dragon tried to lift but the roots had its legs. They went in like worms in soft wood. Black fluid came out of its scales where they took hold.

Triaad came off the dragon's back as the roots took it down—landed clean and rolled up onto one knee. The dragon's head was still loose. Fire came at him from behind. He waved one hand without looking, and the flames in the air went to steam. The clearing dimmed and cooled. The dragon turned on him. Snyp's corruption had it now—Caden could see it in the way the eyes had gone. He knelt and laid his hand flat against the dirt.

A wall of water came out of the ground. It rose past the height of the dragon and held its shape—a long serpent of clear running water, twisting in the air above the clearing. The dragon turned and threw its fire at the water and the water hissed and pulled back and did not break.

The serpent dropped on the dragon like a thrown wave. Black fluid came out of the dragon's nostrils and the corners of its eyes as the water moved through it. When the water drew back, the dragon was on its side, breathing hard, and the corruption was off it.

Caden did not move. He held the trunk so the trunk would hold him.

Snyp lunged. Triaad caught him by the throat without looking and lifted him off the ground.

The dragon came up onto its feet. It put one claw down where Triaad pointed. Triaad threw Snyp into the dirt and flicked his wrist, and a chain came out of the dragon's saddle and laid itself across Snyp's body and rooted into the ground.

"What is this?" Snyp pulled against it. He could not move. He shifted out of his form and back, and the chain was still on him.

Triaad climbed back up into the saddle. "Dark matter. The same as you. You do not slip through what made you."

"You are making a mistake!" Snyp said. "Tagen is using you—"

Triaad did not answer. He let the dragon set the weight of one claw across Snyp's throat.

"Your ego made you stupid," Triaad said. He was not loud about it. "And I have not decided yet what to do with you."

From behind the tree, every part of Caden wanted to break cover and come down the hill with the bundle and not stop until one of them was no longer breathing. He held still. Let them finish each other.

Then Snyp's head turned, and his eyes found him through the trees.

"Mauldrin!" Snyp's voice carried across the clearing.

Triaad's head came around fast.

Caden pulled back behind the trunk. His chest hammered against the bark.

"He is up there!" Snyp shouted. "Let me up and I will bring him to you. I will fix the mistake."

Triaad laughed, low. "I do not trust you."

"Trust me or do not. He is up there. Let me up."

A beat passed. Then Triaad said, "Fine. But I will be looking through you." He cupped his hands. A red light kindled between them. Snyp screamed when the beam went into his forehead and left a small circular mark on the skin.

"Now I see what you see," Triaad said. He turned toward the cave. "Tagen."

That was as much as Caden could afford to listen to. He moved off the back of the tree and went into the trees behind him at a run.

The sun was already going. Light came in patches through the canopy. He kept his feet under him by reading the patches. He did not look back.

Something hit him from the side and took him to the ground.

He hit hard. Teeth went into his back through the fabric. He drove his elbow into the slick hide behind him and felt it give. The thing yelped and rolled off him.

He came up onto his feet and saw the eyes. Two red ones. Snyp.

"Nice to see you again, Mauldrin." Snyp circled him, low to the ground.

"Who are you?" Caden said.

"The one who is going to kill you."

Snyp came in fast, claws out. Caden's hand closed on the wrapped hilt. Something called from within the sheath, a pull to draw the sword.

For the first time since the Witch had laid the sword across his palms, the metal under the cloth let him hold it. The hilt fit into his hand the way a thing fits when it has been waiting.

A pull went up his arm. The pull became heat. The heat became a wave. The wave went out of him and Snyp left the ground and slammed into a tree thirty paces off, and the trees between the two of them bent and cracked.

The bundle had fallen away. He stood with the bare blade in his hand. The metal caught the moonlight, and the patterns on the hilt moved under his hand the way patterns move under water.

Power went through him the way a current goes through wire.

Across the clearing, Snyp came up onto his hands and knees. He saw the sword. The hiss of him changed shape. He took a step backward.

Caden smiled before he knew he was smiling.

Snyp threw himself across the ground at him. Caden stepped to the side and let the sword fall through his shoulder, cutting it clean off. The arm dropped in front of Caden and went to a ribbon of black dust.

Movement at the edges of his vision. A rustling against bark, against root, against the dry leaves of the clearing.

Aniborn came up out of the dark. He counted six.

The first came in low and fast. He pivoted and the blade took it through the chest and it was dust before it hit the ground. The second hit him from behind. He went down with it on top of him and rolled and brought the sword up through it and it screamed once and was gone.

He came back to his feet. The others held a half-circle around him. They were not coming in the way the first two had come. They were watching the sword.

"Come on, then," he shouted.

One broke. He met it with the blade and it went the way the others had gone. Another came in from the left. He stepped through the line of its rush and brought the sword down across it and it went into dust. The smell of it sat in his throat.

One left. It feinted right and Caden held his ground. It came in straight, then vanished. Before Caden knew it, something knocked him to the ground, biting his arm. The sword had dropped. He quickly grabbed it with his free hand and swung it at whatever was biting him. The aniborn materialized as he opened it from collarbone to hip, and the dust of it hung in the air a long beat before the breeze took it.

The clearing went quiet.

His hand was shaking against the hilt. Not from fear. From the pull of what was in it. The blade did not want to be set down.

"Mauldrin."

He turned. Snyp was at the edge of the clearing. He was larger now. His skin gave off a thin steam. The arm Caden had taken off him was growing back.

"You think you have done something," Snyp said. "You have no idea what you have woken up."

"Then come and show me," Caden said.

Snyp came in faster this time. The claws came at his chest. He swung and Snyp caught his wrist and put him into a tree. The breath went out of him. He did not lose the sword.

Snyp's claws opened his chest in two long lines. The pain came up through him bright and hot. Under the pain, the dark matter in his veins came up to meet it, and the sword came up with it, and the three of them together made one rising thing.

He heard the sword. Not in words. The way a man hears a dog he has lived with for a long time.

He pushed against Snyp with what the sword was giving him. Light blew out of the blade. The wave that came off it took Snyp off his feet and put him on his back in the dirt, and this time he did not get up at first.

Caden was already on him.

He brought the sword down once. The cry that came out of Snyp was the last sound of him before the rest of him went into black dust on the wind.

Caden stood over the spot. His chest dripped onto the dirt.

The sword was alive in his hand. He could feel the line between his arm and the blade thinning. The two of them were becoming one thing.

He turned the blade in his hand. He looked at it.

He turned back the way he had come and started walking toward the cave.

CHAPTER 49

Azgiel—The Witch's Woods

A breeze came across the lake and brought a thin chill with it. The moon was full on the water. Small waves moved over the surface in the slow rhythm the lake kept after a long day. Behind him, a few of the trolls pretended to be busy at the shore. They were listening. He let them.

"I do not like it," Azgiel said. He kept his eyes on the water; the edge in his voice did the rest. "If they have taken Mauldrin to Terris—to Triaad—we are finished. Our forces cannot match his, and the sacrifice I made to bring Bridget back will be for nothing."

He lifted his palm. A bead of fire kindled over his skin—obedient, but thin, its edges pulled by the breeze. The weakness nagged him the way a tongue finds a missing tooth. He closed his fist, and the flame hissed out.

Kaz's brow creased. "You never fully recovered after reviving Maselda. Did bringing Bridget back cost you more power?"

"Yes," Azgiel said. "Maselda cost me. This body dulls me. Bridget took more. It is worth it if it gets us Mauldrin—wasted if it does not. We need to be decisive."

Kaz worked a twig with his toe. He kicked it into the lake. "Whatever you decide, we are behind you." His wings shifted at his back, settling.

"I know." Azgiel started to say more. He stopped.

The wind changed. Something carried in on it that he had not felt in a thousand years. Not loud. Not sudden. A pressure in the air the way a body feels a storm before it shows.

The sword. The sword was awake.

He turned to Kaz. "He has drawn it. The curse is broken. Mauldrin has drawn the sword. He is still on the planet. I can take it back now without losing what I have left."

Kaz straightened. His wings came in close. "I will get everyone."

"Send one of the trolls. We do not have the time to walk it ourselves."

Kaz looked over his shoulder at the nearest of the listening trolls and tipped his head. The troll did not need to be told twice. He was up the hill before the dust of his first step had settled.

Behind them, on the path down from the trees, two figures came in a hurry—Maselda and Bridget. Both of them carried a faint light against their skin. In this light, with the moon on the water behind them, they could have come out of the same womb.

"Azgiel." Maselda's voice was tight.

He raised a hand. She did not slow.

"It is about Mauldrin." She came up to him with Bridget half a step behind. "Bridget has seen him."

He looked from Maselda to Bridget. "How? Where?"

Maselda turned and put a hand at the small of Bridget's back, easing her forward. Bridget moved like a person who has not yet learned the floor of a room. "Go on," Maselda said. "Tell him."

Bridget rubbed her hands together. Her eyes went to the lake, then back to him. "I will try," she said. "I do not know what happened. I was in a chair. I heard my name. It was Caden."

"Mauldrin," Kaz said.

She nodded a little. "When I heard him, something pulled. I fought it at first. It startled me. Then it felt peaceful—like he had his arms around me and was drawing me toward him. So I let it. The next thing I knew, I was in a cave. There was a black liquid all over the floor. It pulled back from me as I went. As if it could not be near me."

Her voice softened. She moved a step closer to Maselda. "I looked down at myself and I had no body. I was light, floating above the ground. Like a ghost. There was a door in front of me—a large stone one. I touched it. It blew open. He was on the other side of it."

"What did he look like?" Azgiel said. Quieter than he meant to.

"Terrible." She said it without ornament. "I do not know what they have done to him. The whole place was wrong. I told him to follow me. We went toward the way out. A creature came at me on the way and when it touched me it was thrown back the way the floor had been thrown back. As if it could not put a hand on me."

Azgiel let her speak. Inside, he was working through more than one thing at once. He was relieved. Mauldrin was alive. He was also unsettled. Bridget was carrying more than she knew, and she was carrying it in a body she did not yet know the limits of.

If she ever learns why we saved her—

He set the thought down. He could pick it up again later.

Bridget went on. Her voice fell. "When we got outside the cave there was a tunnel. White light. I do not know how to say where I was. It felt like I was being pulled back into my body. Even after I left him, I could feel him. He is in danger. Something is coming for him." Her hands shook a little. "I screamed at him to run. Then I was back here."

Azgiel waited. "That is all of it?"

She nodded. Her eyes went to Maselda for the answer he had not given her. "When I opened my eyes, everyone was around me. Asking if I was all right."

"Can you go back?" he said. "Can you find out where he is?"

She shook her head. "I think he pulled me. I do not know how to find him on my own."

Maselda's hand stayed on Bridget's shoulder. "The cave she walked through has Snyp's signature on it." She did not look at Bridget when she said it. She looked at Azgiel. "There is something between her and Mauldrin. Something old."

He did not answer her. He looked at Kaz. "The window is closing. Help the troll get the others. We move on the cave now."

Kaz lifted off the ground without a word and was over the trees before the next breath.

Azgiel turned back to the lake. The water held the moon. Below the surface of him, the rest of what Maselda had just said worked.

Bridget had walked through a wall of dark matter without it touching her. The aniborn in the cave could not lay a hand on her.

He had brought her back so Mauldrin would have something to come back to. He had not brought her back to be a weapon. What she was becoming was its own thing, and he had set it in motion, and he did not yet know what he had set in motion.

If Mauldrin had drawn the sword, Mauldrin was walking into Triaad. The war was here. He needed the sword in his hand before Triaad got it in his.

He turned from the lake and went up the path after Kaz.

CHAPTER 50
Caden—Outside Snyp's Cave

The moon was full and gave the forest the color of cold metal. The cave breathed out at him from the dark of the hill. The woods around the entrance were too quiet. He stopped at the mouth.

Should I go in?

The cave gave him no answer. It was a hole. It was waiting for him.

He let the answer come up on its own. The anger he had been carrying since the cell was still in him. Every day they had kept him alive was reason enough to walk through that door.

He whistled once. The sound went into the cave and came back to him. "I am right here," he called.

His voice sounded thin. He let it be thin.

He picked up a rock and threw it in. The clatter of it down the tunnel was a long sound.

Something came out of the dark fast and low. He brought the sword up but the thing was on him before the blade could close the distance. He hit the ground. The breath left him. The sword skittered into the brush.

Teeth went into his shoulder. He made a sound he did not recognize. He found a stone with his free hand and brought it down hard on the side of the thing's head. It screeched and rolled.

He came up onto his knees and went after the sword. His fingers closed on the hilt as the creature came back at him. He turned with the blade and took it through the middle, and it went into the black dust the others had gone into.

A long answering howl came up out of the cave.

He set his feet. He raised the blade.

"Good," he said. "Come on."

Three of them came out of the tunnel at once. He met the first one with the sword and it was dust before it landed. The second he turned through, the third he split. He was getting used to the rhythm of it. He did not like that he was getting used to it.

More came. These came slower. They held back at the edge of the moonlight and circled.

They were learning him.

He put his back against the cave wall to take one direction off the table. Before he was set, one of them dropped on him from above and put him on the dirt.

Teeth in his leg. Teeth in his arm. A third one dropped onto his chest, and a fourth came in low and pinned his sword arm to the ground. He could not move the arm. He had a heartbeat to lose, and he did not lose it. He wrenched the arm free and turned the blade up through the one on his chest, and it came apart on top of him, and the dust of it went into his eyes.

He kicked the one on his leg off and came up onto his feet, and the blade came up with him and took the one that had pinned his sword arm. The last two were already breaking in from the circle. He took them fast, one to the side, one straight in, and the forest fell quiet again.

He breathed. The taste of the dust was at the back of his throat. He could not get rid of it.

That cannot be all of them.

He backed toward the mouth of the cave. He scanned the dark inside. Something was standing a few feet inside the cave that had not moved through any of the fighting.

"I see you," he said. He did not know how many more were behind the one he could see, but he had not come this far to back off. "Do not think I will not come in there."

The shape stepped forward into the moonlight, and he knew the shape before the face caught the light. He had spent more time looking at that face than any other aniborn.

"You."

Tagen did not move. He studied him in the way a tired man studies a long road.

"No one else is coming," Tagen said. His voice was low and tired.

"What does that mean?" Caden raised the sword. "Where are the rest? Where is Triaad? Where is Domblin? Do not tell me they left you here."

Tagen's shoulders went down a fraction. "Triaad is gone. He took the army with him. He left a few of us scattered across the planet to hold the work that was here." He paused. "I am the last in this cave."

"Then I will finish it." Caden set himself for the swing.

"Wait." Tagen went to his knees. He raised both hands. "You do not have to. I can help you."

Caden held the sword where it was. "Help me with what?"

"I know things." It came out fast. "Triaad. The aniborn. Where they are. How to reach them. There is a gate at the back of this cave. They went through it. I can show you."

"And why would I believe a word of that?"

"Because I have nowhere else to go." Tagen looked up at him. "Triaad has no use for me. You have a use for me. You are stronger than him. I would serve you."

He did not trust him. The sword wanted him to take the swing and be done.

He did not take the swing. He kept the blade up. "Do not move. I will tie you while I think about it."

There was a chain in the dirt near where the dragon had stood—the same chain Triaad had laid across Snyp. He set the sword between his knees, wound the chain around Tagen's wrists, and locked it. The chain settled against him in a way ordinary chain would not have. *Made of the same as you,* Triaad had said. He believed that part.

He dragged Tagen up onto his feet by the chain and walked him into the cave.

The portal room sat at the end of the deepest tunnel. The gate itself was a tall arch of pale stone, and inside it a black liquid moved, slow, the way a tide moves under heavy weather. The pull of the gate came up against Caden's chest as soon as he was in the room. It wanted him through it.

"I am surprised he left it open," Tagen muttered. "Unless he means to come back through."

Caden did not answer him. He yanked the chain, brought Tagen close, and lifted the sword.

The first swing took the right pillar of the arch through the middle. The cut went deeper than it should have. The gate gave off a sound like glass under pressure, and the air in the room pulled toward it before it shoved back out.

"What are you doing?" Tagen pulled at the chain. "You will kill us both."

Caden raised the sword again. "It ends here."

He brought the blade through the second pillar. The stone broke. The break ran up the arch in a long line. The liquid inside the gate turned and folded over itself, the way a sea moves before it leaves the floor of a bay. The gate did not want to close.

A long sound came up out of it that was not a sound.

Lightning began to come out of the cracks. Not the lightning he knew. It moved out of the stone the way oil comes up through water—slow, finding its weight, taking its time. Where it touched the air, the air pulled away from it. Where it spread along the stone, the stone began to give up its edges. Blue, and slow, and unhurried, and reaching.

The liquid at the center of the arch pulled itself together—small, then smaller, then a point.

The point gave.

What came out of it did not behave like lightning either. It poured. It moved through the air the way a slow heavy thing moves through deep water, unspooling in long bright strands that bent where they should have broken and held shape where they should have spread. The strands were reaching. They took their time about it. And every part of them was getting farther from the arch faster than anything in the room had any right to move.

Caden saw the contradiction before his body felt it. The lightning was slow. The lightning was already past the walls.

A strand of it found him at the chest, where Snyp had opened him. The warmth of his own blood and the warmth of the sword in his hand and the cold of the cave all became the same temperature at once.

It went through him the way water goes through cloth. Every part of him registered it at once. The wet of his chest. The dust at the back of his throat. The veins running black under his skin. The hilt of the sword warm against his palm—the only warm thing, the one thing the lightning did not take.

He held on to the sword.

The room began to go.

There was no word he had for what came next. It was not dark and it was not light. The pieces of the broken arch that had been in the air around him began to lift away from themselves, and the lifting did not have a direction he could follow.

The sword stayed warm.

He tried to finish a thought, with the part of him that could still try—

—but the thought did not finish, because there was no longer a place where thoughts finished. The room was not there. The cold was not there. The arch and the floating stone and the dark behind the arch and the trees outside the cave and the moon over the trees and the woman who had stood in the doorway in white and the name Bridget were not there.

Only the sword was there. Warm against his palm. Holding.

Then even that went.

**End of Book One, The Battle Continues in:
The DEAD TIME Chronicles
BOOK TWO
FRACTURED FATE**

About the Author

Jason Wilcox is the author of the captivating dark fantasy series, *The Dead Time Chronicles*, blending gripping storytelling with profound insights into human psychology. A licensed clinical social worker (LCSW) and accomplished therapist specializing in cognitive behavioral therapy (CBT), Jason masterfully integrates his deep understanding of the human mind and emotional complexities into every page of his novels.

Known for his immersive scenes, compelling characters, and chilling narrative style, Jason invites readers to explore worlds filled with ominous intrigue and powerful emotional journeys. His professional experience enriches his writing, creating authentic characters and intricate plots that resonate with readers long after the final page.

When he's not crafting his next novel or supporting individuals and couples through his therapeutic practice, Jason enjoys spending time outdoors, engaging in activities like hiking, rock hounding, and fishing alongside his family. He lives with his wife and children, continually drawing inspiration from their adventures and shared love of storytelling.

Book Description

When time stops, something ancient wakes.
Caden Gray's experimental jump into "Dead Time" should have been a measured stride toward the unknown. Instead, he returns with fractured memories, a stranger's name echoing in his head—**Mauldrin**—and a lab mate who swears he's someone else entirely: **Azgiel**, a warlord exiled outside time.

As sabotage rocks the facility and a shadow war spills into the world, Caden's only anchor is Bridget—the combat medic who once saved his life and may be the key to who he was…and what he's becoming.

Hunted by demons, watched by the enigmatic **Domblin**, and racing a clock that doesn't tick, Caden must master Dead Time's rules before a resurrected god claims his body—and the world.

Frozen Shadows launches *The Dead Time Chronicles*—a high-velocity blend of science, sorcery, and shattering secrets where love is the one thing time can't erase.

From Jason's Favorite Author,
C.J. Cherryh, National best-selling author and winner of three Hugo Awards

"A blend of genres. Something different…Edgy…New!…an action-adventure-science fiction-thriller here, with a dose of demons and an inventive,   well-conceived   premise."

www.ingramcontent.com/pod-product-compliance
Lightning Source LLC
Chambersburg PA
CBHW060907250626
47159CB00008B/2906